As The World Dies

A Zombie Trilogy

Siege

Book Three

Rhiannon Frater

Cover Art by Detra

www.myspace.com/nightmarelife

Edited by Michelle Downey and Helen Bibby

Proof Copy Editing by Connie Frater

This is a work of fiction. The characters, situations, and most locations (towns, names of streets, rural roads and country roads) are from the author's imagination.

ISBN/EAN13:   1441405178 /9781441405173

Introduction From Dr. Pus of the Library of the Living Dead Podcast

If you're reading this, you must be a fan of Rhiannon Frater's zombie series "As The World Dies." You must be! You've read the incredible first book "The First Days" and fallen in love with Katie and Jenni. I know I did. When I started reading "The First Days," I didn't get past the first chapter. It was so shocking I had to go back immediately and read it again. And when I finished the book, I read it again!

After what seemed like an eternity, the second book in the series appeared. I had the grand opportunity to read "Fighting To Survive" before it went to print. I was exceedingly humbled when Rhiannon asked me to blurb the novel. What a great second notch in the handle of her literary zombie gun!

Now, I have been asked to write the introduction to the third and final installment of "As The World Dies" called "Siege." This is just an incredible honor for me. Why? Because I KNOW zombie genre novels. I live for zombie genre novels. My podcast and my publishing company are specifically for the zombie genre. My own "Library of the Living Dead" is jam packed with almost every zombie novel that has ever seen print. It is overflowing with zombie goodness except for one spot. One area on the top shelf is reserved for one special book ... the one you are holding in your hands.

"Siege" will answer all of the questions you've been wanting to ask since you read "The First Days" and "Fighting to Survive." Rhiannon addresses them all, but you won't like some of the results. That's because she is such a talented writer that her characters are ones you have come to love, care about, have empathy and sympathy for. Her characters are us. And even though we all want them to win, it just isn't always possible in Rhiannon's universe.

Start reading "Siege" now. When you're finished, your heart will have been touched, and it will be a little bruised, too.

Undead love to you all,

Doc

Dedicated to all the fans of this trilogy

and

my Mother and Husband for your unwavering support throughout the process of writing and preparing this trilogy for publication.

Thank you so much for your countless hours of support, proof reading, and encouragement!

Special thanks to Dr. Pus of the Library of the Living Dead Press and Podcast. Your encouragement and support of this trilogy has been phenomenal. Thank you so much!

And

Special Acknowledgment to my editors and proofreaders. Michelle, Kelly, Julie, Kody, and Helen, you are awesome!

Somewhere in Texas...

In the hills...

Chapter 1

1. Return of the Tiny Fingers

The tiny fingers under the door were missing. Jenni stared down at the dark, terrifying crack under the front door, waiting for the tiny pink digits to suddenly appear and begin straining toward her.

Standing on the front porch of her home, she felt the cool morning air teasing her dark hair and ruffling her pink nightgown and robe.

"Benji?" she whispered.

The hard, steady knocking against the door was a terrifying reminder that her zombified husband, Lloyd, was just on the other side. She could barely make out the dim outline of his form through its frosted glass panes set in the door. Blood was smeared in the inside of the windows, making it harder to see into the house.

"Benji?"

Jenni waited for the tiny fingers, but they didn't come. Slowly, she squatted down, her trembling fingers touching the cold cement of the front stoop. The crack under the door was far too big. She had told Lloyd that many times. It was so easy for someone to slide their fingers under it...or a tiny little hand, trying to reach its mother.

"Benji?"

Lloyd was throwing himself against the door now, and it shook beneath the impact of his body. Benji's tiny little fingers should be pressed under the door right now, reaching for her, straining for her. But they weren't there. The crack under the door, ominous in its promise, did not give birth to tiny bloody fingers.

"Mom!"

Jenni rose sharply to her feet.

"Mikey?"

Her twelve-year-old son ran around the side of the house, barefoot and in his pajamas, clutching his toddler brother tightly in his arms.

"Mikey! Benji!" Jenni stumbled as she rushed toward them.

"We got out the back door, Mom!"

Jenni crushed her sons tightly against her body, their small bodies pressing against hers. Benji's arms wrapped around her neck, and she could feel his tears against her flesh.

"Mommy! Daddy is scary!" Benji wept and thrust one tiny thumb into his mouth.

Jenni smothered her boys with kisses. Clutching them tightly, crying, and thanking God for their survival, she pulled them away from the house.

"Mom, we gotta get away! Dad is crazy! Mom, he's crazy!" Mikey exclaimed.

"We'll get away! I promise. We just have to wait a minute or two and Katie will be here in a white truck," Jenni answered him, clutching his hand.

"Who, Mom?"

"Katie. She's coming to save us," Jenni assured him. She looked back toward the house warily and saw Lloyd was now banging on the window next to the front door. Katie would be here at any moment now. She remembered from...

Scowling, she stood on her front lawn, trying not to think too hard about what was happening, of what had happened before...

Shaking her head, she looked toward the house. The window splintered and glass rained down. Lloyd began to push his way out.

"Mom! Mom! Where is Katie?"

Mikey was holding her hand so tightly, he was crushing her fingers. Benji sobbed loudly, his wet face against her neck, his tiny fingers gripping the collar of her nightgown.

"She should be here! She should be arriving right now!" Jenni dragged Mikey further from the house, her feet touching the cold asphalt of the street. The road remained empty. The white truck was nowhere to be seen. Jenni whirled around, her black eyes scanning her neighborhood for the white truck that should be their salvation.

"Mom! Mom!" Mikey's voice was high and terrified. He was pointing at Lloyd, who had crashed to the ground outside the house and was struggling to get up.

"Katie, where are you?" Jenni screamed.

Lloyd staggered to his feet and looked toward her and the boys. With an unholy screech, he began to race toward them, his hands outstretched. Jenni screamed again and began to run down the street as fast as she could.

Benji clung to her as Mikey ran beside her. She could already feel her body tiring and her lungs burning. Benji felt so heavy in her arms and Mikey held onto her robe as they ran. Her bare feet slapping hard against the pavement, Jenni ran for her life and those of her children. She could hear Lloyd behind her, gaining on them, his terrible screech filling the morning air.

"Mommy! Mommy!" Benji was moaning and she felt his bladder release as warm urine poured down her leg.

"Katie! Hurry! Katie!" Jenni kept screaming, her body tired and sore.

Then the doors of the houses began to fly open. Mutilated, bloody figures began to race into the street toward them, screeching their death cries, hands flung out before them.

"Mommy! Mommy!" Mikey and Benji's voice chorused in terror.

"Run! Run!"

Ahead, the street was beginning to fill with the hungry undead. All of them were racing toward her and her children. Their horrible, bloody mouths were opening wide, waiting to feast on them.

"Katie! Katie!" Jenni sobbed as her leaden legs weakened even more. "Katie, please!"

She ran as the undead began to close in around her.

2. Hitchhikers of the Living Dead

"Katie!" Jenni awoke with a start, banging her head against the passenger side window of the truck. "Ouch! Dammit!" She gripped her head with one hand and forced the nightmare back from her waking thoughts.

Looking up, she gasped.

A badly mauled zombie face was pressed against the window, its tongue licking desperately against the glass where her head had rested a few seconds before.

Drawing sharply back from the window, she fumbled for her gun. The zombie slammed its mangled hand against the window, moaning.

"Fuck," she muttered. She still felt groggy from sleeping.

Out of the corner of her eye, she saw Katarina moving around the front of the parked truck, her pistol out. "I got him, Jenni," she called out.

The zombie, hearing Katarina's voice, turned away from the window and howled. The homely redhead aimed and fired one shot. The zombie's head burst, its body collapsing onto the road.

"Thanks!" Jenni called out, rubbing her eyes, trying to wake up all the way. She had fallen asleep on the way back from a scavenging run. It had been very successful. There had been no loss of life and they were returning with a lot of supplies that were needed to make it through to the Spring.

Katarina climbed back into the truck, slid behind the steering wheel, and slammed the door. She let out a sigh. "Felix *would* have to pee where there are zombies around."

"Couldn't hold it, huh?

"No. He said he was going to explode. I told him to hang it out the window. He laughed." Katarina frowned. "I was serious."

"Boys are dumb. Where is he?" Jenni glanced through the blood-splattered window at the side mirror and saw Felix's reflection. He was just zipping up and another zombie lay dead not too far from him.

"He better finish the hell up so we can get home. This latest cold front sucks." Katarina rubbed her hands over the steering wheel, her knuckles bright red from the cold. "I want some nice hot coffee."

Winter was hitting hard in Texas and it was one of the worst ones in years. Snow had fallen already three times, and Ed was muttering about ice storms. They were barely a week into January, and already Jenni was sick of the new year. It was so damn cold.

"That sounds so good. And a nice warm bed with a nice warm Juan in it." Jenni grinned.

Katarina blushed almost the color of her hair.

Felix wrenched open the back door and slid in. "I urinated on my shoes! Can't a man relieve himself without those damn things showing up. I'm quite irate!"

Jenni slid around in her seat and grinned at him. "Should have held it, huh?"

"When a man has to go, he has to go!" Felix folded his arms across his broad chest and glared at her. He wore several layers of clothing under his usual tracksuit and his black skin looked beautiful against the whiteness of the fabric. Felix dressed like a gangster, but spoke with a sophisticated air most of the time. He was the adopted son of rich white parents from Houston and would have graduated with a masters in literature if not for the zombie apocalypse. Jenni liked him a lot and they enjoyed teasing each other.

After the nightmare she had just endured, she was glad to joke around again. She could not get the final image of her and the boys fleeing down the zombie-infested neighborhood street out of her head. It had been so vivid, so real. If Katie had not arrived that morning, saving her, Jenni would have ended up fleeing on foot alone and she knew she would have perished. The boys had never made it out of the house. Lloyd had killed them.

Jenni laid her head against the backrest and stared at Katarina as she drove the truck back onto the country road to continue the journey home. The rest of the caravan was waiting up ahead. As their truck drew near, those vehicles slowly began to accelerate. Soon the small convoy was speeding down the country roads back toward the fort.

"I can't believe my shoes are ruined," Felix muttered again, then pulled out a book from his backpack. "It will be difficult to find a good replacement."

"You could try to clean them up," Katarina offered.

"I scrape zombie guts off my boots all the time," Jenni added.

Felix just grumbled something that they couldn't make out and began to read the words of Socrates.

"Boys are so moody," Jenni decided.

"And they say we are," Katarina scoffed.

Jenni smiled a little and tried to get comfortable in the truck. It felt odd riding shotgun with Katarina instead of Katie. But Katie was back in the fort, helping with other areas of importance. Jenni suspected Travis had something to do with Katie not being assigned to any of the groups heading out of the fort. Her pregnancy had been a shock when announced. Most of the fort was happy to welcome a new life into their barren world, but others felt having children was irresponsible. The comments were never made around Katie or her husband, Travis, but Jenni heard them.

Her own feelings about the baby were mixed. On the one hand, she was happy for her friend and ready to be an aunt, but on the other she feared for that new life being born into a world full of the hungry dead. Was it really fair to bring a new life into a world so full of death? Would it have been fair to try to raise her boys in this undead world? Jason was older, almost an adult, but Mikey and Benji would have lost whatever remained of their childhood innocence.

Frowning, she felt her stomach tighten at the thought of her dead children. Tears burned in her eyes as she realized she would rather her boys were with her than dead. Juan would have been a good father, and they would have worked hard to give the boys a good life. But that would never happen. Somewhere, her boys were part of the undead hordes.

"Something is going on," Katarina said, pulling Jenni away from her dark thoughts.

The caravan was slowing down.

"We got problems ahead," Ed's voice crackled over the CB.

Jenni snatched up the mouthpiece. "What's up?"

"Bunch of zombies have a van surrounded. Looks like people are up on top of it. Whole way is blocked." Ed sounded peeved by the whole situation.

"We have to save them!" This was Curtis' voice coming through the static. Jenni could imagine the grim expression on the young policeman's face.

"Got any ideas on how to handle it? 'Cause I'm listening," Ed answered.

"Pull up," Jenni said to Katarina.

With a nod, Katarina shifted gears and moved their truck out of the line to drive to the front where Ed's vehicle, a school bus, sat idling at the top of a hill. As they drew up next to the bus, Jenni scowled.

"Fuck."

It was hard to see how many people were on top of the van, but it was easy to see the crowd of zombies gathered around them. It looked like the van had stalled out and the occupants had managed to get on top of it through a sunroof. The door on the side was open and zombies were jostling each other to get inside. Another group was busily consuming someone near the side of the road.

Ed slid open the window next to the driver's seat and peered out at them. His grizzled face looked pissed beneath his battered hat. Jenni pushed the button for the window and it slid down. "What do you think, Ed?"

"Got at least three dozen down there trying to get to those folks. I figure we can either drive close enough to try to get them to come to us, then flatten them. Or we can open fire and risk hitting the people."

"They won't draw off if they've got fresh food in front of them," Jenni reminded him. "What if we get close enough to thin out the outer edge with the guns, then go in and clear out the rest with machetes, spears and my trusty ax?"

Curtis walked up next to the vehicles, his weapon out." His truck was idling behind Ed's. "We need to hurry whatever the hell we're doing. It's getting bad down there."

The zombies were so anxious to get to the people on top of the van, they were beginning to rock the vehicle. Someone on top was trying to stand to wave down the caravan and Jenni gasped as he tumbled off into the zombies. His screams tore through the cold air, then broke off abruptly. The zombies were moaning with delight as they swarmed him.

"We gotta move now!" Jenni shoved her door open, nearly ramming it into Curtis. Yanking her ax out of the truck, she motioned with it for Felix and Katarina to follow her. Shoving the ax into the specially made sheath on her back, she slammed the door shut with her hip. Determined to bust some zombie heads, she headed down the hill.

"We don't have a plan, Jenni!" Ed shouted after her.

Jenni stalked toward the undead swarm. "Kill the fuckers! That's the plan!"

3. Sentries of the Dead

The zombie slammed its mangled hand against the fort wall again, growling with what sounded like frustration.

Katie looked down at it from her sentry post, her blond curls flowing in the wind. Rubbing her cold, reddened hands together, she studied the creature's distorted features. Most of its flesh had torn off and one eyeball rolled up toward her in a gouged socket. How it could see her, she could not imagine, but it howled even more desperately as it caught sight of her. It had no lips, so its bloodied, decaying teeth looked hideously large as they chomped together hungrily.

"I can't even tell if you're a boy or a girl," Katie muttered, blowing on her fingers to warm them.

"So gross," Stacey remarked, peering over the edge of the wall. The slim, young woman leaned her elbows on the cold, cement bricks and stared at the zombie. "I think it's a boy."

"That one patch of hair on the back of its head is kinda long," Katie pointed out.

"Yeah, but lots of redneck boys have long ponytails. Trust me. There were a lot of guys back in my old town with ponytails longer than mine." Stacey reached behind her head to tug on her short braid. She looked far healthier than she had when first rescued. She had been terribly thin, her shoulder blades and collar bone sticking out of her tanned skin in sharp angles. Now she was fit and muscular and recently, the former coach had started sports activities in the fort to keep people fit.

"Clothes are kinda on the neutral side. Yellow shirt, I think."

"Could have started out white."

"Maybe." Katie tilted her head as she studied the creature. "I think it's a girl. Still ugly as sin."

"Uglier. Guess we should put it down."

"Yep," Katie agreed.

Now that her hands weren't cramped from the cold and the bloat from her pregnancy, she reached out for the huge crossbow that was rigged up on a sliding track. It was one of Jason's creations and it made killing the zombies up against the walls a lot easier. Using the mirrors attached to the contraption, she adjusted the crossbow using a lever to get it into the accurate position.

"I'm not saying I miss the big crowds of them, but lone zombies just seem so sad," Stacey decided.

"Until they try to eat you," Katie reminded her.

"Well, there is that." Stacey watched Katie carefully aim. "Jason is like a genius, huh?"

"Jenni says that he's always been one of those kids tinkering with stuff. She said he once took apart his Xbox, put it back together and it still worked. I don't think she's surprised at some of the things he's come up with lately. But I'm pretty stunned. For a teenager, he's pretty amazing." Katie checked her mirrors and saw that she had the zombie perfectly lined up. She squeezed the trigger.

The bolt slammed into the top of the zombie's head and it fell backwards onto the street, limbs askew. Later, a cleanup crew would remove the body and toss it into the landfill on the outskirts of town.

"Penis! I see a penis! It's a boy!" Stacey sounded far more excited than she should be.

"Gross!" Katie made a comical face. "That is so disgusting!" She couldn't help but look. "Ugh! Stacey!"

Stacey giggled and wiped her bangs away from her forehead. "It flopped out!"

"It's not funny! It's a poor dead guy." Despite herself, Katie was laughing. "My God, the gallows humor around here is thick."

"Freud would have had a blast studying us," Stacey agreed.

"Oh, well. Either we be a little crazy and laugh at the absurdities of life or just give into the despair and die." Katie shrugged and reset the crossbow, taking care to show Stacey each step.

"I've done despair. It doesn't help anything." Stacey fell silent for a moment, obviously pondering something. "The fort hasn't really had anyone go nuts and commit suicide or anything has it?"

"Well, a city councilman in the first days tried to save his zombie family and ended up eaten. And we do have the Vigilante pitching people over the wall." Katie slipped her hands into her jacket. Her swelling belly was straining the zipper. She would need to find a new winter coat. "Some of us haven't handled things as well as others." She thought briefly of Jenni. "And others have used the crazy to survive."

"Who do you think the Vigilante is?" Stacey pulled the collar of her coat up a little closer to her face and huddled down into it.

Katie bit her bottom lip, not sure what she should say, then opted out by just shrugging. "No clue. I'm sure everyone has a theory."

"I think it's Nerit," Stacey confided.

"She wasn't here when the first guy got pitched over the wall."

"The meth dealer?"

"Yeah. Ritchie." Katie remembered far too vividly the young man's mutilated body as he stared up at her from the road, duct tape still over his mouth.

"Well, there goes my theory." Stacey watched the street thoughtfully. "A few people think the Vigilante is doing the right thing."

"I had no love for Phil or Shane, but what the Vigilante did to them was inhumane. Stranding them with gimped weapons in the middle of the zombie deadlands." Katie shivered.

"They kinda deserved it." Stacey shrugged. "I'm not gonna cry over them."

"Maybe not. But what if the Vigilante gets mad at you, or Eric, or someone else you care about? What if the Vigilante kills them out of some skewed sense of justice? The Vigilante killed Jimmy because he panicked when we took the hotel. We all have our moments. All of us. We're human. And zombies are so fucking terrifying how can we not be afraid?"

Stacey's brow furrowed at Katie's words. "When you put it that way..."

Katie pulled her cap down on her head a little tighter, the cold wind whistling in her numb ears. "Life is hard enough without worrying about someone judging you and casting you out of the fort based on their own sense of right or wrong."

Stacey leaned her elbows on the wall, avoiding the rebar poking out of the top of the cement blocks. "I just want to feel safe." Her gaze was on the mutilated body of the zombie below. "But I never really do."

They smelled Calhoun before they saw him. The scrawny, old man shoved them roughly aside and looked down into the road.

"Hey, Calhoun, watch it! Katie is pregnant, you know!"

"Checking something," Calhoun muttered.

He scribbled in a battered notebook, making quick notations with a stubby pencil. Katie craned her head to take a peek, but couldn't make sense of the marks.

Stacey covered her nose with her gloved hands, trying not to gag while Katie felt her eyes watering. Calhoun was more ripe than usual.

Calhoun whipped out a strange contraption that looked like rulers taped together at odd angles and held it up, studying various views. Grumbling something about the city planners being imbeciles, he made more notations.

"Calhoun, um, we're supposed to be guarding this area. You need to move along."

"Dear God, woman! Do you understand the gravity of what I am doing? No, you do not! I am trying to make this fort safe from the messed up clones." Calhoun pointed down at the corpse in the road. "Dear God, they don't even have the decency to cover their junk. Heathens!"

Folding her arms over her breasts, Katie stared at Calhoun, one eyebrow arched.

"Fine! I will return later!" Calhoun whipped around, his long coat slapping their legs. His long scrawny legs carried him down the stairs past Travis, who was just starting up to the sentry post. The cold wind ruffled his hair over his furrowed brow as he climbed up the wood steps.

Katie winced. "I'm busted." She fumbled with the crossbow, making sure it was locked into place.

"Oh, yeah. Without a doubt. He has that look, too."

Katie slowly turned to see Travis stepping onto the platform. He looked amused and annoyed all at the same time. He folded his arms slowly over his chest and cocked his head.

"Aren't you supposed to be helping Peggy with the inventory?"

"Yeah, but Stacey needed training and the supply caravan isn't back yet so Jenni couldn't help her so..." She rolled her eyes. "Okay, okay. I'm just sick of being cooped up and not doing anything."

Travis kissed her brow lightly, his hand sliding over her belly. "Yeah, but you're pregnant and, after that bad cold you had, Charlotte told you to take it easy."

"Standing here, manning the crossbow, and shooting zombies really isn't that taxing," Katie assured him. She hated to admit she was a little weak from her illness. "I need to feel I'm doing something."

"Inventory is doing something," Travis assured her.

"You're just saying that because you don't want to do it."

"True," he admitted, grinning. "But it keeps you inside and warm until you're back to full fighting form."

Katie tried not to look as peeved as she felt. Her husband was damn annoying when he was being over-protective, but she really couldn't blame him. This was their first child, and conditions were not the best for bringing a baby into the world. Medicine was limited, and their food supply was not very rich in nutrients. They were living off of a lot of processed food, but there was hope the gardens would have a good yield and bring them healthier meals.

"You better not be trying to keep me off of sentry duty when I am feeling one hundred percent. I don't like being coddled. I already agreed not to leave the fort on supply or rescue runs." Katie gave him a grumpy glare, but let herself lean into him.

Travis hugged her and kissed her lightly on the cheek. "You're so cold. You don't need to relapse. Please get in where it's warm."

Stacey was trying not to pay attention to their discussion, but she was smiling slightly.

"Fine. Then you finish up here." Katie put on her gloves now that she wasn't manning the crossbow.

"Will do."

"And let me know when the caravan gets back. They're running late and I'm starting to worry," Katie added.

His lips were cool against hers. "I will. Now, get going. Peggy was muttering about you not helping her."

"Fine. Fine." Katie waved to Stacey, then climbed down the stairs.

On the ground, she felt even colder. The construction site wasn't nearly as busy or crowded as it had been in the first days. A large area was roped off for a garden, and a few people were working at breaking up the earth. Juan's mother, Rosie, was among them. She looked up briefly and waved.

Katie waved back, then headed to the entrance of the hotel. She felt uneasy despite the security of the walls and she hoped Jenni and the others would be back soon. She shut the door behind her, blocking out the cold wind that moaned like the undead zombies in the world beyond the walls.

Chapter 2

1. Battle of the Undead

H er nickname wasn't Loca for nothing, Jenni thought as she slipped her pistol out of her belt, flipped off the safety and began to systematically shoot the zombies. Gouts of decaying gore exploded out of the tops of their rotting heads.

"Jenni!" Ed sounded pissed.

"We gotta move now!"

The zombies were so intent on their feast, they didn't even look up as she approached. The stench of fresh death overwhelmed the reek of decay, and Jenni tried hard not to gag. She continued to fire at the zombies on the edge of the feeding frenzy. The zombies were tearing at each other frantically, ripping away tattered clothes and rotting flesh, as they tried to get to the freshly dead humans. Their moans were a terrible rumble.

Curtis slid into her peripheral view, also firing his weapon. Felix jogged slightly ahead of her, two pistols firing into the crowd. Behind them, Katarina had taken up a sniper position and was picking off any zombie that got too close to the people huddled on top of the van. As one managed to snag the foot of someone on the van, Katrina's shot severed the zombie's hand.

As Jenni drew closer, she could clearly see the zombies huddled over the dead human. They were stuffing flesh into their mouths with feverish delight. Dead, gray flesh was peeling off of their bones, and their clothes were tatters. Many had limbs missing and a few had odd objects sticking out of their bodies such as knives, pieces of furniture, tree limbs, and, in one weird case, an umbrella.

Jenni felt her throat tighten as a small child zombie staggered into view. It was gripping part of a bloody rib in its hand while trying to fight off the much larger zombies reaching for it. Jenni put a bullet through the child's forehead.

"Reloading," she said, and Curtis moved in front of her to cover.

The old clip slid out with ease and she quickly tucked it into her jean pocket before slamming a new one home. Looking up, she saw their situation had just taken a nasty turn.

The zombies were heading up the hill.

"Keep the line," Ed barked.

The fort people were moving down the hill in two lines. The first group unleashed on the zombies, then the second group took over as first reloaded. At least twenty zombies were heading toward them. These were the old variety, slow and decaying, but they were still a menace. The walking dead jerked and tumbled in a bizarre dance as they were gunned down, bullets ripping through their mottled features and punching out the back of their skulls.

"Nearly got them all now," Ed called out.

"Watch out! Watch out!" a deep voice thundered from on top of the van.

Jenni was reloading again when she heard the fast slap of feet on the pavement and instantly knew what that meant.

"Runners!"

The fast zombies came from behind the van. Their freshly killed bodies glistened with blood in the cold sunlight. Gaping wounds, terrible and grotesque, decorated their torsos and throats, but their limbs were still intact and they were fast.

The slower zombies were now secondary as the group concentrated on taking down the runners before they reached the line. There were at least six zigzagging up toward them.

"Don't panic! Don't panic!" Ed was shouting.

But people were panicking. Runners were so swift it was hard to hit them with a killing shot. The line broke up and Jenni gripped her ax and yanked it off her back as her pistol clicked empty. She had no time to reload and shoved her weapon into her belt before gripping the ax handle tightly with both hands.

"More! More!" someone was shouting.

Runners were now coming up off the side of the road. Men, women, children, their faces snarled into hungry expressions. The gunfire was rapid now. People were firing and reloading as fast as they could.

Jenni met the first runner as Curtis ducked out of the way to reload, not realizing she was on empty. She swung the ax as hard as she could, the blade slamming hard into the thing's neck. It scrabbled at her, its fingers skidding along the leather of her jacket. She shoved it back with one foot, jerking the ax out of its flesh. Blood spewed over her as she slammed the ax back into its neck, this time decapitating it. The head rolled away as the body fell.

Another zombie was almost on her. It was a woman this time, her frizzy, blond hair matted with blood. Her face was partially torn from her skull, and her throat was nothing but strips of flesh and spine. Jenni pivoted on her hip, bringing her elbow up to clip the zombified woman's chin hard. The creature was in mid-scream and the impact of Jenni's blow, shoved her jaw upwards, clipping off the tip of her tongue on her bloody teeth. Shoving the dead woman as hard as she could, Jenni got a little distance between them. Swinging the ax, she neatly decapitated the zombie.

"Help! Help!" Curtis' screams were terrified.

Jenni looked over to see him on the ground, his arm lifted defensively. A zombie had a hold of his forearm and was shaking its head back and forth, trying to bite through the thick leather of Curtis' jacket. Jenni slammed the ax blade down onto its head, splitting it open. It fell lifeless off of Curtis.

Chaos was around her, but the zombies were dying. She could see them falling under machetes, spears, and bullets. Nearby, she saw one of the fort people struggling to get a runner off his back as the thing gnawed away at the back of his neck. Blood rained around the man's terrified face as he screamed.

"Dammit! They got Bob!"

The words had barely left her lips when someone fired two shots, killing both the runner and Bob.

Jenni twisted around as she felt something brush her shoulder. It was Felix tripping over a body at their feet. He recovered quickly and fired two shots into the face of a slower, decayed zombie trying to grab him. The runners were down, their blood making the road slick. Their remains were tripping up the rest of the zombies shambling toward the fort people.

Feeling the heat of battle in her veins, Jenni marched toward the slower zombies, ax poised. Felix fell in beside her, Ed on her other side, and together they decimated the stumbling creatures. The zombies were slow and stupid. As long as she didn't let herself get cornered, it wasn't too hard to get them off their feet and down on the ground. Once there, it was easy for her to plant one boot on their decaying body and slam her ax down on their head.

Felix kicked the feet out from under a zombie and shot it point blank in the face. "I hate these things."

"And we're done," Ed said.

Jenni looked up from the zombie she had just dispatched. A bit of its nose and brain were still sticking to the ax blade, and she shook it off. The road was littered with the dead. She took a few deep breaths and instantly regretted it due to the stench. Jenni felt her heart beating hard in her chest. Suddenly, she was aware of her uneven breathing and her arms aching from the blows she had administered with her ax. When she had been fighting, she had felt nothing but the exhilaration of killing the damned things. Now she hurt all over.

"Anyone bit?" Ed's voice was hard.

The grizzled older man turned, looking over the people scattered along the road. Katarina was standing over Bob, a sad expression on her face.

"I said, is anyone bit? Look yourselves over."

Up on the van, Jenni saw the people they had saved getting to their knees. They had been lying in a heap, holding on to the luggage rack for dear life. There was an older Indian couple, two small children with the biggest and darkest eyes she had ever seen, a huge man with dark hair and unruly chops on his cheeks, a slender young man in Indian garb, and an older woman dressed in a flowing skirt and blouse.

"You okay up there?"

"No one is bit up here," the big man answered her. He was heavily muscled and looked like a wrestler.

The gore around the van was making Jenni's stomach heave. The man she had seen fall from the van was consumed down to the bone. Only his head was partially intact with his skull gleaming under strips of flesh. She was drawing close when she saw the jaws open and close.

"That's fucked up," Felix decided in a trembling voice, then shot it.

"It's brain was intact," Jenni muttered. She felt her stomach roll over and she stopped in mid-step. Gore surrounded her and the stench of death was unbearable. Felix rubbed her back and she closed her eyes, regaining her composure. She heard the little kids on the van crying and she shoved her discomfort away.

"Let's get you guys down," she said, reaching up.

Behind her, Ed and Curtis were checking out the people from the fort. A bite was lethal. There was no cure. Whatever revived the dead was carried in the saliva of the zombies and it always turned their victims if the brain remained intact. But victims didn't always just die and come back. On several occasions, people bitten merely turned and attacked. Maybe a scientist could explain why this sometimes occurred, but as far as anyone knew, the scientists were all dead.

The huge guy jumped down from the van and barely caught himself from slipping on the blood and guts. "Damn. Messy. Poor Jacob."

Jenni reached up to help one of the kids down, but the little girl shied away, hiding her face in the folds of the older woman's sari.

"Jenni, are you bit?"

She looked over at Curtis and shook her head.

"I need to check. Fort rules, you know."

Sighing, Jenni lowered her hands and stepped away from the van. Holding out her arms, legs spread, she let Curtis check her. He even looked behind her ears. With a curt nod, he moved on to check on Felix.

Turning, she reached up again. This time, the grandmother muttered a few words to the little girl and scooted her to the edge. As Jenni's hands went around the child's waist, she looked up into the enormous, black eyes fearfully gazing down at her. "It's okay," Jenni promised.

"Jenni, her hand," Felix said, his voice ragged.

Her eyes fell from the girl's face to the tiny hand clutching the thick leather of Jenni's jacket. Blood was seeping from a wound just below the little finger. A chunk of flesh was missing.

"No," Jenni gasped.

Looking up, she saw the little girl's dark eyes growing dimmer. Beneath her hands, she could feel the tiny heartbeat growing fainter.

"Jenni!" Felix exclaimed.

"What is it?" the big guy asked.

The woman with the flowing skirts and blond hair prepared to jump down off the van. "What's wrong?"

The Indian grandparents began to reach down to grab the little girl.

Jenni saw the fire, the spark of life, the spirit, or whatever it is that makes a human something other than a monster fade out of the girl's eyes. With a scream of anger and fear, she threw the girl away from her.

The child hit the ground and rolled.

Her family cried out in angry tones in their own language.

Then the little girl sprung to her feet, twisted around, and snarled.

2. The Biker From Hell

Rune had been on the road a long time and was anxious to lay his head down for a much needed rest. The big Harley under him roared with power as it raged over the weed infested road. He adjusted the goggles over his eyes and tucked his long braid of white hair into the collar of his leather jacket.

The darkened sky and barren hills were not welcoming. He had a bad feeling the day was going to get worse fast. He was on his way to meet up with his old buddy, Dale, and a bunch of other people who had escaped a rescue center outside of Waco. Since the zombie rising, he had been on the road nearly nonstop. He had been by the rescue center once before, and it had seemed safe enough. Barely any zombies had been stumbling around in that town. But on his last cruise by the old center, he had nearly been dragged off his bike by a throng of zombies. A few grenades into the crowd had cleared his way. His helmet and leathers had kept him safe from hungry mouths and grasping dead hands. It had been a fluke that he had seen the spray painted message and map on a billboard outside of town.

The message had been simple: "Going to the Fort." The map had been a little confusing, but Rune already knew where the fort was located. He had the misfortune of meeting up with some bandits that had designs on a fortified construction site down in Ashley Oaks a few months back. Hopefully, the fort was still standing.

Rune never stayed long in any of the survivor encampments he had come across. He didn't like trusting his safety to others. Most of the time, the survivors had very little food or weapons and were just holding tight waiting for rescue. They were damn fools and they didn't like it when he told them that. People had a tough time figuring out that no one was coming to save them. They were on their own and the longer they waited, the more vulnerable they became to the undead hordes.

In a field next to the winding road, a herd of cows slowly sauntered toward shelter as the wind grew colder. It smelled like an ice storm, and Rune hoped to God in Heaven the fort was still alive and that he'd be able to grab a cot for the night.

The Harley roared around a long curve, and Rune quickly braked as a bunch of vehicles parked on the road came into view. Sliding his Glock out of its holster, he wove through the tangle of big vehicles. As the bike came out the other side, he saw a group of people milling around among the remains of some pretty rancid zombies.

A young man with blond hair and a worried expression looked toward him, surprise filling his features. "Hey, you!"

"Hey, yourself," Rune answered grumpily.

Ahead of him was a van covered in zombie guts and blood. A few people were on top of it, moving to get down, while others were reaching up to help.

"Hey! You! Slow down! Who are you?" the young man persisted, jogging to keep up.

To everyone's surprise, a young woman suddenly hurled a little girl across the road just in front of Rune's bike. He skidded to a stop, one foot planted firmly on the bloodied asphalt.

The child jumped to its feet, whirled around, and let out the terrifying screech of the walking dead. The little girl hurtled across the road straight for the startled humans, all of them raising their weapons. Rune was faster and his Glock barked. The bullet slammed into the side of the kid's head, blowing a pretty good size hole out the other side. The little zombie crashed to the ground.

As the gunshot echoed away into the distance, the surviving humans all stared down at the small, sad figure. One by one, their gazes shifted toward him.

"Name is Rune. Just passing through," he said. The battle appeared to be over, but he was not sticking around for any grand finale.

"Good to see you, you sonofabitch," a gruff, familiar voice called out.

His gaze was drawn to the top of the van where an older woman with waist length hair dressed in a gypsy skirt and flowing blouse was being helped down by none other than his buddy, Dale.

"I'll be damned," Rune exclaimed. "What the hell happened at the rescue center?"

"Got overrun when some people decided to try to get supplies from the grocery store. They brought a whole mess of them down on us. The doors didn't hold," Dale answered. He acknowledged Rune with a short nod of his head, then helped the Indian couple down.

"Okay, people. Let's get off this road and to the fort!" an older, grizzled man called out. "We'll check you for bites and if you're clean, you can come to the fort to stay."

"That was our destination before it all went to hell," Dale answered grimly.

"Let's move. The longer we stay here, the more likely we'll get more of the damn zombies on our asses. C'mon! Let's go."

The pretty woman with the black hair was standing nearby, her head down. She was staring at the little girl she had hurled away to save herself.

Around him, people began talking again, hustling the newcomers from the van toward the vehicles rumbling behind the bike. The Indian woman was howling in agony as she was led away by a woman with red hair. Her husband looked stricken, but was mute as he carried the other small child with him. Rune wanted to feel for them, but he had seen too much to indulge in compassion. It was a fucked up world and fucked up things happened in it.

The witchy older woman that Rune remembered being named Maddie Goode, covered the little girl with her shawl before an older man took her arm and escorted her toward a waiting bus.

"Good to see you, Rune," she said as she walked past his bike.

"And you, Maddie," he answered.

Dale lumbered toward him, waving off the young man with blond hair that was motioning him toward the bus. "Heading to the fort?"

"Yeah. Need to find a place to crash before the ice storm hits." He shook Dale's hand firmly, their leather gloves creaking.

"Been a helluva day. The other van went off the road, and our driver stopped to check it out. Next thing you know, we're overrun and the driver is dead with the keys in his damn pocket. Next time, I'm driving."

"You're going to the fort?" It was the gorgeous woman who spoke.

Rune felt a little flutter in his belly as he looked toward her. Her pale skin was splattered with blood, the ax in her hand still dripping. "Yeah."

"Can I ride along?"

"Sure."

The woman slid the ax into the sheath on her back and slung herself onto the bike behind him. Her fingers gripped his leather jacket and she sat in silence. In his mirrors, he could see she was still staring at the little girl.

"See you at the fort," Dale said, clapping him on the shoulder and winking before walking toward the anxiously waiting people from the fort.

"Hold on," Rune said to the woman, glancing at her over his shoulder.

She didn't answer as she kept staring at the tiny form. The young man who had yelled at Rune earlier grabbed the kid by her ankle and dragged her off the road. Finally, the woman looked away.

Rune gunned the engine and the Harley continued toward the fort. He was strangely entranced by the silent creature behind him. She was beautiful, but grim. Her eyes were large and haunted, but the set of her jaw and lips told him she was a fighter. He wanted to say something to her, but he knew that it would be empty words. She was in her own head, dealing with her own shit.

As they rode, the woman let down her long hair with one hand and closed her eyes as the wind streamed through it. The tension around her jaw alleviated a bit and Rune tried hard not to keep glancing at his mirrors to look at her. He could feel her slowly relaxing and was pretty sure the ride was doing her some good. He found riding to be spiritual and wasn't surprised to see she did too.

The trip to Ashley Oaks was uneventful and free of anymore of the shambling dead. He was impressed by the high walls surrounding the old hotel, newspaper building and city hall. He was even more impressed with the gated entry. As he passed through the two different gates, he looked up to see sentries on the walls watching with interest.

Behind him, the pretty creature smeared in blood was silent, but slightly smiling. He could almost believe she was a ghost, but he had seen enough of those to know she was flesh and blood. It was tough being a medium when the world was full of the dead, but he was slowly getting used to it.

The final gate opened and the bike roared into a busy paddock. The woman pointed, and he directed the rumbling bike over to the empty spot. She slid off the bike and patted his shoulder lightly.

"Thanks, dude. I needed that."

"No prob. Name's Rune," he said, extending his hand to her.

"Jenni," she answered, shaking it briefly. With her dark hair shifting around her and her face splattered in blood, she looked fierce. "Also known as La Loca."

"Loca is good," Rune decided, giving her a rakish grin.

"Sometimes," she answered, winking and walking off.

He watched as she headed over to where people were cleaning off spears, machetes, hatchets and other weapons. A small building had steam rising out of it, and Rune guessed that was where they were cleaning off the zombie gore. Halfway there, Jenni leaped onto the back of a tall, lean Hispanic cowboy. With a grin, the cowboy carried her over to the rest of the returning team.

Rune sighed. Of course a fine woman like that was taken.

"Okay. Who the hell are you? And what's in the bag?" It was the old codger with the grizzled face.

"Rune." He opened the bag to show the old guy the grenades. "And a whole lot of hurt."

The man chuckled. "Name's Ed. Welcome to the fort."

"Just staying until the storm blows over. Then I gotta move on." Rune shifted the bag.

"You sure?"

"Gotta keep moving," Rune answered. He could see the ghosts around him, faint shimmering things. "Gotta keep moving ahead of the dead."

Ed looked at him strangely.

"There ain't no rest for the wicked, man," Rune joked. Or mediums, he thought. Ghosts were everywhere, just like zombies.

"You can't escape the dead in this world," Ed finally said. "You're welcome to stay if you like."

"Thanks, man. I'll think about it." Rune shifted his bag of grenades. "Like I said, we'll see how it goes." The man who could see the dead looked around, studying the fort, seeing the flickering of spirits all around him. "We'll see how it goes."

3. Promises and Shadows

Juan grimaced at the stink coming off the woman he loved. She was hanging on his back, covered in drying blood and gore and reeked of death. She seemed immune to it, having been out in the deadlands all afternoon, but he had been in the nice and tidy dead-free zone of the fort. It amazed him that he had been used to the stench of the dead when they had been under siege in the first days. It was strange how humans acclimated to things like that. But once the dead throngs were cleared out and clean fresh breezes filled the fort, the smell of the dead was again sharp and repellent.

"You ruined my jacket, Loca," he grumbled, trudging toward the clean up area.

"It's ugly anyway," she assured him. "Besides, I'm tired. Spoil me."

"As if I have a choice," Juan drawled, grinning and grimacing at the same time. "What did you do this time to get so messy?"

"Up close and personal decapitations of the zombie kind. I went whacky-whacky with my trusty ax."

"You're supposed to shoot them before they get too close." He felt his stomach coil up at the thought of her fighting with the ravenous dead.

"Yeah, well, sometimes runners see it a different way."

"Shit! Running zombies?"

"Fresh and fast. I think another van of survivors ended up a buffet." Jenni sighed, laying her head against his shoulder.

He tried hard not to be angry with her. Sometimes it was damn hard. She had a tendency to act first, think later. Her rabid hatred of the undead often spurred her to insane acts of heroics.

"I just wish you didn't take so many chances," he said at last.

"Well, zombies need to be killed or they munch on us." Her voice was soft, almost petulant. "A girl's gotta do what a girl's gotta do."

"You mean a loca going loca," Juan corrected.

"It works, doesn't it? Zombies die. I come home to you."

"I just worry."

"I'm not going to die without a fight," Jenni assured him.

"I don't want you to die."

"I'm not gonna!"

"Says the loca."

They reached the fenced in area where the weapons were being cleaned and where Charlotte was attending to any wounded. A bite was deadly. Everyone knew that, but they had two instances where someone had tried to hide their wound only to turn after entering the paddock. It was frustrating to have to implement additional measures to keep the fort safe, but they had no choice. Two armed guards stood watch as Charlotte finished bandaging up a newcomer. A pistol was tucked into the holster on her hip as an extra precaution.

Juan plopped Jenni down onto a lawn chair and stared down at her bloody appearance. "Seriously, you couldn't shoot them in the head before they reached you?"

"Well, I was trying, but they were kinda fast. And then it just got all crazy." A dark and frightening emotion shadowed her expression and then it disappeared.

With a sigh, Juan sat next to her, taking off his cowboy hat. Slouching down in his chair, he pondered demanding to know what had happened out there. Jenni had her moments when it was clear that the grief she felt over the loss of her children was overwhelming her, but he could not say anything when this happened. His beloved tended not to speak of the past at all. Occasionally a snippet or two of information would leak out about her life as an abused trophy wife and mother, but it was never on purpose. It was always worse when she saw something out in the deadlands that reminded her of her children, but she had been handling those situations better of late.

Jenni flipped her hair over one shoulder and stared at him. He had a feeling she knew he was holding his tongue.

"What?" He finally said.

"It was a kid. She got bit. The new guy on the bike had to kill her. I saw the light go out of her eyes. I saw the hunger come into them."

His eyebrows flew up.

"I've never seen that before," Jenni continued. "The life goes out. It was so clear. I could see it. Like a curtain falling over her spark. Then bam. Here comes the hungry zombie." Shaking her head, she pulled the ax off her back and tossed it onto the ground.

"Fucking scary, huh?" Juan muttered.

Nodding mutely, Jenni slumped down in the chair. Nearby, Charlotte was examining the older, Indian woman. Jenni motioned toward them. "It was her grandkid. It sucked." Jenni thought for a long moment, swinging her legs back and forth. "I don't want that to happen to me."

Juan was silent, knowing better than to say a word. It could shut her up and cut him off if he said the wrong thing.

"I don't want you or anyone else to see the light go out in my eyes and the crazy hungry zombie look come into them."

"Jenni, that's not gonna-"

"You can't say that!" Jenni pointed at him, her voice vehement. "You cannot say that! You don't know. None of us know. Bob died today. I'm sure he didn't go out there thinking he was gonna bite it."

"Okay, okay. You're right. None of us can know. You just gotta be extra careful when you go out there."

"I want a bullet right here-" Jenni pointed to her forehead. "-if it ever goes down that way. I want it fast. I don't want to be one of those things. I don't want the light in my eyes to go out and for the hungry zombie to take over."

Juan stared into her dark, luminous eyes, tinged with the Jenni madness that made him crazy for her and love her more than he thought possible. The mere thought of her not being next to him made his throat tighten with emotion. He didn't know what to say, and she seemed to be waiting for words to soothe her. At last, he managed to say, "Okay," his voice cracking slightly.

Nodding, satisfied, Jenni curled up in her chair. She looked so small and so delicate, the blood splatter and the reek of the dead couldn't keep him away. He grabbed her arm and tugged her firmly out of her chair and onto his lap. Holding her close, he nuzzled her cheek. Her body melded into his and she made a small, happy sound that made him smile.

Chapter 3

1. The Boring Things In Life

How many boxes?" Peggy's voice droned.

Katie quickly counted the boxes of ammunition, her fingers lightly touching each stack. "Fifty."

"Damn," Peggy muttered. She shoved her brown hair back from her frowning face and made a notation on her clipboard.

The two women were in the storage room used for the ammunition stock. In recent days, a fresh batch of zombies had appeared out of the Texas Hill Country. There was speculation that they were from one of the fort's neighboring towns. A few of the zombies had been somewhat recognizable as former friends or business acquaintances. Nerit had ordered the horde destroyed, and a good chunk of ammunition had been used up.

"We still got a lot in these other boxes," Katie reminded her.

"Yeah, but if they don't find fresh supplies, we better learn to make our own bullets soon," Peggy responded.

Katie nodded, her hand gently rubbing her swelling belly. In the days before the zombie uprising, she had never imagined being pregnant. It was something her wife, Lydia, and she had discussed a few times, but adoption had always been seen as the route to go. Now, time was more precious and not to be squandered. Death was everywhere as the living struggled to maintain a foothold on the world.

She had been forced to decide when the world ended whether to let her sorrow drag her down into the depths of despair and give up or fight to survive. She had chosen to survive. In the silence of the night, she still mourned Lydia and their old life, but she had also allowed herself to let go of the old world. That had opened the door for her to find love with Travis and now they were expecting a baby.

"Jason and the kids are working on new weapons for the perimeter. It's scary how good they are at inventing diabolical ways to take out the zombies," Katie remarked as they moved to the next box.

"Yeah, well, kids are always good at finding ways to be in trouble. They're just frying zombies instead of ants now." Peggy looked around the room at all the shelves stuffed with battered boxes of ammo. "It never feels like enough, does it?"

Katie shook her head. "No, it doesn't."

Peggy looked down, her expression clouded with fear and pain, and then she shrugged. "Nothing we can do but keep going and hope to God we don't get eaten."

There was nothing really to say to that, so Katie kept quiet. Everyone in the fort had their moments. It seemed to be happening more now. Travis was gloomy about the dampened spirits of the fort, but Katie thought it was probably only natural. There were more cold, overcast days than sunny. Also, illnesses had been working their way through the fort population. The flu had already made one pass and a bad cold had many people stuck in bed. Plus, the safety of the fort allowed people to actually have moments of peace. Strangely, it was easier to shove all that pain and terror away when fighting to live. It was the mundane daily routine that made things harder to handle. Old ghosts and old memories seemed to surface at unexpected moments.

Realizing she may have upset Katie, Peggy looked back at the tall blond standing behind her. "I mean, we ain't gonna get eaten. I mean, look at this place. We got it made compared to the poor bastards out there. I'm sure we're all gonna be safe and sound. And your sweet baby will be fine."

Smiling slightly, Katie reached out to pat Peggy on the shoulder. "I know."

"And that team will come back packed to the gills with ammunition and more supplies, and I won't be such a worried old hag."

"Peggy, you're not old and you're not a hag."

"I feel like it. Worn out and tired. Cody has got that damn cold something fierce, and I was up all night with him. I just hate seeing him suffer. It makes me feel so helpless." Peggy sighed and shook her head. "I miss his daddy at times like these. He was so good at calming him down."

Peggy rarely spoke about her husband who had died in the first days. Katie knew from things Peggy's little boy said that they had seen him transformed into a zombie. Cody was a sensitive soul to begin with and the death of the world had crushed him. For months he had not left his mother's side, always clinging to her and terrified whenever she was out of his view. But lately, with other children joining the fort, he had been braver. He was now able to be away from his mother a few hours at a time without panicking.

The door to the storeroom opened, and Nerit stood in the doorway. The older woman had her yellowed, silver hair drawn back from her face and her sniper rifle was slung over one shoulder. By her reddened cheeks, it looked like she had just come off duty.

"The team just got back, Peggy. I think Yolanda is struggling with the communication center and lost track of them for a few minutes. Could you go check on her? Make sure she has it down?" Nerit asked.

"Sure thing," Peggy answered, handing off her clipboard to Katie. "I told Curtis that one CB was shorting out. But did he listen? Oh, no."

Katie listened to Peggy complain all the way down the hall, her voice fading away.

"How are you feeling?" Nerit asked. She slowly stepped into the room, and Katie noticed that the she was favoring one leg again. She wasn't sure if anyone else realized that the woman in her early sixties was moving more slowly than usual.

"I'm good. I just have a few more boxes to go through then I'll have an updated list for you." Katie motioned to the last shelf of ammunition she had to count.

Nerit tilted her head slightly, looking at the battered boxes nearby. "Well, I'll finish for you. Jenni just got back and she's asking for you. I think it got bad out there. She's down in the paddock getting scrubbed down and checked for bites by Charlotte."

"Ugh! She hates that." Katie handed over the clipboard.

"It can't be helped. Jenni has closer contact with the zombies than most. She punched one last week." Nerit shook her head. "She's taking too many risks again."

"I'll talk to her," Katie assured the older woman.

"Thank you. I would, but she really doesn't listen to anyone but you."

"That's the curse of being her best friend." Katie winked and trudged out the door.

The hotel's ground floor was packed with people as shifts finished. Weary groups were making their way toward the elevators while a few lounged on the plush couches chatting. A new group of people, looking shell-shocked and tired, were being checked into the hotel by Ken.

"Got Muslims now," Curtis said, startling her. She hadn't realized he was next to her.

"What?"

Curtis nodded toward the older man and woman dressed in traditional Indian garb. "Muslims."

"I think they may be Hindu," Katie answered.

"Still heathens," Curtis said, shaking his head. "Don't know if we should be taking in heathens."

Katie turned to gaze at Curtis, her disapproval clearly reflected in her expression. "Really?"

"Well, we're a God-fearing group, Katie. Bringing in other kinds is gonna cause trouble," Curtis answered, his boyish face flush with emotion. "It's rough enough keeping things going as it is."

"Curtis, people are people. We can't start picking and choosing or we'll end up just like the Vigilante. Offing people because we don't approve of them."

A look of horror washed over the younger person's face and he stepped back from her. "I-I-I didn't mean..."

Feeling bad for the harshness in her tone, Katie hugged him. "It's okay, Curtis. We're all freaking out just a bit."

He clung to her for a second, then sheepishly stepped back. His face was so red, Katie felt embarrassed for him.

Jenni stomped in, hair damp, face flushed, dressed in a big bathrobe with a bag slung over one shoulder. She was holding her boots in one hand and wrinkled her nose at Katie.

"Charlotte declared my clothes totaled. I really liked those jeans!"

Katie grinned, snagging Jenni's free hand. "Oh, c'mon. It's just an excuse to go dig a new pair out of the inventory."

"Yeah, but still! They looked good! I looked five pounds smaller!"

"You are five pounds smaller," Katie pointed out. The people in the fort were slimmer now. Food was carefully distributed at each meal. Though people ate their fill, they were not overeating. Also, the hard work that always had to be done was whittling the fat off of beer bellies and strengthening muscles.

Katie noted Curtis making his escape, but she let him go. The poor guy was so easily flustered. She felt bad for the young man. He was the youngest of the Ashley Oaks police force and its only survivor.

"I got stuff to show you!" Jenni patted the bag at her side. "I had fun out there until..." She waved her hand, wiping away the pain that lingered in her eyes. "Enough of that. I'm back. Safe. Sound. Move on."

Katie knew better than to push Jenni. "When do I get to see?"

"In your room. It's top secret stuff."

"I will not be treated in this manner!" The sharp female voice rang out in the lobby, slicing through the drone of conversation. A big candle hurtled through the air and slammed into a painting, sending it to the ground with a loud crash.

Blanche Mann, the town's richest woman before the zombie rising and the meanest bitch most of them had encountered, stomped into the lobby, her high heels clicking loudly against the tiles.

Linda, Juan's younger cousin, ducked as another candle hurtled over her head. "You said you would give me the Imotrex if I cleaned your hotel room!"

"You call that cleaning? That is the most piss poor job I have ever seen! You didn't even polish my shoes or iron Stephen's clothes!" Blanche was in a fury.

"Look, bitch, give me the Imotrex! We need it for the clinic!" Linda was a lithe little thing and easily ducked another candle. She wasn't about to be intimidated. She put her hands on her hips and glowered at the other woman. "I did what you asked. Pay up!"

"I caught you going through my things trying to find something to steal!"

"I was looking for the pills that you promised me!"

"You're a thief and I'm going to report you to Bill!" Blanche tossed back her heavily sprayed hair and began shouting for Bill.

"Call him, you stupid bitch, and I'll tell him how you scammed me!" Linda kicked a chair with agitation.

"You stupid, thieving spic!"

That was enough for Katie. She stepped between Blanche and Linda. "Calm down, Blanche, and give it a few minutes. We'll get this sorted out. You don't need to resort to insults." Katie said in a soft, calm voice.

"Get out of my face!"

Blanche shoved Katie back with both hands. Linda caught Katie as she stumbled back.

The next few minutes were sheer chaos. Jenni swooped in like an avenging angel, shouting in Spanish. Curtis tried to intercept her, only to be pushed out of the way. Blanche commenced screaming about her sister, the Texas state senator, and why she deserved to be treated better. Katie wasn't hurt by Blanche's push, but everyone seemed to think she should sit down, much to her chagrin.

It wasn't until Bill showed up that any semblance of order returned to the hotel lobby. He got everyone separated and ordered everyone not involved to move on.

"She said if I cleaned her pigpen of a room she would give me Imotrex. Manny is suffering really bad migraines, and I wanted to get him some pills. We ran out a few weeks ago, and none of the supply runs have brought in any more." Linda explained with her voice edged with her anger.

"She did a shitty job, tried to steal stuff, and has no right to lip off at me!" Blanche tossed back her hair and glowered at Bill. "Besides, I don't have the Imotrex here. She'll have to go to my house and get it."

"What? You didn't say that!"

Katie caught Linda's arm before she could launch herself at Blanche. Jenni grabbed Linda's other arm and whispered something to her in Spanish.

Bill sighed softly and shook his head. "Blanche, we took everything we could use out of your house."

"You thieves! How dare you!"

"Calm down. We told Stephen all about it. We take what we can to maintain the fort wherever we can. You know that."

"You're a bunch of thieves! I can't believe this!"

"Fuck this," Linda growled. She pulled away from Katie and Jenni, shaking her head. "I can't believe I was fooled by that bitch! I'm not doing a damn thing for you ever again!" She stalked off. Curtis fell in behind her, motioning to Bill that he'd calm her down.

Bill shifted his belt up over his belly. "Blanche, you best just let this drop. You did Linda wrong and everyone knows it. You ain't making many friends around here."

"I don't need friends. I should have left when my sister told me to. I'd be with her, safe and sound, and not dealing with you disgusting hicks." Blanche whirled around on her high heels and stalked off.

Bill let out a long, slow sigh.

"She's such a whore," Jenni decided.

"Her sister is even worse. I had the displeasure of meeting her more than once." Katie rubbed her belly, feeling very tired.

"I didn't vote for her," Jenni grumbled. "Of course, I never voted, but..." She shrugged.

Bill hooked his thumbs over his belt and looked thoughtful. "She's trouble. We all know it. It sucks that she scammed Linda like that, but she's not used to being ordinary folk and taking care of her own needs. Her money is worthless now and she can't get anyone to help her keep her place clean. Stephen is even more helpless."

"I'm not going to feel bad for her," Katie said in a low voice.

"Don't expect you to," Bill answered. "But we need to remember she's a very unhappy viper. She's gonna strike out at whoever is closest to her at any given moment."

"We should make a suggestion box for the Vigilante," Jenni murmured. "I got a name to shove into it."

"Jenni, behave." Katie hooked her fingers through her friend's and squeezed.

With a sigh, Jenni relaxed her stance and tugged Katie to her feet. "Let's get out of here."

Bill's expression was thoughtful as the two women walked toward the elevators. Finally, with a shrug, he walked on.

"Poor Bill," Jenni said softly. "He has to deal with all the crazy shit."

"What isn't crazy nowadays?" Katie asked, arching a brow.

Jenni laughed. "True dat."

2. Rough Spots

Nerit watched as the small bonfire sparked and blew dark smoke up into the graying sky. Another supply run was done and the storage rooms were restocked. But with that gain, came more loss. As she watched Charlotte burning the blood soaked clothing of some of the returning fort members, she couldn't help but think of Bob lying out there beside the road. If possible, some fort volunteers would retrieve him and dispose of what remained of his corpse in the landfill. Proper burial was a thing of the past.

"One loss," Ed said beside her, as if reading her thoughts. "And seven more people to feed and care for."

"It never balances out," Nerit answered.

"Rune, the long haired one, says he's moving on after the ice storm. The rest say they want to stay." Ed was chewing some tobacco he had managed to snag at a convenience store.

Nerit was indulging in another cigarette, grateful the salvage team had brought more boxes. She wasn't picky about the brand anymore. The cigarettes calmed her nerves and were her one small luxury in this life without Ralph. She missed her husband everyday, but she couldn't think too long about his death or she began to feel tired and old.

"Lenore snuck back a whole bunch of beauty supplies for Ken," Ed added after a few beats. "I just looked the other way."

"I would have, too. People need a few pleasures."

"I think they're gonna set up a beauty shop." Ed's craggy face broke into a slight smile.

Nerit laughed. "Honestly, I think that may help morale. Life has felt pretty heavy lately."

In the distance, cold rain was falling in a gray curtain over the hills.

"My boys were hoping I'd ask you out."

She choked on the smoke billowing out of her lungs. "Oh."

"I told them that you're too much of a man for me. That you could probably kick my ass ten ways until Sunday."

Half-coughing, half-laughing, Nerit grinned. "Probably."

Ed crossed his arms over his chest and planted his feet firmly apart. "I ain't gonna ask you out, Nerit. I admire you something fierce and yer my friend. Knowing my boys, they'll be dropping hints like crazy. I thought you should know."

"That's fine, Ed. And I am flattered." Nerit smiled slightly, trying not to think of Ralph and her own adult children. She had hope that her children and grandchildren were still alive in Israel, but hope was all she really had.

"Storm is going to hit hard. Better sound the alarm and get everything tied down."

"Agreed. Please take care of it," Nerit said.

Ed stared at her, studying her calm countenance, then nodded. "You got it."

Nerit continued to stare at the small fire. She was in pain and didn't want Ed to know it. Her hip and leg were throbbing, and she was afraid to move. There was no way she would show weakness. The people in the fort had elevated her to a legendary status, and she would not disappoint them by appearing fragile.

As he walked away, Nerit relaxed a little.

A few minutes later, Travis joined her. He slid an arm over her shoulder and gave her a light hug. Despite her resolve to be a hard ass, she rested her head on his shoulder for a few seconds. He reminded her so much of her eldest son at times. It was nice to feel comforted.

"What's the status?" Travis asked.

"One dead. Six permanent new members. And one guy with a bag of grenades passing through," Nerit answered. "The salvage team managed to get into that gun store in Emorton without bringing the entire town down on them. So we should be set for at least six more months as long as we don't get hit too hard. More boxed and canned food. Two generators. Fuel. And beauty supplies."

Travis laughed. "Let me guess: Lenore?"

"Ed said it wasn't a big thing. He looked the other way."

Travis shook his head slightly. "Well, it didn't cause an issue, so we'll look the other way, too."

"Bob is still out there," Nerit said after a long pause.

"I know. I spoke with that new guy, Dale, and he said there are quite a few bodies out there. He said that they came from a rescue station outside of Waco. Two vans made it away when they were overrun. He says the other van got ahead of them and must have had someone inside with a bite. It went off the road and they were swarmed."

"Ed said there were runners and older zombies. That one area is badly infested thanks to the migration from Hackleburg," Nerit sighed. The migrating zombies were the result of the fort rescuing survivors under attack by the now defunct bandits. It had been a risk they decided to take. They had managed to rescue four people, but now the shambling dead were wandering through the hills seeking them out. "I think we should take a break during the bad weather to get our bearings and decide what our next steps are. We've been in overdrive, and I think people are worn out and cranky."

"Why don't we meet up after the weather clears up? Gather up the council and brainstorm?" Travis tucked his hands into his jacket as he gazed toward the approaching storm.

"I think that would do us a lot of good." Nerit admired Travis. He was not a natural born leader, but he was doing his best. "Having our attention focused on specific goals may help shake people out of their malaise a little."

"And we all prefer that to having a horde of zombies show up on our doorstep to get the old blood pumping," Travis joked.

"Well, this old blood is going in before the sleet gets here," Nerit said, patting his shoulder. She was relieved when her legs moved without much of a limp.

"See you later, Nerit," Travis said, giving her a fond smile.

"God willing," Nerit answered.

It wasn't until she was in her room with her old dog snoring in the corner that she realized Travis had been holding her up, giving her hip a rest, until she could move again. Collapsing into a chair, a book in hand, she lightly laughed and shook her head.

Maybe Travis was a better leader than she had given him credit for.

Cracking her romance novel open, she began to read.

3. Dangerous Times

Katie stared down at the baby clothes strewn across her bed and felt her heart beat just a little bit faster. Her hand settled against her slightly swollen belly as her gaze slid to Jenni's anxious face.

"I did good, didn't I?"

"Amazing." Katie gently touched a blue onsie and her heart beat even faster.

"I got blue, pink and yellow stuff. I figured we have it covered if it's Jenni or Travis, Jr." Jenni picked up a little pink bonnet and set it on top of her head.

"Jenni, huh?"

"It's only natural for the baby to be named after her auntie," Jenni answered. She posed with the bonnet on her head. "Why wouldn't she be named after my fabulousness?"

The bonnet fell onto the bed and Katie slowly picked it up. She traced the tiny lace with one finger then took a deep breath. "Oh, God." She sat down hard on the edge of the bed and tried to calm her trembling hands.

"Hey, you okay?" Jenni immediately crawled over the bed to Katie's side.

"Yeah. Yeah. I think so. I just got overwhelmed there for a second." Katie forced herself to take another deep breath and felt embarrassed by the tears suddenly brimming in her eyes. "Maybe it's hormones."

"Yeah, probably." Jenni smoothed Katie's hair back from her face. "You're okay with having a baby, right?"

Katie was a little surprised by the question, but nodded. "Oh, yeah. I'm sure. I'm very sure. So is Travis."

Jenni kept silent as her fingers kept stroking Katie's hair. She was obviously waiting for Katie to go on.

"We did decide this together. It was a conscious choice to take our chances. We're trying to build a life together and this felt like the right thing to do." It was good to hear the words. Good to be reminded that this was a choice she made and she was responsible for what happened next. If there was a mantra Katie lived her life by, it was to live up to her potential and fulfill her responsibilities.

"Despite the zombies," Jenni said in a soft, worried voice after a long, uncomfortable pause.

Katie bristled slightly. She was very much aware of the criticism by some about her choice to be a mother. "Yes. Despite the zombies. They are here to stay. I don't see them going away anytime soon, do you?"

"No..." Jenni sighed sadly.

"So what are we supposed to do? Stop living? Stop trying to be happy? Stop trying to build a future just because the dead decided we taste really damn good?"

"Hey, you don't have to defend yourself to me!"

Katie stood up, clutching the bonnet in one hand and turned toward Jenni. "Are you sure?" She hated the swell of anger filling her, but she couldn't help herself. She was happy about the baby, overwhelmed at times, but she was happy. It was a piece of Travis inside of her and it made her feel closer to him than she had ever imagined. Before the dead began to attack the living, she had never seen herself as a mother. Her old life had not allowed much room for it. But this life, full of so much grief and terror, was also full of hope. The fort was secure now. It was a place of safety and community.

Jenni didn't answer, her hands limp in her lap, staring off into nothing. "Jenni?"

"My baby died. My baby was eaten," Jenni said in a low voice. "I just don't want anything to happen to yours."

Katie swallowed hard as Jenni's words expressed her own fears. "I don't want anything to happen to anyone I love. Every time you are out there, I live in terror that you won't come back. But I can't expect you to stop doing what you need to do to help this fort survive. And I can't stop my life because of those fucking zombies out there." Irritably, Katie swept a tear off her cheek and sighed.

Jenni finally looked at her and gave her a slight smile. "The old life feels so far away. It did right away, you know. The first day. It just seemed so gone. Like the world was suddenly empty. But it feels fuller now. Like...like...it's coming back to life."

Striding over to the bed, Katie hugged Jenni tightly. "It's because we didn't stop living."

Jenni kissed the growing baby bump and snuggled into Katie's embrace. "I know. Hell, I think I kinda went apeshit crazy trying to feel alive those first few months."

At the memory of some of Jenni's more insane shenanigans, Katie had to smile. "Oh, yeah. Definitely."

"Fuck zombies."

"Fuck 'em."

"You're right, you know. About going on. Hell, look at me and Juan. And you and Travis. And lots of other people around here. The people who stopped trying to live their life are dead now. Like that chick who took a header into the zombies off the crane."

Katie nodded solemnly. "Yeah. That was awful."

Jenni shook her head. "Seriously fucked up."

They lapsed into silence.

"Seriously, what else were we supposed to do?" Katie asked after a few contemplative seconds. "Just freak out all the time, be afraid, mourn the world and just stop trying to live?"

Jenni turned to gaze at her friend, her fingers sliding over Katie's. Holding her hand firmly, Jenni said, "We have all done what we had to do to survive."

It was hard not to think of Lydia at times like these. Hard not to want to feel her soothing touch and her calming voice. Lydia always had a way of making her feel solid and safe. Much like Travis did now. In her heart, she believed that Lydia was watching over her and was proud of her. Much to her chagrin, tears fell down her cheeks.

"Oh, Katie, don't cry!"

"It's okay! Stupid fuckin' hormones!" Katie laughed as she wiped her tears away. "I am damn sure I'm doing the right thing. I know it."

Jenni smiled and squeezed her hand tighter. "I'll teach the baby to be loca. And it will do fine kickin' zombie ass."

Kissing Jenni's cheek firmly, Katie felt her love for her friend fill her completely and totally. It was almost overwhelming. "I know. I know you'll always be looking out for me and the baby."

"You mean Jenni Junior."

Katie rolled eyes. "We'll see."

"It's totally the best name," Jenni assured Katie.

Despite her tears and her overwhelming emotions, Katie found her composure. "We'll all be okay. One way or the other. We're going to take back this world one little bit at a time."

"Now you sound like Travis."

"I am married to the guy."

"And it's so cute!"

"Don't start!"

"He is all adorable with you and-"

Katie punched Jenni's arm. "Don't start!"

Jenni rolled around on the bed laughing, scattering the baby clothes.

Chapter 4

1. A little Taste of The Old World

Ken was in a fabulous mood. The air was filled with a combination of the harsh scents of bleach and hair dye and the fruity fragrances of shampoo and conditioner. His dark hair now had blond tips and his fingernails were carefully manicured. He felt more like himself than he had in ages.

The big room that had been reluctantly turned over to him for his beauty salon was buzzing. Music played softly from a big, ancient boom box in the corner. Next to him, Lenore twisted Yolanda's hair into a tight French braid that wound around her head while Yolanda flipped through a year old copy of a fashion magazine. They were both sassing Felix, who was trying to ignore them as he read his book. With ebony skin and dark eyes, Felix was a good-looking guy, but painfully straight. Ken had tried flirting with him to no avail. He had been down in the dumps about his single status, but now that his beauty salon was up and running, he felt better. He was much happier doing hair than working on the construction site. Besides, he felt he was helping raise the spirits of the people in the fort.

Now, nothing could dampen his mood, not even the sleet pinging against the curtained windows. Another storm had blown in during the morning and was still going strong. But it was nice and warm in the hotel and the nastiness of the deadlands seemed far away. If only Curtis would sit still so he could give him a decent haircut, all would be well.

"Sit still!"

"I think you took too much off the side," Curtis complained.

"No, I didn't. Sit still!"

He was having a horrible time trimming Curtis' hair. The boy kept fidgeting nervously in the chair. He had asked for Lenore to do his hair, but she was halfway through a ten hour marathon sewing in Yolanda's new extensions. The young police officer had finally submitted to letting Ken do his hair. Ken considered poking at the guy's homophobia, but decided against it. He was working hard to make friends and find acceptance in the fort. Riling Curtis wouldn't do him any favors.

Curtis grumbled under his breath, watching Ken's scissors like a hawk.

Yolanda flipped through the magazine for the fourth time. "When are you going to get the stuff so I can get rid of these damn press on nails? I need some decent nails, Lenore. I've glued them onto my nails so many times, they're wearing thin."

"Maybe next time. I can't grab stuff unless the coast is clear or I'll get in trouble. Don't need no Vigilante tossing my fat ass over the wall." Lenore's nimble fingers kept braiding as she spoke. Ken marveled at her patience and stamina.

Curtis squirmed around his chair. "You're taking too much-"

Ken grabbed Curtis' head firmly between his hands and aimed his gaze straight forward. "Stop moving."

"Your ass is fine," Felix drawled from behind his book. There was a pause as everyone looked at him and he slowly lowered it to peer over the well-worn edges. "I meant that it's not fat. Not that it's..."

"You saying my ass ain't fine?" Lenore shot him a cross look, her fingers still braiding.

"I didn't mean that!" Felix sighed heavily.

"So it is fine?" Yolanda arched both her eyebrows, gazing into the mirror in front of her at his reflection.

Ken giggled.

"Just don't answer them, Felix. They got you trapped," Curtis advised. "They're just being wicked."

"You have no idea how wicked I can get." Yolanda winked.

Ken was amazed at how red Curtis' scalp turned under the golden strands of hair. "You made him blush, Yolanda!"

"It ain't that hard. Curtis is our sweetie, ain't you?"

Curtis blushed even more.

Ken wondered how red he could turn.

"He's always making sure everyone minds themselves and he is always super sweet and gets me coffee when I'm on duty in the communication center." Yolanda smiled affectionately at Curtis.

"It's no big thing," he answered awkwardly.

"Maybe he's sweet on you," Ken teased.

"Nah, he's sweet on Linda," Yolanda answered.

Curtis darted out of the chair so fast, Ken almost stuck him with his scissors. "Hey!"

"I...um..I can't pay nothing and can't tip you. I feel bad about that. Maybe I can get Bill to let Lenore get more supplies-"

"Just gimme a kiss and we're even," Ken said, trying to sound and look serious.

Blinking hard, Curtis stammered, backing toward the door, "I think...I'll..."

"I'm just teasing, Curtis!" Ken burst out laughing. "I wasn't done. Sit your ass back down."

Turning, Curtis ran his fingers over his hair, fussing with it a little. "It will do. I'll see you later." He was moving so fast, he nearly shoved Peggy back out the door as she entered. Mumbling an apology, he darted past her and vanished.

Peggy screwed up her face, frowning. "What is up with that boy?"

"I just teased him a little about Linda," Yolanda answered.

"Oh, Lord. You didn't!" Peggy looked aghast.

"Oh, there is dish here. Spill it!" Ken began to clean up around the chair, sweeping up the tiny bits of hair he had trimmed.

"I caught him consoling Linda in the communication center." Peggy paused for dramatic effect. "They were naked."

Ken almost dropped his scissors. "No!"

"Oh, yeah. They were buck ass naked and going at it. Well, actually Curtis' pants were around his ankles, but they were doing the naked tango just fine." Peggy smirked as she slid into the vacant chair in front of Ken.

"I will never sit in that chair again," Yolanda declared. "Curtis' nasty, naked pasty ass on that chair is too much for me to deal with."

Lenore murmured in agreement.

Felix sighed loudly.

"Were you next?" Peggy asked.

"I have nothing better to do, so you might as well go first." Felix cracked his book back open with dramatic flair that impressed even Ken and went back to reading.

"I just need a little trim and some fresh bangs." Peggy messed with her hair a bit, showing off her abundance of split ends.

"Okay, I suggest taking two inches off the bottom, skip the bangs and do a little bit of layering in the front instead and let me put a little bit of a lighter color in."

"Honey, I ain't got a man to impress no more. Just chop it so it's easy to deal with."

Ken frowned at the back of Peggy's head and ran his hand slowly over her hair. He wanted to hack it off and make it stunning. The thought of a mere trim was too terrible to bear.

"Hey, you got an opening for me? I need a serious shave and some of this hair whacked off." The voice was big and booming, yet strangely comforting and warm.

In unison, everyone in the room looked toward the doorway. A stranger stood there filling it completely. He was tall, muscular and shaggy. Ken thought he looked like a big ol' cuddly bear. And he wanted the big man to cuddle him right up. He felt his jaw drop, but didn't care.

"Twinkle toes is gonna trim my hair, but you can take a seat," Peggy answered.

"I'll check back in then. I gotta go check in with some Juan guy," the big man answered.

"I can make time for you," Ken managed to squeak out.

"When he's done with my hair," Peggy added, giving Ken a dark look.

35

He ignored her and took a step toward the newcomer. "I'm Ken and more than willing to help you fulfill your grooming needs."

"If that ain't a come on, I don't know what is," Lenore muttered.

"Um hmm," Yolanda agreed.

Ken flipped them both off.

The big guy laughed and shook his head. "It's all good. I'll just come back. Name is Dale. I'm glad to meet all of you."

"I'm Ken, and the rest of these bitches are Peggy, Lenore, Yolanda, and that's Felix."

"I'll be back, Ken. Thanks." The big guy flashed a wide grin, then left.

"You could have let him go first!" Ken wailed, whirling around toward Peggy.

"Oh, no way am I supporting your sinning ways. You practically threw yourself at that poor man." Peggy folded her arms, giving him a disdainful look

"Ugh! I hate you," Ken pouted. "I'm chopping off your hair and dying it, you old bat!"

"Fine! But make it snappy!" Peggy smiled slowly. "Besides, he was kinda cute in a bear-like way. Maybe I should look a little more presentable."

"I'm going to shave your head," Ken growled.

Peggy just chuckled and waved a hand at him. "You'd like to, but you won't. Cause then I could tell everyone you ruined my hair."

"Ugh! You're evil!" Ken frowned, but began his work. Soon he was consumed in his task, but he still couldn't help but think of the big, brawny guy with the great smile.

Hopefully, he would come back for a shave and a trim. Smiling at the thought, Ken continued to snip away as the ice continued to ping against the window.

2. Making Demands

Travis sighed the second he saw Stephen Mann briskly walking down the hall toward him. This wasn't going to be pleasant. The sleet was coming down hard and he contemplated ducking out into it to escape the determined man bearing down on him. The thought of being pelted by the ice rain and the harsh wind was enough to keep him from opening the door. He was trapped and knew it.

Slowly, he turned away from the door leading out onto the construction site and headed down the hall. As he knew he would, Stephen fell into step beside him.

"We need to talk," Stephen started.

"Make it fast. I got things to do other than to hear your latest complaints," Travis answered.

"Okay, I deserve that. I know that I have complained at times-"

"-everyday-"

"-since we arrived here, but it has been very difficult for Blanche to adapt. She struggles to fit in and she's not doing too well."

Travis stopped, turned, and regarded Stephen with raised eyebrows. "You're joking, right?"

Stephen ran his hand over his hair nervously. "What do you mean?"

"Blanche does not try to fit in at all. She yells at everyone all the time and is a right, royal bitch. She lied to Linda about the Imotrex and accused her of stealing. She also shoved my very pregnant wife when Katie tried to calm the situation down. So do not tell me that Blanche is trying."

His brow puckering, Stephen averted his eyes, obviously weighing what his next words should be. "Okay. So maybe she's not trying, but this has been difficult for her. She was raised dirt poor, but her Mama always took good care of her and treated her like a princess. When she married me, I made sure she got everything she deserved."

Travis sighed, rubbing his tired eyes. "Stephen, why are you telling me this? What do you want?"

Stephen fumbled with the buttons of his shirt nervously. "We want to go home. Blanche hates it here. She wants the Hummer back and anything you guys took from our estate and she wants to go home."

"No. The Hummer is an important part of our defense and anything salvaged from your home is part of the fort's inventory now. If you want to leave, we can get you a car, a few days of food, and a gun, but then you guys are on your own." Travis hated the words coming out of his mouth, but this was the law of the new world. As mayor of the fort, it was his responsibility to keep its inhabitants safe and as healthy as possible.

"You can't do that. It's our property." Stephen's voice rose in pitch and a few people walking by hurried on. "We paid for all of that. Our money. Our property. Give it back."

"Stephen, no. We took food and anything else the fort needed when we salvaged your place. It's part of the stores now. How are we supposed to know what we took at this point? That was months ago. We probably ate the food by now." Travis set his hands on his hips and gazed steadily at Stephen. "And why do you want the Hummer?"

"Because it's ours!"

"Are you going to use it to drive you and Blanche out to areas to salvage? Where are you going to get your food? Your supplies? Chances are, we give you the Hummer, you take off, and we'll find you two moaning outside our walls in a few days."

"Don't underestimate us, Travis."

"Blanche won't even clean her own damn room right now. Who is going to cook?"

"Actually, Blanche thought maybe we could get a few people to go with us if we promised them some jewelry and other valuables," Stephen answered in a cold, angry voice. He was growing impatient. He was used to being able to push around local officials. He did not like being rebuffed.

"You mean stuff that is worthless now that the zombies have risen." Travis shook his head. "Unbelievable. Really."

"Why do you want us here? You hate us! Everyone does. You hate our wealth and our prestige."

Travis gripped Stephen's arm tightly with one hand. "Stephen, you're not wealthy or prestigious anymore. Now, you're just another living human being. You're a part of this town. This fort. I wish to God you two would settle down and just adapt. Look, I get that you used to be spoiled rotten, but those days are gone. All of us need to carry our own damn weight and help everyone out here in this fort. Do you get that? Do you understand that? We can't afford to be selfish anymore."

Wrenching his arm away, Stephen looked unsure of what to say next. He rubbed his arm, his eyes cast downward.

"The old world is gone. This is the new world. You gotta adapt. Be a part of us. Settle down. Learn some useful skills. Chip in. Make some friends, Stephen."

"You know, everyone keeps talking about the old world being gone. But it's really not. It's just waiting for us to push back the dead then everything will go back to the way it was. I will rise to the top again. I will take care of my wife. You'll go back to being a foreman of a construction site, working for me, not strutting around acting like you're the mayor." Stephen's voice was angry, but defensive. "All these people you want us to be friends with will go back to their pathetic lives. You think everyone is equal, but people with power, like me, have that power because we worked hard to gain it and we deserve it."

"Stephen, you got your money cause your great-grandpa was smart enough to take advantage of the railroad when it came through these parts way back in the day. He worked his ass off to be a success and bring commerce to this area. He put this town on the map. He built this hotel. He brought jobs into this town and he made it happen. Hell, this town is named after your great-grandma. I've been in that little museum down the hall that shows him working side by side with the townspeople. So maybe you should follow his example and join us in making this fort a success. Let that be your legacy."

"You don't get it, Travis. You think I'm just a spoiled, rich man who never did anything to earn my keep. Well, I have. I have worked damn hard. And I love my wife. I want her to be happy and she is not happy.

She wants our supplies back and our Hummer. She wants an armed escort and some people to come along to work the estate. I think she deserves those things. Being here is hard on her. And being a good, decent husband, I plan to do what she needs to make her safe and happy." Stephen was close to being enraged.

Travis shook his head, frustrated at not being able to get through to the man. "You go out there and it will be just you and her unless someone is dumb enough to fall for your ruse."

"I am not a man to be trifled with, Travis." Stephen stared at Travis for a long, piercing second, then turned and stomped off without another word.

Travis raised his hand to rub his very tired eyes. When he lowered his hand, Bill was staring at him. "What's up?"

"He isn't an easy man, Travis. You can't make him be what he doesn't want to be."

"You heard that, huh?"

Bill nodded, his hands resting on his belt. It was cinched tighter than in the past and his once round face was now more oval, with a hint of jowls. "They ain't never been easy people. Stephen is the younger brother who wasn't supposed to inherit his Daddy's mantle, but his older brother managed to get his ass killed doing some fool stunt in a race car. He's always trying to prove himself, and his wife ain't much better. She's from the trailer park and got lucky becoming a beauty queen. Stephen has been smitten with her since the day he saw her. He has poured tons of money into making her sister's political career work. They don't wanna be here, Travis, because this is what they wanted to avoid all their lives. Being common folk."

Travis inclined his head, acknowledging this was probably true. "Do you want to give them a bunch of supplies, the Hummer, an armed escort, and maids?"

"Nope. I say we give them a decent car, though. A week's worth of supplies. Weapons. Ammo. And let them go defend their home. They won't last long. We both know it. Either they'll get their asses eaten or show back up in a week or two begging to come back in." Bill's expression was somewhere between amusement and anger.

"We're agreed on that point then. I told him as much, but..."

"Let him simmer down then tell him again." Bill shrugged slightly. "It's the humane thing to do, I guess."

"Never gets easier, does it?"

"It will. One day."

"As long as it's not when we're all dead," Travis said with a weary grin.

"I was trying to catch ya and let ya know ol' Calhoun got his specs down for those flamethrower weapons for the walls. I can't make heads or tails of his scribbling, but I figured you, Eric and Juan could let him know if it's doable."

"Mind rounding up the others?"

"Can do."

"Thanks." Travis walked on toward the old hotel manager's office that he used as the mayor of the fort. He felt tired and wanted a bit of a nap, but he could tell already that wasn't going to happen. It had been hard to climb out of the warm bed he shared with Katie this morning. His wife's body had felt so comfortable tucked next to his, and the sound of the ice rain tapping against the window had almost lured him back under the covers. Now, he was wishing he had stayed there.

Travis passed the front desk where Peggy hung out during a lot of the day trying to contact the outside world on what was left of the internet. He noted that she had a cute new hairdo.

"Looking good, Peg."

Without looking away from her game of Solitaire, she handed him a bottle of Febreze. "Calhoun is looking for you. I think he was rolling in dog shit."

"This day just keeps getting better."

3. Tangled Webs

Calhoun skirted around the lobby and ducked down one of the lesser used hallways. The voices in the lobby were echoing and mingling with the ones in his head, causing his brain to hurt. Falling against the wall, he was dimly aware of the two people standing behind a plant nearby, whispering to each other.

Clutching his head, he tried to get his thoughts together. He envisioned all the thoughts moving through his mind like long, colorful threads, twisting and looping, sometimes weaving together. Sometimes they made perfect sense, other times they became a jumbled mess. When that happened, his head throbbed and those threads all sang in wild voices, demanding his attention. Gripping the wall with his dirty, gnarled hand, he tried to find the strongest thread, the strongest thought, and hold onto it.

Then it came to him.

His eyes snapped open and he became vividly aware of the two people staring at him with disgust. It was that blond bitch and Ray, one of the salvage crew guys.

"Blanche Mann, you're the whore of Babylon!" He could see it so clearly. Her twisted soul was a black miasma of goo around her neck and evil was vivid in her red eyes. With a cry of despair, he twirled around and ran from the hallway.

He barely heard Blanche order Ray to, "Get the old fucker."

It was painfully clear to him what was going on now and what he needed to do. There was evil in the halls of the fort, and he had to rectify the situation.

Running across the lobby, his battered boots beating on the marble floor, he wailed an agonized cry.

Out of the fuzzy world around him, a face came sharply into focus and he skittered to a stand still.

"What's up, Calhoun?" Travis looked at him quizzically.

Calhoun felt his mind slip off the thread he was clutching and swirl downward into the maze of brightly colored thoughts. It took a few seconds for his mind to snap onto a new one.

"Flame throwers!" Calhoun snapped his fingers. "Flame throwers to protect the gate! That's it!"

"You seemed a little upset there."

Calhoun tapped his chin as he tried to remember what it was that had terrified him so. Whatever it was, it had escaped him. "Don't rightly know."

"Okay, but you're ready to talk about the flamethrowers? Eric is in my office with Juan." Travis looked at him worriedly.

Fumbling with his jacket, Calhoun managed to find the pocket he had made by sewing a kerchief into the lining. Tugging out his notebook, he waved it in front of Travis. "Got it right here! Let's go!"

The big red thread in his mind, full of fire and the destruction of messed up clones, throbbed and opened up, pouring out all the information he needed to guide the young ones to proper defenses.

For the next thirty minutes, he was vividly sane.

Five minutes after the meeting, he was lost again in the web of his own mind, feeling uneasy that there was something trapped inside that was very important and dangerous to the fort.

4. The Scales

After the meeting with Calhoun broke up, Travis found himself consumed with helping Juan and Bill build an extensive list of supplies the fort would need to expand. Walking in the cold, notepad in hand, he had to marvel at the high walls that encompassed their world. Strange how the first makeshift wall made up of construction trucks had given birth to high, concrete walls patrolled by armed sentries.

It was nearly dinnertime when he finally made it back into the hotel and up to the room he shared with his wife. He felt half-frozen and was dying for a hot shower. When he pushed open the door, he saw Katie sitting in a chair near the window, holding a baby blanket, and staring wistfully toward the hills.

"Katie?"

"Do you ever wonder when it happened? When the tide turned against us?" Her voice was soft, thoughtful, and melodic.

"What do you mean?" He shrugged off his heavy jacket, glad that the heater in the room was working.

"There had to be a moment, a flash, a second, when it all turned against the living. When the future of the world was precariously balanced between the living and the dead. And then the scales tipped in favor of the dead." She looked toward him and he saw she had been crying.

"Katie, honey," he said, feeling utterly helpless all at once. He was confident and strong when out on the walls, planning, plotting, building, and fighting, but seeing his wife crying made him feel desperately weak. He moved to comfort her, wondering if he could.

"I was just sitting here, looking at the blanket, and wondering about the baby and then it hit me. What if our baby is the first of the new generation that will grow up with the dead walking? He or she will never know what it is like to live freely outside of these walls. And then it occurred to me that there must have been just one deciding moment in all of this."

Travis knelt beside her chair, his hand rubbing her fingers lightly. "Maybe, but we'll never know what it was or when it happened. This insanity had to be happening for some time before what we call the First Day. It couldn't have gone to hell in just twenty-four hours. Jenni's no good husband was bitten the day before. There was that weird plane crash in Chicago. Riots were being reported for days before the First Day."

"Why didn't they tell us?" Katie's green eyes were so big and beautiful with tears sparkling in them. "Why don't you think they warned us?"

"Maybe they thought it was under control. Or maybe they didn't understand how fast it was spreading."

"Do you think they wanted it to happen?"

Travis pondered this, then shrugged. "I may sound like Crazy Old Calhoun, but maybe they wanted it to happen so they could seize full control, but it went too far. I don't know, but if there was a moment when the scales tipped, then maybe it will come again. But this time those scales will tip in our favor."

Katie leaned her forehead against his and stroked his cheek lightly. "I want to believe you."

"Then do," Travis whispered, and kissed her lightly.

"I'm sorry I'm being so hormonal," Katie said, pouting.

"Nah. You're just saying what everyone else thinks. We're all in a weird funk. We need to get ourselves out of it. Focus on more positive things. Like the fact we are alive. We are inside fortified walls, not outside them. We have food and supplies. We have ammunition. We have each other." Travis felt better just expressing those few thoughts aloud. It was all true, but so easy to forget when the days were cold, gray and full of unexpected dangers.

"You're right," Katie said after a beat. "And maybe we will have our moment to claim it back. For our sake and the baby's."

Travis leaned over the armrest to kiss her swelling belly. He was in awe that his baby was growing inside of her and of the magic of that reality. His little family meant the world to him, and he never would have had it if not for the zombie rising. It was a strange, wondrous truth.

"I'm going to take a hot shower, then take my favorite girl out to dinner."

"Oh, that sounds good! Where are we going?" Her bright smile washed away all the shadows that had been haunting her expression.

"Well, there is this quaint little place downstairs that has some of the best food around."

"Sounds amazing! I can't wait!" Katie grinned and wiped the last of her tears away on the baby blanket.

"And then maybe we'll get crazy and go watch a movie. I hear there is a Burt Reynolds double feature tonight."

"Oh, wow! I don't think I can stand the excitement!"

Travis grinned, stood, and pulled her out of the chair. Holding her close, he kissed her tenderly on the lips. "You know you want to hear Curtis heckling The Bandit for his lawbreaking ways."

Katie snuggled up against him, laughing softly. "We're just one big crazy family, aren't we?"

Laying his cheek on her blond hair, Travis smiled. "Yeah. We are. And it will be okay."

Katie sighed, her body relaxed against his and Travis was glad that she trusted him so completely. He would never let her down. It was his sacred vow. He would never let Katie down.

5. No Peace for the Living or Dead

Rune sauntered into the dining room and looked around with a cautious eye. The hotel was full of shimmering patches of light and shadows, but he was trying not to let on that he could see them. He was relieved to see the dining room full of people lining up against one wall for dinner. People from the kitchen were loading up the buffet with big bins of food and it smelled like it was chili tonight.

The soft whisper of a ghost glided past him and he kept his eyes straight ahead and didn't acknowledge it.

"Hey, Rune!"

Looking around, Rune caught sight of Maddie and Dale waving at him from the line. He nodded his head at them in greeting and took up the last place in line. He wasn't too surprised when Maddie and Dale joined him. Maddie had her long hair braided down her back and had found a long flowing skirt and comfortable sweater to wear. Rune wasn't too sure how old she was, but he thought she was pretty, wrinkles and all. Dale was clean-shaven except for razor sharp chops. They were impressive.

"How are you, Rune?"

"Good, Maddie. Slept all day. I was tuckered out."

"Figured you were taking the time to rest up. I volunteered to help with the garden."

"Good for you!"

"I got a nice little shave and a haircut. They actually got a beauty salon here. Can you imagine?" Dale shook his head, looking floored by the idea. "I was pretty fucking amazed."

An old man in a wheelchair glided by to the front of the line. His arms were covered in tattoos and he looked older than God. Rune was impressed with how things were run in the fort. It almost felt like normal life.

"Maybe I'll drop by and get my hair properly done. Wind is hell on it after awhile." Rune folded his arms over his chest, edging up in line a little.

"You could stay here, you know. Not head back out there. It's so dangerous. So many people have died." Maddie shook her head sadly. "Like that poor little girl."

"Can't. Once they figure out I can see them, they won't stop badgering me," Rune said in a soft voice.

"Oh, right!" Maddie's eyes widened and she looked around the dining room cautiously. "Are they here now?"

"A few. Over by the bar," Rune said, trying hard not to look at the bar.

"Has to be a bitch having what you got with this shit going down," Dale growled. "Damn, man. Glad I ain't you."

"We all got our crosses to bear." Rune shrugged.

A tall, homely redhead walked into the dining room and right behind her was a perfectly formed ghost of an old, angry woman. Rune caught himself before he shivered.

"More, huh?" Dale shook his head. "Nobody is getting to rest in peace nowadays."

"Whole world is full of the dead. Nobody, living or dead, ain't getting no peace," Rune answered.

A boy in his teens entered the dining room, closely followed by a big German Shepherd. Something about the boy made Rune take notice and he felt a strong premonition hit him. "That boy is special. Real special. People gotta take care of him."

"You're weirding me out again," Dale grinned. He folded his big arms over his wide chest. "All creepy and mysterious. That's Rune."

"I'm sure he doesn't have the name Rune for nothing," Maddie said, laying her delicate hand on Rune's arm. A huge moonstone glimmered on her finger and Rune covered it gently with his hand. He could feel the energy in it and he smiled.

"My mama nicknamed me that when she found me making my own set when I was three. Got a bunch of rocks from the backyard and was trying to draw on them with a marker. We got old Nordic blood in our veins." Rune looked around the dining room again, feeling the energy of the living filling it and pushing away the presence of the dead. It felt fantastic.

Maddie peered up at him. "Stay until you need to go, Rune. Everyone deserves a little rest."

Rune nodded and looked at Dale. "Maybe we can rustle up a bike for you somewhere and get you back to riding."

"You have no idea how happy that would make me, dude."

A young, black woman and young man with his hair tipped with gold walked by, both clutching trays heaped with steaming food. The young man gave Dale a flirtatious smile and slightly waved with his fingers. Dale waved back.

"That boy is so sweet on you," Maddie teased.

"Yeah, but I'm sweet on her." Dale pointed across the room at a grumpy looking woman.

"That's the city secretary, Peggy," Maddie told him.

"She's hot."

Rune shrugged. "She ain't much to look at but she's got that vibe."

"Oh, yeah. She does. That hellcat vibe." Dale grinned even more.

Maddie shook her head and laughed. "Oh, boys."

An older, black gentleman stepped into the center of the dining room and loudly cleared his throat. "Before we start tonight's dinner, I would like to say grace and thank God for the blessings we have received. We have new people among us and a bounty of new supplies in our storeroom. I would also like to commend the soul of our brother, Bob, into the hands of God. He lost his life yesterday and was laid to rest today with the others who died trying to make it to the fort. Let us thank God for our lives and our safe home."

There was a round of amens, and then the Reverend pitched into a prayer that boomed through the room. Rune lowered his gaze, staring at the tips of his motorcycle boots. They were pretty battered and probably needed new soles. He listened to the prayer in silence, taking peeks around the room as it continued. He saw the pretty woman that had hitched a ride with him hugging the tall teenage boy as the German

Shepherd leaned against her legs. Behind her, the tall Mexican in the cowboy hat had his eyes closed, his arm around an older Hispanic woman. The leader of the fort and his pregnant wife were last in line. They were hugging each other, her head on his chest, and they looked so happy it made Rune's heart twist in his chest.

The community around him felt unified and strong. He yearned to be a part of it. But he knew it would only last so long before he would have to move on. It was moments like these that reminded him that he was not a lone survivor and that there was a bit of hope left in the world.

"Amen!" the voices chorused around him, then someone shouted, "Let's tear this chili up!"

Laughter filled the room and Rune slightly smiled. Maybe staying around a bit longer would be a good thing.

Chapter 5

1. Making the New Eden

Travis yawned as he joined the rest of the fort council on top of the hotel for a planning meeting. Another cold front had blown in during the night, dropping temperatures, but not bringing any dreaded ice, rain or snow. It would probably warm up by ten o'clock. He shoved his hands into his leather coat to keep them warm. The wind was fierce and blew his curls into disarray. Behind him, Juan cursed as he held his cowboy hat down on his head.

"Fuckin' Texas weather," Juan grumbled.

"Schizophrenic, isn't it?" Travis grinned.

"I just love how it teases us with the promise of good weather before crushing our enjoyment with a nice cold front," Eric, the fort's engineer, said in a disgruntled tone.

"Men. You're so cranky," Nerit chided them. She slung her sniper rifle over one shoulder and headed over to where Peggy and Bill sat waiting for them.

Katie and Jenni stepped out into the cold air, both bundled up in heavy coats, knit caps, and gloves. Per the usual, Calhoun was taking up the rear, determined to film what he regarded as a secret city council meeting. Jenni and Juan stood nearby, snuggled up to each other.

Travis slid into a patio chair and tried to ignore the cold emanating out of the metal frame. Katie sat next to him and he took her hand in his.

"Okay, let's get this meeting going. It's freaking cold out here, but I think if we can actually view what we want to alter, we will have a better understanding of the task at hand."

"Agreed," Eric said.

"I'm all for it. Let's hurry though. I'm dying for some coffee." Juan finally gave up trying to hold his hat on his head and took it off. His long hair was ruffled by the wind as Jenni tucked her head under his chin.

Calhoun was already filming, muttering in a low voice to himself. Travis tried not to pay attention to the crazy, old coot. "Okay, we have already expanded outward, taking in a block on the west and enclosing it with new walls. That is our planned entertainment and recreation area. Our attempt to help morale. We have the main fort centralized on this block. We have the Panama Canal, the garage, the hotel, city hall, and the construction site blocked off from the rest of the expansion. To the north, we have the Dollar Store and empty buildings that we are now using as a storage depot."

"We definitely need to reinforce the back of those buildings," Eric said in a grim voice. "I still think it's a weak point." He still dressed like he was going to the office. He was wearing a red sweater with khakis under his long wool coat and leather loafers. His girlfriend, Stacey, had worked hard to get him into jeans and a t-shirt. It hadn't lasted long.

Peggy quickly scribbled down everything that was being said, her face pale, her jaw tensed.

"We got the windows and doors all bricked up," Juan pointed out.

"But those structures are old. Rot has set in. I firmly believe we should build a new wall behind those stores that connects with the wall we have going across Main Street." Eric shoved his glasses up on his nose and looked at Travis for support. "We need to reinforce that area."

"Nerit, what do you think?" Travis looked toward their head of fort security.

"We haven't had the amount of zombies that we had in the first days, so we know it's secure for the level of threat we've had recently. But if we end up with a larger horde descending on us, we may have issues. Especially if our engineer fears for the structural integrity of the buildings," Nerit answered.

"We'll have to find more building supplies. More rebar, more bricks, more cement," Juan said. "Construction supplies are low after the last wall we built."

"We may have to go further out and risk bringing a crowd of those things our way to get those supplies in," Bill said in a somber tone. "Every time we go out, it gets harder to come back with everyone alive."

"We don't have a choice though, do we? If we're to be safe," Katie pointed out.

Travis felt her hand tighten on his, and he gave it a reassuring squeeze. "The interior walls to the main area of the fort are pretty solid. We can always fall back to the main area if there if there is a breach."

"I say reinforce the interior walls behind the Dollar Store before starting on the outer perimeter," Bill said.

"We need to make sure the internal walls will stand no matter how large the onslaught." Nerit chimed in.

Travis wondered if she was playing all sorts of terrible scenarios in her mind. "The zombie population has been really low. We need to take advantage of that." Travis tucked his hands into the pockets of his leather jacket and gazed over the dead town toward the hills. "We should work on the outer walls. The expansion."

"We need to build outside while we have the chance," Juan agreed.

"We don't need to expand so far that we don't have the resources to support it though," Eric said. "We should reinforce the walls we have up now."

"And we need to be able to defend it," Nerit added. "We're working on bows and arrows, catapults, and fire pits, but we still need more time to make sure people understand how to use them."

Travis sighed and rubbed his brow.

Peggy sat nearby. She looked tired as she clutched her notepad. "We'll need space for another garden and the sooner the better. We need to plant soon."

"If we bring in some of the surviving livestock, we'll need that big empty lot behind the Dollar Store," Bill said.

"Another reason to build a new wall back there," Eric interjected. "That will make sure that the area is secure."

"We definitely need to think about our food supplies." Peggy looked up, her expression one of worry. "We got enough for now, but what about the future?"

"Do you think having multiple entrances into the fort is wise? We already have the Panama Canal and the loading dock on the side of the hotel," Eric added. "If we expand, maybe we should consider that as well."

"We don't want to be trapped either," Nerit answered. "Should something go wrong."

"I think I have a headache," Travis said with a wry smile.

"No one ever said recreating Eden would be easy," Katie responded.

Nerit cleared her throat and said in a steady, firm voice, "Look, the zombies are not smart, nor are they that fast anymore. But they are dangerous when in a large group. They are persistent. They don't give up. If there is any weak spot in our defenses, we better get it shored up now before we have something more to worry about."

"I agree with what she said," Jenni piped up, ignoring Juan's look of disapproval.

"I say we expand while we got the chance," Juan ignored Jenni's look of disapproval.

"I know the fort defenses are very important. But so is food. We need to build up our stores. We need a garden. We need livestock," Peggy said worriedly.

"She's right. I was working on the food inventory with Rosie. We have to make long term plans," Katie added.

Calhoun raised his hand high over his head.

"Yeah?" Travis looked at him bleary-eyed. He hated being Mayor. It wasn't easy making the tough choices.

"I got chickens," the old man offered. "Automatic feeder and water probably have them doing just fine."

Everyone laughed. Travis knew they had all been expecting something crazy. He had been ready for some insane conspiracy theory.

"Got my whole place rigged up on timers and thermal detectors."

"Fresh eggs would be great," Peggy said with an almost desperate tone in her voice. "We could all really use the protein in our diets."

Travis stood up and wandered over to the rail. Looking across the empty lot in front of the hotel, he saw a zombie staggering down the road. It had its hand out, reaching toward the fort. Another stumbled into view further down the road.

The undead never stopped coming, did they?

"Inner wall first, then we need to move fast on the expansion. Can we really afford to not make sure we're completely secure?" Travis decided aloud. He had to admit to himself he was thinking of Katie and the baby.

The new fort council took this in, then everyone slowly nodded.

"Well, I'm going to go ahead and send out more supply missions," Bill decided. "Juan, we'll need a complete list of building supplies and we'll pull some of those construction trucks out."

"Any more people out there?"

Peggy shook her head at Travis' question. "Not within a fifty mile radius. And people beyond that are going quiet. No one is reporting heavy zombie activity, but everyday it seems like less and less people are on the horn."

"Okay then. Inner wall it is."

Travis watched as the first zombie disappeared from view behind the outer wall. Silently, he watched as a guard walked over with a long spear and got into position. The guard brought the spear down hard into the head of the out-of-sight zombie and gave it a firm wiggle to make sure. When he drew it back up, gore decorated the end of it.

He hated the violence of this new world.

2. Rebuilding the World

"Stupid freakin' Texas weather," Jenni huffed.

She tossed out a bag of garbage from the second floor window of the old movie theater into the dumpster below. She was clad in jeans and a tank top and sweat was pouring down her face.

Katie swept more debris into a dustpan, then dumped that into another garbage bag. Her hair was pinned on top of her head with blond tendrils poking out at odd angles. Her face was flushed and she was breathing hard. The ice and cold were gone. It was eighty degrees outside.

Leaning out the window, Jenni craned her neck to look over the new wall that cut off the street just after the theater and stretched across to a clothing store on the other side. A block in every direction from the fort was reclaimed territory, and their world suddenly seemed much larger. They weren't necessarily spreading out, not yet. The hotel was comfortable and safe, but they needed to have more leeway in defending their home.

Meanwhile, the restoration of the theater was purely for entertainment. Peggy and Rosie, Juan's mother, worked hard to put on social events every week to help the fort's inhabitants blow off steam and relax. But there was an awareness that people needed something closer to the world they had once lived in. A place to walk, a place to hang out, a place to go to the movies, and the such. It would be an enormous stress reliever to get the theater up and running. People needed a diversion from the day in, day out stresses of surviving in a world infested with the hungry dead.

The theater was a mess and needed a lot of work. When the owner had died, his wife had shut up the theater, leaving it as it was. She then pretended he wasn't dead, just busy at work. The fort people had found everything just as he had left it, including the upstairs room they were cleaning out. It was full of the old man's porn mags and fetish gear. Jenni almost died laughing when she found the secret stash.

"Can you imagine this old guy hanging out here all the time with all this stuff while his wife thinks he is working?" Jenni grinned at Katie as she shoved more fetish magazines into the trash.

Katie blew a strand of hair out of her eyes and looked around the room at the piles of trash bags. "I would hate to know what all he was up to."

Jenni dangled some shackles and handcuffs in front of Katie and tossed those in a box for Bill, the police officer, to look at. "And who with?"

It had taken awhile to clean out the room. Now they were bagging up the trash. Downstairs, they could hear people talking as the theater was cleaned thoroughly.

Jenni looked out the window again. "Hey, that nurse is still up on the roof across the street taking notes."

Katie tied off the bag. "Really?"

"Yeah," Jenni adjusted her gloves, then grabbed another bag and hurled it out the window. "Do you like her?"

Katie pondered this, then shrugged. "She's different. Very...methodical. She's kinda abrupt during my examinations, but she's thorough." So far Katie was in good health and her pregnancy was going well. She leaned down to pick up a full, black trash bag.

"Her name is Charlotte, right?"

"Yeah."

Jenni lifted the big bag, shooing Katie away. "You're pregnant. No heavy lifting."

"Yes, Mom," Katie said, rolling her eyes. "I swear, between you and Travis, I don't know how I am allowed out of bed."

"You're just lucky we don't use those shackles on you!"

Jenni looked out the window to see the Reverend Thomas pulling up to the front of the building on a power mower with a large cart attached to the back. The cart was loaded up with sacked lunches. Jenni liked the Reverend. He was always smiling and laughing. Plus, his sermons were actually good and not at all boring.

"People need God in times like these," he had said to her at lunch one day. "We're in the new Eden...just got more than that damn snake to deal with."

Jenni yanked her gloves off and tossed them onto a pile of cleaning supplies. "Let's go eat. I'm hungry and need a break."

"Sounds good," Katie answered. "I'm pretty tired, too." She rubbed her swelling belly absently and chunked her gloves into a corner.

Together, they trudged down the narrow staircase. The fading black and white pictures of old movies stars were strangely comforting. Jenni blew a kiss at Cary Grant as they passed his photo. She tried not to think about the fact that Hollywood was now gone and movies were now relics of the past. Maybe someday humanity would get control of the world again, and new movies would fill old theaters.

Outside, the workers gathered around the cart. They were cleaning their faces and hands with damp hand towels. Jenni grabbed one from a laundry basked and pressed the moist cloth to her face. It felt amazing and refreshing. After cleaning her face, she ran it over her hands and arms, already feeling much better.

Katie tossed her used one into another basket for the dirty towels. "That felt good, but I'm dying for a shower."

Jenni nodded and draped the towel over the back of her neck to cool her down. She was starved and when the Reverend Thomas handed her a lunch bag, she clutched it gratefully.

"Thank you!"

"You're welcome. Make sure to drink plenty of water." He motioned to the cooler packed with water bottles.

Sitting on the curb next to Katie, she eagerly tore into the her lunch bag. Jenni bit into her peanut butter and jelly sandwich hungrily while Katie gulped down a bottle of water.

"Oh God, when did water start tasting so good!" Katie grinned and wiped her mouth on the back of her hand.

"When peanut butter and jelly started tasting like manna from heaven," Jenni answered. "Everything just tastes better now days."

Three of the new people joined the group. The older woman looked like one of the artist-types that used to inhabit South Austin with her long flowing hair and funky way of putting clothes together. Rune was with her and a tall, massive guy with chops on his cheeks and long dark hair.

"Hey, Rune!" she waved, smiling and munching on her sandwich.

"Hey, Jenni. Good to see ya," Rune answered, sitting on the curb.

"They got you working?"

"Volunteered. Figured I might as well stay a short spell."

Maddie gratefully accepted a lunch and bottle of water from the Reverend and found a place to sit with her big friend.

"Rune gave me a ride into town the other day. His bike is very cool," Jenni said to Katie.

"I heard that. Nice to meet you, Rune. I'm Katie."

"Good to meet you, Katie."

Jenni liked his smile and thought he seemed pretty nice. As he tore into his sandwich, she happily chewed on her own. She was hoping she could get another ride on his bike if the good weather kept up.

Charlotte came over, sat down next to them, and started to eat slowly. She looked very thoughtful, her hand straying to the pocket where she kept her notes. She was a rather plain woman with mousy hair and a bland face. But her brown eyes were keen and her gaze intense.

"How are you today, Charlotte?" the Reverend asked as he handed out water bottles.

"Figuring it out still, Padre," Charlotte answered.

"Figuring what out?" Jenni asked.

"The zombies. I've been studying them," Charlotte answered around a mouthful of food.

"Yeah, we noticed that," Katie said as she pulled the crusts off her sandwich. "Jenni said you were up on the roof watching some."

Jenni snagged the crusts and shoved them in her mouth.

Charlotte swallowed a bit of sandwich and drank a little water. "I'm trying to figure out how they tick. We have to know our enemy after all."

"True words for a sad time," the Reverend agreed. He continued to hand out water and bagged lunches as more workers arrived for lunch.

"Notice anything?" Rune asked.

"Well," Charlotte hesitated, then bobbed her head. "I noticed a few things. I'm planning to put it all into a report for the council, but basically there are a few fundamentals. The first one is that they are decaying very slowly. The regular process of decay is just not happening: the bloat of the body as the gases inside build up, rigor mortis, et cetra. I really expected there to be some exploding zombies. But not one."

"Exploding?" Jenni blinked.

"Gases build up in the body as it decays normally. You see it in road kill. Sometimes those gases burst the body. But no, nothing like that. Just...slow...slow...rot."

"And they're fast in the beginning. That is so breaking the rules," Jenni said with disappointment, then let out a huge hiccup.

Rune handed her another bottle of water as he said to Charlotte, "I noticed that they kinda beat themselves ragged real damn fast in the first days. They don't stay fast long."

"Well, they do slow down fairly quickly. The truly dangerous ones are the new ones that are just turned, especially if they've only suffered minor damage to their limbs. They can have their whole throat torn out and nothing left in their body cavity, but if their arms and legs are fine, you better be able to run fast. The fast ones are why so many people died in the first days." Charlotte shook her head. "But, you're right, Rune. They don't feel pain so they just go and go, breaking apart their ligaments, tearing apart muscle, literally ripping off limbs as they try to get to prey. The older they get, the slower they are."

"Ha! I knew Romero had it right!" Jenni grinned with satisfaction and hiccuped again. She knew she shouldn't have eaten so fast.

Katie rolled her eyes.

"He did. C'mon. They are so much slower now. Everyone knows it. And it's so much easier to kill them now. They are stupid and slow."

"They are very fascinated by our Christmas lights. I seriously don't think we should take them down." Charlotte pulled out a bag of chips and opened it. "They will stare all night at the lights and only move when they are turned off."

"Really?" Katie lifted an eyebrow.

"Really."

The Reverend whistled. "Then we could string up a lot of lights."

"Well, give them enough humans in visual contact, they'll shake out of it, but seriously, they'll just stare. The fireworks on New Year's Eve, that had them completely stone cold still."

"Why haven't you said anything to anyone?" Katie demanded, an edge in her voice.

"I wanted to make sure." Charlotte popped a chip in her mouth. "They aren't smart. They don't really think. Most likely their brains are the least decayed part of them and I have a feeling it's all instinct. They do things but don't know why. Their need to feed is basic. It's the reptilian brain speaking. Why cannibalism? That I don't know. I watched one zombie try to mow the lawn at the school the first day of the rising. I don't think it was doing anything more than something it had done in life. It wasn't a reasoning action. It was just an action. But it may have been some sort of residual memory that was sparking in his brain. But a few days later, he was just banging on the windows."

"So, you think in the first few days after they change, they might have a memory? Of how to do things?" Jenni frowned at this thought, not really wanting to know what it meant.

"Not a conscious thought, Jenni. I don't think they are actually processing information like we do. It's their dying brain firing off in weird ways. Maybe neural pathways looping as the brain transforms into...a zombie brain." Charlotte shrugged and stuffed more chips in her mouth, crumbs flecking her lips and chin.

"So, if a zombie tried to open a door on the day it was turned, it doesn't mean it will the next day?" Katie looked at Jenni. "Like that girl who tried to open the truck door."

"Oh, right!" Jenni remembered that moment well. The fort had been terrified that the zombies were actually thinking and plotting.

Charlotte nodded her head. "In the first days, I theorize that as their brains are dying or transforming or whatever they are doing to make zombie, residual memory pathways may have zombies doing very mundane human actions. In the end, those neural pathways die and we're left with a creature that has only the instinct to feed left."

"So they're stupid," Jenni said with satisfaction.

"Yes. So that works for us. We're much smarter." Charlotte continued to eat her chips, looking thoughtful.

Jenni gulped down more water, washing away the salty taste of the chips from her palette. "Oh, that I'm sure of, but they are damn persistent."

The people around them had been silent for most of the conversation as they ate, but the tension in the air was palpable. Jenni felt it, but didn't really want to know what the others were thinking. She liked things being nice and simple. And Charlotte's theories made things nice and simple for her.

"Do you think there is anything left that is human inside of them? A spark of who they were? Have you seen that?"

It was Maddie who had spoken up and from the expressions on the faces around her, Jenni understood that it was the question others had been afraid to ask.

"What do you mean?" Charlotte wiped her lap off and took a long drink of her water. She was fairly oblivious of how disconcerting the conversation had become to the others.

Katie set down her sandwich and swallowed hard. Slowly, she raised her eyes. "She means, do you think there is something left of the person they were still inside. Are they aware at all of what they were?"

Hearing the fear and pain in Katie's voice, Jenni reached out and grabbed her hand. "Of course not! Right, Charlotte? They're just dead things!"

"I haven't seen any of them acting remotely like they have a memory of who they were. Like recognizing family members or anything like that? No. Have any of you? I mean, most of you saw friends and family turn. All they want to do is eat you."

"No. No. I haven't seen any of my old friends or my family members even so much as look at me as anything other than food," the Reverend cut in. "Their souls have moved on. They're free of this world."

"Actually, Reverend, not to correct you or nothing, but they haven't really moved on. They're all around us. All the time. Some are stronger in this world than in the other, but they are all caught between the world of the living and the dead." Rune looked at everyone steadily. "It got messed up. All the dead rising like that. The natural order of things got screwed up."

"Kinda like that line in Dawn of the Dead when they said there was no more room in hell?" Jenni could feel that Katie's hand was trembling and she felt terribly for her. She didn't even want to think of her kids not being in heaven. That was the thought that made her feel better when the nightmares came.

"I don't know rightly." Rune slowly set down his water and rubbed his mustache with his long fingers. "All I know is that I see 'em. I see the ghosts. And everywhere I go, they're there. Trapped."

The Reverend looked like he was about to say something, but as he gazed at Rune's face, he seemed to think better of it and averted his eyes.

"I think they are all waiting for something to happen so they can move on. Something big. I don't know what it is, but they're trapped here until it gets done."

"I don't know if it's a consolation or not, thinking of our loved ones being ghosts as their dead bodies try to eat us," Katie finally said. "But it makes me feel a little bit better than living in fear that our loved ones are trapped in those rotting things."

"I'm real sorry for y'all losing your loved ones. But y'all got a good thing going on here. And good things are rare in this world," Rune decided.

There was an awkward silence as people pondered what had been said and slowly they began to talk amongst themselves. Maddie took Rune's hand in her own and smiled at him softly.

"At least we know the zombies are stupid," Jenni said at last. "Stupid is good, right?"

"And they are afraid of fire," Charlotte added, as if the conversation had not taken a strange, metaphysical turn. "Another primitive fear of the reptilian brain."

Jenni thought about it and imagined bonfires all around the fort. It appealed to her.

Katie hesitated then, said, "So, we have a few...really weird new weapons." Her voice didn't sound shaky anymore.

"Uh-huh." Charlotte took another bite of her sandwich.

"Christmas lights," the Reverend said, slowly smiling.

"Christmas lights," Charlotte agreed.

Jenni grinned. "Damn. That's just kinda funny."

Chapter 6

1. Jenni's World

"And what do you do if you see a zombie?" Nerit asked in a loud voice.

"Poke it in the eye!"

The chorus of children's voices made Jenni look over from where she helped lay cement blocks on top of the old wall. A group of twenty kids, all ages, had gathered around Nerit and a dummy made up to look like a zombie. The kids all held the fort's makeshift spears.

"And then what do you do?"

"Shake it hard!"

"Why?"

"To make their brain soup!" some little wise-ass called out.

The kids broke up into wild peals of laughter.

Nerit smiled slightly, then ordered, "Okay, line up! Let's make zombie brain soup!"

Jenni looked over at Juan. He was sweating hard, his long curly hair slipped free from his ponytail. Feeling her gaze, he looked up at her then over at the kids.

"They need to know how to fight back," he said finally.

"Yeah," she answered, looking back at the kids.

A young boy, about Mikey's age, walked up to the zombie effigy and rammed the end of his spear into its cloth eye as hard as he could, then shook it hard.

Again, the children laughed.

Jenni sighed and spread more wet cement with the trowel. "I wish Mikey hadn't turned back to defend me."

"He didn't know, babe," Juan said in a soft, cautious voice.

"I know, but...you would have liked him," Jenni fought back a few tears and lifted the heavy cement block into place. She rarely spoke to Juan about her kids. It was hard to speak of a piece of her life she could not ever share with him.

Juan kissed her cheek softly, causing the makeshift platform they were on wobble a little. "I know, Loca. I know."

"If I could find a way to give you kids..."

"Loca, it's okay. Really. I got you. I got Jason, even though he does hate me, and I got Jack. And Jack is a pretty bad ass kid. Kinda furry, but a great kid."

Jenni laughed despite the lump in her throat.

"Besides, Katie and Travis are probably going to be spitting out kids left and right and we'll end up with babysitting duty." He wiped the sweat from his brow, managing to get a little cement in his hair. "I just want to be with you. Okay? If we're together, I'm happy. Even if you are batshit crazy."

Jenni laughed and leaned against him. "Crazy is good."

"Crazy is good. And fun in bed." Juan grinned at her lovingly.

"You're such a pervert," she teased and kissed his salty cheek.

"And you like it." He pressed a kiss to her forehead, then moved to lay another brick.

Jenni looked back down at the kids and Nerit.

"Okay, who's next?"

A slew of kiddie voices shouted, "Me!"

2. Time to Move On

"Hey, Mom." Jason slid into the chair next to Jenni at lunch. He peered out at her from beneath his long bangs and looked a little embarrassed.

"Hey, baby, what's up?" Jenni shoved a couple of homestyle fries dunked in mustard into her mouth and ignored Jack staring at her longingly from Jason's side.

"I was wondering if I could have Shelley over to watch movies tonight?" the teenager whispered, his cheeks blushing.

"You gonna make out?" Jenni asked around a mouthful of fries.

"Mom!"

Jenni grinned at him. "Are you?"

Ducking his head, Jason looked up at her through his bangs. "Maybe."

She playfully nudged him with her elbow and grinned. "My sexy son is getting some loving!"

"Mom!"

Jenni rolled her eyes, shrugging. "Okay, okay. Have your make out session, but she has to leave by eleven."

"You're so embarrassing, Mom," Jason grumbled.

"Hey, I gotta tease you when I can. You're always off with Roger and your crew making crazy mad scientist zombie killing stuff." Jenni hugged him and smothered him in kisses. He squirmed with discomfort.

"Mom, fine. Okay. I get it. And thanks, Mom," her stepson said, and quickly kissed her cheek. He ducked out of her grip and stood up.

Jenni saw Shelley standing nearby and gave her the thumbs up.

Jack laid a paw on her knee and looked at her plaintively. With a sigh, Jenni gave the dog her dessert, two peanut butter cookies. Graced with a doggy grin, she smiled back.

The boy and his dog jogged over to Shelly, leaving her to finish her fries alone.

* * * * *

As her best friend dug through a pile of supplies, Jenni giggled. Katie looked up at her, holding baby wipes in one hand and diapers in the other. "What?"

"You look cute."

Katie frowned and put her items into the growing stack beside her. Jenni remembered her own anxiety when she was pregnant with Mikey. She felt envy mingled with happiness as she watched Katie search for necessities in a large unsorted pile. The pile had been designated as unnecessary goods and was left in a storage room. It was from the WalMart truck. Baby supplies just hadn't seemed important in the first days. Months later, Katie was desperate to find what she could.

Jenni, meanwhile, eyeballed what looked like lingerie, WalMart style, but slinky nonetheless.

"Do you want a boy or a girl?"

Katie was deep in the pile again and had to straighten to speak. "Uh, either. Travis wants a girl though. He actually offered to name her Lydia."

Jenni looked at Katie in surprise. "Really?"

Katie nodded. "He said it was okay with him. I told him I'd think about it." Sitting back, she pressed a hand to her belly. "I know that if this nightmare hadn't happened that Lydia and I would still be together and that Travis..." She hesitated and then wiped a tear from her eye. "I know I never would have met him."

Instantly, Jenni crawled across the piles to hold Katie. She held her friend tightly, feeling the other woman trembling.

"I'm so damn emotional!"

"It's hormones," Jenni assured her.

Katie laughed and wiped another tear away. "I love them both, you know. Lydia and Travis. And I'm very happy with Travis, but...I miss her." She paused. I can't... give the baby her name. It doesn't feel right."

"Then if it doesn't feel right, don't do it. Travis is trying to be a good guy. It can't be easy living in Lydia's shadow."

"Oh, I know that. And he's so good about it. He really is! And I love him! If I hadn't lost her, I wouldn't have him and it feels so fucked up! And I'm such a hormonal mess!" Katie was half-laughing, half-crying.

Jenni kissed Katie's cheek firmly, then snuggled her tighter. "I know, I know. If I hadn't lost my family, I wouldn't have you and Juan. I'm so grateful to have Jason, and it feels really weird to be happy cause the world is definitely hell right now."

It did seem weird to Jenni. She found this world almost comfortable compared to the suburban lifestyle she had once lived. Lloyd had controlled every aspect of her life from what she wore to what she ate. She had been a trophy wife and his punching bag. Her former life was devoted to her children and pleasing Lloyd. He hadn't even allowed her to have friends. She now had someone who loved her, good friends, and a purpose in life. The only thing that would make it better was if she could have Benji and Mikey with her. Juan would have been such a great dad to them.

Katie nodded and wiped more tears away. "We're lucky to have each other, aren't we?"

"Absolutely!" Jenni agreed and held her best friend tightly against her. "Without a doubt, Katie. You saved me. And I love you."

Pressing a kiss to Jenni's cheek, Katie whispered, "I love you, too, Jenni. You're the best friend I could ever have."

"So the baby is Jenni, Jr. right?"

Katie burst out laughing and Jenni smiled with relief.

The rest of the afternoon was light and fun. By the time they left, they were both weighted down with baby supplies and Jenni had red lingerie tucked into her back pocket.

* * * * *

Jenni loved the aftermath of the lovemaking with Juan. They always lounged around in the bed, naked and tired, grinning at each other. She painted her toenails, one foot propped on his knee as he read a book, buried under the covers. A cold front had finally hit just after dark and the room was cold. The covers were wrapped around her waist, but she enjoyed the coolness on her skin.

"Blanche was giving me shit again today," Jenni said after a long bit of silence.

"Yeah? Why?"

"She was clean up crew tonight after dinner and ragged on me for not putting my plate into the proper bin. Then she ragged on me for a bunch of other stuff. I stopped listening after the 'stupid spic' comment."

Juan looked over at her and frowned. "I thought she just called me that."

"No, no. She calls everyone she thinks is Mexican a spic. Including Rashi, the Indian guy we picked up the other day."

"That woman is such a bitch," Juan growled. Putting his book down, he rubbed Jenni's leg gently as she finished polishing her toenails. "Her husband has just been sulking, but she's on a fucking warpath."

"Too much drama," Jenni said with a frown. "Though, her husband actually did something nice today. He stopped trying to file a claim for the return of their Hummer. Peggy told me."

Juan laughed and shook his head. "You wonder if they realize what is really going on."

Flopping back on the pillows piled behind her, Jenni giggled. "Stupid people doing stupid things, huh?"

Juan flipped the book off the bed. "Yeah, but we are keeping them alive for some reason."

"Entertainment value!"

"Are your nails dry yet?"

"Um...no...why?"

Juan looked at her toes, then said. "Eh, fuck it. You can redo them." He leaned over and kissed her deeply, pulling her close.

With a grin, Jenni wrapped her arms around him and returned his kiss.

3. Time to Go

Rune awoke with a start. His hand automatically gripped his Glock as he sat up and pointed at the figure at the end of the bed. As his brain sputtered into wakefulness, he blinked his eyes to focus them. The room was dark, but the figure at the end of the bed was a black blot. He nearly expected it to moan and reach for him, then realized he wasn't facing a zombie.

Flipping on the lamp next to the bed, he stared blearily at the man standing at the end of the bed. Expect for being transparent, he looked just like any other person living in the fort. Setting the Glock down beside him, Rune sighed softly.

"What do you want, buddy?"

The man opened his mouth, silent words forming.

"You need to speak up. I can't hear you."

The room grew steadily colder as the apparition tried again. It managed one word.

"Help."

The figure then lost its tentative hold on the physical world and vanished.

Sliding his legs out of bed, Rune shivered as the room grew steadily colder. His breath turned to mist and he whispered, "Dammit." Standing, he grabbed up his jeans and boots.

The room began to fill with shimmers of light and shadow. He felt the whispery touch of the dead as they gathered around him.

"I can't help you," he said shortly. "I can't hear you. I can't help you. Stop pestering me. Either talk to me or leave me alone." Frustration and despair filled him as he shrugged on his leather vest and reached for his heavy jacket. The delicate touches of the dead fluttered over his skin. He tried to shrug them away, but they were persistent.

The room was unbearably cold. Cussing under his breath, he grabbed his motorcycle bags and headed toward the door of his hotel room. He had never unpacked, anticipating this moment.

Striding down the hall, he saw the air rippling around him. A few of the spirits drew enough energy to actually grab his arm, but he shrugged them off.

In the beginning, he had tried to help the ghosts he encountered. Slowly, he realized that the spirits were simply trapped. Nothing he said to guide them helped. The whole world had been filled with death, altering everything beyond the world of the living.

Ignoring the elevator, he headed down the stairs. His boots heels sounded like thunder rolling through the stairwell. The spirits were losing energy quickly, basically burning themselves out trying to hold onto him. He hit the bottom floor, cut across the lobby, and headed toward the door exiting to the construction site.

As he entered what had once been a janitor's closet, he was startled when a hand grabbed his arm in an iron grip. Yanking his arm away, he was hit with a gawdawful stench. His Glock was already in his hand and coming up for a killing shot when he heard Old Man Calhoun mutter, "I can't remember!"

"What the hell, Calhoun?" Rune shoved his Glock back into his holster, frowning at the old codger. He had given him a terrible fright.

"I can't remember something important. And it's eatin' at me!" Calhoun let go of him and shoved open the door to the construction site. "I saw something long ago and then again a few days ago, and I know it was something important. It's important because..." He faltered, obviously struggling to grasp a flitting thought. Plunging into the night, the old man seemed to be chasing after that thought.

Rune sighed and followed. He headed toward the stairs that would lead him over the wall into the area where the fort secured all its vehicles.

Calhoun ran back and forth in front of him, hands outstretched, grasping at the air.

He didn't feel the ghosts anymore, but they would catch up. His only real hope for any peace of mind was to head out into the deadlands and keep changing his location. Leaving the fort so soon was an annoyance. He had allowed himself the luxury of becoming a part of the community for a few days. Maybe he had even deceived himself into believing he could stay. It was a damn shame he had to go. He would miss Maddie and Dale.

Calhoun suddenly came to a stop and turned around. "The Whore of Babylon. That was what it was about. She was cohorts with the one that ended up killed in a woman's dress. She..she..." He faltered, his eyes rolling wildly in their sockets. Clutching his hands to his face, Calhoun wailed. "I can't remember. It was...it was..."

In the distance a rooster crowed, long and loud.

"Chickens!" Calhoun exclaimed. "Chickens!"

Rune blinked, then shook his head. The old guy was in a tizzy and there was nothing he could do for him. It had to suck to have lost your mind. He climbed up over the wall and entered the huge parking area from which the teams were launched. His bike was in one of the old newspaper garages. The doors were open and he headed inside to uncover his bike.

As he pulled the tarp off, he heard a noise behind him and quickly turned. It sounded like a door opening, but he didn't see anything through the gloom.

"Hello?"

There was no response and he shook his head. The damn ghosts had him spooked. Securing his bags to the bike, he took a deep breath. It was that time again and that was all there was to it. No time for regrets or fear. He rolled his bike out into the open air, noting that the sun had began to slowly peek over the horizon.

"Heading out, Rune?"

It was the old guy named Ed.

"Yeah. Time to go."

Ed stared at him thoughtfully. Behind him, the sentries were charging out on the wall; the early morning crew was arriving to work on the wall reinforcements. In Ed's gnarled hand was a steaming cup of coffee. Rune would kill for a cup right now, but he didn't feel like stirring up the ghosts anymore than he had. It was hard enough keeping focused when he had to deal with one or two. He couldn't deal with a whole town's worth.

"Well, you're welcome to stay," Ed finally said.

"Yeah. I know that. But it's time to move on. I can't stay long in one place. My nature don't permit it." Rune felt that was explanation enough.

"I understand. I'll see about getting the gates open for ya." Ed moved off.

Rune straddled his bike and tugged on his thick leather gloves. The braid of white hair fell over one shoulder as he zipped up his leather jacket and made sure to keep his neck covered. As he finished getting ready to head out, he sensed someone standing near him.

Looking up he saw a woman with short brown hair smiling at him. Her long black dress flowed to her shiny black boots and ornate jewelry decorated her neck and wrists.

"Damn," he whispered.

"We'll let you know when it is time to head back," she said in a clear, melodic voice.

Rune slowly bobbed his head, mesmerized by the woman. "Okay."

"You'll be needed later," she continued.

"I'll keep that in mind."

"Stay alive. You're needed on this side."

"Okay." Rune noticed that the edges of her figure blurred slightly. Still, he swore he could touch her if he tried.

Ed stepped through the apparition and she vanished. "Get ready. We'll open the first gate and once you're inside, close it, then open the second. Area is clear of zombies, but be careful. Got Katarina, the sniper, watching out."

"Gotcha. And thanks, man." Rune clasped hands with the older man, then gunned the motorcycle to life.

"You're always welcome to come back."

"I think I will head back one day. Kinda...got that feeling." He pulled on his goggles as Ed nodded his head and walked on.

Once free of the gates, his bike roared down the abandoned streets of Ashley Oaks, away from the fort and into the deadlands.

4. The Whore of Babylon

For once, Jenni dreamed blissful dreams. Secure in Juan's arms, she slept deeply and did not awaken once.

Juan left early in the morning, leaving her to sleep in. Jenni briefly remembered him kissing her lips before sliding out of bed. She also remembered him kissing her again before he left. When the alarm clock went off two hours later, she groggily climbed out of the bed, naked and disoriented.

After a long hot shower, she pulled on her work clothes and fussed with her hair. The night before had been wonderful and she felt amazingly at peace. Juan was too wonderful for words and she couldn't help but be happy.

The knock on the door startled her and she walked over and flung it open expecting to see Katie. Instead, it was Blanche.

"Oh, hi, bitch." Jenni couldn't imagine what Blanche wanted.

Blanche smiled at her. "Hi, spic," she answered.

Jenni never saw what hit her, but suddenly the world swirled into darkness and she felt herself falling.

* * * * *

The two men with Blanche pulled Jenni up off the floor and half-carried, half-dragged her down the hall. Blanche walked swiftly behind them, her hand gripping the kid-sized baseball bat she had used to club Jenni. Her husband was cowering near the service elevator down the hall, and she gave him a fierce look.

"Are you sure-" he started.

"Yes, Stephen" she said sharply.

She was very sure. After all her hard work the last few months, she was damn sure. Things would have gone much better if that idiot Shane hadn't gone after the lesbian, but oh well. Blanche had been paying Shane, Philip and three of their buddies in money and sexual favors (she always did like it rough). In return, the men stored food and supplies at her mansion in preparation for her return. The fort never realized how much the men had diverted to her old abode. Then Shane screwed up, leaving her to make do with his three lackeys. They were simple men who worked on the salvage runs when they weren't working on new construction. After Shane had called the wrath of the fort down on his head, Blanche had kept a tight reign on her three remaining minions. She liked to think of them as minions. It empowered her.

"Ray, go get Juan. Meet us in the garage near my Hummer," she said to one of the men. He was the scrawniest of the three, but amazingly good in bed.

"Gotcha," he said, and hurried off.

"I don't understand why we need her," Stephen said in a voice that made her want to claw his eyes out.

Blanche was good at manipulating people and she had done her best to keep herself and Stephen isolated from the rest of the fort. It allowed her to plan her return to the mansion without much interference. Stephen had been the easiest to manipulate. God help the poor man, but he really did love her.

"Because, her spic boyfriend controls the gate and if we have her with us, he will do what we say."

God, he was a total idiot. The only thing he was good for was managing her money and making more of it. He definitely had not done anything to help her out during these hard months at the fort. He had tried to get Travis to give them the Hummer and supplies behind her back, but he had failed, of course. He was lucky he had not brought the fort authorities down on them or ruined her plans. That had nearly happened when Linda, searching for the Imotrex, almost found the contraband the boys had been smuggling to Blanche. The scene she had to make afterward to cover up had been ridiculous, but it had worked.

"Then we let her go?" Stephen asked.

"Of course not. I need someone to clean the mansion," Blanche said with a laugh.

The service elevator opened and they stepped inside. Brewster and Johnson flanked her, Brewster holding the unconscious woman under one arm. Blanche straightened her dress a bit and checked her shoes. She was wearing snake skin boots with her dress and she admired them with a sigh. Soon she would have all of her lovely things back.

Including her Hummer...

The doors snapped open to a back hallway and they moved swiftly through it. Stephen followed, clutching their bags. He was at least good for that.

Pushing open a back door, she stepped into the small courtyard between the hotel and the newspaper building. The new wall rose up enclosing the courtyard and blocking her view of the town, but she didn't care. She was done with this shit town.

Johnson ran ahead of them and opened up the doors to the newspaper office. He had picked it open the night before and it swung open on freshly oiled hinges. Blanche strode confidently inside and walked down the long narrow hallway, barely paying attention to the old offices. Again, Johnson ran ahead and opened up the door to the loading dock that was now used as a garage. Her Hummer sat there, beautiful and waiting for them among the rest of the shitkicker vehicles the fort vermin had collected.

Stephen rushed over to the board where all the keys hung and grabbed the ones for the Hummer. At least he was good for that much, Blanche thought bitterly.

"Pack the Hummer, get ready to go," Blanche said tersely. "And do what we planned, okay?"

Stephen nodded and obeyed.

"Hey, once we're out of here, what are we doing with him," Brewster whispered to Blanche.

"I'll take care of him. He's deadweight in this world."

Johnson handed Blanche the revolver with the silencer she had specifically requested from her mansion. She took it with a smile.

"Keep to the plan," she said.

The door on the far side of the room opened and Juan walked in with Ray. Ray looked nervous, but Juan looked almost frantic. Blanche wondered what the hell Ray had told him to get him down to the garage.

"What happened? Is she okay?" Juan asked as he drew near. "How did she get hurt?"

Blanche calmly pressed the muzzle of the silencer against the underside of Jenni's chin.

Juan stopped cold, his eyes growing wide. "What the fuck?"

"We're leaving and you're opening the gate," Blanche said coolly.

Juan blinked, taking it all in. He looked sharply at Ray, who backed away, ducking his head. "What the hell is going on, Ray?"

"We're leaving," Brewster said in his loud booming voice. "And you're letting us out."

"You could have just asked," Juan hissed at them.

"Oh, like you would have let the Hummer go," Blanche said mockingly.

"This is about your fucking car? Travis said your husband was all crazy to get it back."

Blanche just laughed. "It's about my fucking treatment around here. I am taking my car, my men, and I'm going home."

"Fine, but you can't take her!"

"I'll give her back to you once we're through the gate. I'll leave her off on a corner somewhere in town and you can hurry your little ass out there to get her before the zombies do," Blanche assured him.

Of course, it was a lie. Blanche had come to hate Jenni about as much as she hated anyone. She was going to enjoy making the little bitch her...well...slave. She wasn't sure why she hated her so much, but it was probably because everyone seemed to adore the fucking crazy spic.

"Bitch," Juan spat.

Blanche nodded and shrugged. She flipped the safety off. "Now, I have no problem shooting her if you don't do as I say."

"You shoot her, I won't let you out."

"No, no, someone else will let us out because then you'll be our hostage," Blanche assured him.

"I don't believe you," Juan said after a beat. "You don't have it in you. You wouldn't even do guard duty."

Blanche shrugged, then looked over at Stephen. "Stephen?"

"Yes, dear?" he replied softly. He was obviously uncomfortable with the whole situation.

Blanche shot him four times in the chest and watched with some satisfaction as a look of surprise gave way to horror on her husband's face, then he collapsed.

"I will shoot her," Blanche said calmly.

Juan backed up a few steps, shaken. Even Ray looked horrified.

"Damn," Brewster muttered.

"I didn't sign up for this," Johnson said unexpectedly.

"What?" Blanche turned toward him, startled.

"I didn't sign up for you killing people. You said we were leaving, that's all." He was backing away from her, his hand moving toward his gun.

Blanche fired at him, hitting him twice in the chest. She made a mental count of her rounds and patted her pocket for the other clip. She was uncertain if she had started with a full clip or not.

"You're fucking crazy," Juan shouted at her.

"Start the car," Blanche told Ray.

He hesitated, then obeyed, moving to the Hummer and picking up the keys from Stephen's limp hand.

Well, at least her favorite two were left, Blanche decided.

Brewster still had a good grip on Jenni, but he was looking unsteady, unsure.

Blanche wondered if she had read these men wrong. She had expected them to be more ruthless. She sighed. Stupid Shane. He would have had her back.

Juan took a step forward. "Just take me, okay? Let her go. I'll tell them to open the gate and you can drop me off somewhere. Okay?"

Blanche considered this. It was tempting but she really needed a maid to upkeep the mansion. Though she was loathe to admit it, she envied Jenni. Juan may be Mexican, but he was rather hot.

She shook her head, trying to concentrate on the here and now.

"Now, Juan, don't go messing up my plans," Blanche ordered.

He stared at her, then shook his head, fear in his eyes. "You're lying. I can see it. I don't trust you. Give me Jenni and then just go. Just go."

Blanche hesitated. It sounded so easy when he said it. But it wasn't. She had a point to make here. They had not treated her as they should have, plain and simple. They had all treated her like shit. Yet, they weren't worthy to lick the heels of her $14,000 boots. She had been forced to mop, dust, clean dishes, and put up with stupid people. She and Stephen had to share a room and she wasn't even given any sort of personal maid.

There was a fucking point to be made here.

These stupid people did not realize who she was! She was a shining daughter of the fucking damn state of Texas. She moved in circles with the gawddamn Hiltons and Donald Trump. She was a fucking somebody and they were fucking shitkickers.

"Just, please, put the gun down and let Jenni go," Juan said softly.

"Don't tell me what to do!" Her infamous temper flared and before she realized what she was doing, she swung the gun around and shot Juan.

He staggered backwards, then collapsed against the wall.

"Why the fuck did you do that?" Brewster demanded.

She turned to tell him to shut up.

Jenni's head came up sharply, snapping back and bursting Brewster nose with a deafening thwack. Blood sprayed everywhere and Blanche ducked away, trying to avoid it. Brewster grunted and went down with a thud.

Blanche started to turn to bring the gun up when she felt something hard slam into her temple and she was sent spinning. The revolver slipped from her hand, then she landed on the disgusting, oily floor. Gasping, she tried to get up, but she was flipped onto her back and she saw a blur of long black hair and a pale face, then something hit her cheekbone with a sickening thud. Pain splintered her thoughts as she was pummeled into senselessness.

Her last real thought before the darkness washed over her was that she should have taken the pregnant woman instead.

5. Winter Sky

Jenni staggered away from Blanche, her hands bloodied and her face splattered with red drops. Her hands were bruised, battered and her knuckles torn open, but she didn't care. The bitch was down and not moving.

She reached over and grabbed Blanche's fancy gun and pivoted on her heal to take aim at Ray and Brewster. But Brewster was unconscious and Ray was moving toward Juan.

"Stay away from him!" Jenni's voice sounded faint and hoarse to her own ears.

"He's shot...I...I..." Roy faltered.

Jenni was crying, her tears hot on her face. She stumbled forward, her head throbbing. "Leave him alone!"

She regained consciousness after Blanche had shot her own husband. Remaining limp, Jenni had waited for the right moment to try to escape. Keeping her eyes slitted and watching through her hair, she had seen Juan get shot. It was then in a fit of anger and desperation that she had made her move.

Her head still hurt where she had rammed it into Brewster's nose. In fact, her head felt huge and swollen and when she walked, she swayed. Blanche had nailed her pretty hard.

Juan looked so still where he lay slumped against the wall. Blood was pooling around his body and his shirt was stained red. Ray stood a few feet from him, looking unsure. Though he had a sidearm at his side, he made no move for it. Jenni staggered to Juan's side. Falling to her knees, she whispered to him in Spanish.

Juan was barely able to lift his head. "Loca," he barely managed to say.

Pointing the gun at Ray, Jenni struggled to get her sweater off.

"Look, let me go get help," Ray said finally.

"Shut up!"

Juan's hand feebly touched her leg and she looked at him, tears in her eyes, struggling to think straight.

"I'll go get help," Ray said again. "Look, I didn't think Blanche would pull this shit. Let me go get help!"

Juan moaned and Jenni stroked his hair, trying to calm him. "Okay, go! Go!"

Ray nodded and ran toward the door that would lead to the construction site.

Once he was gone, Jenni put the gun down and quickly removed her sweater and wadded it up. The wound was ugly and bleeding hard on the left side of his chest. Jenni didn't even want to think about the damage the bullet may have done. Pressing her sweater against the wound, she tried to staunch the bleeding.

"Tengo frio," Juan whispered.

"We'll get you somewhere warm," Jenni promised. She stroked his hair and lay kisses on his clammy brow.

"I...always...thought...she was...a stupid...bitch..." Juan muttered, and tried to smile.

"Shh...don't worry about her. I beat the hell out of her. No one messes with my man," Jenni answered.

"That's...my...Loca..." Juan smiled, but he looked too pale and his eyes were growing glassy.

Jenni could feel his blood, hot against her flesh, soaking into the sweater. She looked toward the door and knew Ray wasn't coming with help.

That was when she began to scream.

* * * * *

There were moments that would be forever seared into the memories of those who lived and worked in the fort. The terror of the first day, the raising of the first wall, the battle against the horde of zombies from the school, and countless others. But one that would haunt those that survived the coming terrors was the vision of Jenni, covered in blood, dragging Juan into the winter sunlight that cold morning.

Jenni would always remember the terror that she was losing the love of her life. But she would also remember how her screams brought the fort members running to help her.

And for some reason, until her last day on earth, she remembered the color of the white winter sky and the single bird flying over head, riding the cold winds.

Chapter 7

1. Eyes I Dare Not Meet In Dreams

Travis couldn't bear to look at Jenni. As she was guided into the hotel, he thought of the T.S. Eliot poem "The Hollow Men." The line that came to him was: "eyes I dare not meet in dreams." He had seen the utter hollowness in Jenni's eyes when Katie had helped her into the hotel, and he had gone cold inside. She had looked almost as lifeless as Juan.

Through the doorway, he could see Katie and Rosie gently cleaning and bandaging Jenni's hands. Jenni's hair was covering her face; her shoulders shook as she sobbed.

The lobby was loud with voices as word got around about what had happened in the garage. Nerit and her people were looking for Ray while Bill had Blanche locked away. The bitch was unconscious, but alive despite the incredible beating Jenni had given her. Travis hadn't even recognized Blanche when they had carried her in to the hotel.

Travis felt sick to the pit of his stomach as he looked at the long line of blood donors. Charlotte was working feverishly to save Juan with Belinda assisting her. Brewster was in another room with Peggy and Stacey trying to clean up his shattered nose. The Reverend was leading a prayer vigil nearby. He wasn't sure how bad off Juan was, but he knew the fort did not have the medical facilities needed to save his life.

Travis tried to remember how did the T. S. Elliot poem ended. Didn't Stephen King quote it in one of his books?

> *This is the way the world ends*
> *This is the way the world ends*
> *This is the way the world ends*
> *Not with a bang but a whimper*

The fort was abuzz with people talking about Blanche being the Vigilante. It was a consensus that she must have had help, but that she was the mastermind. Case closed.

Travis rubbed his brow and looked up as Ken rushed up to him. "Did you find Ray?"

"No. And Calhoun is gone, too. We can't find him anywhere. He was supposed to help with some wiring today and never showed up. Juan sent me to find him right before that bitch shot him," Ken answered. His eyes widened and he pressed one hand to his throat. "Shit, Travis, think she

71

offed him? Ed said Calhoun was acting weird this morning. He was all muttering stuff about the Whore of Babylon right before that biker guy left."

Travis shook his head, exhaling slowly, trying to keep calm. "Keep looking. He's a wily, old man. He could be anywhere. I can't see Blanche and her goons taking him out that easily."

"Yeah, but she hated his guts," Ken said, tears glimmering in his dark eyes. "Yesterday, Calhoun stepped on her boots, and she shoved him into the wall. She's a psycho bitch. I refused to do her hair because she's so mean!"

Travis rubbed his brow slowly. "Just keep looking. Hopefully, we'll find him and Ray and figure out what the hell is really going on."

Katarina strode by, her rifle slung casually in her arms, as Ken departed into the crowd. She just merely shook her head at Travis as she passed and moved through the crowd on her way to another part of the building.

Curtis, looking nervous and very young, appeared next to him. "I'm hearing he's at death's door."

"Yeah," Travis said softly. How where you supposed to react when your best friend was dying? He wasn't sure. He just felt strangely numb, yet angry.

"I can't believe it was Blanche and her goons all along. Guess we should have seen it?" Curtis shook his head. "It's kinda obvious now. She's one messed up bitch. Always been a mean one."

Travis sighed and rubbed his face again. "Yeah, I suppose. But everyone just thought she was a spoiled bitch...not a dangerous one."

With a nod of his head, Curtis agreed. "What are we going to do with her and Brewster? And Ray if we find him?"

"I have no fucking clue," Travis answered.

One of the older black women, who's name eluded Travis, stepped out of the makeshift clinic and motioned for the next person in line. They were using a lot of blood donors to try to save Juan.

The crowd parted automatically for Nerit as she moved toward Travis. He noted her slight limp, but knew better than to ask about it. Nerit's yellowish white hair was in a tight bun on her head and she looked fierce.

"No sign of Ray. I suspect he went over the wall. Dixon says he swore he heard a car start up in the distance. I have a feeling this little group had some contingency plans."

"Dammit," Travis murmured.

"We should send out patrols then! Round his ass back up." Curtis looked fierce and very bloodthirsty. His hands were clutched tightly at his side and he kept pivoting back and forth on the balls of his feet with agitation.

"Won't do us any good, will it?" Nerit's gaze was cold. "We'll just set his ass back outside the wall again."

"But we need answers! A confession!"

"We have Blanche and Brewster. I think that is sufficient."

Travis looked over at the Reverend and his prayer group. "Nothing is sufficient anymore," he said bitterly.

"We gotta go after him and find out what was going on!"

"Curtis, it's obvious what was going on. Blanche wanted her damn Hummer back." Travis shook his head. "And she was stupid and crazy enough to kill for it."

"It was more than that, Travis," Nerit said in a low voice. "It was a grandiose move on her part to make a point."

"And what was her damn point, Nerit? That the Hummer was hers?" Travis glared at Nerit, trying not to direct his anger at her and failing.

Nerit shrugged. "She is clearly not sane. And how can we anticipate or understand the actions of the insane?"

Travis rubbed his face with both hands, growling with frustration. "I should have given them the damn Hummer!"

"It may not have satisfied her, Travis. Maybe this is all about revenge for not treating her as she believed she should be."

"She was just a freaking beauty queen," Curtis exclaimed. "Who happened to marry a rich guy! She weren't no damn Queen of England."

"All this arguing is pointless. Juan is dying. Ray is missing. Calhoun is nowhere to be found. There are two dead men in the garage. And that bitch is unconscious. And none of this makes a bit of freakin' sense!" Travis whirled on his heel and stalked off. He didn't want to talk about any of this anymore. He didn't even want to deal with it anymore, but he had to. For Juan's sake.

He walked into the room where Jenni sat trembling, sobbing, and whispering to Rosie in Spanish. Katie stood up and came to him. He allowed himself a brief moment of comfort in her arms.

"We can't find, Ray," Travis told her. "Or Calhoun."

Katie frowned. "Calhoun? I don't--"

"Ken thinks Blanche did away with him. Maybe she did. I don't know. This is so fucked up."

Jenni looked up, her lips trembling. "Is Juan...is he..."

"They're still working on him," Travis answered.

Rosie looked pale and her mouth was clenched shut. She and Jenni were holding hands, united in their fear and grief. "My son is strong. He'll come through."

"I have no doubt that Juan is determined to live," Travis answered.

Jack was under Jenni's chair, his sad eyes looking at all the humans. Jason was on guard duty and Jack had come to be with Jenni. It was almost as if he knew she needed him. Travis leaned down and petted the dog's head.

Charlotte entered the room, covered in blood, looking tired. Letting out a desperate, horrified gasp, Rosie grabbed Jenni in her arms. Both women looked on the verge of collapse.

Travis straightened and reached for Katie's hand. She clutched it tightly. Travis forced the words out. "How is he?"

Charlotte let out a long sigh. "Stabilized. For now. We actually stopped the bleeding and have him on transfusions. I have some ER experience from my nursing days and I managed to get him stable. The bullet is still in him and it definitely collapsed a lung. I used an empty pen as a tube to get it re-inflated, and Belinda is manually pumping air into his lungs. I have Peggy looking for an oxygen tank she swears she has in storage. He has lost a lot of blood, and I don't know what other damage is in there."

"Is he going to live?" Rosie whispered.

Charlotte licked her lips, then said, "I did my best with what I have. But the bullet is still in there and there is risk of infection. He's also in shock and we're treating him for that."

Jenni pulled away from Rosie. "I need to go to him. He needs me."

There was a moment when Travis thought Charlotte would deny Jenni, but then she nodded. "He probably does. Just don't get too hysterical in there. Keep it calm. Keep it soft. Encourage him to fight. He's not conscious, but he may hear you."

Rosie and Jenni held each other hands tightly as they went into the next room where Juan lay. Jack followed to the door and whimpered when the door shut, cutting him off. Katie moved to comfort the dog as Travis looked at Charlotte.

"What's up for real?"

"I need surgical tools and resources we don't have," Charlotte answered truthfully. "I need to get that bullet out. I need equipment to monitor him and keep him alive. I need medications to fight infections."

Travis nodded. "Okay, get me a list. We'll get it."

"Travis?" Katie's voice sounded frightened.

Charlotte blinked. "You realize the hospitals are death traps."

"There is a small hospital about fifty miles from here. Real small. It's a possibility. It'll be volunteer only"

Katie stood up, looking fearful. "Travis, you can't go."

"Why not?" His voice sounded harsher than he meant it to be.

"The fort needs you to be our leader," she answered. She ran her hand over her belly. "And the baby and I need you."

Sitting down hard in a chair, he covered his face. He felt tears on his cheeks, and he whispered, "I can't just sit here."

"Katie is right. You're not the only one who cares about Juan."

Charlotte looked weary as well as anxious. "We can't afford to lose our leader."

"Some leader. It's my fault this happened."

"Travis, no!" Katie moved toward him, reaching out to comfort him, but he pushed her hand away.

"No, it is my fault. I should have realized what was going on with those two. If I had given them that damned Hummer-"

It was then Bill entered the room, interrupting. "Travis, the bitch is awake. Want to be there when I question her?"

Travis stood up slowly. "Yeah. I do." He kissed Katie and she wiped his tears away. He regretted pushing her hand away and stroked her cheek softly, begging for forgiveness with his eyes. "Let me know if anything changes."

Katie nodded, her eyes full of love and desperation. "Of course." She sat back down, Jack at her side.

Travis walked out of the room feeling the fear and anxiety in that room still clinging to him.

2. The Broken World

Maybe it was the way she spit out a tooth onto the table or the way she kept laughing at them, but Travis could not see Blanche as human anymore. The longer they questioned her, the more insanely confident she seemed in her lying tales. She barely looked like herself with her swollen and bruised face. Jenni had done a real number on her and Travis was glad for it.

"Look, she attacked me and killed my husband! She's a crazy spic," Blanche shouted at them. "I just want to go home! Give me my Hummer and let me go home!"

"Blanche, we know that isn't true. You took Jenni hostage. We know the truth." Bill's voice was even and very calm.

"Do you really? Do you? You know, I think you're too stupid to know the truth."

Despite Bill's quiet persistence, it soon became evident that Blanche was not about to divulge anything but her version of the story.

"Blanche, we know you had this set up. We know you have been doling out your own special justice," Bill said shortly, finally close to being angry.

She just laughed in his face. "You stupid fucks. You have no freaking clue what is going on. You think you're so smart, but you're all just a bunch of dumb rednecks. I don't know how I ever let Stephen drag me out here with you morons."

"Is that why you decided to kill off a few of us undesirables before striking out to your own promised land?" Travis could feel his temper rising. He wanted to smash her arrogant face into the table.

Blanche smirked. "Do you even realize who I am? You are all so beneath me I shouldn't even waste my time talking to you. You can't even see how dangerous that stupid spic is. Look what she did to my face!"

"What did you do to Calhoun? He's missing." Bill glowered at Blanche, his doughy face flushed red with anger.

"Really?" Her bloody, swollen face was a terrible parody of a clown. "Well, that's a bit of good news."

"Is this really all about the Hummer? Is that damn car why you killed two people, including your own husband?"

Blanche stared at Bill, slightly smiling. "Exile me. Send me home. In my Hummer."

Travis shook his head and walked into the corridor. Bill followed in silence. Travis looked grim and pale and Bill just looked tired.

"What do we do?" Bill asked aloud.

Travis shrugged. "Send her home. Let the bitch go rot in her mansion."

Bill nodded. "Okay. Let her rot."

Travis set his jaw grimly. "And not in the Hummer. Fuck her and that car."

"I'll send Curtis and Katarina out with her then."

"Good. I don't have time to deal with her. We've wasted enough time on her. We need to get hospital supplies to save Juan's life."

Bill arched his eyebrows and adjusted his belt nervously. "Really? A hospital?"

"I know. I know they're death traps, but..." Travis faltered. "I gotta do something."

"I'm in. I'll go." Bill shrugged slightly. "We need more supplies anyway."

"Thanks, Bill."

"You ain't going though, right?"

"What is this? A conspiracy?"

"You're the fearless leader. You can't go."

"We'll discuss this later! Just...get the word out that we're doing this. Okay?"

Bill shrugged again. "Okay. I will."

"Meeting in an hour in the dining room, okay?"

"Gotcha."

Travis walked away, rubbing his neck, wishing to God he could restart the day. Instead, he went to check in with Peggy.

* * * * *

Katie could hear the arguing through the door and had a good idea what it was about. Her eyes hurt from crying and she felt a little sick to her stomach. She had left Jason and Jack to wait for Jenni and Rosie to come out of Juan's room while she went in search of her husband.

Peggy hadn't been at her regular haunt at the front desk, so Katie had gone on down the hall to the old hotel manager's office. Now, the voices on the other side of the door were getting louder.

The second she opened the door, the people inside went quiet. Travis was leaning against his desk, glaring at Nerit and Peggy. Bill was standing with his hands on his belt, glowering at Travis. Eric was seated, legs crossed, cleaning his glasses while looking quite pensive.

"What's going on?"

"Your fool husband wants to go out and get himself killed and leave us without a leader," Peggy answered, her voice harsh with her frustration.

"Why should I ask other people to go out into the deadlands and risk themselves if I'm not going out myself? Huh?"

Katie looked at her husband and raised her eyebrows. "I thought it was settled that you weren't going."

Throwing her an annoyed look, Travis flung up his hands.

"Your most trusted advisers and good friends are telling you that you need to stay." Eric donned his glasses and looked up. "Don't you think you should listen to us?"

Picking up the volunteer sheet, Travis shook it at the co-conspirators. "We have only seven people on this list."

"Katarina and Curtis wanted to go, too, but they're getting rid of Blanche," Bill reminded him.

"I would go, but I'm needed here," Nerit added.

"And I would have no idea how to handle myself out there," Eric admitted, reddening slightly.

"Linda I can understand going because she's Juan's cousin. Lenore and Ken have me surprised, but they're good people. Who is Dale?"

"The big guy that was rescued the other day. Has long hair and chops," Bill answered Travis.

"That's kinda weird, him volunteering," Travis said, obviously perplexed.

"He told me he wants to get involved and he might as well start now." Bill shrugged. "I think he'll do fine."

"Okay, I guess." Travis returned his gaze to the piece of paper. "Felix always volunteers. I'm a little surprised by Roger though. Should Roger be going out?"

"He does well on scavenging runs," Nerit pointed out. "He's competent."

"He is probably going out for Jason," Katie added. "They're pretty close."

"They are always working on defensive weapons together." Nerit sat down slowly, settling the sniper rifle at her side. "What is your point in scrutinizing the list, Travis?"

"I'm closer to Juan than all these people except for Linda. I should be going out there. He is my best friend!"

Katie stepped toward Travis, her hand reaching for his. He had already pushed her away once today and though he seemed ready to do it again, he relented and let her take his hand. "Travis, we all know you care about Juan. I know what it feels like to be helpless in the face of death, but you are needed here. Everyone in the fort knows you're willing to put your life on the line. You helped bring weapons back to the fort, you helped clear the hotel, you helped bring down the bandits. That is why people trust you."

"She's right, Travis. If you're trying to prove anything to us, you don't have to."

"Eric, it's not about proving anything to you guys. In fact, the Travis Fan Club in this fort freaks me the hell out! It's about..." Travis struggled with his emotions. "It's about me. How I feel. I want to help my friend. I want to help save him."

Katie ran her hand gently over his hair and let it rest on the back of his neck. He looked toward her, his expression anguished. She could feel tears filling her eyes, but she struggled not to let them fall. "We understand more than you realize. But we need you here. You may not like it, but you're our stability. You make us believe we can survive and flourish in this world. It may not seem like much to you, but it's everything to us."

"Listen to your wife and stop being a bullheaded idiot," Peggy said shortly. "She's right. If you were to die out there, do you know what that would do to us?"

Travis stared at Peggy angrily, then shook his head. "Dammit."

"And don't say one of us can take over. We got our job to do and none of us can do what you do." Bill crossed his arms over his chest.

Eric nodded his head vigorously. "That is very true."

"I am the one who fucked up! I'm the one who didn't let that psycho take that damn Hummer and leave. And she shot my friend because of it!"

"So it comes out. You feel guilty," Nerit said, lifting an eyebrow.

"Gawdammit, Travis! Blanche is unhinged. That girl hasn't been firing on all cylinders for a damn long time. You can't blame yourself!" Peggy looked ready to smack him and Katie couldn't blame her.

"I can't help but feel it is my fault."

"So you're going to go out into the deadlands and risk not coming back to soothe your guilt? You should feel guilty for putting yourself at risk. We all need you. I need you. The baby needs you." Katie tried to keep her voice even and not let her own anger and desperation leak into it.

Travis looked down at the volunteer sheet. His fingers were trembling and his jaw was clenched. Finally, mutely, he nodded and gave in. Setting the paper aside, he leaned forward, setting his hands on his knees and exhaling, long and slow.

"It's the right thing to do, Travis," Nerit assured him.

"Charlotte is drawing a map of the hospital interior and marking where they need to go. She has Belinda photocopying pictures of the equipment the team needs to bring back." Eric motioned toward Bill. "Bill is organizing the teams and debriefing them. It's a dangerous run, but it's being handled. You're needed here. People are still freaking out over all of this. And you may not like it, Travis, but you are a calming force."

Travis straightened and pulled Katie into his arms, resting his cheek against hers.

"It's the right thing to do," she whispered in his ear.

"It doesn't make it easier," he answered softly.

"It never does." She slowly ran her hands over his hair and tucked them behind his neck. Pressing a soft kiss to his lips, she felt his body slowly relax.

"Oh, you two make me sick," Peggy declared.

Resting his forehead against Katie's, Travis said softly, "Get the volunteers together. We need to get them out there and fast. We're burning sunlight."

"I'll get them to the dining room."

"Thanks, Bill."

"I'll get the map and photocopies from Charlotte," Peggy said, heading toward the door.

Katie kissed Travis' forehead, feeling his body slowly melding against hers.

"I will go check on the search for Calhoun and Ray," Nerit said, standing up to leave.

"Thanks, Nerit."

She patted his shoulder then followed Eric out the door.

"Forgive me?" Travis asked his wife.

Katie kissed him firmly on the lips. "Nothing to forgive. You're a loyal friend, a good leader, and a man with a huge heart. There is nothing to forgive."

Travis laid his head on her shoulder. "Katie, I'm so lucky to have you."

"Yes, you are. So don't go running off doing something stupid."

"I'll keep that in mind."

"I'm going to go check on Jenni."

Travis straightened, rubbing his neck. "Ok. I need to go to the briefing anyway."

Running her hand lightly over his arm, she reluctantly drew away from her husband. "I'll see you later."

"I love you, Katie."

"I love you, Travis."

As she slipped out the door, she stole one more look at her weary husband. Travis sat on the edge of his desk staring into space. She could see that he was resigned to not going out, but it was hard on him. With a soft sigh, she shut the door behind her.

* * * * *

It was nearly one-thirty when the volunteer teams were briefed on the medical supply run in the dining room. The volunteers studied the layout of the hospital Charlotte had drawn and listened to her explain exactly where they needed to go. They looked over the photocopies of the equipment and surgical instruments as well as a list of medications that would be useful.

Travis stood in the back of the room trying not to feel frustrated and guilty for not going along. He had put up a good argument only to be shot down. Even Roger had told him the Captain needed to stay on the ship and not go out with the away team when he had expressed his regrets in not going with them.

Finally, Charlotte finished her briefing and said, "Anyone have anything to say? Ask? Suggest?"

"Yeah," a voice came from behind them. "When are we leaving?"

Everyone in the room turned to look at the pale, determined face of Jenni.

"Shit," Roger muttered.

"You're not going," Travis said automatically.

Jenni frowned and pointed at him. "You can't tell me what to do.⨍"

"C'mon, Jenni. Shouldn't you be with Juan?" Travis walked toward her, wondering if the sick feeling he had in the pit of his stomach is what others had felt when he announced he wanted to go with the team.

"And do what? Watch him die?" Jenni shook her head. "Fuck that. I'm going. I am good at this sort of thing. How many rescue teams have I been on?"

"You're still new at scavenging and it's a little different," Roger answered. "Death rates on the scavenging teams are higher than the rescue."

Everyone in the room looked at him obviously wishing he hadn't spoken that particular bit of truth.

"Sorry, but seriously, there are a lot more redshirts on the scavenging teams," Roger said a tad defensively.

Travis took hold of Jenni's arm lightly and gazed down into her face. "You are a good fighter. We all know that. But wouldn't you rather be with

Juan right now?"

"Doing what? Crying? Praying? Staring at him, hoping he moves?" Jenni again shook her head, almost violently. "I can feel myself going crazy in there waiting. At least this way, I'm trying to do something to save his life other than waiting for him to die."

Travis stepped back, his eyes lowering. "Jenni..."

"Travis, don't keep me from going out there. I'm begging you."

Katie slipped into the dining room behind Jenni. She looked pale and frustrated. "She won't listen to me."

"She does have a point," Bill interjected. "Watching the one you love die slowly and not be able to help is a hell unto itself." His eyes held incredible sadness. "I would have done anything to save my wife from cancer. I would have climbed Mount Everest to save her."

Travis could feel all the eyes in the room on him. "Jenni, if you go and something happens..."

Jenni whirled on him, her tear-filled eyes flashing with anger. "I can't just sit there and wait! I can't! I fucking can't be helpless this time! Okay?"

"She's made her choice." Dale spoke up for the first time. "Everyone has got a right to make a choice."

"We could use her," Linda finally ventured. "Juan is my cousin and I love him. Yeah, I'm scared knowing the risks, but he has always treated me like his little sister. I gotta do what I can to save him. Let her go, Travis."

Lenore and Ken were seated side by side and by their lowered heads and averted gazes, it was obvious they did not want to get involved. Felix just sighed deeply and looked away. Charlotte fussed with the printouts she had used for her debriefing, obviously refusing to say a word about the situation.

Travis reached out slowly to Jenni, and she flung herself into his arms. He held her close, feeling her trembling. "Jenni, can you keep it together out there?"

She nodded vigorously. "I can out there better than I can here."

Katie slid her hand over Jenni's long hair slowly. She looked agonized, but said in a quivering voice, "She'll do fine out there."

Travis held Jenni tightly, laying his head on the top of her head. He could feel her anguish pouring out of her, filling the room. What would he do if Katie lay dying? The answer was obvious. Even he wanted to go to help his friend, but was held back by his position. But Jenni should have the choice, despite his personal misgivings.

"Okay, go, Jenni. I don't think we could stop you if we tried," Travis finally said.

Katie wiped away tears and Jenni turned and wrapped her arms around her. Holding each other tightly, the two women wept.

"I gotta go,"Jenni whispered.

"I know," Katie answered, looking at Travis. "I know."

Travis reached out and touched her cheek lovingly. "Be careful out there, Jenni."

"I will. I promise."

"Then it's settled. Jenni, get over here so I can catch you up, then we gotta go," Bill said firmly.

Jenni pulled away from Travis, wiping away her tears. Walking toward Bill and Charlotte, she threw a smile back his way that was both grateful and terribly sad.

Travis slightly smiled back. Turning, he saw his wife staring after Jenni. She had huge tears rolling down her cheeks, and it broke his heart to see her in pain.

"She'll be okay. She's more of a badass than I'll ever be."

"True, but I can't help but worry." Katie turned away, moving toward the hall. "I hate today. I hate everything about it."

Travis hurried after her, his hand gripping her elbow lightly. "Honey, go lie down for a bit. Okay?"

"How can I? With Jenni going out and Juan in there..." Her voice caught and she covered her mouth.

"Have you eaten yet?"

Shaking her head, she looked quite guilty.

"Okay, I want you to eat something, then go lay down. You have to think about the baby."

"I can't until they leave, okay?"

Travis nodded, frowning slightly. "Okay, but after they go-"

"I promise." Katie blinked the tears from her lashes and let out a soft moan of despair. "God, Travis..."

Taking her in his arms, he held her tight, kissing her face and hair. "We'll make it through. I promise. We'll make it."

Chapter 8

1. Bless Me Father

J enni leaned over and gently kissed Juan's dry lips. Her fingers played over his curls and she took in a deep shuddering breath. Resting her hand lightly on his chest, she could feel the faint thudding of his heart.

"Keep strong, baby. I love you."

With one last kiss, she straightened and stepped back from the bed.

Rosie reached out to touch her hand. Jenni clasped the older woman's and squeezed it. They shared a quiet moment, then Jenni kissed her cheek and left the room.

Her long black hair fell freely around her shoulders as she walked toward the chapel. People looked toward her, but no one spoke. She was wearing the red sweater that Juan liked to see her in and her lucky jeans. Her stomach was rolling with nerves, but she didn't care anymore. She was going to save Juan.

Ken stood near the open door to the chapel and smiled slightly as she approached. "Bill says we got ten minutes."

"Okay. That should be enough time. I just don't want to go out there without having God at my back."

Walking inside, she found the Reverend waiting for her with a Communion of saltines and red Kool-Aid. She had specifically asked for Communion and he had quickly agreed. She was surprised to see some of the other members of the teams gathered as well. Taking a seat, she pulled out her rosary and threaded it between her fingers.

The Reverend did his best to improvise a Catholic Communion, and she adored him for it. She knew he struggled to be all things to all the different denominations in the fort and she thought he did an amazing job. He was even wearing a white robe made from a tablecloth. It touched her.

When it came time to partake of the Communion, she felt her hands shaking. Despite her need to go out into the deadlands and bring back the things that would save her love, she was terrified. Juan's injury made her feel vulnerable. She hated that feeling.

Taking the piece of stale saltine on her tongue, she closed her eyes and tried to concentrate on the Risen Christ and the Blessed Virgin. The Kool-Aid was a bit tart, but she downed it. Crossing herself, she whispered fervent prayers to the Holy Trinity and the Queen of Heaven.

"Just let him live," she whispered.

Rising to her feet, she turned to see Roger, Linda and Bill taking Communion as well.

Walking on leaden legs, Jenni strode out of the chapel.

* * * * *

Katie's expression when she saw Jenni enter the staging area broke Jenni's heart. Jenni walked straight up to her and hugged Katie hard. She could feel Katie trembling and she buried her face in Katie's soft curls.

"If you don't come back, I'll be really pissed," Katie said finally, a catch in her voice.

"I know. But I gotta go."

"I know." Katie pressed a string of fierce kisses to Jenni's cheek. "You love him. I would do the same for Travis. And for you."

With tears in her eyes, Jenni drew back. "I would do the same for you, too."

Katie wiped her tears away and shook her head. "I just can't believe all of this."

"It'll be okay," Jenni said, her voice firm. "Juan will live."

With a small smile, Katie said, "Of course he will. He's tough."

Jenni pushed her hair back out of her face and lifted her chin. "I'll be back. One way or the other."

"I know. I can't help but worry. You're my best friend."

Jenni flung her arms around Katie again and snuggled her. She kissed Katie's forehead firmly. "And you're mine."

Travis walked up, looking a bit awkward, trying not to interrupt.

Jenni slung her arm around his neck and kissed his cheek, too. "I'll be back."

"You better be. Juan needs you," Travis said.

"Yes, he does. He's lost without me," Jenni declared with false joviality.

Her son staggered up to her and flung his arms around her, holding her tightly. "Mom," he whispered in her ear. "Mom, don't go." She squeezed him so tight it hurt both of them.

"I have to go," Jenni whispered. "I have to do something to save him. I couldn't save your...brothers. I have to try to save him."

Jason backed away, ducking his head, trying to hide his tears beneath his bangs. From the agonized look on his face, she knew he understood. "Be careful, Mom."

"I will be," she promised. She grabbed him close again and kissed him firmly on the forehead. "I love you."

Jack pawed at her knee. She leaned down and kissed his furry head. "I love you, too."

With a fake grin and trying not to look scared shitless, she walked toward Roger and Bill as they waited for her by the truck. Pivoting on her heel, she turned and waved to her small family: her best friend, her stepson, and a dog named Jack.

She tried not to think of Juan lying in that bed looking so vulnerable.

Climbing into Ralph and Nerit's red truck, she nodded at Bill. "Let's do this."

"Just like old times," he answered her, gunning the engine.

Jenni sighed. It felt nothing like old times and it scared her to death.

But she would come back.

She had to.

2. Beer and Strawberries

Bill drove in silence. Jenni sat in the back of the truck's cab, staring out the window at nothing. He doubted she was seeing anything other than Juan's face in her mind's eye. Felix was passed out asleep beside her, slightly snoring, while Roger was deep into a Star Trek novel.

The drive was over an hour, so maybe it was good to be silent. They were heading into a highly dangerous situation. They all knew that hospitals were death traps and had been from day one. Bill was eternally grateful his wife had passed on by the time the dead rose. If she hadn't, he knew she would have been one of the first to rise. That would have destroyed his will to live. It was hard watching her die of cancer, but seeing her as a member of the revived living dead....

No, he couldn't think about that now.

Despite the fact this hospital was very small, it didn't take away from the fact it was probably a deathtrap. They had two, four-member crews going in. The odds weren't with them, that was for damn sure.

Bill gripped the steering wheel harder and concentrated on the road.

In the first hours of the infestation, he hadn't even been sure he wanted to survive it. The first zombie he had seen had freaked him out so thoroughly, he could barely move. Luckily, he had been in his patrol car. It had banged on the window for a good ten minutes before he got the nerve to do something about it.

A six-year old zombie just wasn't right.

He could still remember how it thrashed under his foot after he had knocked it flat on its back and pinned it so he could get a good shot at its head. It was one of the worst moments of his life.

With a weary sigh, Bill concentrated on the road. He could see a few zombies moving through the dried brush. They seemed disoriented and sluggish. Charlotte was right. They were slowing down as the elements got to them. That didn't keep them from being fiercely terrifying if they got close to you.

Glancing in the rear view mirror, he could see Jenni leaning her head against the window, staring blankly.

He felt for her. All too clearly, he understood her distress and why she had to be part of the rescue group. It was just something she had to do. He would have done the same for his wife.

Once more, he had to admit to himself that just living had been hard when his wife had passed. He was just back to work and on patrol when that dead little boy banged on his patrol car window. He had almost given in and let the zombie take him, but then he had started to worry about Ralph and Nerit and that had been the end of that. Those two had been friends through thick and thin with his wife's illness, and he had to make sure they were okay.

Now he was glad he had made his way to them. He had found some incredible friends in the fort. They made this life worth living.

Behind him Felix let out a snort in his sleep and Bill smiled to himself.

"Check that out," Roger said.

Bill glanced over to see a commercial plane rammed into the side of a barn. There was no sign of life or unlife.

"Bet they're trapped in there," Roger went on. "What a way to go."

"I'm sure jets went down all over the world. I heard, right before the TV went black, that the planes over DFW were going down into neighborhoods. Just dropping right out of the sky," Bill said.

"So many ways to die," Jenni said with a sigh.

"Yeah," Bill answered, and they all fell silent again.

They passed an overturned car. Inside a figure was flailing around. They drove on.

A figure darted out in front of the moving truck behind them and it was immediately flattened.

How easy it was to kill them now. So very easy.

Katarina again came to mind. He had seen her right before they had left. She had been walking into the hotel as he exited.

"Good luck,"she had said.

"Thanks," he had answered grimly.

"Come back, okay?"

"Try to," he said, then hesitated. He wasn't sure where he had gotten his nerve, but he had actually said, "Hey, Katarina, want to have a drink with me when I get back?"

She had smiled and said, "Yes, that sounds nice."

Then she had walked on and so had he.

He kept thinking of that moment. He wanted to survive, go back to the fort and have a drink with her. He was ashamed to admit it, but he wondered what her hair smelled like. He hoped he would find out. Maybe someday, if she could ignore his plain looks and beer belly.

He turned the wheel and the truck slowed down as they hit the outskirts of their destination. Closed restaurants, gas stations, and a truck company lined this road. Then, up ahead, the two story modern hospital that served this town and several others loomed over an old laundromat. It was small, but that didn't mean shit in this world.

The truck came to a stop.

Jenni leaned forward. "Looks like fun."

Just inside the glass doors, two zombies in wheelchairs clawed at the glass.

Bill sighed.

He bet Katarina's hair smelled like strawberries.

3. Possibilities

Lenore and Ken were jostled around as the moving truck made its way down the country road following the first team's red truck. They sat on a long bench secured to the interior wall, holding onto straps someone had drilled into the side.

"So why did you come?" Lenore fussed with her hair, wishing her new weave wasn't already getting smashed under a hat. It had been a relief to get some beautiful lush hair after months of dealing with her own short hair without any decent products or styling tools.

Ken crossed his legs and gave her his most annoyingly cute look. "Guess."

"Dale."

"That was easy!"

Lenore scowled at him. "You do realize, twinkle toes, that we are going into a highly dangerous situation where we will most likely get our asses eaten."

"He's really cute, don't you think? All rugged and strong. Dreamy," Ken said, smiling widely.

"Eaten. By zombies. Not a cute guy. A zombie."

"You do realize I only heard the words 'eaten' and 'cute guy' just then."

"I hate you." Lenore tried to get comfortable on the bench, cursing herself for volunteering.

"Why did you volunteer?" Ken fussed with the laces of his boots, retying them as he bounced around on the bench. He made it look easy performing this feat. She would have landed on her ass.

"You volunteered, so I volunteered. Someone has to watch out for you. You'd be all staring at Dale and some zombie would bite you. Then I would have to beat you for being stupid and then kill you for being a zombie. Which would be annoying."

Ken laughed with delight. "Besides, I'm your best friend and your fag."

"I ain't your hag."

"Oh, yes you are."

"Oh, no, I'm not."

"Yes."

"No."

"Yes."

"Do not make me feed you to the zombies!"

"Feed me to Dale," Ken whispered, winking.

"I am going to pound you." She winced the second the words were out of her mouth and she saw Ken's opening. She hastily added, "No, don't you say it!"

Ken rolled his eyes and began to check his weapons. "You love me."

"Maybe."

"Felix volunteered because you volunteered."

"No, he didn't. He doesn't like me like that."

"Uh-huh."

Lenore frowned. "No, he doesn't." She hated how the thought of Felix having interest in her made her pulse speed up.

"He likes you. Why else would he sit in our beauty shop for hours waiting for you to trim his hair?"

"Because he knows I know how to trim his black hair and that your white ass does not."

Ken shook his head. "No, no. He likes you. Which is kind of funny if you think about it. Dale signed up to be part of the fort. I signed up to impress him with my prowess. You signed up to save my ass. And Felix signed up to watch yours. It's the circle of life."

Lenore wasn't too sure about that, but she didn't want to think about much more than getting into the hospital, grabbing what they needed and leaving. She wasn't just doing this for Juan, but for everyone in the fort that may one day need the supplies.

After awhile, they lapsed into silence. Ken dozed off with his head against her shoulder. She loved the idiot, but she hated to admit it. He was the most loyal friend she had ever had, even if he was annoying. Sighing, she checked her crossbow and the bag of bolts.

When the truck came to a stop, she mentally prepared herself for the worst.

The doors opened and Dale looked up at them. "It's pretty clear except for some dead guys in wheelchairs inside the front doors. Weirdest shit I've seen in awhile."

"Thank God for that," Ken said with relief. He hurried over to leap down, while Lenore pulled herself to her feet and grabbed her bag.

"Let's get this done so we can go home," Lenore grumbled as she tried to get down off the moving truck and still maintain some dignity.

Dale grabbed hold of her and helped her down with surprising ease. She flashed a grin at Ken's jealous expression and slung her bag over her shoulder.

Felix, Bill, Jenni and Roger walked toward them, their weapons out, looking around cautiously. Lenore also swept her gaze over their surroundings. It was surprisingly calm and zombie free except for the two creatures inside the glass doors of the hospital. Linda came around from the front of the truck, braiding her hair back from her face.

"Kinda feels too easy all at once," Dale decided.

"Never say that!" Ken chided him.

"It's bad luck," Linda added.

"Oh, sorry." Dale looked sheepish despite his huge size.

Bill pulled his belt up over his stomach and looked grim. "We go in. We get the stuff. We come out. Alive."

"Sounds like a plan," Felix said as he fell in beside Lenore.

Feeling shy after Ken's declaration about Felix's intentions, Lenore cautiously stole a look at him. Felix flashed a big smile and lightly took her hand in his. Giving it a soft squeeze, he seemed amused by her startled expression. Since she was not very good at the whole flirting thing, she ended up scowling at him, which elicited an even bigger grin.

"So, it's zombie killing time," Dale declared, stretching, his huge muscles flexing under his t-shirt.

"Yep. Better zip up your jacket and pull on your gloves." Bill motioned to Dale's exposed chest. "T-shirt ain't protection."

Lenore made sure her thick wool scarf was tight around her neck and yanked on the thick leather gloves that would allow her the flexibility to fire her crossbow. All of them were in zipped up leather jackets, jeans, and heavy shoes. Leather gloves protected their hands and anyone with long hair had it braided and pinned up on their heads.

"We should use motorcycle helmets," Ken pouted.

"They'd limit our hearing," Bill answered.

"And they get ya from behind easier. I've seen it," Dale added.

They had yet to come up with an effective way to protect their faces and necks, though a few people back at the fort were working on some ideas.

Lenore finished messing with her clothes and looked up to see that everyone else was ready, too. Jenni looked pale and worried as she stared at the hospital. Linda cocked her shotgun and looked toward Bill, waiting for the word.

"Let's do it," Bill said grimly. "Let's get it done."

4. Banished

Pain is what brought her to consciousness. Sitting up sharply, she was startled, then pleased to see she was in her bedroom at the mansion. Her face was throbbing and the coppery taste of blood filled her mouth, but she was home.

The fucking hicks had finally seen the light and sent her home.

The last thing she remembered was Charlotte, that fat nurse, coming in to tell her that she was going to give her a shot for the pain. Blanche never should have believed her, for almost immediately she had felt herself slipping away into darkness.

But now she was home, so she supposed she could overlook that fat bitch's deceit.

Blanche rolled off the bed and set her feet down on the velvety softness of her Persian rug. It took some work standing up without feeling nauseous, but slowly she regained her sense of balance and moved into the bathroom. The sun was going down and she was annoyed to see that the generator was off. The lights were dead. She caught her reflection in the mirror and felt a fresh surge of fury well up in her. She had paid good money for her nose job, veneers, and cheek implants. Hopefully once the swelling went down, she would be able to see the full extent of the damage. There had to be a good plastic surgeon out there somewhere still alive and serving her kind.

In fact, she was sure the rich and famous were somewhere safe. She had told Stephen they should try to head out on the road to find the enclave of the rich. She was sure it was Malibu. But no, her stupid husband had dragged her out to the godforsaken town he had sunk so much money into in a ridiculous effort to revive it.

Finding a box of wet wipes, she took off her clothes and tried to clean off her body to the best of her ability. She slipped on a silk robe and opened her bedroom door. The house was very quiet and she moved slowly through the hallway to the grand staircase.

She hadn't even considered if she was alone or not, but now she was curious. The stupid hicks had brought her home, but she wasn't sure what it meant. Reaching the main floor, she saw that the doors to the dining room were open. There were boxes on the table and what looked like a piece of paper taped to one of them.

Curious, she moved closer and saw that it was a note. Then, slowly, she realized the boxes must be all the supplies Shane and his men had been stockpiling. Looking into one, she saw that it was empty. Frowning, she grabbed the note.

"Thanks for the food, thanks for the liquor, thanks for the sex. If you ever make it back here, know that I took the stuff to survive. Good luck, babe. You're going to need it. By the way, you're a fucking bitch. Ray."

Blanche growled in anger and grabbed the nearest box. It had been full of fine champagne at one time.

All the boxes were empty of all the fine things she had paid Shane good money to collect. Moving into the kitchen she saw one can of chili sitting out. Another note was left on it. Grabbing the note she saw her gun under it.

Confused, she read the note.

"Here is dinner. Here is your gun. Hope you enjoy both. – Curtis."

Curtis must have dropped her off here.

"Dammit."

She was furious now. Picking up the can of chili, she hurled it across the kitchen and watched it shatter the lead glass of her china cabinet.

Turning on her heal, she stalked to Stephen's office. She would just have to get money out of the safe and take Stephen's car. It shouldn't be too hard to find another dumb ass to do her will.

When she opened the door, she blinked then swore furiously. The safe was open and empty. *Dammit!* Shane had said that Ray had once been in prison and would do as she wanted if she paid him. Now she had a good idea what Ray had been in prison for.

Stomping to the back hallway, she headed for the garage. She had a horrible fear that Ray had taken Stephen's Mercedes, but she had to be sure. When she opened the door and found the garage empty, she screamed with frustration.

Swearing, she charged back into the kitchen. Grabbing up the notes, she studied them again. Ray had fucked her and so had Curtis. She couldn't believe they had taken her things. And what the hell had Curtis meant about her enjoying the gun?

The sun would be going down soon. She scrounged around until she found a flashlight and some candles. She set up the candles and took a deep breath. The stupid fort people didn't know who she was and what she was capable of. She had some money stashed in her closet as well as some jewels. She could go out to the stable and get the work truck. They had their own gas pump and she could gas up and leave in the morning.

She just wouldn't be traveling in luxury, but things would be fine.

Comforted by this thought, she began to look for something to eat other than the disgusting can of chili. She did not want to be reminded of that gawdawful food from the fort. Finally, she found some chocolates and a bottle of wine. It would have to do.

She was halfway through the box of somewhat stale chocolates when she heard the yelling. Moving to the front door, she tilted her head and caught her own name in the shouts.

Slowly, she realized it was Ray's voice. He was yelling for her.

"Blanche, open the gawddamn door! Blanche! Open the door!"

Hesitating, she turned back and grabbed her gun.

"Blanche! Open the door! Open the gawddamn door!"

Blanche peered out into the dusk looming outside her window and saw Ray running up her driveway. She started to unlock the door, then considered what his note said.

With a snort she stepped back from the door.

He hit the door full force. "Blanche! Open the door! I know you're in there! I saw Curtis drop you off. Open the fucking door!"

"Oh, really? And why didn't you come to save me instead of ripping me off?"

"Blanche, the car broke down, okay? I was stuck up the road and saw them leave you off. I came back as soon as I could. Now open the door! Blanche, open the door! They're coming!"

"So, you steal my things and then Stephen's car breaks down and you come running back here because they are coming, huh?"

"Blanche! Open the fucking door!"

She smirked. "Ray, let me get this straight. You come to my house, steal from me, take my dead husband's car, it breaks down, but you happen to see them leave me off, and come running back here expecting me to take you in?"

"Blanche! Open the door! Open the door!" Ray's voice was near hysterics now.

"You stole from me, you son of a bitch! You fucking pathetic hick! And you expect me to take you into my home?"

"Blanche! Just open the door! Just open the door! I'm out of bullets!" He was pounding hard on the door, desperate, terrified. "Open the fucking door, bitch!"

Blanche opened the door and lifted her gun. For a moment, she saw Ray's terrified expression and figures moving up the drive out of the growing darkness.

"Thank God, Blanche, I-"

She fired her gun and his head snapped back. He looked suitably shocked before his eyes went utterly blank and he fell back. It was then she saw the mottled, decaying figures moving up the steps toward her.

"Stay off my property,"she screamed and aimed her gun.

Her finger squeezed the trigger, but the gun only clicked empty.

She was hit full force by the horrible reek of the undead creatures, then they were on her, knocking her back into the house and onto her expensive Persian rug. She raised the gun again, pulling the trigger over and over again.

One of the zombies, screeched at her and she slapped it. "Get off me!"

It didn't recoil, but grabbed her hand and bit down.

Screaming, she tried to get away, but then more were on her and suddenly she realized what Curtis had meant in his note.

He had left her one bullet.

She had killed Ray.

Fuck!

Her screams of fury filled the night until they finally gave way to screams of pain.

Chapter 9

1. Gateway to Death

The front door to the hospital swung open and the zombie in the pink housecoat growled and thrust her hands outward to grab the tasty human before her. Something long and sharp came straight for her and in the next second her muddled brain became nothing more than mush.

With a grunt, Ken yanked the spear out of the old woman's eye socket.

The old man in the other wheelchair fumbled toward the open door, trying to reach the enticing opening where the humans were.

Roger put his sneaker squarely on the gnarled knees of the dead old woman and shoved her and the wheelchair back.

With a loud hiss, the old man launched himself toward Roger, but the delicious human flesh stepped back through the door and the old man landed flat on his stomach. Clawing at the floor, he tried to move through the doorway, but something hard came down on his head. He growled in frustration as the object came down over and over again. Soon, he lay silent, unmoving, his head squashed nearly flat.

"That was truly disgusting," Ken muttered. He watched Bill walk over to the lawn to try to wipe the gore off his boot on the dry overgrown grass.

Bill shrugged.

Lenore leaned down slowly, her gaze divided between the long expanse of white hallway and the dead old man. Tilting her head, she studied his bracelet.

"He's tagged as bitten," she said finally.

Jenni studied the sign on the door. "They took off and left the infected behind."

The sign read: **Evacuated to Madison Rescue Center. Do Not Enter Hospital. Go to Madison Rescue Center.**

Still rubbing his boot over the rough brown grass, Bill looked up. "That will make it easier for us. Less zombies."

"Of course, we don't know how many infected they left behind," Roger pointed out, looking uneasy.

Jenni checked her weapons one more time: her ax, one dagger in a sheath on her thigh, two revolvers, rifle, and a short spear. "There will be enough to kill us," Jenni said honestly.

Lenore looked down the long white hall beyond the glass doors. At the far end there were smears of blood. "The same old, same old."

Staring down at the two corpses, Ken shuddered. "Truly gross."

Moving back over to the group gathered in the hospital doorway, Bill said, "Okay, no guns unless absolutely necessary. Do not open any doors that are not in our brief. If you run into trouble, radio it in immediately. We're here to get the supplies and get out."

Linda moved closer to the front door and peered past the two dead zombies. She shoved the old man's body aside and stepped inside. Her large brown eyes looked terrified, but her chin was set with determination.

"We should hurry," she said. "The sun will go down soon."

Slowly, they all filed in, walking slowly down the white hallway. From the diagram they had been given, they knew the hallway ended in a large reception area. From the reception area, the hospital divided into four areas. The doors straight across from them led into a long wing with patient rooms. To the left was a cafeteria and gift shop. To the right was the admissions area, the doors to the emergency rooms, and then a stairwell and elevators. Upstairs were the operating rooms, examination rooms, and ICU. The hospital was efficient.

Jenni and Linda paused as they reached the end of the hall. The spacious waiting room was illuminated by the dim emergency lights. The chairs in the waiting room were overturned and dried blood was smeared over the walls. To their right, behind a glass window where people normally would have checked in, an armless woman hissed.

"Eww," Ken said with distaste.

"Someone ate that girl's arm," Lenore observed. "Nasty."

The nurse began to claw at the window with her remaining hand, clearly not remembering how to slide the window open. Behind her, a man stood jawless and eyeless, turning in a circle.

"Okay, no one goes into the receptionist's office," Linda muttered.

"Don't worry. Not planning on it," Dale answered.

Jenni looked back and forth between the double doors leading into other areas of the hospital. They looked daunting and she took a breath, reminding herself this was for Juan. Moving toward the stairs on the far side of the room, she stepped over a truly dead body. A security guard, it looked like. He had been shot in the head. She signaled to her group to fall in behind her.

Roger followed her, looking around the room nervously. He spotted a headless corpse shoved under a pile of chairs and shook his head. Too weird to think about now. Behind him, Bill let out a soft curse. Felix took up the rear with his crossbow at the ready.

"Head," Jenni whispered from ahead of them.

Looking up, Roger saw a decapitated head snarling at him. It was in a potted plant.

"I don't wanna know how that happened," Bill decided.

Felix aimed and a crossbow bolt sliced through the zombie's eye. "Man, now that's fucked up."

"Gross," Ken's voice said from behind them.

They had to pass the door to the emergency room to reach the stairs and Jenni raised a hand to bring everyone to a halt. The stench of death was strong. Cautiously, she moved closer to the door and realized it had been chained shut.

"Look," she whispered, pointing to the chains.

Everyone froze.

Hesitating, she looked around, then pulled a framed picture off the wall behind her. Holding it up, she used the reflective surface as a mirror to see through the windows set in the chained doors. Adjusting it slowly, trying to stay out of sight of the windows, she finally managed to get a look.

She almost dropped the painting.

Immediately, she slid down to the floor and motioned everyone down. They were already on their way to the ground the second they saw her expression.

"It's full of them,"she mouthed.

Everyone's eyes widened.

"Packed. They're just standing there," she continued to mouth, trying to form words in a way that everyone could read her lips.

Lenore crossed herself and Ken gulped.

Bill motioned to everyone to crawl along the floor. Ken and Lenore began to crawl with Dale and Linda right behind them. They were heading to the doors on the opposite side of the room and not the stairway. Hopefully, they could stay out of sight until reaching the doors on the far end.

Jenni tried to hold her breath and crawl past the chained doors without gagging. Roger, Felix, and Bill moved right behind her. The stench was so bad she found it hard not to gag. Keeping close to the waiting room chairs, she crawled up to the stairwell and looked up. It appeared clear.

Across the room, the others were relieved to see the doors to the patient rooms were not chained. After a wordless debate, it was Lenore who finally stood up and took a peek into that hallway, trying to do it fast so as not to rile the zombies across the room behind the doors to the emergency room.

Jenni watched Lenore motion that it was clear, and then the other team slipped out of sight.

Bill moved up beside Jenni and squeezed her arm gently. She smiled back at him and tried to steady her nerves.

"We do this and go," he said softly.

She nodded silently.

They climbed the stairs.

2. Death's Doorway

Ken was relieved that it was relatively easy going once they were in the patient ward. Every room they passed appeared empty. Ken suspected whoever had evacuated the hospital had locked up all the infected in the emergency room. Per orders, they opened no doors that were not marked on Charlotte's maps.

"Don't hear them," Lenore whispered. "It's all quiet here. I bet they're all stuffed in the emergency room."

"And they can stay there," Ken answered. He made a face as they passed a decomposing corpse surrounded by dried blood and brains. "They were shooting everyone in the head."

"Smart move," Dale said in a low voice. "But they must have decided not to waste anymore ammo and just got out."

Lenore gingerly pushed an empty stretcher out of her way.

"Okay, we get what we need and get back to save Juan." Linda blew her dark bangs out of her eyes and passed out the lists. "Just what is on the list. No more."

Collecting items, Linda, Lenore and Ken began to strike off entries on their "grocery" list while Dale knocked out a window at the end of the hall and began to lower equipment onto the lawn. It seemed like a good idea considering the danger in the reception area. There were probably enough zombies to break through the chained doors if they were provoked.

Moving quickly, the team did their job, being careful with every move. Lenore warily avoided closed doors and grabbed up everything she could in a tote bag. Ken wheeled equipment down the hall to the window to Dale, sashaying as prettily as he could. Dale didn't notice.

Finally, Linda slid out the window and ran to bring the big moving truck up to the window, her gun in her hand as she moved. Ken thought she was hot for a girl, but his eyes kept straying to Dale. He was a big hunk of a man, just like Ken liked them. He had tried to catch the big man's eye a few times, but had failed so far. It was getting truly annoying that no one was out of the closet in the fort, aside from him. Ten percent of an average population was supposed to be gay. There had to be at least one more of his kind and he was hoping for a nice hunky man.

"Stop staring," Lenore chided him.

Ken waved a hand at her and rolled the heart monitor down to the window. Dale nodded, picked it up, and lowered it outside.

"Thanks," Ken said with smile.

Dale barely looked at him.

With a sigh, Ken moved down the hallway and checked his map. There was supposed to be a supply room at the end of a short hallway that branched off from the main corridor. Charlotte had provided a list of medications she wanted from the room.

Edging toward the end of the hallway, he looked down the shorter hall and saw two more sets of double doors. The emergency lights made the windows in them glow an eerie red.

"Cover me," Ken ordered Lenore.

Holding his spear firmly in one hand and his map in the other, he moved down the hallway, keeping close to the wall. The door to the supply room was near the very end. Beyond the double doors was another hallway to...

He unfolded the map just as he reached the double doors.

...the emergency room.

Heart pounding, he looked up into the face of a zombie snarling on the other side of the glass. Ken's gaze swept down length of the doors. They were unchained.

The door burst open so hard that when it hit him, he was slammed into the wall. Falling sideways, he lost his spear. Ken was trapped, wedged into the tiny area between the door and the wall. He was in a perfect little triangle of hell.

Ken felt tears spring into his eyes as he cowered in the tiny sliver of space. The zombies were snarling at him through the window as they pushed hard against the door, pressing him into the corner. His body barely fit into the space and the pressure was beginning to cut off his breathing.

He heard Lenore screaming and he cried out in fear. The twisted dead zombie faces pressed hard against the glass, teeth champing hard together. Blood and spittle smeared the slowly cracking glass.

Trembling violently, he felt his body being pinched as the space behind the door grew smaller.

He was going to die.

The first gunshot made him jump. The volley made him hopeful. The distorted gruesome zombie faces turned away toward the shooters. With loud moans, they began to shamble down the hall. Finally, Ken managed to get a breath as the undead staggered away from the door.

At the last moment, he realized the door would swing closed now that the zombies were not holding it. He would be exposed. Grabbing the door firmly with his fingers, he held it in place the best he could. More zombies staggered past him, moving toward those shooting. His sweat slicked fingers slipped on the handle.

One zombie noticed him through the smeared glass and reached out. It was an old man, his face eaten away on one side and his throat shredded into dried strips of flesh. Instead of pushing the door toward Ken, he began to try to pull it away.

"No, no, no," Ken whispered, struggling to hold on. His adrenaline rush had left him now and he felt weak as a babe.

The zombie persisted, its slow movements agonizingly terrifying. Ken could hear its bones cracking and its muscles tearing with the exertion, but it didn't feel pain. It gripped the side of the door firmly and began to pull it outward. Ken tried to hold onto the door, but his fingers were so wet, they slipped free. Falling back into the corner, Ken screamed as the zombie reached down for him.

"Die, fucker," Lenore said in her low voice from behind the zombie.

The zombie lurched forward and fell onto Ken.

Ken began to scream in terror, then realized it was dead. A bolt had shattered the back of its head. The rotting brains slid out in a slimy pile as he shoved the creature off him and struggled to get up.

Grabbing Ken's arm, Lenore pulled him to his feet. "Run!"

He ran with her, stumbling and sliding over the dead bodies littering the floor. He heard growls behind him and glanced over his shoulder to see zombies staggering along behind them. The undead were reaching out with desperate hands as their mouths groaned in hunger.

Running down the hallway, Lenore guided him to the open window. She pushed him forward and it was Dale who lifted him up and through it. Ken clung to him relishing the moment, then Dale set him down and shoved him toward the moving van. Lenore was heavier and harder to lift through the window and the zombies were almost to her, when she finally fell out onto the dry grass. Grabbing her hand, Dale tugged her after him as the zombies filled the window and began to tumble out.

Standing next to the truck, Linda fired at zombies, her shotgun barking loudly.

Ken scrambled into the back of the truck and looked back to see Dale dragging Lenore behind him. The zombies were falling out of the window and struggling to get up.

"Hurry! Hurry!" His voice sounded shrill, but he didn't care.

Dale shoved Lenore up into the truck as Ken pulled on her arms. Lenore cussed at them with impressive insults, but they got her in. Dale slammed the doors shut, securing them.

Within seconds, the moving truck lurched and headed off at top speed.

Silently, Lenore sat down beside Ken on the bench and took his hand.

He sobbed silently beside her. He was surprised to see she was crying too, her big body shivering.

"You are one stupid faggot," she finally said.

Ken threw his arms around her and wept into her large bosom. "I know!"

Clutching him tightly, Lenore rocked him. "I love you, anyway."

"You saved me," Ken sobbed. "You saved me. I thought I was gone, but you saved me."

"No zombie is eatin' my best friend," Lenore declared through her tears.

Ken lifted his head. "But...what...oh..God..what about Jenni and the others? They're still back there!"

Lenore just shook her head. "I don't know, Ken. I don't know."

As the truck headed back to the fort, the two friends clung to each other and hoped for the best for the other team.

3. Death's Doorway Opens

It was evident from the chaos in the operating rooms that things had gone to hell fairly quickly. Dead bodies lay everywhere. Every single one had a gunshot to the head. Someone had meticulously gone through and killed every single person in ICU. Some, Jenni suspected, had not even been zombies.

"Why kill all of these, but not the ones in the ER?"

"Ran out of time, I suspect," Bill answered Jenni.

"Can we hurry it up? This place is making my skin crawl," Felix said from across the room.

"Yeah, this place is damn creepy," Roger agreed.

Jenni unfolded her map and held it up against the wall to study it. The eerie lighting made her look very pale and almost dead. Roger felt uneasy by her appearance and took a step back.

"Bill, you and me can take care of the stuff in the O.R. Roger, Felix, you get those drugs from the pharmacy," she said firmly.

Felix studied his map, then nodded. "Let's roll."

Things were very messy in the operating rooms. They entered very cautiously, but only found dead bodies. The corpses were terribly decomposed and they tried hard not to look at them too closely. Together, Bill and Jenni loaded up operating tools in a bin, careful to get the ones Charlotte had requested.

Bill's walkie-talkie hissed to life.

"Sorry, Bill. Ken's my best friend," Lenore's voice said.

"What?" Bill fumbled to grab the walkie-talkie off his belt.

"What did she mean?"

"Hell if I know, Jenni."

Bill was just about to call Lenore back when they heard gunshots down below and what followed turned their blood cold. The bellow of a hundred zombie voices rising.

"We're out of here," Bill said firmly.

Jenni slipped the safety off her rifle and grabbed the bin. She followed Bill out into the hallway just as Roger and Felix came running from the direction of the stairs.

"Just run," Felix hissed.

It was then they heard the footfalls on the stairs.

"Shit!" Jenni ran, clutching the gun in one hand and the bin in the other. She could hear the scalpels and other tools rattling around in it, but she didn't dare drop it. Juan needed these things.

Felix hit a door and shoved it open. They all piled into it and Roger quickly turned and locked it.

"Way out!" Felix ran toward the windows on the far side of the room.

Looking around, Jenni realized they were in some sort of dorm room. Probably for doctors on long shifts.

"Felix!" Bill shouted.

The slender man didn't turn around, but ran across the long room. Sections were curtained off and Jenni realized a form was moving behind one at the far end. She could just make out its silhouette highlighted by the fading sunlight coming through the windows.

"Felix, no!"

He looked back just long enough to run straight into the last curtain. And beyond that curtain was something that reached out for him. He went down in a tumble of grunts and moans, the curtain falling over him and a dark figure.

Roger ran to help, his heavy body sweating profusely. "Felix, no, no!"

Behind Jenni, the door was struck by something large. Then the pounding began. Bill immediately pushed her aside and shoved a large metal wardrobe over in front of the door.

Felix shouted as Roger grabbed the curtain and yanked it back.

Tumbling out, Felix gasped in large breaths of air as he struggled to his feet. Behind him, a terribly mutilated and decaying soldier was chewing on a bit of Felix's ear.

"Shit," Roger screamed.

"What? What?" Felix exclaimed, leaping away from the zombie. "Kill it!"

Jenni shot the soldier as it lunged forward. It jerked backwards as the bullet tore through its chest. The second bullet sheared off the side of his head and it tumbled to the ground. Its brain slid out through the shattered skull, falling wetly to the floor. A bit of ear, with a gold earring still attached, fell out of its mouth.

"Oh, shit, no," Felix said as his hand came up to his ear. "No, no. He ripped it off with his hand. He didn't bite me!"

Roger raised his gun. "Sorry, Felix."

"No, the fucker ripped it off! It didn't bite me!"

Pushing a desk in front of the door to brace the metal wardrobe, Bill swore under his breath. It continued to buckle and push into the room. "We don't have much time!"

Jenni threw the contents of the bin onto a bed and rolled it up in a sheet, then tied the ends to make a backpack. With a sigh of regret, she yanked her ax from her back and tossed it onto a bed. Pulling on the makeshift backpack with the surgical tools in it, she hurried toward the men fiercely arguing back and forth.

Felix screamed at Roger, holding his torn ear, as Roger obviously tried to get up his nerve to fire.

"You can't do this to me. It tore it off. I swear it did. It didn't bite me! I promise. Dear God, I promise!" Felix shouted. Tears streaming down his face, he raised his gun, pointing at Roger. "Put the gun down, Roger. I mean it! It didn't bi-"

Jenni raised her gun and fired. Felix fell, silent and dead, over the soldier who had already effectively ended his life.

"You make it fast," Jenni said to Roger in a low voice.

"God, Jenni. He's my friend."

"It doesn't matter. You make it fast!"

The pounding on the door was increasing.

"Roger, some help," Bill said from where he was still stacking things against the door. "Jenni, get us an escape route!"

Roger ran over to help barricade the door. More and more decayed hands were reaching into the room through the slowly opening door.

Jenni looked out the window and saw a fifteen foot drop onto the roof of the first floor wing. The red truck sat silent on the grass just within view.

Sliding the window open, she punched out the screen.

"We gotta jump."

Pulling the mattress off the nearest cot, Jenni pushed it out the window and watched it fall. Satisfied, she grabbed another one off another cot, and also pushed it out.

"Let's go, guys!"

Bill and Roger turned and ran as the door gave way. The first of the zombies shoved itself into the room.

Jenni pulled herself up onto the window sill, her trembling hands gripping the frame tightly. With a deep breath, she lowered herself as far as she could, then let go. She dropped hard onto the mattresses and felt the wind get knocked out of her. Rolling onto her side, she managed to get to her feet and struggled for her next breath.

Seconds later, Bill fell beside her. Despite his beer belly, he managed a better landing. Climbing to his feet, he scanned the top of the roof they were on, then looked up at the window.

"Roger! Hurry!"

Roger appeared above them, looking terrified. Wordlessly, he began to climb out of the window. The howling of the zombies seemed quite near now. Jenni saw a gray chewed hand reach out from behind Roger and make a grab for him.

"Jump!" Bill and Jenni shouted at the same time.

Roger screamed when he saw the hand about to close on his neck and jerked to one side. He fell wildly. Instead of striking the mattresses, he hit the hard gravel surface of the roof feet first. Jenni not only saw, but heard his legs break as the angry, white splinters of bone erupted from his shins.

"No!" She rushed to his side as he screamed in pain and collapsed.

"Fuck, shit! I shouldn't have worn the red shirt," he cried out. Tears streaked his face and she saw his red turtleneck peeking out from his leather jacket.

"I wore red, too. But we're not going to die!" Jenni turned to Bill, her expression desperate. "Bill, help me!"

Bill was looking up toward the window. "We need to go," he said in a desolate tone.

"Help me!" Jenni repeated, trying to drag Roger.

The injured man howled in agony.

"Now, Jenni," Bill ordered. "We need to go now."

She looked up in time to see the first zombie plunge out of the window. Luckily, it landed head first, splitting its skull open. But the second landed on the first zombie and immediately crawled toward them.

Roger looked at her, terror in his eyes. "Make it fast," he said, his voice cracking. "I can't jump down to the ground. It's over, Jenni. Make it fast."

"No, no!" She tried to drag him, but he kept screaming in pain.

Another zombie landed on the mattresses. Then another. They were tumbling out of the window faster now. Some were crawling across the roof, others struggling to their feet.

"Jenni, do as he says!" Bill's voice was urgent and stricken all at the same time.

"Make it fast!" Roger screamed at her, his eyes fastened on the zombies crawling toward him. "I don't want to be eaten alive! Do it!"

Jenni rose to her feet, her gaze sliding to the zombies. Their teeth were snapping together in anticipation of their feast.

"Roger, I'm sorry," she whispered.

She felt her finger pull the trigger and saw him fall back just as one of the zombies grabbed the bone sticking out of his leg.

Bill grabbed her, yanked her around, and they ran together to the edge of the roof. Looking back, she saw that Roger's dead body was giving them time to escape. The undead were swarming him, tearing him apart.

"Roll when you land," Bill ordered.

With a nod, she sat down on the edge of the roof, her legs dangling. Taking a breath, she pushed off. She landed hard again, but managed to roll. Sharp swift pain hit her side. When she rose, she felt blood on her hands, warm and sticky. Looking down, she saw she had landed on the makeshift bag and something inside had sliced through the fabric and cut a two inch gash in her side.

Bill landed with a thud next to her and managed to get to his feet. "Just run," he said.

There were zombies all over the front lawn and climbing out of a lower window. The shambling figures were already moving toward them. Bill and Jenni ran, weaving through the dead, avoiding their grasping hands, all the way to the red truck. Leaping inside, they slammed the doors shut. Bill had barely locked the doors when the banging on the sides began. Turning on the engine, he floored it before the wave of zombies pouring out of the hospital could block off their exit.

Pulling off her jacket, Jenni tried to staunch the flow of blood from her wounded side.

"What happened?" Bill demanded.

"Cut myself on something in the bag," she answered. She lifted her t-shirt to show him the even slash in her side.

"Okay," Bill said with relief.

Looking into the rear view mirror she could see the throng of zombies crowding the front lawn of the hospital. There had been far more than they realized. They had been incredibly lucky to escape.

They fell into silence as the truck roared down the road. The sun was setting and the sky was ablaze in pinks and purples.

"We had to leave him," Bill finally said. "His legs were broken. We couldn't have carried him."

"I know."

"We all knew the risks," Bill continued.

"I know." Jenni was crying and her side was killing her, but she had the tools needed to save Juan. At least she hoped what she had salvaged was enough.

Bill nodded grimly and kept driving.

An hour back to the fort then Juan would have his operation.

"Did you see the moving van?"

Jenni shook her head. "It was gone."

"They must be ahead of us then," Bill decided. Reaching out, he snagged the CB mouthpiece. Turning it on, a screech filled the cab.

"Shit!"

Bill tried to change the channel, but the electronic screech continued. Finally, he turned it off.

"Must be something interfering. A storm or something," he said in confusion.

Jenni nodded and checked her wound. It was not bleeding as badly.

The darkness of the night washed all around them, chasing away the brilliance of the sunset and soon they were submerged in inky blackness.

"I liked them," Jenni said, finally.

"Me, too," Bill answered. "They were both great guys."

Abruptly, the cab was filled with a bright, white light and they were both instantly blinded. The red truck veered off the road, through the brush, and impacted hard against a fence post.

Inside the truck, nothing stirred.

Chapter 10

1. Full Circle

Jenni swam up from the depths of unconsciousness, her mind spinning and her body spasming. She fought to wakefulness, pushing her eyes open, straining to see.

There was a loud ringing in her ears that made her feel sick to her stomach.

Something bad had happened, but fragments of memory eluded her as she grasped for them.

Where was she? Was she in a truck? The truck had crashed! But she wasn't in a truck; she was on a bed or cot. She had been in a hospital, but they had escaped. Hadn't they? Suddenly, she wasn't too sure.

And were there zombies around?

She forced herself to sit up completely, her eyes fighting to close. Everything was white and bright around her, blurring her vision, making her feel even more woozy. A dark figure lurched toward her and she could barely discern the mottled green that covered it.

With a short scream, she kicked out, striking the shape firmly in the chest with the heel of her boot. She heard it moan and fall back.

Dimly aware of her surroundings, she staggered to her feet and saw another figure moving toward her.

"Fuck off," she growled, and backed away from it.

It continued toward her and her swimming vision made it hard to see. It grabbed her wrist firmly and it made a noise, but she could not hear it through the ringing in her ears. Her elbow came up sharply into the thing's face.

With a startled cry, it let go of her, dropping back.

Spinning away from it, she stood on unsteady legs trying to figure out where the hell she was.

Finally, her vision slightly cleared and she made out the red of an exit sign over the door.

Then the door opened and another mottled creature entered. Her hand hit something hard as she scrambled to get out of its way. She grabbed it, with the dull realization that it was the back of a chair. She swung it hard, but the creature was ready and deflected it. Then she saw the dark shape raise something.

Seconds before she lost consciousness, she realized the shape was wearing army fatigues.

"How did it go?"

"She hurt two of my people," the First Lieutenant responded. "I think she thought they were zombies."

"She caught them by surprise. She's the weaker one. Try again."

"Yes, sir."

* * * * *

The smell of ammonia brought Jenni to wakefulness sharply and painfully. Her temple was throbbing and she felt like throwing up. She was sitting on a cot and a soldier was leaning over her. The woman in the army fatigues with short cropped blond hair looked at her kindly.

"How you feeling?" she asked Jenni.

Jenni promptly slugged the woman in the face. Diving off the cot, she rushed toward the nearest door.

"Grab her!" the army nurse shouted.

One of the guards managed to grab Jenni around the waist and hoist her off the ground.

"Let me go!" Jenni kicked her legs and twisted frantically.

There was a sharp prick in her arm, then the world swam and went dark.

* * * * *

"Tell me you had success this time."

"I would like to, sir, but she fought back the second she was awake. Sir, I seriously believe we should question the man first."

"The woman is the weaker link. Try again. Restrain her this time."

"Yes, sir."

* * * * *

Jenni jerked away as the smell of ammonia assaulted her senses again. She found herself sitting in a chair before a table, her hands restrained behind her with plastic cuffs. Trying to move, she found her ankles were also cuffed.

"Shit!"

Across from her sat a very handsome black man with the kindest green eyes she had ever seen. He was staring at her curiously, his expression quite intense.

"Fuck you."

"We hardly know each other," the man answered, flashing a brilliant smile.

Jenni set her jaw, her gaze steely.

"You know, we're just trying to get to know you."

"You fucking kidnapped me!" Jenni nearly growled the words. She was so pissed she wasn't even sure why she was so angry. Thoughts of Juan were jumbled with the disaster at the hospital and then the bright light blinding her and Bill. "Where the hell is Bill?"

"Is that his name?"

Jenni clamped her mouth shut.

"We've met before. You and I," the man said. "On a road, long ago. You were in a pink bathrobe and you had this dog that looked exactly like my dog when I was a kid. And there was a blond woman with you. I have a photographic memory. I remember people. I remember you."

Taking a deep breath, Jenni glared at him and said nothing.

"I told you to come here. To Madison. But you didn't. You went somewhere else."

The man opened up a folder and began to show her photos of the fort. Then the photos became more personal, showing people. Obviously the photos had been taken with a telescopic lens. She saw herself and Juan in one. The sight of the man she loved brought tears to her eyes.

"Tell me about your home, Genevieve," the man said in a soft, warm voice.

"Fuck you, puto."

The man just smiled a little, then said, "Like I said, we hardly know each other. Besides, my superiors have me in here visiting with you to find out more about this enclave you live in than trying to get lucky with you."

"I'm not going to tell you a gawddamn thing," Jenni snapped at him. "You fucking kidnapped me! You had no right!"

"We're under orders to bring any civilians we find outside of the designated rescue center back here. For your protection."

Jenni began to try to twist her hands. She knew it was fruitless, but she needed to remain angry or she was going to cry. Juan needed her and these assholes had kidnapped her.

"Genevieve, please, you need to talk to me. Tell me about your friends," the man continued in his soft voice.

"How do you know my name?"

The soldier silently drew a folded sheet of paper from the folder. "My Darling Genevieve, you're still a loca bitch, but I love you. Juan."

Jenni screamed at him with raw hate and struggled to get free. "That's mine!"

With a sigh, the soldier stood up. "Well, I see you don't want to cooperate. I'll give you a little time to cool off."

Jenni never heard his complete sentence. She somehow managed to flip herself backwards and hit her head with a resounding thud.

The nurse sighed. "She's going to have a concussion from that."

The First Lieutenant nodded. "Thank goodness she has a hard head."

"She's a feisty Latina, what can I say," the First Lieutenant said with a bemused smile. "And she has a reason to be mad. As far as she is concerned, we kidnapped her."

The Major General scowled at him. "She's clearly unhinged. Question the man."

"Yes, sir."

* * * * *

Bill stared at the photos, then up at the soldier with the kind eyes. He sat in a chair, his hands folded on his lap. So far the treatment here had been good though he had heard Jenni screaming more than once since he woke up. But, in a way, that was to be expected.

"We're just civilians," Bill said at last. "Survivors making our way."

"Are you a militia of some kind?"

"No. No. Just trying to survive, really."

"Religious affiliations?"

"You mean a cult? No. No. We have some Christians, Catholics, a Jewess, a few Hindus, an agnostic or two...maybe even an atheist. And some guy who believes in aliens," Bill answered honestly.

The black man looked thoughtful. "And you did all this yourself? No pre-planning? Just spur of the moment?"

"Out of necessity, sir. Really. I mean, you gotta survive somehow when the dead come back." Bill shrugged a little.

"Did you hear the order go out in the first days to report to Madison?"

"Honestly, no. I was just trying to live," Bill answered.

The soldier nodded again, looking thoughtful. "Well, martial law was enacted and all civilians were ordered to report to rescue centers. Madison was the one the people in your 'fort' should have reported to."

Bill just stared at the soldier, not understanding.

"It is our responsibility to ensure the safety of the civilian population and keep our nation alive in any way possible," the soldier continued. His expression was grim now.

"Yeah, so?"

The soldier sighed. "My superiors plan to take over the fort. They want to know if there will be an armed response."

Bill blinked slowly, then lowered his head. He thought long and hard, swallowed a few times, then looked up. "It's our home."

The soldier nodded sadly. "Yes, I know. What are the chances of an armed response?"

Bill sighed. "I don't know."

The soldier looked surprised, then nodded. "All right. Thank you."

2. The Pendulum Sword

Katarina studied the fancy bottle that read "hair gloss" and with a shrug, began to pour the clear liquid onto her palm. She had taken it from Blanche's bathroom and figured it had to be good stuff. Hell, most of the writing on the bottle was in French so it had to be good.

The thought of Blanche made her frown. Nothing had been as satisfying as leaving that bitch stranded in her big swanky mansion with one bullet and a can of chili. Curtis and Katarina had considered taking bets if Blanche would actually use the bullet on herself, but then they both started laughing when they both realized she wouldn't be smart enough to do that. It was a cruel thing to do, but after Blanche had done so much harm, she didn't feel any guilt.

Katarina spread the clear glob over her hair, rubbing it in per the instructions. She was dressed in jeans and a pretty green sweater. Bill had asked her to join him for a drink when he got back and she wanted to look her best. Nervously, she ran her fingers through her red hair, trying to tame the frizziness that made it look like a lion mane.

She was disappointed she and Curtis hadn't run into Ray. They had spotted a car crumpled against some trees at the base of the hill where Blanche's mansion sat and suspected he had rolled it on purpose. Steam was still billowing out from under the hood. Most likely he had taken off in Stephen's car. They had found a stash of empty boxes inside the house. After what had happened to Juan, she had an itchy finger. She had originally lobbied to put Blanche down like a rabid dog, but Travis' idea to dump her at home with just one bullet had been all too delightful.

Her hair wasn't looking much better yet.

Just as she had gotten back from dumping Blanche, Bill caught her by surprise with his talk of a drink. He was such a nice man she hadn't expected him to really pay much attention to her beyond her job at the fort. She wasn't used to nice men even noticing her that much.

Frowning into the mirror, she again put more glop on her hair. It was still frizzy.

All her life she had been teased because of her unruly red hair. All sorts of names had been tagged onto her throughout her life. All of them were annoying. "Bozo" was probably the worst.

She had been a walking bulls-eye in school. Her mother was almost fifty and her father well into his sixties when she was born. He had died before her tenth birthday. Katarina had tried to believe they had her out of love, but years of hard housework made her wonder if they had been lucky enough to give birth to a live in maid that would help them through their twilight years. All her older siblings, nearly 20 years her senior, ignored her parents and her. With good reason, she thought. Her mother had been a nagging shrew, but Katarina had stayed with her faithfully until the end...

She sighed.

..until the end of the world.

She still couldn't believe Bill wanted to have a drink with her. It just wasn't that he had asked her, it was how he had asked her.

Men didn't usually hit on her. At least good men.

Of course, in her entire life she had been with only two men and both of them had done a good job of ripping out her heart. It wasn't until she finally got a job outside of her mother's stuffy home that she had even mingled with men. In high school, she hadn't had one single date.

Her mother had sculpted her life to be her helper and Katarina had dutifully fallen into that role. When it became apparent to her mother that her retirement check wasn't stretching far enough, Katarina had been ordered to work.

Katarina, the ever faithful and long suffering daughter, finally had an excuse to escape the house and work at the local diner. It was then she learned how cruddy men could be. And worse yet, she had learned how to avoid dangerous situations. Sometimes out-of-towners were the worst. Some of the truckers seemed to think she was easy pickings because she wasn't "that purty" and had to be hard up. More than one had told her that, "You're damn lucky to have any man wanting to stick it to ya."

She had smiled and bore it all. That was what she always did when things were tough. She took care of business. In Nerit, she had found someone just like her. Yes, Nerit was different, darker, and more confident, but Katarina knew Nerit understood her immense sacrifices and her inner strength.

Katarina always did the dirty jobs. The hard jobs. And without complaint.

The day the first zombie rushed into the diner and latched onto a customer, it was Katarina who had picked up the cleaver and brought it down on its head. And when the customer rose up and lunged for her despite the huge gash in his throat, she had once more brought the cleaver down. Looking outside, she saw what was happening and ran out to her little car, blood splattered, and with the cleaver in one hand.

When she reached the quaint house she shared with her Mom, she found her mother lying on the sidewalk, struggling to get up as two neighbor kids tore at her. Katarina had coldly slammed the cleaver down on their little heads, and then looked down at her dying mother.

"Sorry, Mom," she had said, and delivered her mother from the world.

Then, somehow, fate had led her to the fort.

With a sigh, she officially gave up on her hair and braided it back from her face. Resigned, she went down to the lobby to wait for Bill.

She was just about to enter the dining room when Ken was carried in, bruised and battered, Lenore trailing behind the stretcher. Linda and Dale followed carrying what looked like monitoring equipment from the hospital. They all looked frazzled.

"Where's Bill?" Katarina asked as they passed her.

"Don't know. We never saw the other team after we left the hospital with a horde of zombies on our trail," Linda answered. Seeing Katarina's expression, she quickly added, "But I'm sure they are okay. Bill and Jenni alone are enough to hold off a horde of those things."

"Yeah, yeah. They're tough. I'm sure they're fine."

Katarina forced a smile and moved on. She headed down the hallway that would lead out to the old newspaper building and the fort's garage.

The Reverend was busy posting the bulletin for the next church service outside the doorway to the convention room where the church was located. He immediately noticed her tense expression.

"Are the teams back?"

"Only one. And Ken was hurt. I'm heading out to see what's up."

"I'll go check on Ken and the others," the Reverend decided, tucking the rest of the announcements in his pocket.

Katarina could feel her heart beating harshly in her chest and she took very deep breaths to calm herself. It was too soon to think the worst quite yet. Things did go wrong on runs and sometimes teams were delayed. She had been on plenty of outings where her team had to take another route home or had to fight its way to safety. Jenni, Bill, Felix and Roger were tough. She had to remember that and have faith in them.

Nerit, Travis and Ed were standing near the moving truck when she walked into the gated entry. They both looked toward her, their expressions grim.

"Where are the others?" Katarina asked as she joined them. "Have we heard?"

"We don't know. We can't raise them on the CB," Nerit answered.

"The other team reported that a horde of zombies was in the hospital behind secured doors. They broke out and attacked the teams." Travis took a deep breath, obviously trying to steady his nerves. "Lenore said it got bad really fast."

Katarina hesitated, then said, "I'll take a crew to go get them. They may be delayed out on the road and need backup."

"The airwaves are full of static. A norther is blowing in. We'll wait until morning." Travis' tone was forlorn and full of regret. "We can't chance a bad storm and losing more people."

Katarina swallowed hard. "What if they need help? Need back up?"

Travis folded his arms over his chest, lowering his head slightly. He was obviously torn over the matter and finally shook his head. "We can't risk it."

"Everyone heading out knew there was a chance they weren't coming back," Ed added grimly. "That's why I didn't volunteer. I got my boys to think about. I didn't feel like a suicide run. The teams knew that they may not come back. No use risking other people to get them back when the conditions ain't good."

"That's pretty cold of you, Ed," Katarina snapped.

The old man shrugged. "So what if it is?"

"Chances are, they are fine," Nerit said with a smile that didn't reach her eyes.

Katarina knew Nerit was only trying to calm her down and give her hope. But Katarina didn't feel calm or hopeful. "I'll go alone. I know the roads around here well. I can handle it."

"No," Travis answered simply. "We can't risk it. Weather is kicking up fierce. Lightning is flashing on the horizon. We still got those zombies on the outskirts wandering around. If something went wrong-"

"Something has already gone wrong," Katarina reminded him. "And those are our people out there!"

"You can go out in the morning with me to look for them," Nerit said in a tone that was all ice. Her fake smile was nowhere to be seen.

With a slight bob of her head, Katarina stepped back, turned, and headed back to the hotel. She struggled to breathe and regain her composure.

Of course it had been too good to be true...

Straightening her shoulders, she walked back into the hotel. She'd head out with the crew in the morning. She wanted to know what had happened. But then again, she suspected she already knew the fate of Bill and the others. Her Mom was right. Happiness was not her lot in life. She had been born for hard work and sacrifice.

Bill would not be coming back to her. Their date would never happen.

Good things never happened to those who did what had to be done.

3. Revelation

First Lieutenant, Kevin Reynolds, gazed solemnly at the Major General, Senator Paige Brightman and Chief of Police, Bruce Kiel.

"They're just civilians," he repeated.

The Senator looked unimpressed, her pinched face looking even more pinched. For the hundredth time Kevin wondered how she got her pale blond hair so poofy. "I can't believe they're not some lunatic cult or a militia. They're too well organized for ordinary people. Seriously, are ordinary hicks capable of this?"

"Ordinary people are capable of great things," Bruce said softly. "And if this is my daughter in this picture, I know she wouldn't be with a cult or a militia."

"Maybe she doesn't have a choice. Did you think of that, Chief?" The Senator raised an eyebrow and crossed her legs. "We've dealt with well-organized crazies before. Anyone remember Waco or Eldorado? Those cultists had nice little compounds a lot like this one. How do we know that most of the people in this fort aren't being held hostage waiting for us to rescue them?"

"Bill is very adamant that they are just ordinary people trying to survive," Kevin answered.

"What if he is one of the cult leaders?" The Senator tapped her nail on the photo. "They are well-armed."

"Well, the dead are trying to eat the living," Bruce pointed out.

"If you are planning to take control of the fort, I suggest that we do our best to avoid any sort of armed confrontation. We are in Texas. We are dealing with Texans. They aren't going to take kindly to someone from the outside trying to take over." Kevin sat back in his chair, looking grim.

"I'm a Senator of this great state, Kevin. I know my people. And I know that the rural areas are full of crazies." The Senator flashed her winning smile. "If we have to go in and disarm them, we'll do it."

The Major General's craggy face wore his usual disgruntled expression. He had been retired, working his way into the political arena, before all hell had broken loose. The President had assigned him to coordinate the rescue centers in this part of Texas. The only thing he had managed to coordinate was his escape from Austin with the Senator. "The First Lieutenant is right. The situation needs to be dealt with in a calm and logical manner. I think we should let the two captives into the civilian population. Let them see what we're about. Let them see we are organized and prepared to take on the added responsibilities of leading the fort. After they have seen our operation here, I'll question this Bill personally tomorrow."

"We should just contact the enclave and speak with them," Bruce Kiel said in a low voice. "Why all the cloak and dagger bullshit? Why snag their people? Just contact them!"

The Senator looked at him reproachfully. "You seem to forget the kind of people we have already encountered since this incident began. Consider the hoodlum that gave us the information on the fort and his merry band of methheads. He said they shot his people, blew up one of their trucks, and shot two innocent people when he tried to seek refuge with them. Now, I'm not saying that the fort people didn't show a bit of class not letting him into their facility, but they showed aggression that we cannot consider lightly."

"The Senator is correct," the Major General agreed. "They are well-armed and ruthless."

"According to a criminal," Kevin pointed out. "A man who we found with two women held captive in his truck."

"We need an accurate picture of what is going on before we make our move," the Major General said finally. "Take care of it, First Lieutenant. Then report back to me."

"May I have the discretion to do as I please?"

The Major General nodded. "Just get me the truth."

* * * * *

Bill was the one who went in to get Jenni from her holding cell. She had attacked everyone who had tried to enter, but when she saw him, she collapsed into tears and clung to him. Together, they followed the tall, handsome man who had questioned them down a long narrow white hallway.

Another soldier handed them two bags. Inside were rations and a blanket.

"Your sleeping assignments are in the folder at the bottom of the bag. It also holds your schedule and what work detail you are on," the soldier explained. "We'll talk more later about your fort, but for now, I think you need to see the world we have built here."

Holding tightly to each other, Bill and Jenni stepped through the glass double doors and gazed over the railing down into the world of Madison.

"Fuck," Jenni whispered. "It's a mall."

Chapter 11

1. Waiting

Peggy slammed her cup of coffee down on the table, a little sloshing onto the wood. The people gathered around the large table in the dining room looked up at her curiously and she shrugged.

"No word. Nothing. It's quiet out there." Tucking herself into a chair next to Dale, she grimaced.

Lenore reached for another biscuit and shrugged. "That ain't good." Her expression was grim and her eyes close to tearing.

Tenderly, Ken rubbed her shoulder and leaned against her. "It'll be okay. They'll come back."

"We shouldn't have left them," Linda whispered, pouring whiskey into her coffee. "It was the wrong thing to do."

"We had to get out of there. Had to get the equipment back," Dale said firmly. "Plus, the damn zombies were coming out of the woodwork."

Maddie Goode ran her delicate hands down over her long tousled hair. It was a pretty mix of white, silver, and strawberry blond. It was hard to tell her age. Her smile was youthful, but the skin around her eyes and lips was finely lined. "You can't second guess yourselves. You did what you felt was right."

Peggy grabbed a biscuit from the Tupperware container in front of her and reached for the butter and peach jam. Rosie had put out the day old biscuits for a late night snack. Coffee and hot tea were set out on a counter nearby. "Well, there ain't nothing out there tonight but static, so I have no clue where the hell our people are. Storm is kicking up a lot of wind and the lightning isn't helping."

Passing the liquor bottle over to Dale, Linda set her elbow on the table and leaned her chin on her knuckles. "They just came at us so fast. It was so quick. I still don't know how we got Ken out of there."

"It was a blessing you did," Maddie said patting Ken's hand.

With a sigh, Ken shook his head. "Not if it got the other team killed."

"I did what I had to. I was not letting my best friend die."

"No one is blaming you, Lenore," Dale assured her. "I would have done the same damn thing. It got crazy fast. You did what you thought was right."

Lenore wiped a tear away from her eye and her jaw set in a stubborn line.

"Felix, Jenni, Bill and Roger all kick ass on a regular basis," Linda decided. "If anyone can make it out of a hospital full of dead people, it's them."

Another tear rolled down Lenore's cheek and she shook her head. "If they died..."

"Oh, Lenore, don't cry!" Maddie slid to her bare feet and rushed around the table to hug her. "You did what you thought was right."

"I may have gotten Felix killed," Lenore whispered. "And Jenni. Bill. And stupid ol' Roger always going on about Star Trek and..."

Ken covered his face with his hands. "I'm so sorry! I didn't know the doors led to where they were all stashed! I wouldn't have gone down that hall even though it was on the map if I knew the zombies were there!"

"It was on the map. It was on your instructions. What else could you have done?" Linda downed her coffee and this time poured straight whiskey into the cup. "You were doing your job."

"It's okay, li'l buddy. You were a tough hombre out there and you did good," Dale declared. "I was damn proud of you."

"Really?" Ken peeked through his hands at Dale.

"I sure was."

Lenore leaned into Maddie, holding onto her and looking more emotional than most people had ever seen her. Peggy felt awkward about the whole situation. She was torn between being spitting mad and sobbing terrified. It was her family out there and though they had been trying to do their best for Juan, she was pissed at everyone involved to some degree. She was tired of losing people. Tired of the pain of loss. Tired of the whole damn mess.

"It's not like we didn't know the risks," Linda mumbled. She downed her whiskey and poured more. "We know the risks. Every time we go out there, we know the freaking risks."

"Should we cut you off?" Dale eyed the cute little Latina thoughtfully.

"Try it." She gave him a sly smile.

"No flirting!" Ken pointed at her accusingly.

"You stop first!"

Dale chuckled as Ken sputtered.

Peggy sighed and stuffed the whole biscuit in her mouth. Dale looked at her with an impressed smile on his face and she chewed the wad of white flour goodness slowly. With a shrug, she said, "I was hungry." The truth was she was about to say something that would have pissed everyone off. She was in a bad mood and knew it. Yet, she didn't want to be alone.

Looking harried, Curtis walked into the dining room. He spotted them and headed over, his hand shoving his thin blond hair back from his face. Peggy thought he looked about as pissy as she felt.

"Linda, there you are. I thought you were going to come down and join me in the communication center," he said, reaching the table.

"I'm getting drunk," she answered. Clicking coffee cups with Dale, she dismissed Curtis with a look.

"Oh, well. You could maybe come down to the communication center and we could talk," Curtis said, a little more gently. He looked peeved at Dale as he drew up a chair and sat next to Linda.

"Felix was such a great guy," Linda declared. "He was my buddy. And Roger, that fucking perv, taught me how to swear in Klingon and told me all about Vulcans and sex. And Bill...man...Bill..."

"We don't know what has happened yet. We shouldn't start having their wake just yet," Maddie said gently.

"You didn't know them. How would you know?" Curtis crossed his arms and glared at the older woman.

"I may not know them. But they're people and I do care. I believe we should not mourn until we know for sure," Maddie answered in a tone that was a little more firm than one would expect from her delicate appearance.

"And don't get in Maddie's face. She's a good one," Dale said shortly. He folded his big arms over his chest. "Besides, who the fuck are you, you punk ass kid."

"I am a police officer here in this fort and I will let you know that I know those people who are out there and-"

Peggy put her hand on Curtis' arm and squeezed. "Shut up."

"What?" He looked at her in surprise.

"Just shut up. We're all sitting here, upset, pissy, and just trying to get a little comfort from each other. We don't need you wagging your badge or your dick in our faces."

Linda snorted whiskey out of her nose, laughing loudly.

Curtis looked at her with a hurt expression on his face.

Slamming her hands down on the table, Lenore glowered at no one in particular. "I did what I thought was right."

"I wouldn't be here if not for you," Ken said, hugging her arm.

"But maybe the rest of the team would be here if you hadn't gone off firing your gun," Curtis snapped.

"That's it!" Peggy grabbed Curtis' wrist and dragged him out of his chair. "Go back to the communication center and do your job. Now!"

Curtis sputtered, but the look on Peggy's face shut him up. With a dark scowl, he stomped off.

Linda downed the last bit of whiskey and stood up, swaying on her feet. "I'll go calm his ass down."

"Is that what they call it now days?" Peggy felt a sharp pang of disappointment as Linda started after Curtis. She wasn't sure if she was jealous that Linda and Curtis were going to mess around or if it was because Linda deserved better than a surly boy with a badge.

With a shrug, Linda kept walking after Curtis.

"I'm not going into the communication center until tomorrow," Ken decided.

"Let them get naked. As long as they are listening for our people," Peggy sighed.

"Nothing wrong with comforting each other in our time of need," Dale said.

"No, not at all," Maddie agreed. She was seated next to Lenore now, gently stroking her hair.

"You remind me of my grandma," Lenore said in a low voice.

"Thank you, hon."

The people at the table lapsed into silence and Peggy began to butter another biscuit. She should get up to check on Cody soon. He was sleeping over with a friend and she wanted to make sure he was okay before his friend's parents turned in. Maybe it was the manly scent of Dale next to her or the smell of the biscuits, but she was feeling a little more relaxed now.

"I hope they come home okay." Ken reached out to grab the peach jam.

Lenore wiped another tear away.

Peggy had nothing to say that would be productive, so she just ate.

2. The Thoughts of One Man

Kevin Reynolds leaned against the railing of the second floor of the mall watching the newcomers. He could tell the woman was still reeling from the blow to her head. Her companion, Bill, had not left her side all night. They were now settled into what had been a children's clothing store, both of them lying down on the army issue cots they had slept on during the night. He could barely see the very pretty Latina's red sweater standing out amidst all the other people in the store.

Rubbing his hand over his head, he felt the prickle of his closely cut hair tickle his palm. He felt bone weary. His brain felt overwhelmed. Without a doubt he was going on pure adrenaline at this point. It was certain sleep would be long in coming.

An army private wandered past him, gun slung casually in his arms, and they both acknowledged each other with half-assed salutes.

Kevin wondered if this how Fletcher Christian felt on board the HMS Bounty. Knotted up inside until he felt like he could barely breathe?

Below him the soft voices of the four hundred people living in the mall murmured. It was past noon now. Rations were passed out. Water bottles, half full, were being dispensed. Work crews would be changing shifts. The few children that had survived the flu were in school.

Everyone looked drawn, tired, and scared.

And after what he had recently discovered, they should be.

His fingers traced over the flag on his jacket thoughtfully. America didn't exist anymore, but the people did. They were gathered down below, struggling to make it through. They were fighting tough. He could see that, but they were getting worn down by the powers that be.

He was worn down by the powers that be.

The Senator and her cronies formed a parade as they walked across a bridge nearby. They headed into Foley's, where they were headquartered.

They were the 'haves;' below were 'have nots.'

How the Major General did not see this was beyond him. Ever since the rescue station started up the Major General had been intent on preserving "the American people," and yet, he was helping the Senator create a new world where the American people were...

As a black man it made him cringe...

...but they were making slaves.

If the Senator was truly in touch with the President and this was what the government had planned under martial law for the American people, then the world he had known was truly dead.

The very pretty Airman Second Class named Valerie Gomez strode up to him. She always looked impeccable in her uniform despite its lack of washing and her closely cropped hair set off her Native American features beautifully.

"The fort is broadcasting, sir," she said.

"Right on schedule," he said with a sigh.

She nodded, her keen eyes reading his expression.

They were, despite their immense differences in background, best friends and sometimes more.

"Then we're on schedule."

"Yes, sir."

"Carry on," he said, watching her eyes give him a soft, imaginary hug.

He looked back down over the people below...

Yes, this must be how Fletcher Christian felt as he considered mutiny...

The knot in his stomach wound tighter...

3. Hell is Other People

The words of Jean-Paul Sartre flitted through Bruce Kiel's mind as he walked among the survivors living in the Madison Mall.

Hell is other people.

Yes, this was hell and this had been created by other people. The original intent of those who had started the rescue center had been to preserve life and keep the citizens taking shelter safe from the cannibals outside. That was a noble and good cause he could support. But now things were changing. Since they had established contact with the remains of the government, the Senator had new goals that he could not agree with. He still carried his title of Police Chief, but what good did it do him? Only two of his men actually survived the massacre at the police station. The only reason he held any clout at all was because the Senator was an old political ally. Frankly, he didn't trust her one bit.

A group of twenty children was tucked into a store that now served as a school. A teacher read to them from a children's book she had found in the bookstore. The sight of the little ones made him sigh.

The world had gone to hell very quickly. Nothing had worked right. Nothing had gone right. All the precautions, all the plans had fallen apart. The county bio terrorism expert had called to inform him that he would need security the next day for the distribution of medication that would bring the pandemic under control. There had been, of course, no next day for anyone, but a scant few survivors.

The National Guard had fallen quickly. FEMA held press conferences and announced rescue centers, then went silent. The CDC rattled on about 'reanimates' then vanished from the airways.

The only rescue that had ever appeared had been a small convoy of brave Marines who had liberated him and his men from the roof of the police station. Half of them had not survived the throng of the dead overrunning the city.

The mall was protected and manned by what remained of factions of the military stationed in Texas. They were mostly Army and National Guard with a few Airmen and Marines tossed into the mix. The soldiers had barely survived the early engagements against the dead, but they had held the line at the mall for months now. They were tired and overwhelmed, but tough. They were heroes in eyes of the people in the mall. But the Senator now wanted to turn them into something much more.

Bruce Kiel paused and looked for the newcomers. They were assigned to an old clothing store and he looked at the store names, trying to remember which one.

He was afraid for everyone in the mall. The threat from outside was persistent and constant, but now there was a threat from within that chilled him almost more. He was an ambitious man by nature. All his life he had pushed himself to do his best and achieve his goals. He had raised his daughter the same way. As a former Marine, he believed in serving his country. A firm believer in the law, he had worked hard to make society safe once he had entered the police force. He understood the concept of service to one's country and people.

But, there was no real structure left anymore. The old ways were long gone. When the dead rose and attacked the living, the old ways had passed away like leaves on the wind. He recognized and understood this reality. The soldiers standing post did so because they chose to do it. The people in the mall trusted them because of that dedication. It was truly a volunteer force now. He understood that. The Senator did not.

Everything had changed once Central had come on the air and begun broadcasting to any surviving military.

What was known was that the Vice President, now the new President, had survived with some of the Cabinet and a few members of Congress. They had all been on a hunting trip in East Texas during the initial outbreak. These people of power had taken refuge with what remained of the army in their area and were now firmly ensconced in a city eight hours east of Madison. The city was heavily fortified and had managed to seize most of the resources in the area.

Once Central was secure, they had began broadcasting via military channels to any surviving rescue centers. It was now known there were also four surviving rescue centers across the state that were still manned by the remnants of the military, the Madison Mall being one of those. The other three were closer to Central and ran supplies to it. Madison was not considered an asset to Central and was informed they were on their own. Because of the large mobs of zombies in the big cities and the risk of cross state travel, it had been deemed unnecessary to open supply lines with the mall on the edge of the Texas Hill Country. Bruce knew, that essentially, they were left on their own to die.

This was not acceptable to the Senator. She originally wanted out of the mall to join her cohorts at Central. It was difficult for her to understand that Central saw them as expendable despite her presence. She had been one of the big movers and shakers just before the zombies rose. As far as she was concerned, her star was still rising. She just had to find a different way to ascend Now, she was working on making her case to Central that her area of the state was a viable resource to them and worth establishing a trade route. Under the guise of "protecting the American people" she had persuaded the Major General to bring in all surviving pockets around the area to the mall. Once her labor force was large enough, the Senator planned to offer them all to Central. Bruce had seen a rough draft of her proposal. It talked of "labor force" and "breeding stock."

It had been a flimsy case and the Senator knew that. But the fort changed that. Photos taken of the fort showed those inside tilling the earth getting ready for planting season. It showed a good, solid fortified structure with the possibility of expansion. Generators, fuel, and building supplies had been seen secured within the walls. Now the Senator was keen on taking over the fort and offering up its resources to Central as well. She was enthralled with the idea of establishing a major human colony under her control to vie for a position of power within Central's new government. Always a power player, the Senator was positive that providing both a work force and breeding stock to the new government was just the right ticket.

Bruce thought it was all ridiculous. He didn't give a rat's ass about what was going on in East Texas. The world was over. The old governments had fallen. The enclave in East Texas had power only because people allowed it to claim power. His opinion was fuck them, fuck that, and keep fucking moving. If he had his way, they would just move to the fort and be done with the damned mall.

But the Senator and Major General seemed determined to be a part of whatever the Vice President and remains of the government were doing out in East Texas.

Finally, he spotted the correct store and entered. People were getting ready to bunk down for a nap and a few greeted him as he headed toward the newcomers. After a little chitchat, he finally managed to reach the two people sitting on their cots.

"Excuse me," he said in a soft voice, his nerves almost getting the best of him.

Both the man and the woman looked up. The man was a big guy and the girl was stunning with huge black eyes.

"Can we help you?" The man stood up and stood slightly in front of the woman.

"My name is Bruce Kiel. I want to know if Katie Kiel is at your fort," he said, trying to keep his hands from shaking.

The man glanced at the woman then back up at Bruce. "Why do you want to know?"

"Because I'm her father," he answered.

The woman stood up sharply, then grabbed her head, wincing. "The Police Chief?"

"Yes," he answered. "You know my daughter?"

"I spoke to you that first day! I was in the truck with Katie! We escaped the city together!"

Bruce sat down sharply on the cot nearest him. "She's alive then? She made it to the fort and she's still alive?"

The woman grinned. "Yeah! And married and pregnant!"

"My Katie? She was married to Lydia," he stuttered in shock. It was too much to comprehend. He had allowed himself to hope his daughter was alive, but to hear she was in the motherly way was a shock.

"Yeah, but Lydia died the first day. You knew that, right?" The woman sat next to him, her hand resting on his.

"Yes. Yes. Katie said she didn't make it." Bruce nodded. "I told her to run into the hills."

"And we did! And we made it to this town where they had built a wall.

And she met this guy named Travis. It was rough for her at first, but they fell for each other. They got hitched up and pregnant. They're very happy together. Oh, my God! She's going to be so happy you're alive!"

Bruce felt his body trembling and he lowered his head. With a sob of relief, the big man let his tears flow. "My Katie-girl is alive! Dear God, it's a miracle."

He had to get out of this gawddamn mall.

Chapter 12

1. Choices Made In Haste

I t was nearly 5 AM when Travis finally climbed into bed beside Katie. She was curled up on the bed with Jack. The German Shepherd gave him a petulant look as Travis scooted him to the end of the bed. Spooning his wife, Travis kissed her shoulder and sighed into her blond curls.

"Are they back?" Her voice was thick with sleep and emotion.

"No. They're not. Nerit is taking a team out soon," Travis answered.

Katie rolled over slowly, her green eyes scanning his face. Tears were glimmering along the edges of her lashes. "You think they're dead, don't you?"

"No," Travis answered slowly. "No I don't. I don't believe that. I think there is a good chance they're out there and that they're okay. We'll find them."

"I don't want her to be gone," Katie said in a low voice. "I keep thinking about her. How I found her that morning in that ugly pink nightgown and robe, nearly catatonic, and how she changed into someone that was amazing and fierce. That morning, when I saved her, she saved me, too. She gave me a reason to go on. To live."

"I know, honey."

"I just don't want her to not be a part of my life anymore. I don't want her to be lost." Katie sniffled loudly and rubbed her eyes. "I know we never would have been friends if not for all of this going down. We never would have met and if we had, we would have had nothing in common. Our lives were so different until that morning. And I keep thinking of her, sitting next to me in the truck, and how I knew she was important. That I had saved her for a reason."

"Baby, don't work yourself up. We don't know anything yet. You can't flip out." Travis gently tucked her hair back from her face and kissed her brow.

"I should have been there with her. Helping her. We are always better as a team," Katie declared.

"You got the baby to worry about. And like you told me along with everyone else, you have a job to do here."

"And what's that?"

"Keeping me sane," Travis said and smiled wryly.

Despite her tears, Katie laughed. She rubbed her eyes again, wiping away her tears and vestiges of her makeup. "That's a pretty rough job.

Between you and Jenni, it's amazing that I'm sane."

Travis yawned and laughed at the same time, making an odd sound. "Didn't sleep, did you? Are you just coming to bed?"

"I didn't mean to wake you." Travis pulled the covers over him, kicking off his boots as he did so. They hit the floor with a resounding thud.

Jack again gave him a disapproving look.

"I had trouble sleeping anyway. Jason told Jack to stay with me. He figured you would be up half the night anyway."

"I'm that predictable?"

"Pretty much, yeah."

"How is Juan?" Katie's voice was hesitant, as if she wasn't sure she wanted to hear the answer.

"Stable. For now. Charlotte is doing the best she can."

"Thank God, he's still alive." Katie wrapped her arms around his neck and kissed him lightly.

He sighed with weariness and contentment as she snuggled against his side. He could feel her rounded tummy pressing against him and the gentle movement of their baby inside her. "I felt wired, so I stayed up working on some ideas. Plus, Ed made me feel like a shit for not taking the situation about Blanche to the fort."

"You mean dumping her at home?"

"Yeah. With a gun with one bullet." He looked at her, expecting her to be angry, but she just frowned a little. "I was pissed. I was done with her. We had dead people and my best friend was dying. All over that damn Hummer. Nerit, Curtis, Katarina, Bill and I just decided to ditch her out there."

"You decided on a death sentence," Katie corrected him.

Travis moaned and covered his face with one hand. "I know. I was just...done."

"Ed was upset?"

"He said we should have taken it to the fort."

"I agree. But it's done now, isn't it?"

"I should send someone out to check on her, shouldn't I?"

Sighing softly, Katie shrugged. "I don't know. I don't give a damn what happens to her, but if it adversely affects the fort..."

"Maybe we should bring her back for justice at the hands of the fort people." Travis sighed. "Just when I thought I would get some sleep."

"You're not going out there, are you?"

"Nah. I'll send out some of the volunteers who were going to go with Nerit." He glanced at the clock. "I'll head downstairs and meet up with them. They should be going to breakfast soon."

"Then you'll come back up for at least a few hours of sleep?"

"Yeah. Yeah. Unless something else happens." He kissed her soundly, then her belly, and gave the reproachful looking German Shepherd a pat on the head. "I'll be back."

Bone weary, Travis pulled on his boots and headed back out the door.

2. Walking Hamburgers and Helicopters

The morning was very cold and a light mist flowed over the ground. Occasionally a dark figure lingered in the wispy grasp of the haze, but mostly the world seemed strangely empty as the Hummer sped along the country back roads.

A herd of cows gathered around a pond huddled together for warmth. They looked relatively well fed considering how long they had been on their own.

Just since last year, the world had changed drastically. The few houses they passed were desolate looking creatures. Before winter had set in, nature had already begun the process of dismantling the man made buildings.

Katarina drove the Hummer dressed in warm clothes with her hair braided tightly and slung over one shoulder. Beside her, Nerit stared out at the dead world with a thoughtful expression on her face. Curtis and Dale sat in the back, quiet and half-dozing. Despite hot coffee and donuts, it was too easy to want to fall back to sleep on a cold morning.

"It won't take too long," Nerit decided.

"Huh?"

"For nature to take back the planet." Nerit motioned to the fences that were already down.

Katarina looked over at a farmhouse and its listing front door. "Yeah. It's already going to hell."

"Not surprising. Americans do not build to last," Nerit said, wiping her nose with a Kleenex. Allergies were hell on everyone it seemed.

"Yeah. Expendable society is what it's called, I think," Katarina said with a nod.

"Humanity. That is what is expendable." Nerit shook her head. "We went down so easily."

"Some of us are still here," Katarina pointed out.

"The lucky and the too damn stubborn to die," Nerit said with a laugh.

"I know which category I'm in."

"Me, too. Me, too..." Nerit said.

"Damn lucky?"

"Absolutely," Nerit laughed.

"Me, too."

"If I had still been living in Houston, I would be eating someone's nose right now," Nerit decided.

"Weird how it worked, huh? If you made it through the first day, it got easier somehow."

"The initial shock of it all wears off and the survival instinct kicks in." Katarina ran a hand over her hair, then sighed. "It almost feels like this is normal. Ya know? Like this is just how life is."

"This is how life just is now. The old way is just that...old. Gone. Lost."

"And now people are hitching up and having babies..."

Nerit bobbed her head. "And expanding our home...planting gardens..."

"Falling in love..."

With a tilt of her head, Nerit regarded Katarina. "You like Bill."

"He's nice," Katarina said after a moment. "I did like...I do like...he is just nice."

"Nice is good. Ralph was nice." Nerit suddenly stiffened, looking ahead. "The next turn pull over!"

The Hummer came to a slow stop just after a curve on the country road. A few cows were walking down the road. Deer were strolling casually across the meadow and, somewhere in the distance, a bird was calling out. The mist was now just wisps along the ground.

Ralph's truck was smashed firmly into a fence post. Its deer guard took most of the damage and Nerit was fairly certain it would drive. But both doors were wide open and it was obvious the truck was empty.

"Shit," Curtis said sleepily, straightening up. "This isn't good."

Dale woke up in mid-snore and sputtered a few incoherent words before saying, "Hey, cows."

"They must have got out when the truck took the fence down," Katarina said.

Nerit ignored the cows and stared at the truck thoughtfully. "Get out slowly. Cover all sides. I doubt there is any activity out here, but be on guard. Let me examine the area around the truck."

"You got it," Dale said, stuffing the rest of a stale, cold donut he had fished out of his pocket into his mouth.

Katarina slid out of the truck, holding her gun easily in her hands. Curtis stumbled out and worked a crick out of his leg as Dale strode in a slow circle keeping his eye on the cows.

"Them's good eating," he said finally.

"Keep to the objective," Nerit responded.

Moving toward the truck, she squinted a little, focusing her gaze. With a little groan, she squatted down to look at some shoe prints in the mud. Curtis joined her, looking perplexed.

"Jenni was in cowboy boots. So was Bill."

"Roger was in sneakers," Curtis added to Nerit's comment. "So was Felix."

"What do these look like to you?" Nerit motioned to the footprints.

"Honestly? Combat boots."

"Exactly." Nerit stood up slowly, feeling her hips and back protesting, and moved to the truck. Gazing inside, she saw the dried blood, sticky in the humidity of the morning, smeared along the passenger side.

"Someone was hurt."

"Shit," Katarina whispered.

Curtis was instantly at Nerit's side. "Think they got bitten and went at each other?"

Pulling what looked like a wadded up sheet to her, Nerit looked it over. "No. This is full of surgical tools. See that neat slice in the fabric. I think someone got stabbed by one of the instruments." She fumbled with the makeshift bag a bit more. "My guess is Jenni."

"You can tell that by the blood?" Dale asked in surprise.

"No, sweetheart, by her wadded up, bloodied leather jacket," Nerit answered pointing to where the article of clothing lay on the floor of the truck.

"Oh."

"There are drag marks through the grass." Katarina pointed.

"And along the side of the truck," Curtis observed.

"And a helicopter settled down in the pasture," Nerit added.

"What? How?"

"Look at the grass, Curtis. Flattened in a circle. And it was not one of Roger's crop circles." Nerit sighed and moved around the truck slowly.

"Only two bodies," Curtis said from behind her as he studied the drag marks.

"Yes," Nerit answered. "Just two."

"So they got Jenni and one other person," Katarina said in a soft, low voice.

Nerit's intense eyes looked toward her. "Yes."

"Who?" Katarina asked.

"I can't tell that." Nerit sighed and climbed into the truck. Turning the key, she furrowed her brow, listening to the engine try to turnover. Then it suddenly roared to life and she sat in silence in the cab.

Katarina was stoic, but Nerit knew she was in pain. Curtis just looked a little lost. Dale was still staring at the cows like they were walking hamburgers.

"What do we do now?" Curtis finally asked.

"We go back. We tell everyone we are not alone. We tell them the military is still functioning somewhere out there and they have Jenni and one other survivor."

Curtis shook his head. "Fucking shit! If Lenore hadn't tried to save Ken and kept with the mission--"

"She did what I would have done, fucktard," Dale growled. "You don't let your friends die in front of your eyes."

Flinching from the harshness in Dale's voice, Curtis drew back. "Okay, okay."

"We do what comes instinctively. Lenore saved her friend. But we lost two others. That is the nature of this world," Nerit said firmly. "There are no second guesses, Curtis. We just do our best."

"Yeah, but Bill, Jenni, Roger and Felix...they're fucking gone now," Curtis said in a low, tight voice.

"Yes, they are," Nerit answered in her calm tones. "Now, let's go home."

Wordlessly, Katarina returned to the Hummer and climbed in.

"Can I have a cow?" Dale asked.

"No."

"Shit," Dale sighed, but obeyed Nerit. He climbed into the truck with her not minding the drying blood one bit.

Curtis moved back to the Hummer. The young police officer was tense. When he slid into the other SUV, he hunched down and looked away from Katarina.

Nerit slammed the door shut and backed the truck up slowly.

"She did what I would have done," Dale repeated.

"I know," Nerit said.

"It's not fair that doing something like that can get others killed or kidnapped," Dale said gruffly.

"Yes, but life is not fair."

"So the fucking military is out there, huh?"

"Yes," Nerit answered, following the Hummer, her hands gripping the steering wheel tightly.

"Great. Fucking great. And who do you think controls them?" Nerit shrugged her shoulders. "People of power."

"Dammit," Dale cussed. "I was kinda hoping Congress got ate."

3. Only Questions

Katie ran across the lobby avoiding some of the old timers taking up their morning bingo spots. Her blond curls were pulled up into a ponytail and she was clad in one of Travis' shirts. Her swelling belly was beginning to pop out the bottom of her tops. Though she felt sheepish to admit it, she loved it. Instinctively, she placed a hand against her stomach as she ran, almost as if she could protect the baby from whatever news had returned with Nerit and the others.

Travis had never returned to bed and she had woken up groggy and disoriented. She had called down to the front desk to find Peggy grumpy and cursing about Travis making her nuts. It was then she found out the two groups Travis had sent out earlier were in route to the fort. After changing her clothes, she had rushed downstairs.

Catching sight of Nerit talking with Travis, she knew instantly the news was not good. Travis' expression was grim as he rubbed his brow. Nerit looked calm, but her gaze fierce.

"What happened?" Katie asked as she reached them, her voice raw. She feared the worst and the tension in her face clearly revealed that.

"We found the truck and they weren't in it," Nerit answered simply.

Katie blinked at the bluntness of that statement. "Were they...was there..."

"They were taken," Nerit answered. "Apparently by the military. At least Jenni and one other man. We don't know which of the men it was though."

"So we lost two people at the hospital," Katie said softly.

Travis nodded, his mouth pressed into a grim line.

"And the military is out there," Katie continued.

"That is likely," Nerit answered.

"How do we know they have Jenni, but we're not sure about which of the guys they took?" Travis asked.

"Jenni was injured by a piece of surgical equipment she was holding," Nerit, explaining quickly what she had observed. "I gave the surgical equipment to Charlotte already so she can try to save Juan."

Katie felt a little dizzy at the thought of Jenni being hurt, then carted off by some unknown military force. She leaned against Travis for comfort. His arm snaked around her and he held her tightly, his lips briefly brushing over her forehead.

Ed and Linda walked toward them briskly. Both looked grim and Katie wondered if they were the ones that checked on Blanche.

"What did you find?" Travis looked nervous.

"A Mercedes packed to the gills with supplies on the side of the road. Ray busted the axle trying to off road it. Maybe he was trying to avoid being seen by Curtis and Katarina yesterday," Ed answered.

"And what looked like maybe the remains of Ray on the doorstep of the mansion. Gunshot wound to what was left of his head." Linda shivered. "There were a few zombies milling around still. Front door was open. Zombies on the inside. We didn't go in."

"We didn't stick around. No sign of life and once the zombies get you in their sights, they get all feisty," Ed added.

"Think she got away?" Katie wasn't sure if she wanted Blanche still alive out there or not. She wasn't very happy about the choice that had been made the day before, but at the same time it was hard to find sympathy for Blanche.

Ed shook his head. "Nope." His keen eyes looked toward Travis. "Nope. I think she's dead."

Travis squirmed under his gaze and Nerit shrugged.

Linda shook her head. "I don't feel bad for the bitch. She shot my cousin. Killed two men, including her husband."

"Justice has got to be fair for everyone or it ain't justice," Ed said in terse voice.

"Hey! Hey, Travis! Nerit! There is word the army is coming to rescue us," a man said running up to them.

Katie couldn't remember his name, but knew he had survived with his son in a farmhouse not too far out of town.

"No, they took two of our people," Travis answered, struggling to keep the edge from his tired voice. He and Ed were still locking gazes.

"Are they coming for the rest of us?" The man looked excited, but anxious.

"They took two of our people and we don't know what that means," Nerit answered truthfully.

"Yeah, but they are coming to rescue us, right? They know we're here now. Our people will tell them where to come to get us. Right?"

A crowd was beginning to form around them as the word spread. Katie clung to Travis, feeling his body leaning heavily against hers. He was so tired and she knew he was not in the mindset to deal with yet another crisis.

"Travis, is it true?" This was Belinda, Juan's former crush, and she looked hopeful.

"We don't know. We just know that the military took two of our people. It could mean anything," Travis responded.

"But if it's the army, that means we're saved!" This from an older black woman, clutching her hands together. Her expression was rapturous.

"Where would they take us?" Travis asked the fast growing crowd.

"A place safer than what we got here," Belinda said, and the people around her nodded.

"This may be bad," Peggy pointed out. "What if their base isn't as nice as this. We have a good thing here."

"Besides, maybe it's not the army at all. Just rogues. Deserters," the Reverend added.

Things were becoming very agitated now. Voices swelled as arguments broke out. Some people seemed almost desperate to believe this was good news while others looked dubious.

Katie was one of the doubters. She couldn't see how someone taking Jenni could possibly be a good thing.

Nerit held up a hand and things quieted somewhat. "The truth is, we do not know the situation. We do not know why Jenni and the others were taken. We just know for sure that they were and that it was most likely a faction of the military."

"We shouldn't get overly excited yet," Travis added. "We're not sure what this means for the fort."

"But they'll rescue us," someone said persistently. It was Janice, a local. Her face was flushed and anxious. "They kept saying on the radio they would save us!"

"Save us how?" Travis asked her point blank.

"Take us to where it's safe," Janice answered.

"But it's safe here," Katarina said, stepping out of the crowd. "It's safe where we are."

"But they'll have real weapons. Real ways of defending us," another voice said from the back.

Katie noticed it was the newer people who clung to this idea of a rescue more tightly than the townsfolk. Also, the people from larger towns or cities seemed to immediately embrace the idea of the army coming to the rescue.

"What is true is that we don't know what is happening yet," Travis said in a loud voice. "And that is where it stands."

Pulling Katie with him, he moved into the manager's office, Nerit following.

"I don't like how this feels," Travis said grimly, leaning his hands on his desk.

"Until we know what is going on, we need to keep people calm," Nerit said.

Picking up the phone, Travis dialed Peggy's line. "Gather the council, please."

"They're going to go ape shit," Katie decided. "The idea of being rescued is going to have people completely nuts." She leaned against Travis, comforted by the gentle touch of his fingers through her hair and down her neck.

Peggy slipped in the door followed by Curtis. Katarina entered, standing in for Bill. Eric arrived last, wearing his usual khakis and a sweater. He ran a hand over his dark hair as he sat in a chair. There was a moment of tense silence as they realized how many of the council was missing. Jenni, Juan, Bill...Katie even missed Calhoun whipping out his camcorder.

"Rumor is that the army is coming to rescue us," Eric said, starting the conversation.

"We're really not sure what the military wants," Nerit answered, and quickly filled him in on the details.

Curtis looked tense, sitting near Katarina. "Can we trust them? Right before it all went to hell they were killing people left and right in the streets."

"Killing infected people," Katie corrected.

"We don't even know if it's the real military," Katarina pointed out. "What if it's just a bunch of AWOL guys like the Reverend said?"

"And acting like gods," Curtis chimed in.

Travis nodded solemnly as he leaned back against the desk. "That is my fear."

"Or they could be men and women doing their job and rescuing civilians," Nerit interjected.

"I can't see how their fort could be better than this," Katarina said defensively.

"Maybe it's the Madison Rescue Center," Peggy said finally. "They've been looping the same message since all this started to stay in our homes and they would eventually rescue us."

Glancing toward Peggy, Katie pursed her lips. "Madison? Oh, yeah. I remember that. Jenni and I were told by some soldiers in a convoy to go to Madison."

"Where is Madison?" Eric adjusted his glasses on his face. "I've never heard of it."

"It's a small city near here. 'Bout seventy-five miles or more to the northeast." Curtis was staring at his hands as he rotated a statue of Lincoln on the table next to him with his fingers.

"We don't go in that direction because of the mass amounts of zombies in some of those towns, right?" Eric looked around the room. "So going that way is dangerous."

"We never had no one calling in from that area, either." Peggy shook her head. "It got ugly out that way according to what we heard on the radio. When we lost our phones, there was speculation it was because of that area going dark."

"What was so special about Madison? Why did they send people there?" Katie had wondered on the first day of the rising why they were directed toward an area with a denser population. "Is there an army base there?"

"There's no base there." Curtis stopped fiddling with the small statue. "There ain't nothing there that is that special."

"Yeah, but there had to be some sort of rescue center if they sent us there," Katie said.

"There is a convention center there. And a mall." Katarina flinched. "Damn. A mall. Just like the movies."

"There is a message on the emergency broadcast system. It repeats over and over again, but I figured they were all dead long ago," Peggy admitted.

"I did, too. Overrun like the rest of the rescue centers," Katie agreed. "We never thought about it twice after we decided not to go there."

"But they may be still there. Still operational." Eric looked thoughtful as he considered this prospect. "Perhaps they have established a safe haven just like we have."

"And," Nerit said, "that would make them close enough to have taken our people."

"So what do we do?" Eric asked.

"Try to contact them?" Katie offered.

"We've been monitoring the airways. I never heard a thing," Curtis said in a soft, angry voice.

"Military channels are not accessible to civilians," Nerit pointed out. Her expression was stoic, but her eyes were fierce, bright, and thoughtful.

"Besides, the closest military anything around these parts is about two hundred miles away. That National Guard base." Peggy shook her head. "Why should we even think about them? Once all the shit hit the fan and no one showed up, we took care of ourselves."

"But a military presence is obviously out there," Travis finally said. "And they have our people. So what do we do now?"

"Maybe we should start sending out a message of our own," Katie suggested. "Requesting the return of our people. They must be monitoring us."

"If that's true," Travis sighed. "I gotta ask why they didn't come knocking before?"

"Too many questions, no answers." Katie ran a hand over her hair.

"Back when the world had order and things worked properly, we may have found each other much more quickly. But if they are operating on channels that we are not and vice versa..." Nerit slightly shook her head. "We can't apply normal world expectations to the situations we are experiencing now. This new presence in our lives is not a known quantity and we don't know what it will hold for us."

"They're the United States military. Sworn to serve and protect. Why should we fear them?" Eric looked up and stared at Nerit. "They're our people."

"I think we should start asking for our people back," Peggy said. "Maybe now that they know we're here, they'll be listening for us. Looking for us. And we can start talking like civilized people instead of freaking out."

With an angry sound, Curtis rose to his feet. "If Lenore had not blown the plan at the hospital and opened fire--"

"That is a moot point now," Travis snapped. "Jenni and whoever else survived are in the hands of the military and we cannot be going off second guessing what Lenore did!"

"We cannot afford fuckups that cost us our people, Travis!" Curtis shouted.

"Everyone makes mistakes," Katie said, stepping toward Curtis. "I love

Jenni! And this is killing me, but Lenore did what I would have done in her place. I would have saved my best friend."

"Back down," Katarina said in a low voice.

Curtis shot her a fierce look, but her gaze was so cold, so chilling, he visibly shrank away from her.

"We're off topic. This isn't about Lenore," Eric said in a firm voice.

"I say we send the messages," Nerit said after a beat. "Because if they have our people, they have a reason behind it. Let's start talking."

Katie felt tears threatening as she bobbed her head in agreement. "Yes, please, let's do that. Let's bring Jenni home."

Eric nodded. "I agree."

"We gotta find out what is going on out there. I say send out an invite." Katarina pushed her heavy red hair out of her face. "Won't do us no good worrying and not doing."

"I ain't got no issue calling them up and asking them to give us our people back," Peggy declared. "I am so sick of this bullshit."

Travis took a deep breath. "Then let's do it."

Chapter 13

1. The Mall, Zombies, and the Alamo

D *amn lot of zombies*, Bill thought.
After an hour of listening to the Major General carry on about building a new tomorrow, a greater America, protecting the native soil, and on and on, he had finally escorted Bill up onto the roof of the mall.

"What do you think?" the Major General asked, sweeping his hand out in front of him.

Bill took in the white wall that surrounded the mall, the blockades over the entrances, the cars, buses, and a combination of army, marine and national guard vehicles of every shape and color. Every entrance into the mall parking lot was heavily fortified with multiple guards on duty.

But beyond the wall...

Zombies...a whole lot of zombies...

"We can eradicate them," the Major General said in a decisive voice.

"Or just get eaten," Bill added.

The Major General frowned.

"It's happened before," Bill said. "In at least two movies. Malls, just bad...bad news.."

"I'm not sure what you are talking about, but I can assure you, we can overcome the undead scourge," the Major General declared.

Bill wasn't too sure. It looked like a lot of Madison was outside the walls. He glanced over the mall defenses, then back over toward the throng of zombies.

Yep, that was a whole lot of zombies...

Damn.

Now, he knew how the people in the Alamo felt.

Shit. He hoped he died well. For a moment, he wondered if the Major General, who spoke with a thick East Coast accent, would understand if he told him "You can go to hell -- I'm going to Texas." He was tempted to paraphrase Davy Crockett's famous words to "You can go to hell--I'm going to the fort."

Damn.

Whole lot of zombies...

"Once we take control of the fort, you will see that we can make things a lot better for everyone. The Senator has a definitive plan on how to build a new society on the ashes of the old one. The military forces will take over the security of the fort so your people can get out into the fields and start preparing for a new future."

Bill squinted at the guy and wondered if he realized what the hell he was saying. "You want us out in the fields. Growing crops?"

"And expanding the fort. Getting a cattle ranch secured. Everything that will be needed to create a new tomorrow. We can work out assignments for the men and create a schedule for the women."

"Schedule?"

"Yes. Which ones will help with the fort household and which ones will have children."

"Really?"

"Yes. Every woman that can have a child will need to produce a future citizen of the fort. We must get our population up so we can make sure to keep things moving toward a secure future." The Major General gave him a warm smile. "It'll be rough at first, but the good old American know how will get us through."

"So, you guys will kinda divide us up, tell us what to do, take over the running of the fort?"

"Yes. Your people won't have to worry about it. You'll have an experienced Senator to govern and a trained military force. Sounds good doesn't it?"

Tilting his head to one side, Bill took a deep breath, eyeing the throng of decaying dead outside the walls.

"What do you think, Bill?"

Bill took a deep breath and in his deep Texan drawl, that he deliberately twanged out, answered,

"Born, raised, and lived as a Texan, sir. Aim to die as one. So, about America, she was good to me, but this is frontier land again. And if you don't see it that way, yer fucked. This is Texas. We don't take kindly to being told what to do."

The Major General blinked at him. "I don't understand."

"This is Texas, sir. We aim to do what is best for ourselves and our family. Your government, your military, they don't exist anymore to us. We'll do our own thing. Find our own way."

"You're saying the people at the fort won't welcome our leadership?"

"No, sir. I am saying they will tell you to fuck off."

The man's eyebrows lifted in surprise.

"Think I'm done now," Bill said firmly.

The Major General slowly nodded and motioned to a soldier to lead Bill back into the mall. Bill was more than glad to get out of the view of all the zombies outside the walls, but the mall wasn't that welcoming either. People were eating breakfast and heading off to their work assignments. The heat was off and the cold made him shiver. It felt more like a prison than a home. He didn't know how the people had mentally survived so long in such a sterile and cold environment.

He spotted Jenni at a table, sitting down to breakfast, and headed over to her.

"Well?" She flipped her long dark hair over one shoulder. "What was the big deal with that guy wanting to talk to you?"

"He wanted to talk my ear off and show me what is going on outside." He slid onto the chair next to her and shook his head.

"What is going on outside?" Jenni poked at her congealing oatmeal, her expression one of slight disgust.

"We're in the gawddamn Alamo," Bill answered gruffly.

"Seriously?" Jenni grimaced.

"Only difference, Mexicans didn't eat the people in the Alamo," Bill muttered.

Jenni leaned her head on his beefy shoulder. "Damn. We sure are good at getting ourselves into trouble."

"Yeah, tell me about it. This place makes the hospital look like a cake walk." Bill exhaled long and hard. He slid his arm around Jenni's shoulders and hugged her to his side. "It'll be okay, Jenni. We always figure something out. We'll figure a way out of this."

"I don't think my old method of whacking zombies with my ax is going to work," Jenni decided grimly.

"Nope. But we gotta trust our friends are going to be looking for us and hopefully something can be worked out."

Jenni lifted a spoonful of the oatmeal and slowly turned it over. The oatmeal clung to the spoon. "Ugh. I hate the food. I'd kill for something sugary and crunchy."

"Did you notice the people around here?"

Turning her gaze from her spoon, Jenni looked around. "Hmm..."

Bill smiled at a woman sitting across from them, but she looked away. "They all have given up hope. They're like ghosts. Just wandering around. Kinda empty."

Jenni slowly swiveled around in her chair, looking at the people seated around them. There was barely a whisper of conversation among them. Side by side, they sat in silence watching the people all around them talk, eat, and drink.

"I want to go home," Jenni whispered.

"We will, Jenni," Bill vowed. "We'll go home."

2. Speaker of the Dead

Travis sighed and tried hard not to look at the clock hanging over the check-in counter in the lobby. He hated waiting. It was sheer torture. It always made him feel as though someone had decided to churn butter in his gut. Charlotte, Belinda and the Reverend were operating on Juan in an attempt to remove the bullet and the suspense was killing him.

He was also completely exhausted even though it was just ten in the morning. He was having trouble focusing. Of course, he hadn't slept a wink the night before. Rubbing his eyes, he yawned. At least he wasn't alone as he waited to hear if Juan would pull through. A collection of Juan's friends and family were gathered in the lobby waiting for the word.

Rosie sat nearby, clutching her rosary, and softly whispering, "Hail Mary, Full of Grace..."

Nerit sat next to her, her hand gently resting on Rosie's, eyes closed, seeming to meditate.

Jason was sprawled on the love seat next to the couch Travis was sitting on reading a Star Trek novel Roger had loaned him. The boy looked absolutely morose and Travis couldn't blame him considering the drama encompassing the boy's life. His mother was in the hands of the military, his friend and teacher was missing, and his somewhat stepfather was in surgery. Despite his surly teenager routine with Juan, Travis had noticed a considerable thaw in how Jason felt about Juan. It was just too much for anyone to handle. Jason's way of handling it seemed to be to sink down into the love seat and read, his hair falling over his eyes to hide his tears while Jack lay next to him looking very sad.

Travis looked down at Katie. She was sprawled out on the sofa, her head resting on his thigh as she slept. He slowly drew his fingers through her hair, once more marveling at the softness of her silky curls. It was a relief that she had fallen asleep. The stress of the last twenty-four hours had worn on her. She had began to suffer from vertigo, and Travis had made her lie down. He knew she had slept fitfully the night before. He was relieved to see her soundly sleeping.

Again, he tried hard not to look at the clock.

Picking up the pencil on the end table next to him, he started to write notes and sketch a possible extension to the fort. Yes, he was most likely a workaholic, but working made him feel more in control and relaxed. He hated feeling helpless. He hated feeling there was nothing he could do to remedy a bad situation.

Most of his life he felt helpless. It wasn't until the fort had risen from the ashes of the former world that he felt he had found his place.

It had been Travis' misfortune to be born good-looking. He had even won baby beauty contests that his grandmother had entered him on the sly. His parents were too busy working to save the earth to notice he was anything more than their smart little boy. But others saw a golden child. The good-looking shall inherit the earth and all that.

In kindergarten he had been chased around by little girls determined to kiss him while all he had wanted to do was build sand cities in the sandbox.

In junior high, girls had bugged him continuously as he tried to draw buildings and cities of the future.

In high school, he had been stalked relentlessly by the popular girls. He had finally resorted to growing his hair out and being as scruffy as possible his sophomore year. This had just landed him bad boy status, which had the girls mooning over him even more.

By his junior year, his love for running landed him the role of track star. His enjoyment was short-lived when the school's football coach decided he wanted to put Travis' speed to use on the football field. Out of frustration, Travis had quit altogether.

Even his choice of Leilani, an exotic belly dancer, who was also on the school newspaper, had been protested by others. A teacher even told him, "Travis, you could so easily have Jennifer if you'll give up on Leilani." Of course, Jennifer was the head cheerleader. He had managed to keep his alternative girlfriend until graduation, but she had to deal with being called "bitch," "whore," and "slut" until graduation day by those who felt spurned by Travis.

College had been a bit of a relief. He was finally able to just blend in and he had found joy in pursuing his political interests. He had plunged whole-heartedly into the laid-back, alternative lifestyle community that lived around the University of Texas campus in Austin and spent too many hours stoned out of his mind down near Town Lake.

He had surfaced from the madness a year later, tattooed, long haired, and feeling quite satisfied with his year of wildness. It was then he felt free to jump fully into academia, pursuing a double major. He studied architecture out of sheer love for the art of it and studied to become a city planner for the love of helping people. Things had gone well until he had met Clair, the woman that would change his life.

Her beauty and sparkling personality had worked magic on him. By the time he had graduated, he found himself ensconced in her father's architecture firm building high rise buildings in Houston and living a life he had never imagined for himself. He won awards and was given huge bonuses. He dined at the finest restaurants and vacationed at the best resorts. But one day he woke up and it all meant nothing. He realized he had lost his soul and forgotten his desire to help people.

In months everything was sold, the girlfriend was in the past, his expensive suits were at Goodwill and he was in a truck heading into the Texas Hill Country to help restore an old historical town.

Now he was helping rebuild the town in a way he never imagined.

People in the fort saw Travis as a leader. He saw himself as a helper. He was helping build a new life and making sure it was safe. He was Katie's husband and their child's father and that was good enough for him. All the rest of it, the looks of admiration, the looks of disdain, the arguments, the accolades, were meaningless when he looked down into Katie's face and understood his role.

"I always loved looking at her when she slept," a silky, deep voice said.

Looking up, Travis saw a very tall woman gazing down at them. She was very slim and wore a black dress with long sleeves and a skirt that brushed over the toes of her black boots. She sat down next to Jason and smiled at Travis.

Blinking, he took in her short cropped brown hair with auburn highlights, amazing cheekbones and shining eyes. Ornate native jewelry decorated her throat and wrists.

"She just looks so innocent when she sleeps, though every once and awhile, she gets this furrow right here," the woman said, leaning over to point between Katie's eyebrows. "That is when you know she's arguing a case in her sleep."

"Lydia," Travis whispered.

"Yes," she answered with a dazzling smile.

He noted her hands were long and elegant. She wore a diamond wedding band.

"Then I must be asleep," Travis decided.

"Yes, you are," Lydia assured him. She tilted her gaze to look at Katie. Her eyes glimmered with unspoken love and she smiled a bittersweet smile. "She looks beautiful pregnant."

Travis knew this was a dream, but he felt awkward. Meeting the-well, she wasn't really the ex--but his wife's former wife was odd.

"We...eh...oh...um..."

Lydia laughed. "Don't worry, Travis. Life goes on for the living. I know that. I would never want to hold her back from loving again. From living. I will always love her and I just want her happy."

"But," Travis rubbed his brow, wincing with embarrassment. "I'm a guy."

"Yes, you are." She laughed with delight.

Travis continued to grimace.

Lydia's hand reached toward him, but she didn't quite touch him. "It's all right, Travis. The heart loves without boundaries. It is the mind that can trap the heart with cages constructed by society's rules. Katie always had a beautiful open heart."

Travis forced a smile, feeling nervous. "Why am I dreaming about you, Lydia?" He understood he was asleep and this was all a dream, but somehow it felt important. It felt amazingly real.

Lydia's smile faded a little and she sat back, crossing her legs. "Travis, you need to understand something important. I'm here to give you a message."

"About Katie?"

"About you." She tilted her head and gazed at him with a serenity that was both comforting and disconcerting.

"Oh?"

Leaning forward, her eyes gazed steadily into his. "You need to understand that the world has changed. The veil between the living and the dead is very thin now. The worlds have blurred and nothing is as it was. Many have died and will die as the world tries to regain balance of some sort. The dead are all around you. Not just the empty shells that are trying to kill you, but the spirits of those trapped by the massive upheaval that took place when the dead seized the world from the living."

"Like you," he said softly.

She nodded. "Yes. I have yet to move on. But soon the world will find a new balance and I will."

"I'm so sorry about what happened to you, Lydia."

"Being a good Samaritan sometimes gets you killed. Trust me. I know." A shadow of pain flitted over her features, then she swept it away with a wave of her hand. "This is something you need to learn."

"What are you saying?" He narrowed his eyes.

"You want to save everyone, Travis, and help all of them be safe. But this world is not safe. Nothing is as it was. Very soon you will fully understand the sheer fruitlessness of trying to control everything around you. You will need to make choices for yourself, Katie and the baby. Others will make choices for themselves as well. These choices may lead to life or to death."

Frowning a little, Travis looked down at his wife, then up at Lydia. "They are my priority, Lydia. Katie and the baby."

"Are they?"

He swallowed hard, remembering how anxious he had been to risk his own life to try to help Juan. Tears filled his eyes and he looked up at Lydia. His voice caught in his throat and he said, "You're right. I just want to help everyone."

Lydia smiled at him tenderly. "I know. I know. But it is time for you to begin to let go of all the reins you have been holding and concentrate on your family. Soon, very soon, everyone will have to make choices for themselves. You, Katie, and everyone around you."

"And they may die," Travis said in an agonized voice.

"Travis, what you need to understand is that people will make choices for themselves. And sometimes, the right choice, the good choice, will lead to their death."

The truth of this statement startled him. "Who will die?"

Lydia tilted her head and looked at Katie for a long tender moment. "She will need you."

"Who will die, Lydia?"

"I can't tell you."

"Tell me! I don't care if you are a dream."

Lydia hesitated. "The future isn't set yet. It is constantly changing, evolving based on what people choose."

"But you know something. Who is going to die?"

Lydia sighed, then said, "Not Juan."

"Not Juan?"

"No, he is going to be all right. The operation was a success," Lydia said softly, then suddenly she was gone and Charlotte was standing over him.

"Did you hear me, Travis? Juan is going to be all right. We got the bullet and he is stable. I think he will be all right." Charlotte repeated.

Katie sat up groggily and when she heard Charlotte's words, she leaped up and hugged her tightly. "Thank you, Charlotte! You saved him!"

"Oh, thank God!" Rosie wailed.

Then everyone was crying and hugging each other.

Travis felt relieved, but strangely disconnected from all around him. His dream still felt tangible and, despite himself, he looked around for Lydia.

Katie threw her arms around him, kissing his cheek. "Love you."

"Love you," he answered, his gaze still sweeping over the lobby.

"You look a little strange," Katie decided.

"I had a weird dream."

"Yeah, me, too. I dreamed you and Lydia were talking while I slept," Katie said with a little shrug. "Strange, huh?"

3. A New America

Kevin walked briskly along the walkway leading to the mall's offices. The Major General had sent for him and he had an ominous feeling about this meeting. Down below, he could see people moving about, talking in groups, or moving to their assigned duties. Already he could see one group of people washing the glass of the window displays. In an effort to keep people from going stir crazy, all sorts of ridiculous chores had been thought up for the populace. The fear and stagnation in the mall was terrible. He felt it pushing on him everyday.

Sliding his hand over the stubble on the top of his head, he tried to focus himself the best he could. He could see the Senator's entourage on their way across the bridge from Foley's and knew this meeting was not going to be one bit pleasant.

Kevin knew that he would have to keep his tongue in check. It was hard to do with the increasingly inflammatory comments being made by those in power. It was obvious to him that the people in Central had no compassion to those outside their walls. What had once been the

American populace were now merely commodities to be divvied up into neat little categories.

A group of short, dark skinned men were being herded toward the outside doors as he drew near the offices. He hesitated as he watched the indigenous men group tightly together, obviously afraid. For some obscene reason, the migrant workers were forced to work on the mall's landscaping. Supposedly, it was to keep them busy, but no other people in the mall were forced to go outside and endure the blood curdling moans of the undead.

Frowning, he turned and moved down the short hall that would deliver him into the Major General's office. The men on guard gave him sharp salutes and opened the door for him. Walking in, he felt everyone's eyes on him. He had originally been the senior officer in charge of the mall until the Senator had shown up with the Major General. They were constantly suspicious of him and he did his best to make them feel he was a faithful drone.

"Kevin, thank you for joining us," the Senator said with a brilliant smile. She was heavily made up as usual with her blond hair forming a big bubble around her head.

"Senator," he said in a soft voice.

"Sit down and let's begin," the Major General said.

Kevin sat down and looked down at the stapled sheets of paper before him. He flipped through it and saw a heading that read "Distribution of Human Assets."

"I spoke with Central last night," the Senator began, her grin wide. "And they were very excited about the photos of the fort I sent them. And what is truly wonderful is that they have accepted my proposal to relocate the populace of the Madison Mall Rescue Center to our newly named Fort Bowie Work Center."

Kevin blinked blandly and glanced around the table. The Major General looked impressed. Bruce Kiel was scribbling on the proposal in front of him. The Senator's eagle-eyed, sharp tongued, cunning campaign manager, Raleigh Tullos looked smug.

"So they don't expect us to maintain the mall anymore?" the Major General asked.

Kevin realized in that moment how much of a puppet his commanding officer was.

"Exactly. Upon further examination of the photos I realized the hotel in the shots is the same hotel my sister and her husband were financing for restoration. It is a luxurious hotel that harkens back to the beginning of the last century. There is plenty of room for us to settle in there. We can secure the Governor's Suite immediately and use all its resources to provide us a safe and civilized home," the Senator said with relish.

"What of the people living in the hotel?" Kevin asked.

The Senator looked toward him with her shrewd blue eyes. Her smile remained plastered on her face. "They have obviously cleared other buildings. If we bring the cots from the mall with us, there will be sufficient room for the working force."

"Working force?"

"Why, yes," Raleigh said smoothly. "The Senator pointed out to the President that it is time for the people of America to return to their values. Hard work has always been a part of that. Together we must build a new America. This fort is near cattle ranches and farms. Using the military as guards, we will help the people start building a new world."

"We can begin supplying Central with fresh meat and vegetables in a matter of months," the Senator said with a wink.

Bruce Kiel was making notes on the proposal. "And what is this estimated birth rate gibberish?"

The Senator's fake warm smile was frozen on her face as she shuffled her papers. "We must begin to breed if we expect to survive."

"Isn't it the American way to have babies when you want them?" Bruce Kiel looked up, his expression quite dour.

The Senator laughed a little and Raleigh leaned past her to speak. "We are in a new world, Mr. Kiel. If we intend to survive the undead uprising, then we must have a future generation ready and willing to assist us."

Kevin flipped through the proposal as fast as he could, scanning it. He found the estimated birth rate data as well as the breakdown of ages among the surviving women in the mall. Women over forty-five were to be part of the regular workforce, since they were not considered optimal breeding age. Women thirty-five to forty-four would be given a six month window to become pregnant, or they, too, would be sent out into the fields. Women, married or single, were expected to produce one child per year. Scanning further he was horrified to see what looked like a formula that estimated an acceptable loss of life to productivity ratio.

"You're talking about these people as if they are cattle," Bruce said in a low voice.

Again, the Senator laughed, flashing her beautiful smile. "Bruce, please. I'm being realistic. We all must be realistic. The days of freedom of choice are over. The people must look to us to guide them or we are doomed."

"How do we intend to convince the people living in the fort to turn it over to us?" Kevin looked up from the data. He felt sick to his stomach.

"They are Americans. They will do what their President asks them," the Senator answered. "Besides, there is no clear indication of resistance from them. They are calling us every hour asking for the return of their people and have not uttered one threat."

"That is true," Raleigh agreed. "They may initially resist, but when they see our overwhelming firepower, they will concede."

The Major General cleared his throat and shook his head. "We may have more resistance than you anticipate. Bill from the fort said-"

"Bill from the fort is one man. We must speak with the leaders. The leaders will see that it is in their best interests to turn over the fort," the Senator said smoothly.

Kevin sighed and rubbed his chin thoughtfully. "When are you going to start negotiations with them to turn over control of the fort?"

"We're going to let them wait just a bit longer," the Senator answered. "They need to see we are the ones in power."

"You do realize that evacuating this mall will be dangerous and the loss of life may be high," Kevin said.

"I saw the evacuation plan. The charges go off, the barricade comes down and as the zombies flee the fire as many vehicles as possible break their ranks," Raleigh responded.

"Also in that evacuation plan it is stated that those in the last vehicles are at risk of being overwhelmed by the undead hordes as the fires die out and the zombies close ranks again," Kevin said.

"They have that in here," Bruce said softly. "The elderly and sick fill the last vehicles."

"The expendable population," the Senator explained. "We have to protect the healthy and the young."

Kevin nodded, then said, "I see."

"This fort is more of a godsend than we originally realized. Instead of maintaining the mall and the fort, we can merely take over the fort," the Senator said with a grin. "It will be a civilized environment that we can nurture and grow into something the President will be proud of."

Kevin nodded again. "Very well. When do I leave to negotiate?"

The Senator leaned across the table toward him. "I knew you would understand. Contact them in the morning. Make arrangements to see them tomorrow afternoon."

"Excellent, excellent," the Major General said.

Kevin forced himself to keep his expression as neutral as possible.

Bruce Kiel muttered "Fuck this," stood up and left.

"He may be a problem," Raleigh sighed.

"I'll deal with him," the Senator said. "We're old friends."

"He'll come around," the Major General said firmly. "They all will. It's a new age. A new America."

Kevin looked at the proposal, flipping slowly through it. Land of the Free seemed not included in this new America.

He had no choice. He would do what needed to be done to protect the American people.

Chapter 14

1. The Return of the Living Dead and More

The morning was quite cold with a thick mist covering the ground. The fort was completely enshrouded in fog and the fading darkness of the new day.

"Hate it when it's like this," Katarina muttered as she stood watch on the wall.

"Should clear up once the sun is fully out," Linda, her partner on the watch, answered her.

"Just makes me nervous," Katarina sighed.

"...if it was really her, then it means she's not trapped in a rotting corpse out there..." Katie's voice trailed out of the mist.

Katarina felt the floor beneath her quiver as the joggers approached. The extensive catwalk that had been built around the interior of the walled in fort was finally finished.

Katie and Travis emerged from the mist, huffing and puffing, jogging at an even stride.

"I don't know if I believe in ghosts," Travis answered his wife.

Everyone nodded a hello to one another as the joggers shot by.

"Look, we live in a zombie infested world...I think that ghosts are not that far a stretch anymore..." Katie answered then they were gone.

Katarina returned her gaze out over the mist. She couldn't see into the street and field beyond the hotel. It was so very thick. She wasn't sure what Katie and Travis were talking about, but on a morning like this she didn't want to think about zombies and ghosts. She had a rough enough time dealing with her mother's ghost glowering at her at the worst times. Already, her skin was pricking and she didn't dare look behind her.

"This is the kinda thing that goes down in horror movies right before the monsters show up," Katarina muttered and lit up a cigarette.

Linda laughed. "Oh, c'mon, you're not going to get all spooked out by some mist?"

Katarina gave Linda her coldest eye and she laughed in response.

"Zombies exist. I think we have the major spook factor covered, huh?"

The Christmas lights blinked on and off, tiny halos of red and green light illuminating the mist.

"Something isn't right. I feel it," Katarina finally answered.

Linda glanced into the mist. "Yeah, I feel it now, too."

Almost as if on cue, the mist parted and at least a dozen zombies staggered into view. Decayed and gruesome, they reached toward the fort wall with low, rumbling moans.

Once again, Katarina was grateful for the wall. "Not too bad a group."

"Bullets or spears?"

"Save the ammo," Katarina decided.

They both grabbed their long spears that were screwed into extensions to ensure their reach. Katarina braced herself against the railing and slid her spear into position.

The first group of zombies looked up and froze at the sight of the lights. They stared with wide glazed eyes, their mouths gaping open as they reached upwards toward the lights. Some of the zombies behind them seemed to be more aggressive and shoved past the ones staring and began to beat against the wall.

Katarina took a breath, ignoring the stench, and began to aim, shoving the spear downwards as hard she could. She killed three of the creatures before a fourth managed to grab the spear. Releasing it instantly, she didn't fight the creature for it.

Whirling about, she reached for another one.

"Katarina, they're pulling back!"

Leaning over the rail, she could see most of the zombies turning slowly back into the mist leaving only three behind staring at the Christmas lights

Katarina stared in shock, blinking, then whispered, "Someone is alive down there. That is the only thing that would make them back off."

"Shit!" Linda pulled out her walkie-talkie. "We have a situation outside the wall. Possible human survivors approaching."

Moving swiftly, Katarina dropped the spear, raised her rifle and dropped the three zombies staring up at the lights. She then hit the spotlight and it lit up the mist like a beacon.

All around the fort, the spotlights switched on. Katarina cursed as nothing became visible except mist. Hopefully whoever was out there would clearly see them now.

The sun broke the horizon, the sky cracked by rays of yellow and pink. The world began to slide from shades of black to gray. Katarina strained to see into the fog, but could see only a few tree limbs beginning to poke through the thick soup.

In the distance, Katarina could hear the rumble of what sounded like an engine. Linda began to swing the spotlight back and forth.

"See anything, Kat?"

"Not yet, but I hear it."

The yapping and barking of what sounded like a pack of dogs began. The moans of the zombies seemed to echo hungrily up from the street below.

"Hello!" Katarina called out.

The dogs began to growl down below.

Travis and Katie appeared out of the fog. "What's going on?"

"Zombies were attacking the wall, but then took off," Linda answered.

"We think someone alive has to be down there," Katarina added

"What's that noise?" Katie asked.

A huge chunk of the mist broke off and floated down the street as the sun's rays began to slowly penetrate the fog. The area they had cleared of buildings was now visible, as was Bowie street that intersected with Morris.

"I'll be damned," Linda whispered.

A huge tractor was slowly coming down Bowie. A strange, cage-like contraption had been welded around the driver's seat. The tractor was towing a flatbed piled high with chicken coops and pet carriers. Attached to that flatbed was another one piled with several bales of hay. Following the bales of hay at an even, slow walk was a small herd of black and white cows. Weaving in and out of the parade was a large pack of dogs of every size and zombies.

It was almost comical to see the zombies trying to get to the tractor through the herd of cows. The undead seemed utterly oblivious to what these moving obstacles were and would bounce back and forth off of them as they struggled to get to the person driving the tractor.

The dogs, even the little Chihuahuas, seemed almost rabid in their hatred of the zombies. They would grab hold of the dead, tearing at them viciously. As the stunned onlookers on the walls of the fort watched, the pack of dogs took down a zombie with primal savagery. When a little terrier walked out of the fray with the thing's head, Katarina began to laugh.

"Calhoun," Travis decided.

"And we thought he was dead!" Katie covered her mouth with her hands, giggling.

"Are you sure?" Linda asked, squinting, trying to see the driver.

"That cage thing's top is covered in foil," Travis pointed out.

"Oh, yeah, it's Calhoun." Linda shook her head. "Old Crazy Calhoun."

A zombie scrambled up onto the side of the tractor and began to shake the cage. It suddenly stiffened, then tumbled over dead. Another zombie, an elderly woman, tripped and fell over a dog and immediately was trampled by the cows.

"I'm going to start picking off the zombies on the outer edge," Katarina decided. There were at least a dozen struggling to get past the dogs and cows to Calhoun.

The sun was higher now, the mist rolling back as the grayish light of dawn filled the streets. The old man seated in the cage erected on the trailer was now visible as Calhoun, complete with a foil jumpsuit and cowboy hat.

Katarina and Linda began to steadily pick off the zombies as the tractor drew near. Calhoun began to slowly turn in front of the wall before the hotel. He noticed the people up on the wall and slowed down to shout up at them.

"Thems here dairy cows for milk and chickens for eggs. Nobody eats 'em or I keep driving," he called out.

Katarina could now see the pet carriers tied to the flatbed trailer were filled with cats. They were snarling and hissing and not too happy.

Meanwhile, the little dog was still dragging around the zombie head while a bigger dog made attempts to steal it away.

"Okay, Calhoun, just get inside," Travis shouted back.

With a salute, Calhoun shifted gears and the parade continued. "Leave that nasty ol' head alone, Pee Wee, and get along little doggie," Calhoun shouted.

The little black dog heard his master, hesitated, then lifted its leg, peed on the zombie head, then trotted after the rest of the dogs.

Katarina thought she would die laughing.

* * * * *

Travis met Calhoun in the courtyard after the old coot successfully managed to get in the gate. The snipers on the walls had picked off the zombies mingling with his herd and all the dogs, cows, chickens, and cats were accounted for to the old man's satisfaction.

"So you went for your animals," Travis decided with a wry smile.

"Yep. Realized feeders were about empty," Calhoun answered.

"I see."

"Figured we need fresh milk and eggs anyway," Calhoun decided. "Keeps your brain sharp against the aliens."

"Yeah, right," Travis said dubiously, staring at the grizzled old man in the foil jumpsuit.

"'sides, army has been circling my farm. Don't need them taking my stuff," Calhoun said in a dire voice. "I don't take kindly to martial law. I didn't vote for that yokel in the White House."

"I think that yokel is dead," Travis answered.

"And leading the messed up clone hordes? Their undead master? Damn! It all makes sense now," Calhoun decided grimly.

"So you saw the army?"

"Saw their helicopter flying around. Told you them folks were up to no good," Calhoun said, and gave Travis a hard look.

"Yes, you did."

"Obeying their Amazonian overlords," Calhoun sighed. "Well, anyway. I'm back."

Travis laughed a little and said, "Yes, yes, you are and we're glad for it. Even though we're going to have to figure out how to deal with the animals now." He looked down at a Chihuahua busy sniffing his foot. "We honestly thought Blanche had killed you."

"That bitch? Hell, no! But she were up to no good right before I left. Did you know she was doing ol' Shane back in the day? I think she got some men sneaking stuff out to her mansion and shit like that. But I've seen her wandering around on the roads, so I guess that plan failed, huh? I think someone dern ate her."

With a grim expression, Travis nodded. "Yeah, probably."

"Almost feel bad for them zombies that ate her. Must have been a bad case of indigestion," Calhoun decided.

2. The Twilight World

Jenni's head hurt.

Rolling onto her side, she felt her brain swim around in her head before settling at a weird, annoying angle. Bill was snoring loudly in the cot next to her and the soft breathing of the others hummed around her.

She couldn't believe she was in a freaking mall. At least the damn mall music wasn't on.

Wiping a tear away, she tried to get comfortable, but it wasn't easy on the hard canvas cot. It was hard for her to believe she was spending another night in this godforsaken place. She missed Juan. Missed him terribly. She missed him with the terrible ache that comes with death or abrupt separation. She knew in her heart he wasn't dead. Somehow she knew he was alive and waiting for her to go home.

Staring up at the high ceiling, she sighed again. The mall's emergency lights were still on and it was annoying. She needed pitch-black to sleep. She needed her Juan next to her, warm and slightly snoring. Again, she shifted on the cot and this time rolled over so that her back was to Bill.

Next to her, on another cot, was Mikey. He was fast asleep, his sweet face that was slowly transitioning from little boy to teenager made her heart beat faster in its innocence.

No, no, Mikey was dead.

Yet, he lay next to her. He was deeply asleep, his mouth hanging slightly open.

She pressed her eyes closed, then re-opened them.

Mikey was still there.

"You see, Jenni, it wasn't you I saved that day on the lawn. It was Mikey. He was crying and staring at the house. I saw him and pulled over," Katie said as she sat down on the edge of Mikey's cot. She looked thin and a little haggard. Her belly wasn't swollen with her pregnancy and she looked like a pale shadow of herself.

"No, it was me," Jenni whispered. "Mikey..Mikey...he was...you know what he was."

Katie sighed and shook her head. "You shoved him out the door and your husband took you instead. You slammed the door shut and it was Mikey I picked up that day."

"No, no. I...I..." Jenni sat up sharply. Her head swam fiercely and she had to steady herself. "He turned back to defend me."

"Mikey told me about his brother, but we didn't know where to find him. Jason died out there at the camp. We found our way here to where my Dad is," Katie continued. "I never met you."

"No, we're best friends! I...I..Mikey..."

"You never met Juan. I never met Travis. I've just been here rotting away with the rest of them, trying to take care of your son and remembering my dead wife."

"No, no," Jenni whispered. She sat up and reached toward Katie. "I didn't push him out the door. I...I...heard him turn back to fight his dad, but I kept running. I...went out the door alone. I didn't save him."

"But this is the outcome you believed should have happened. Mikey alive and you dead." Katie's image blurred a little and for a moment, Jenni saw another form behind it, but just for a second.

The words were true, yet horrifying. Seeing Katie here, not pregnant, without Travis seemed wrong.

"You're not Katie," Jenni whispered. "You're someone else. Something else."

"I'm here to tell you the truth," the form said, now merely a shadow.

"No!" She awoke with a start, gasping, her head feeling like a bobble head. Looking over at the cot next to her, she saw a little girl tucked in with an oversized teddy bear.

Her heart was thudding so hard she could barely stand it. Tears flowed freely as she covered her face with both hands and wept in silence.

She hated the mall. Hated it! It made her feel helpless and it made her think of that horrible day. She should have found a way to save her son. But she hadn't. She had been terrified and had run. She had not once turned back to see if he was behind her.

"It's about second chances," a soft voice said. "Do you understand?"

She looked up to see Lydia sitting at the end of the bed.

"It's about choices made and not made. It's about what we do with our life and the impact we have on others."

"I...ran..."

Lydia nodded. "I know."

"Wasn't Mikey the one who was supposed to survive? Didn't I steal his life from him?"

"Right or wrong, you made a choice that day and because of it you had a second chance to find happiness. To save others. To fight to survive with those who love you. To live a new life."

"With Juan," Jenni whispered.

"To love and be loved," Lydia agreed.

"But why are you here telling me this?" Jenni asked.

"Because very soon, Jenni, you are going to have to make that same choice again."

Jenni shivered so violently, her teeth chattered. She looked up at Lydia. "I know. I have been feeling it."

Lydia nodded. "It's going to be okay. I believe you will make the right choice."

Jenni smiled with relief, crossing herself. "Thank you for telling me that."

Lydia gave her a sweet smile. "Jenni, sleep. You need to rest and heal. The wheels are turning faster. Events are moving quickly toward the moment of decision."

Lying back down, Jenni reached out toward the ghostly woman. "Lydia?"

"Yes, dear."

"Will I make it back to the fort? To see Juan?"

Lydia gently smiled. "Yes, you will."

"Then I am not afraid now."

The ghost's expression became tinged with sadness. "I know, honey. But you will be."

Jenni woke up with a start. She was startled to realize she had been dreaming. The mall was full of light and voices drifted around her. The smell of weak coffee and maybe something close to oatmeal wafted in the air. Sitting up slowly, she looked across the store at all the people gathering in line for breakfast.

Running her hands through her long dark hair, she lowered her head and prayed.

3. John Wayne, the Alamo, and the Republic of Texas

"We have cows," Katie said in a somber tone.

"Yep. We have cows," Nerit answered.

They stood at the guard post overlooking Main Street looking down into the corral that had been thrown up on a cleared lot near the hotel. Safely ensconced in the fort's walls, the cows looked rather comfortable with all the attention they were getting. People were lined up around the roped off area trying to pet them while Calhoun proudly strutted among the small herd.

"And cats," Katie said pointing to a cat walking daintily across the old construction site.

"And dogs," Nerit added. She gave the Chihuahua trying to mate with her boot a dark look. It just grinned up at her and kept going.

"Did we want him back?" Katie asked scrunching up her nose.

"Unfortunately, I think we did."

"We're on crack," Katie decided.

"Absolutely," Nerit answered.

*****

"Calhoun, seriously, I want to talk to you," Travis called out.

"Can't talk...milking," Calhoun answered.

Travis climbed over the rope and pushed between two cows that barely acknowledged his presence.

Calhoun was on a short stool milking away. He was still in his foil suit and smelled of sour milk and sweat. Three cats and two dogs sat patiently on the other side of the cow waiting for their master to send a squirt their way.

Travis had been voted as the one to debrief Calhoun since he didn't trust the "Amazonians." He was having a rough time getting the old timer to talk to him. Calhoun was definitely on his own agenda.

"Calhoun, seriously, we got to talk," Travis repeated drawing near.

Calhoun looked up at him through the long, crazy threads of his busy eyebrows and said, "You wired?"

"By who?"

"That old woman with the devil's eye."

"Nerit?"

"I figured it out. She's the Amazonian queen."

Travis considered this, then shrugged. "Probably, but no, I'm not wired."

"Eh...what do you want to know?" Calhoun asked and shot a cat with a spray of milk.

The cat lapped up the rich milk from its whiskers with relish.

"The army. How long have you known about it?"

"Um, army has been around for a long time," Calhoun answered. "Started back when we fought against the alien overlords that were possessing the English king."

"I mean, recently. The helicopters."

"I TOLD you the government was kidnapping people for cloning. And the clones got fucked up and now they're zombies."

"Do you know where the helicopters were coming from? Which direction maybe?"

Calhoun looked up, studied Travis long and hard and said, "Madison."

"Madison? So they are at the Madison Rescue Center!"

"Yeah. Madison. They're always blathering on the radio to each other."

"The radio?"

"Military channels. I monitor all the time. I will not be caught unaware again!" Calhoun squirted the two dogs. He muttered for a few seconds about zombies, clones, the mayor and the possessed government.

"You've been listening to military channels?" Travis blinked slowly and almost laughed.

"Yep. Madison Mall. They're all holed up in there and some Amazonian overlord is running the whole shabang. She wants the fort so she can buy her way into paradise. Talks all high and mighty to some nitwit out in some place called Central. They keep telling her that they want her to stay put."

"Why doesn't she take a helicopter to Central?"

"Cause they'd shoot her ass down. BAM BAM BAM!" Calhoun made a great show of this happening, complete with a demonstration of how the helicopter would fall to earth. "Zombies would have barbecue. Anyway, she's all sweet talking them, telling them how important she is, trying to do her voodoo. They told that old bitch that the clones follow any kinda vehicle. Car, truck, motorcycle, plane, helicopter and they don't want her dragging stinkbags down on them. I think they got alien spaceships patrolling."

"This Central place?"

"Yeah. Because between the overlord and Central are butt loads of what they call zombies. Messed up clones is what they are."

Travis frowned and said, "Okay, so this Amazonian overload is at this Madison Mall place and she has the military working for her?"

"Something like that. I don't listen too much to her. She's just begging to get out. I just listen so I know where they are gonna be. I don't want them near my stuff. Bad enough dealing with the aliens and the zombie-clones. Don't need to be dealing with the Amazonian overlord's helicopters. I seriously think she has mental powers to control people." Calhoun pointed to his hat made out of foil. "She ain't gonna get me."

"Do they have Jenni?"

"Yep. And Bill. Heard that this morning," Calhoun began to milk with earnest now.

"Bill?" Travis felt a sense of relief, but he knew what that meant for Roger and Felix. His stomach did a slow roll. "Okay. And what are they gonna do with them?"

"Use em as pawns, Travis. What else? Yer kinda slow sometimes. Lucky yer woman is smart. Okay, gotta fix the kiddies chocolate milk now," Calhoun said standing up and snatching up the bucket.

"Anything else to tell me? We've been trying to contact them, but there hasn't been an answer."

"Yep. They are a coming to visit. That's why I brought the animals in.

Figure if we're gonna pull an Alamo might as well have fresh eggs and milk." With a grin, the old codger was off toward the hotel, a trail of kids, dogs and cats behind him. "Y'all should have listened to me when I first told you all this. Now we're gonna have to fight down to the last man."

Travis walked slowly, turning over Calhoun's words in his mind, trying to make sense of them. Katie and Nerit came down from the guard post to walk with him.

"Well?"

"He's plum nuts, Nerit."

"Yes, Travis, but did he say anything enlightening?"

"He says the military is at the Madison Mall like we suspected. He's been monitoring the military channels." Travis hesitated and took Katie's hand gently. "He says it's Bill and Jenni at the mall."

Katie took a deep breath and let it out slowly. Nerit merely nodded her head.

"He says they are going to use them as pawns. He said something about a woman being in charge of the military and the mall and that this woman is trying to get to a place called Central. I'm not sure how much to believe. He sees the world in a really warped way. He's convinced we're about to do another Alamo."

Nerit shrugged. "Maybe. I have a feeling that a lot of what he is telling you is important, just twisted to fit his theory of how the world runs."

Katie shook her head. "Okay, what do we do?"

"I guess get ready for the military to come knocking," Travis decided. "Calhoun says he overhead them talking about coming to see us today. Maybe they're gonna finally answer us."

"And I get to be John Wayne," Nerit decided with a gleam in her eye, but a stoic expression

"Oh, no, no, no, Nerit. I want to be John Wayne," Travis protested.

Nerit considered this. She shook her head. "No. I'm John Wayne."

Katie looked back toward the people gathered to pet the cows. She knew in these moments of ridiculous brevity there was serious concern. They were going to have to take to heart something she had read somewhere that John Wayne had said, "Courage is being scared to death - but saddling up anyway."

They were going to have to saddle up.

Sweeping her hair back from her face, she could only wonder what Bill and Jenni were experiencing in this very moment.

What were their thoughts? Were they saddling up?

Chapter 15

1. Tales of the Madison Mall

J enni poked at the lumpish gray stuff in her bowl that she was certain was supposed to be oatmeal. It looked nothing like oatmeal, though the smell was similar.

"Army food," a woman said sitting down across from her.

Jenni was surprised that someone was talking to her. Everyone the day before seemed to regard her with suspicion. But she was grateful for the company. "Not all that great."

"Makes me really appreciate the army," the lady said with a wry smile. Her eyes flicked to a soldier strolling by in full battle fatigues. "Where did they rescue you from?"

"I wasn't rescued. They kidnapped me," Jenni said with a frown.

The woman blinked in confusion. "Huh?"

Jenni lifted her eyes to truly look at the woman. She was probably a few years older than Jenni, but those had been hard years. She had lank dark blond hair and pale blue eyes.

"We were returning to our fort and this helicopter swooped down and blinded us. We had an accident and woke up here. We were pretty much kidnapped."

"Fort? Do you mean a real fort?"

"Well, more like four blocks of a downtown walled in, but the big hotel is pretty damn nice," Jenni answered.

The woman double-blinked. "Are there lots of people?"

Jenni furrowed her brow. "I think may be close to two-hundred and fifty people now. I'm not real sure."

The woman slowly exhaled. "Wow. We really thought we were the only ones still alive out this way. But why would the army take ya if you weren't in trouble."

"I think whoever runs this place wants the fort. Or at least that is what my friend Bill says."

"Well, damn, that would be the Senator. But then, it has been real tough here," the woman confessed.

"How long have you been here?" Jenni shoved her plate of food away with one hand and tried to eat something that looked like toast.

"Since the first day. We were over at that yonder civic center first. When the news started getting bad, FEMA said to go there. It was a rescue center. At first we didn't pay no attention. It was just crazy talk on the TV, but then this man came and started trying to get in our back door. Troy, my husband, he shouted at the man to get lost, but this guy kept hitting the door. Hitting it so hard he was busting his hands open. We could see it through the window. My kids started screaming. Troy keeps threatening to shoot the guy with the shotgun, but the guy keeps banging and making these noises."

"Oh, God, what did you do?"

"Well, Troy grabs the shotgun off the fridge and opens the door and waves the gun at the guy. But this guy has his guts falling out and he just lunges into the house. Troy shouted for us to run,. So me and the kids run out the front door. Troy runs, too. That guy, the messed up one, falls on his own innards."

Jenni made a face and shivered. "Damn."

"So we get into the truck and Troy is getting into the truck when he sees Mabel, our neighbor running to us. She's got some nasty folks after her. Troy shouts her name and reaches out to her. And she bit his hand! So he cold cocks her one and we see her back is all tore up. He gets into the truck and we hauled ass to the civic center."

"So if the rescue center was the civic center, how'd you end up here?" Jenni was enraptured by the story and reached for another piece of stale toast.

"Soldiers came and got us after FEMA took off."

Jenni mulled this over. "FEMA took off?"

"Yeah. They gave us milk and cookies and told us to sit down in the auditorium. They took the worst of the messed up people into this reception hall or something. I dunno. They said Troy wasn't hurt enough to go back there with the volunteer doctors and nurses. I heard all sorts of rumors that the hospital wasn't taking no more patients." The woman sighed. "We just sat in there and it was real scary. All we heard was gossip and shit. I heard someone was gonna come and give us all shots so we wouldn't get rabid, too. Troy starts getting a fever and the kids were all antsy and it was just plain shitty. Then the damn FEMA people started packing up their stuff and told us that we need to sit tight and wait for the Army to come get us and take us to another place. So they bail and we get stuck in the auditorium just waiting."

A few other people began to draw closer to listen. Jenni became aware of one older black woman vigorously nodding her head. "Oh, yeah. I remember that!"

"So Troy gets sicker and so do some other people. Finally the Army does show up, but it's just a few guys. They start getting on the radio trying to figure out what is going on. One of them comes in saying that the doors to that other room are locked and there are those things in there."

"FEMA just up and left us with a whole bunch of those zombies in that back room. All those doctors and nurses got ate up," the black woman cut in.

Jenni thought back on Katie's decision not to go to the rescue center in Madison and was she ever grateful for her friend's intuition.

"Right, right. So then more soldiers show up, but they are looking for a place to be safe, too. Then a few more. And it gets real clear to us that none of them know what is going on. Then that one guy shows up."

"That handsome Kevin," the black woman put in with a grin.

"Yeah, and he finds out about those things in the back room and he just says that we are all going to the mall. So they load up the old people in the trucks. The soldiers start going and asking people if they are bit or not. And all the bit people are made to go to another room. Including my Troy," the woman took a breath, looking ready to cry. "The kids are crying and it's just bad."

"Uh-huh, real bad," the other woman agreed.

"Well, we got into lines and filed outside. The trucks were taking people back and forth to the mall. It's only like two blocks away, but they wanted us to be safe. You got a ride on a truck, didn't you, Ethel?"

"Thank you, Jesus, yes, or I wouldn't be here today," Ethel answered.

"My kids were crying real hard for their Daddy. We younger folks were the last to go and just as the trucks left with some people, the doors behind us start banging hard. We look and those things are trying to get out of the Civic Center. So the soldiers shouted 'run.' And, girl, we ran."

Ethel nodded her head. "We got into the mall and the soldiers were all shouting and telling us to keep moving. Was bad."

"We were running like crazy down the street. A whole bunch of us with some soldiers. Then those doors got knocked down and those things came running. And everyone was screaming and crying. People were tripping. The soldiers were trying to shoot..." The woman steadied herself emotionally and Ethel took her hand.

"Take a breath, Amy, take a breath," Ethel said softly.

Jenni looked around to see their table was now not only packed with people but others were gathering around to listen. Most were nodding their heads, obviously remembering the horror of the first day.

"And my little boy said, 'Look, Mommy, Daddy is coming, too' and I looked back. It's not my Troy anymore. He is all messed up and screaming. We just keep running and I could barely breathe. One of the soldiers grabbed my kids and just yanked them up into his arms and ran. And I was running hard. And people...started...to fall back...then we could hear them getting...getting...ripped up..."

A big black man leaned forward, taking over the story as Amy sobbed into Ethel's shoulder. "So we made it to the mall and the soldiers were closing the gates the city council had put in to keep vandals from doing graffiti on the mall."

"Probably the only thing they ever did right," someone huffed.

"We just had that one gate to get in and the soldiers were shooting and we just ran, ma'am. We just ran," the black man continued.

"They shoved cars up against the gates to keep them closed and kept those things out," Amy said.

"Later, the helicopters came," the black man added.

"Oh, yes, they were shooting those undead bastards for hours. Almost ran out of ammunition," Ethel added.

"Those soldiers didn't know what they were doing at first," another woman said. "They were scared, too, but once they got it safe and those things weren't getting in, they tried to calm us down.

"Fed us..."

"Got us safe..."

"So this wasn't the rescue center?" Jenni asked. "They just brought you here and made do?"

"Exactly," Ethel said.

"It was real scary. Every time new people showed up to get saved, it was real scary. Lots of shooting. I heard the helicopters went and got more ammunition and soldiers until the National Guard base got taken by the dead things," a middle-aged man said. "And they had to...shoot...the people who got bitten."

Amy, the first woman who started speaking, nodded sadly. "They had to. Cause they'd die and just get right back up."

Jenni's back was a coil of nervous knots. Hearing what these people had been through brought back all her memories of the first day. When Bill touched her back, she jumped, then looked up with relief to see him. He slid onto the bench next to her and looked very solemn.

"So you folks have been here all this time with the soldiers taking care of you?" Bill asked.

"For the first week," Amy answered. "Then the Senator came with her soldiers and that Major General. They made Kevin step down. He did such a good job in the beginning, too. When they came, they brought a lot more zombies with them. They went through the damn town and dragged them down on us."

"So you don't like the Senator?"

Everyone looked nervous now, looking around warily.

An old Mexican woman, probably almost a hundred years old said, "Tonta! Pendeja! Stupid. She makes the Mexicans do the...the...work of the gutter. She don't like us cause she says we're wetbacks. My family has been in Texas since it was Mexico!"

"Total bitch," a woman said who looked like she had been some sort of professional. "She won't talk to any of us. She stays up on the second floor and looks down at us. I know she's behind them doing some sort of weird questionnaire on everyone."

"Yeah. That was kinda weird and scary," Amy agreed.

"Esta tonta! Pendeja! Tocha," the old Hispanic woman muttered.

Jenni giggled, reminded of her own late Mexican grandmother. The woman was on a roll with her insults.

"Things are not good here," Amy said to Jenni. "Not at all. We're all hungry. We're all scared. Nothing is getting better. It only gets worse."

Bill folded his hands on the table and looked at the people gathered around. "The fort has room for everyone here. I just don't think the Senator will let y'all go there and live with us. I think she's gonna try to take over our home, too."

Murmurs of discontent spread through the group.

"Is it really better for y'all? Really?" Amy's expression was hopeful.

Jenni looked around at all the tired, smelly people with their desperate expressions. "Yeah. It is."

The old Mexican woman hit the top of the table with her cane. "Then we go with you. The puta stays here."

Everyone laughed until Bill coughed nervously as the Senator appeared on a walkway above them. Everyone lapsed into silence, a few people drifting away.

"I'm not sure what is going on," Bill said at last, when the Senator walked away. "But I'm sure if we can get you good people to the fort, you are more than welcome there."

Expressions of hope appeared on the faces around them and Jenni looked at Bill nervously. She leaned toward him and whispered, "Bill, how are we going to get all these people there?"

"Dunno...but...damn..they gotta have hope," Bill answered.

Jenni looked up to see the people talking around her and realized that what had been missing since she had arrived was a sense of hope. Now it was spreading like wildfire and the very desperate expressions were giving away to smiles.

"Gotta have hope, Jenni," Bill repeated. "Gotta have hope."

2. Preparing the Way

Travis could always tell when his wife was on edge. She'd stand with her legs slightly apart, arms crossed, one hip shifted to one side, her chin set firmly. Walking into the lobby of the hotel, he saw her posture and thought "crap." Moving up behind her, he looked over her shoulder to see at least fifteen people sitting around on the sofas and love seats, backpacks, suitcases and even pillow cases, all packed up and ready to go.

"Do I want to know?"

"They're waiting for the army to come rescue them," Katie answered in a low voice. "Ingrates."

"Katie," Travis chuckled.

"They are! We risked our asses to go out there and rescue them and this is the thanks we get? Them ditching their chores and sitting around waiting for the army?" Her eyes were flashing with indignation.

"You know," Travis said with a slow smile. "You're kinda sexy when you're feisty."

Katie frowned and narrowed her eyes at him. "Don't make me hurt you."

"Hormones," Nerit whispered walking by.

"I am not hormonal!" Katie said passionately.

Travis grinned and chuckled. "Right."

Katie narrowed her eyes even more and pointed at him with one long finger. "You're just lucky I love you." Turning on her heel, she stomped away.

"Pregnant lady coming through! Step aside!" Calhoun shouted as Katie walked toward the dining room. "She's loaded and dangerous."

Katie flung up her hands at Calhoun before vanishing down the hall.

"She's really cute pregnant," Travis decided to no one in particular.

"I can't believe they're pulling this shit," Curtis said joining him. "There are more coming down the stairs, all excited that the army is going to come rescue them."

"You can't take offense, Curtis. I'm a little peeved, too, but they just hope things are better somewhere else."

"But it's bullshit. After everything we've done for them!" Curtis' young face was scrunched up with his anger. "Rescuing them, bringing them in, giving them shelter, giving them food..."

"We've all done it together. Just some of the latecomers don't realize how much the original group did." Travis tucked his hands into his jacket pockets and watched the little crowd grow larger. He noticed some dark looks among those walking by. This was not going to be a pleasant situation, he realized.

"They're not country folk. They're not used to having to pull it together and keep going. Working together to beat the odds," Curtis said in a low voice.

Looking over the group Travis realized it consisted mostly of people from either larger towns or the city. "Well, I'm from the city and so is Katie and Jenni and a few others."

"Exceptions. They're just lazy," Curtis scoffed.

"Curtis, you're too young to be so bitter," Travis said with a little frown.

Peggy appeared out of the hallway that led to the hotel offices. She was flushed and anxious, "Travis! Travis! The military is calling us back."

"Told you!" Calhoun whooped. "I told you!"

Travis ran across the lobby as the small group of people began to applaud. Curtis threw them a nasty look, then followed Travis into the communication center.

* * * * *

Katie sat down next to Juan's bed and gave him a smile. In her hand she had a bowl of grits, hot and buttery, for him. He had awakened early in the morning and it was her first chance to see him.

"Katie," he whispered in a dry voice. "Anything yet?"

Katie shook her head and stirred the grits slowly. "Not yet. But you know Jenni. She's okay."

Juan looked better than he had, though a bit pale. He sighed and ran a hand over his curls. "I wanted to wake up and see her beside me. I was hoping the stupid shit with that puta shooting me was just a nightmare."

"Blanche was a total bitch," Katie agreed. "And according to Calhoun, a dead stupid bitch."

Juan slightly smiled. "Can't say I feel bad about that."

"Me neither."

"I miss Loca, Katie. I just want her home."

"We're working on that," Katie answered softly. "I miss her, too. I want her back here with us."

"If she doesn't come back, I don't think I can take that," Juan said after a beat.

Katie set the bowl down and took his hand between hers. "Juan, there is one thing I know about Jenni. She will do everything in her power to get home to you. She loves you."

Juan exhaled slowly. "I know. I know. She's just so loca."

"You need to get better so when she does get home she can jump your bones at will," Katie added with a grin.

"She is a horny little loca bitch," Juan conceded with a smile.

Katie grinned and picked up the grits, stirring them again. "So, are ya hungry?"

* * * * *

Jenni watched the handsome black soldier leave with a small entourage. She could see the tension in their faces and suspected they were leaving for the fort. Within minutes she heard one of the helicopters lift off. She sighed, running her hands through her long dark hair.

The people of the mall had definitely seized upon the idea of the fort and their excitement was growing. Jenni couldn't blame them as she heard about the horrors they had endured. All she wanted was to get back to Juan and get back to her life. Sadly, she realized these people had no life since that first terrible day.

Being in the mall was beginning to affect her. She remembered all too vividly the first days she had experienced with Katie. Even worse, she was remembering those first moments on that horrible day.

The horrible gurgling, slurping noises had drawn her to Benji's room after she had wakened Mikey. She had stood in the doorway, horrified at the sight of her husband eating her precious baby boy. Then he had looked up at her, growled, and she had run. She remembered Mikey shouting, "Mom, Mom, Mom!" as she had grabbed his hand and dragged him down the hall with her. She remembered the sound of her husband's feet against the floor behind them.

When had she let go of Mikey's hand?

She wasn't sure.

She remembered vividly the flight down the stairs to the front hall, fumbling with the lock to the front door.

Mikey had still been with her. Hadn't he? Or had he turned back on the stairs?

And then...

She had been on the steps staring down at those tiny fingers under the door...

Jenni pushed her hands through her hair slowly. She couldn't go back and change that horrible morning, but she could do her best to help these people.

But how?

She sighed and sat back to watch some kids running around the chairs, playing games, oblivious to the deadly world beyond the mall.

* * * * *

The zombies stared upwards at the helicopter as it took off. Some continued to slam their rotting, battered hands against the wall, others just continued to moan. As the helicopter angled away from the mall and flew toward the horizon, some zombies turned and began to follow.

3. The Dead World

As the helicopter banked over the dead town of Madison, Kevin gazed down at the streets feeling a sense of dread. Staggering figures reached up desperately toward the helicopter, their fingers closing on empty air. Slowly, the walking dead shambled after the helicopter.

They had anticipated this and planned to turn around out of sight of the zombies toward the fort after reaching the outskirts of town. The dead seemed mindless in their treks after food. Usually, they stood in one place, rooted until they caught sight of the living. Once they started off in the direction of perceived food, they just kept walking.

"It never gets easier to see," Valerie decided. She was seated near him, her gaze also on the world below.

Kevin silently agreed. They had spent a good chunk of the night before curled up together talking about the old days and what they needed to do to make sure there were new days. She was his constant comfort in this world. They had both lost so much in those first few days. Kevin tried not to think of his wife and kids. He knew Valerie struggled not to think of her boyfriend, a mechanic at the base in San Antonio.

They had bonded when she had found him in a service hallway sobbing uncontrollably. After they had secured the mall and managed to feed all the people they had saved from the civic center deathtrap, he had found himself alone for the first time since he had woken next to his wife early that horrible morning. Overcome, he had collapsed. Valerie had come and sat next to him to comfort him.

Looking down, he saw a segment of the highway. This far out of the big cities most of the traffic was the big rigs. There was one rig flipped on its side and a few cars pulled over to the side of the highway. One or two zombies stood staring up at the helicopter. He shuddered, remembering vividly the escape from the city and the clogged highways. This scene was a relief compared to that horror.

The Texas sun was muted by the dark clouds moving into the area. The weather was definitely colder these days. The helicopter began to make its long roundabout turn back toward the fort.

"Do you think they will believe you?"

Kevin looked at Valerie. "I hope so. We can't hold the mall much longer. Supplies are so low right now and the ammunition isn't going to last very long either. That crowd outside only gets bigger every day."

Valerie ran a hand over her skimmed back hair. "The Senator is a crazy ass bitch. She's not going to just let us do this."

"I know."

"There are at least twenty guys who will go along with her. She's promised them a lot and they're desperate," Valerie added.

"I know."

Valerie sighed and he knew she just wanted him to make her promises he wasn't sure he could keep. He decided to anyway, just to make her feel better. "It will be okay. Something will work out."

She smiled slightly at him. He reached out and squeezed her shoulder.

The minutes slid by slowly as the helicopter flew over the dead world. They saw the hotel almost immediately when they crested a hill. It stood tall and imposing over the ranch and farm land. The little town around it wasn't immediately visible, but the red-bricked building was. As the helicopter drew nearer, the town slowly emerged from the trees. They could see the slim farm roads cutting through the countryside.

"Make a pass," Kevin said into his headset. "I want to see it."

The helicopter did a slow turn as they looked down at the now abandoned town. There were dead in the streets, slow and lumbering, moving toward the fort. He hated how the dead seemed to sense where the living were once they were within a certain range. The town's trees were bare of foliage, so it was easy to see the small, old fashioned homes that were nestled in weed ridden yards. The downtown area was not very vast, but most of it seemed to have been reclaimed. A high wall encircled a few blocks of the town and most of the buildings immediately around the wall were now rubble. As they flew over the enclave, Kevin was startled to see what looked like a pasture of cows munching on hay. Some children were running around in the streets, a few were on bikes. As the helicopter roared overhead, the kids looked up and waved.

"We've been instructed to land in front of the hotel," the pilot's voice said in his ear.

As the helicopter flew over the hotel, Valerie whispered in awe, "A pool."

The wall extended in front of the hotel. The block in front of the wall had been cleared and was nothing more than an empty lot now. Slowly, they began to descend just outside of the fort.

"Watch out for zombies," Kevin ordered, even though he knew it wasn't necessary to do so.

Valerie, Kevin and Thomas were the only ones on this expedition. The pilot, Greta, was their fourth. She wasn't too pleased about having to leave the helicopter, but he had promised the leaders of the fort they would all go inside.

Valerie zipped up her jacket and shoved her helmet on her head. Thomas did the same before taking the time to double check his weapons.

As expected, the helicopter drew the dead out and toward them. Some staggered, some crawled, and a few did a weird little skip, but none ran. The older they got, the slower they were.

"I hate this," Greta hissed.

As the rotors slowed, Kevin thought briefly of that zombie movie where a zombie had the top of his head whacked off by the blades.

"I got four on this side," Thomas said.

"I got nine," Valerie responded.

"They should be out here with a vehicle in a few," Kevin assured his people.

Then the zombies began to fall. One by one, a plume of bone and brain exploded out of their heads and they slumped to the ground.

"Snipers?" Valerie looked shocked.

The zombies kept falling and Kevin said, "Shit. Dead on aim."

Greta watched through the window and looked toward Kevin. "Think they got military here?"

"They didn't say anything," Kevin answered.

Another zombie tumbled to the ground as more appeared from the side streets.

"We're drawing a crowd," Valerie said, her voice growing tense.

Suddenly jets of flame exploded up out of the street and sent the zombies into retreat, some of them on fire.

"Fire traps," Thomas said with a grin. "Bad ass."

A civilian version of the Hummer came racing around the corner at top speed. It ran over a few of the crawling zombies then roared up to the helicopter.

"Out," Kevin ordered.

They slid the doors open and leaped to the ground. Racing toward the Hummer, they saw more zombies falling near the edge of the lot. Piling into the Hummer, they sat in amazement as country music flooded their ears.

"Hi," a woman with bright red hair said. "Hold on."

She floored the vehicle and the Hummer flew over the ground, smashing into a few zombies, before the woman whipped the wheel around and headed back toward the hotel.

"My name is Katarina," she said.

The Hummer hit an old man zombie and sent the creature's broken body careening off into a tree.

"First Lieutenant Kevin Reynolds," Kevin said as he held onto the dashboard.

The Hummer turned sharply and slid through an opening in the wall. Kevin briefly glimpsed heavy metal gates beginning to slide closed as they breached the perimeter. A few zombies tried to enter, but jets of flame erupting from the ground sent them fleeing. The Hummer was in a lock of some kind with another set of gates closed in front of them. Once the gates behind them closed, he watched as a man and woman on the wall extended long poles with mirrors on the ends and examined under the Hummer. Satisfied, they signaled and the second gate opened.

"You are all civilians?" Valerie finally asked.

"Except for Nerit," Katarina answered. "She was a sniper for the Israeli army."

Kevin blinked as the gate opened to reveal a large courtyard. A block down, garage doors were open into the bottom half of a building.

A tall handsome man stood with a pregnant blond and an older woman.

Thomas was busy looking around, his mouth slightly open. Greta was still pissed over leaving the helicopter, but was looking a bit more impressed than mad now. Valerie craned her head to look up at the top of the wall.

Katarina slid out of the Hummer and Kevin followed. His crew climbed out behind him and they stood in a small, amazed group looking around.

The man walked over to Kevin and held out his hand. "I'm Travis. Welcome to our home."

Kevin looked around before he slowly took the man's hand. "Kevin Reynolds, glad to be here."

"So, how can we help you?" Travis asked.

Kevin could feel the older woman's eyes studying him intently. He pegged her as former military. She seemed far too keen for a mere civilian. Probably the Israeli sniper.

"I'm here to negotiate. I was sent by my superiors to ask for you to surrender the fort."

The man's face grew solemn and the pregnant woman's eyes narrowed. The older woman just looked calm and deadly.

"But I'm here, on the behalf of the people at the Madison Mall and the men under my command to ask for your permission to relocate here and join your town. My superiors, frankly, can go to hell."

Travis looked surprised, then said, "Well, then, sounds like we got a lot to talk about."

Kevin smiled slightly. "You have no idea."

Chapter 16

1. The Bridging of Words

This world was far different from his own.

As they were escorted out of an area where all the vehicles were maintained and stored in the fort, Kevin could not help but think of the vehicles in the mall's parking lot that could not even venture past the gates where the zombies groaned and wailed. His men would turn on the cars once a week just to make sure the battery didn't die. But here, there was a whole fleet of vehicles that seemed ready to go at a moment's notice.

The only way out of the fort's entry was a staircase that led up over the wall that separated it from the rest of the fort. Levers at the top and bottom of the staircase made it clear the stairs could be collapsed at a moments notice.

"Is this the only way in and out?" Valerie asked.

"When the garage doors are down, yes," the older woman answered. "And those are reinforced."

When Kevin reached the top of the stairs, he found himself looking out over the reclaimed downtown of the small town. He felt tears come into his eyes and fought them back.

All the way from the secured courtyard where the trucks were kept and over the wall into the actual town, Kevin absorbed it all. He noticed how internal walls and gates divided the town up. He took in the guards on the walls and the construction workers. Children ran in the streets, shouting and laughing. Old people sat in a gazebo enjoying the cool air and warm sun. Young people were walking down a sidewalk outside of an old movie theater, talking and sipping sodas. The marquee read "Family Night Tuesday Night. Monster's Inc and Shrek Double Feature." A pack of dogs ran around playing, yelping and carrying on as a cat sat calmly in the sun cleaning its paw.

As they walked, people stopped to look at the soldiers. A few people waved, others just stared. An old man, with navy tattoos covering his arms, gave them a salute. Kevin saluted back.

"Are you going to kill all the zombies, mister?" a little boy called out. He was playing with toy soldiers in the dirt.

"We're working on it," Kevin answered.

They walked past the back of city hall where a woman stood with a little boy, watching them suspiciously. The hotel loomed large and imposing. When they entered, he glimpsed a young couple was kissing in a corner. On the wall was a hand drawn poster announcing "Disco Night Friday Night."

This was far removed the mall and he felt a lump in his throat.

A large chalkboard in the hallway announced lunch as "Egg Sandwiches, homestyle fries, and chocolate milk shakes."

"Eggs," Thomas gasped behind Kevin.

Nothing in this world was similar to his. His world was near starvation, mindless tasks to keep people moving, children dying of the flu, and zombies moaning endlessly outside the walls of the mall. It was power struggles. It was hell.

To his surprise, a group of people was seated in the hotel lobby with their luggage around them. When they saw him, they all rose to their feet and began to applaud.

"What the hell is this?" Valerie muttered.

A middle-aged man rushed over. Kevin saw in his peripheral vision Travis sigh and rub his brow in embarrassment.

"It is so good to see you! We are ready to go! We have all our things," the man said in a torrent of words as he grabbed Kevin's hand.

"Um...why?" Kevin looked at the man clutching his hand and shaking it vigorously.

The man blinked and his grip lessened. "Why what?"

"Why are you ready to go?"

"Yeah. And where to?" Valerie tilted her head and looked at the man curiously.

"To go to your base, of course. Away from here!"

The soldiers laughed and Kevin patted the man's shoulder. "Trust me. You don't want to leave here. You don't want to go to where I came from."

The people looked confused and began to whisper among themselves. Then an older black woman said loudly, "We want to go where it's safer!"

"Ma'am, this is about as safe as you are going to get. Trust me. This is heaven compared to where I came from." Kevin turned toward Travis and the blond woman and saw amused expressions on their faces. "Trust me, they don't want to go there."

Travis led him down a hall, past the check-in desk, and into a large office that most likely had belonged to the hotel manager. There was a young man in a police officer uniform waiting along with a man that looked every inch the city official. The woman, who had stood outside of city hall looking suspiciously at them, came around from behind Kevin and took a seat. Travis motioned to the soldiers to sit down as he sat on the edge of the desk. The blond woman slid onto the desk next to him, her legs dangling, watching all of them curiously.

A little nervously, Kevin and his people took up seats in the creaky leather chairs, feeling awkward in their helmets and body armor. Kevin took off his helmet and the others followed his example. Next to him, Valerie shoved her weapon under her chair.

"My name is Nerit," the older woman said. "And this is Katarina. We head up the fort security."

"I'm Peggy. The fort secretary. I deal with making sure the people here are comfortable."

"Curtis, I'm the last cop from the town's force. I assist in law enforcement. Bill usually works with me on that."

"Eric, fort planner and engineer," the well-dressed man said.

"Juan De La Torre is in charge of construction, but he is recovering right now in our clinic," Travis said. "Katie, my wife, serves on the fort council. I'm Travis, the Mayor."

"First Lieutenant Kevin Reynolds," Kevin answered. "I have been serving at the Madison Mall Rescue Center since the first day."

"Valerie. I don't think my rank means much anymore," Valerie, the perpetual smart-ass, said with a grin.

"Thomas. I was a Private," Thomas said with a slight wave.

"Greta. That's my copter out there," came the surly response from the redhead.

"We're taking care of it," Nerit assured her.

Travis had his arms folded across his chest and looked very thoughtful. "So, what can we do for you folks?"

"Like I said, we were ordered to come here and demand you surrender the fort to our superiors. But we can't agree with that." Kevin sighed wearily.

"And why are we supposed to believe you?" Katie arched an eyebrow.

Kevin pulled out a letter from his jacket. "This is from Police Chief Bruce Kiel. He was told his daughter is still alive and here at the fort. If she reads this, she'll be able to vouch that what I am saying is true."

The blond woman's face paled and she reached for the letter. "Give that to me."

Travis reached out to lay a calming hand on her shoulder as Kevin handed over the folded bit of paper.

"You're Katie Kiel?"

"Yes," she answered, and unfolded it quickly. She let out a gasp as the familiar handwriting came into view. Covering her mouth with one trembling hand, she read quickly. Tears shimmered in her eyes and she handed the letter to her husband in silence. Travis bundled her up in his arms and read the letter over her shoulder.

"Katie-girl, It's me, Dad. I'm alive and safe in the Madison Mall. Safe for now at least. Your friends Jenni and Bill told me you are alive and doing very well in the fort they came from. They tell me that you are even married and have a little one on the way. It makes me very happy to hear you are okay. I have lived these last months in sheer terror that you died with the rest of the world. Senator Brightman is in charge at the mall and wants your fort. Don't let her have it. The way she treats people is despicable. I would never want her to have any say in your life or the lives of the people around you. Especially in the life of your baby. Listen to Kevin. He's a good guy and know that what he says is the truth. Love you, baby. Your Dad." Travis finished and kissed Katie's forehead, holding her close. She was sobbing loudly and openly with relief.

Nerit stood up and Travis handed her the note. She looked it over. "It is good to know that ones we love survived."

Kevin lowered his gaze. So far, he had not found one survivor of his former life. His family was long gone and he knew it. That is why he wanted to make sure these good people and the people at the mall had a chance.

"So what do you have to tell us?" Travis finally asked.

Looking up, Kevin saw all eyes were on him. He felt old and tired, but knew he had to press on. Where should he start? What should he say?

"I guess I should start at the beginning," Kevin finally said as the images of the first day horror unfolded in his mind and his hand slightly shook as he ran it over the top of his head.

"I woke up next to my wife with the phone ringing. We were being mobilized to deal with civic unrest. Of course, what I didn't know then, was that it was the last day of everything..."

2. Kevin's Story

He opted not to tell them how he had reluctantly climbed out of his bed to dress as his wife sat on the edge of the bed talking to him softly in a sad voice. He had just returned from overseas and she had hoped he could make a normal life with his family. There had been plans to see his son play basketball in the early evening followed by dinner at their favorite barbecue dive. Of course, that would never happen.

Instead he had found himself rushing to make it to the base. He took the time to open the doors to the bedrooms of his three children one by one. Trying hard to control his emotions, he tried not to remember how their skin and hair felt under his touch as he had kissed them goodbye as they slept. He had left his home for the last time, promising his wife that he would contact her as soon as he could. He would never speak to her again.

The briefing at the base had been quick and his orders simple. At a truck stop near a small town a riot had broken out. The local police and sheriff had responded, but were overwhelmed. The military was being sent in to quell the violence and bring it under control. There were rumors it was one of many riots breaking out in the pre-dawn hours in the country.

The convoy of trucks had departed the base, the headlights sluicing through the darkness like a blade. Looking back, Kevin had to admit he had seen some odd things as they traveled out into the hills. At one point he saw two people running down a street at such a quick pace he had thought they must be training for some sort of sprinting event. Now he wondered if they were running to or from something.

By the time they had arrived at the truck stop, which was a small city unto itself, they found a scene out of hell. Vehicles were smashed into each other, one truck was overturned, and a fire was spreading inside of the restaurant. But what was worse was the human carnage. There were dead people everywhere, but they weren't lying down. Instead, to his horror, they were running about. As soon as the convoy came into view, it was rushed.

Those minutes were a blur. The sound of weapons being fired, screams, growls, and the horrible chewing sounds filled his ears. Blood had sprayed through the air and he had to wipe it from his face mask. Somehow, they managed to tear a swath of destruction through the horde of undead. But mostly, they only damaged them enough to slow them down. Finally someone had shouted to aim for the head. It wasn't until that moment that Kevin fully realized what they were dealing with. He had seen the armless man running toward him and the woman with an empty chest cavity ripping the eyes out of a soldier, but it had not fully hit him until then.

The soldiers swept through the truck stop, guns firing, bullets ripping apart heads, blood and gore splashing over the pavement and sides of trucks like gruesome artwork. There had been losses as men fell under the onslaught of the zombies. Once they realized what they were up against, the soldiers were more methodical and soon they stood wearily triumphant among the truly dead.

The true horror started when the wounded soldiers suddenly attacked the living. Kevin had fired four bullets into the face of one of his best friends to keep him from attacking him. It was then he discovered a bite was lethal.

Reporting in, Kevin found himself defending what he had seen. Finally, he was told to help the National Guard in the nearby city at the downtown rescue center. As he sat in his truck, covered in blood, his men waiting for his orders, he looked up to see the sun rising over the hills.

Little did he or his superiors realize that the world was already dead.

They had traveled along the back roads toward the city, occasionally stopping to eliminate any zombies or any infected they ran across. Now he realized it was fruitless to eliminate all the bitten, but at the time they had tried to do their best. The number of undead was probably overwhelming at that point, but they didn't know that.

Looking at Katie as he spoke, he recognized her as the woman he had seen with the German Shepard. The two women with their dog in the big white truck had impressed him that morning. They both looked so shell-shocked yet determined to survive. He remembered petting the dog and thinking briefly of his family. He had told them to go to the Madison Rescue Center. Yes, there had been others much closer in the area, but that one seemed the farthest away and therefore, possibly the safest.

When the convoy had reached the city, it was like entering the gates of hell. The trucks had barreled through snarled traffic, run over raging zombies, smashed through barricades, all in an attempt to save the living. They had reached the police station just as it was overrun. The police chief and some of his surviving men had leaped from the roof of the police station onto the back of one of the trucks. It was terrifying to see how few people survived. They had met up with what remained of the National Guard and made an attempt to get out of the city. Nearly half of their vehicles and men were lost when waves of zombies filled the roads.

Shattered, overwhelmed, and near panic, the soldiers had fled into the hills. A few had jumped ship at the first sight of an abandoned car to try to go rescue their families. It was tempting to do in the face of so much horror, but Kevin knew their efforts were fruitless. He understood what those men and women did not.

The world was dead. Their families were dead. His own family would have taken refuge in the hospital where his wife worked. There was no hope for them, but he could try to save others.

He had let those soldiers go. The world was ending and every man and woman deserved to make a choice as to their own fate.

So those who remained followed him into the hills. They found their way to Madison, driving through dying towns, and watching with weary eyes as the zombies followed the trucks howling. Bullets had struck down the walking dead, but nothing could alleviate the pain the soldiers felt.

It was the most bitter of any defeat.

They had found the Rescue Center abandoned by FEMA, a few military survivors and townspeople inside, and a locked door in the back barely holding back a horde of undead. Kevin had made the choice to get the people to the mall. All the businesses were closed due to the outbreak spreading so fast so it seemed like a secure location. The high wall around the mall provided them a chance to hold back the undead.

He had stood at the gate of the parking lot and watched the last group of people running from the civic center with the zombie horde behind them. In his mind, he could still hear his voice shouting orders as he watched the slowest of the survivors be dragged down and consumed. It was a terrible sight, but each person who fell bought a little more time for the ones still running. When the survivors were all inside and the gates shut, Kevin had looked through the bars at the undead snarling at him. He had felt all hope leave him, but he was determined to do his best for the survivors.

For a week he had run the mall as best he could. The surviving soldiers worked hard to secure the mall and keep the zombie population down. Other survivors showed up on occasion and sometimes successfully made it to safety. More often than not, they were torn apart trying to scale the high walls into the mall parking lot. The National Guard helicopters arrived the second day and managed to airlift supplies and ammunition until the National Guard base was overrun.

He had felt as though he was on the edge of losing his mind. Working hard and keeping focused on what needed to be done kept him from thinking about his family. But at times, he would find himself alone weeping until he felt he would die of the pain.

A week later, the Senator showed up with the retired Major General. The Major General carried orders from the President giving him the power to run the FEMA rescue stations in the area. Kevin had stepped aside, not knowing what else to do. He was at a loss how to run a rescue station or how to keep things running. Or so he had thought at the time. Now he wished he had never relinquished authority. The Major General obviously had his eye on a political career and wanted to be in good standing with the Senator. Kevin just wanted the people to be safe.

When he told the fort leaders of the Senator's plans, he saw his own horror reflected in their faces. He told them honestly about her disregard for the survivors and her regard of them as "assets." He was brutally honest about her ambitions. It felt good to speak of her so harshly.

It was hard not to cry, remembering what he had seen, but he knew they had all seen their share of horrors. When he finished telling his story, his voice low, his eyes full of tears. He could see that that the people in the room believed him by the tears in their eyes.

"I just want to do what is right," Kevin finished. "I want to give those people a good home. I failed them once. I don't want to fail them again."

"And you won't," Travis promised him. "Let's bring your people home."

3. A Terrible Thing

Katie stood holding her father's letter in her hand, listening to Kevin tell his horrible story, her fingers slowly tracing the edges of the paper. Her tears were dry now, but she felt them close at hand.

It was too wonderful and too miraculous to fully accept that her father was still alive and yet, she held a piece of paper with his easily recognizable scrawl covering it.

Looking up, she could see the weariness in Kevin's face. The months in the mall had probably aged him a bit. She didn't think he was actually as old as he appeared. His shoulders were stooped slightly as if with the great burden of protecting those people in the mall weighed them down. The other soldiers had a weary look about them as well.

"I appreciate this more than you know. We are getting low on ammunition and the gates won't hold forever against the zombies," Kevin said.

"The crowd gets a little bigger everyday," Valerie added.

"For awhile we would thin them, but ammunition became an issue when the National Guard armory fell to the dead," Kevin continued. "So we've been holding the line up until now."

"Did you consider trying to get the people out before now?" Nerit asked.

"Honestly, yes. I talked to the Major General and Senator Brightman. The Senator told me to make sure the zombies didn't get in and that was the end of that. Every time we went out for rescue with the helicopters, we'd try to find a new location, but nothing was really workable."

"Zombies are thick the closer you get to the cities," Greta agreed. "We stopped trying to even go within seventy miles of any of the major cities."

"The bigger towns are just as bad. Most of our rescues have been from small towns," Kevin said with a weary sigh. "We knew supplies would become an issue soon, so we sent out scavenging raids. We lost people when we went east, so we started coming out this way, west. That is when we realized someone had been there before us. We found this one group in a grocery store making a meth lab in the back. They were seriously messed up. We interrogated their leader. He is the one who told us about the fort. He said his group had tried to join yours, but had been refused. That you had attacked them instead of helping them."

"The bandits," Curtis hissed.

"We could tell his story was fishy, but the minute the Senator heard about the fort, things became very intense. She's been trying to get her free pass to the compound where the President and the remaining government are ensconced. Her goal was to make the mall seem like an asset to the President so that we would receive more assistance. But it was clear to me that the powers that be considered us a lost cause. But the fort changed that. With the farmland and ranches around here and the lower population of undead, this area is now seen as a viable supply outpost. The Senator is determined to take over and implement some FEMA plan." Kevin shook his head. "When you realize that your superiors see the surviving human population as assets, that is when you know that the country has truly fallen. She even came up with some crazy invasion plan that had us invading the fort to seize control."

"So what do you suggest we do?" Katie asked. "Don't you think the

Senator will try to block you coming here."

"She probably has about twenty military people on her side. They're scared. They want out. Some of them are from East Texas. I think they are hoping to find their families. Desperate times bring out the fear in the best of people. She'll try to stop us, but we have more military on our side."

Travis sighed. "Will her side respond with violence?"

Valerie and Kevin exchanged glances.

Thomas laughed. "If they're stupid they will. C'mon. This place is heaven compared to the stinking shithole we're in."

"It doesn't mean they will be able to switch allegiances that easily," Nerit said softly. "People have a tough time admitting when they are wrong."

"The reality is that the mall is full of desperate, terrified people, supplies are running low, and the zombies outside are growing in number. Nobody is in their right mind," Kevin said. "I feel on the edge of insanity every day."

"Which means there could be a forceful response to your request to relocate the mall population," Nerit decided. "They could panic seeing their own ticket out being removed."

"Tensions are high, ma'am," Kevin said softly. "I won't lie. The people are restless. Scared. The Senator is a determined woman. Ruthless. She has no regard for the people. They are statistics in her plans. That's all."

"If there is any sort of gunfire, innocent people may be hurt," Katarina sighed.

"And chaos could follow. It could get dangerous real fast," Eric agreed.

Katie took a deep breath. Her father was alive and trapped. She wanted him here, with her. She wanted to see him meet Travis and love him as he had once loved Lydia. She wanted to see her father hold her child in his arms. She wanted Jenni and Bill home. She wanted Jenni at her side when she gave birth. She wanted her family to be whole again.

"I'll go and speak with her," Katie said at last.

"What?" Travis looked at her startled.

"I was a prosecutor and leader of the debate team in college. I can be very persuasive. I will speak to the Senator and Major General and make them see that the fort is open to everyone as long as they are willing to work hard to keep this place safe and a decent place to live."

"Katie," Travis whispered.

"I can do it. I can make her and her supporters at least see the possibility. So that there won't be bloodshed or death. I may personally despise the woman, trust me, I know her, but if this is all that remains of the American dream and Texas independence, then we should at least give her the option to see the truth. Besides, if the President is really, truly alive in East Texas, then maybe we can find a way to open communication and figure out what the hell happened and what the future holds."

Everyone was staring at her, taking in her words.

"The Senator did ask me to return with the fort leader for negotiations for the turnover," Kevin said finally.

Katie felt her jaw set and knew her eyes were determined. "I can talk to her. I have argued her into corners before. I had the displeasure of meeting her at more than one dinner party. She had a real issue with me being married to a woman and I argued her into a corner on that subject," Katie said in a low, terse voice. "I can face her again."

This comment elicited raised eyebrows and looks of curiosity, but Katie didn't care.

Travis kissed her temple softly Travis's lips were warm against her skin and she looked up into his eyes. He smiled sadly down at her. "Okay, then I go, too." He immediately turned and pointed at Nerit. "And you are not stopping me this time!"

Nerit inclined her head. "I agree with you. This time."

Katie smiled at him and kissed him lightly. His body was tense and she knew he wanted to argue with her, but she loved that he respected her enough not to.

"So if the Senator says yes and there is a horde of zombies outside of the mall, how do we get the people out?" Curtis was looking very uncomfortable with everything going on and his foot was rapidly tapping the floor.

"Airlift. We got three other helicopters other than my bird," Greta answered.

"We've been using an abandoned commercial airstrip for refueling. We cleared out the zombies and have been refueling there regularly," Kevin explained. "It will take a lot of trips, but it would be the safest. We do have explosives on all the gates out of the mall, but if we do that, there is a good chance of the last part of the convoy being overrun."

"We can coordinate and figure out how to make the airlift work then," Nerit assured Kevin. "As long as the helicopters don't pull in any zombie mobs, we can run regular pickups out to the helicopters to pick up the people."

"Sounds like a plan," Travis said in a low voice. " A workable, needs to be fine-tuned plan."

The tension in the room had dissipated and now there was a sense of tentative camaraderie. It would be rough bringing everyone here, Katie knew that, but they could do it. And perhaps they could use the Senator's contacts within the East Texas compound to their advantage.

Travis rubbed Katie's back gently as she leaned into him. She loved him so much, but it was time for her to do what she did best. Beyond that, she felt a great need to go to the mall. She wanted to see what had happened there and see her father. She wanted to bring him home as well as Jenni. The thought of both of them trapped there made her feel sick to her stomach.

"We should get to planning then," Nerit decided.

Kevin nodded. "Absolutely."

Calhoun burst into the room, wide-eyed, jabbering, and wielding his camera. With a scream that made Katie jump, Calhoun raced toward Kevin, his hands stretched out.

Valerie swung her rifle out from under her chair, rose easily to her feet, and nailed the old man with a sharp crack to the forehead. Calhoun fell back, blood running down his face, the camera falling to the floor. Thomas aimed his revolver at Calhoun's head and everyone heard the safety snap off.

Everyone began shouting as chaos erupted.

Nerit calmly stepped in front of Thomas, blocking Calhoun. "Stand down."

"It's a fucking zombie," Thomas shouted at her.

"...damn clones..." Calhoun muttered.

"He's just a crazy old man!" Katarina had her gun pointed at Thomas. "Stand down!"

"He looks like a fucking zombie," Valerie protested.

"Do zombies talk?" Katie stepped forward and she felt Travis holding her arm, making sure she didn't rush forward.

"...Government set them free...Amazonian conspiracy...gawdamn aliens..." Calhoun was saying in a low voice as he lay on the floor.

Kevin gently pushed the weapons down that his people had trained on the old man. "He smells dead."

"But he's not," Nerit assured them. "He's just crazy."

Thomas and Valerie slowly relaxed, looking confused.

"Curtis, get Charlotte," Travis ordered. "I think he's hurt pretty bad."

Katie leaned down and moved the broken camera out of the way. Gently, cautiously, she touched the old man's matted hair. "Calhoun?"

His eyes, dazed and filled with blood, glanced toward her. "...they are hiding secrets...aliens...you know...and clones...and my head hurts real bad."

"Sorry," Valerie said uneasily.

"I think it's broken..." Calhoun whispered and his eyes rolled up.

"Stop the bleeding," Nerit ordered as she pulled a small pillow from a chair and handed it to Katie.

"He looked like a zombie," Thomas said softly.

"Shit," Kevin muttered.

Calhoun lay silent, blood seeping into the carpet around him.

Chapter 17

1. Entering the Parlor

This is hell, Jenni thought as she walked through the mall after a few hours of scrubbing toilets and sinks with five other ladies. The mall stank of human sweat and fear. Despite all the cleaning they did, personal hygiene was not a luxury the common people enjoyed. According to one of the ladies she had been working with, only a few showers existed in the mall and most of them were upstairs where the Senator and her entourage lived. The two showers on the main level were rigidly scheduled and each person was allowed a two minute shower every four days.

She felt nasty and raw, but according to the schedule, she wasn't to have a shower for another two days.

The mall was a weird design. Its bottom floor was v-shaped with a long corridor connecting the two sides of the v halfway to form an "A." The crossing corridor was the food court and public area, complete with a two-story waterfall that fell into a pool of water. Jenni had already been told the waterfall was off limits. It was seen as a reserve water source. Considering how little water they were given, she wondered why it wasn't being used yet.

As she entered the food court, she saw people sitting down silently eating their rations. It looked like beans with bits of hot dog was the meal. A few kids were running around in the playscape near the waterfall, but otherwise, the scene was depressing. Soon after the news of the fort had spread, other news had countered it. Word was out that the Senator was seizing control of the fort. Hope had slowly sizzled out of everyone.

An enormous skylight let in the outside light and illuminated the area. She noticed a crisscross of catwalks that sprawled over the entire court. What looked like a fire escape-like metal stairway snaked up the back wall and over the empty fast food stalls.

She fell in behind other people waiting for food and let her hair down from its ponytail. After a few minutes in line, she was handed her bowl of beans and wieners and headed over to sit with Bill. He was eating slowly, watching the children with a sad look on his face.

"They're just waiting to die," he said as she sat down.

"Aren't we all?" she answered a tad flippantly.

"No, not really. At the fort we were actually living. You and Juan together. Katie pregnant. Folks do things like movie nights and special dance nights. We actually live." Bill spooned more food into his mouth and chewed.

"True," Jenni admitted. She shook her head a little to clear her thoughts. Without Juan and Katie, it had grown easier for her to hide inside herself and disassociate from her surroundings. Much to her distaste, she was reverting to the old, quiet Jenni who waited for her husband to unleash on her. Except now, she was waiting for something very wrong to go down. The Senator scared her shitless. Every time the attractive, yet imposing woman appeared looking down at the main floor, Jenni felt her skin crawl.

"No, no, you're right. We are different at the fort," she admitted. "We actually are living. This is just existing. It's not right."

Bill sighed. "I was gonna ask Katarina out to disco night. I actually asked her out for a beer when we got back from the hospital."

"Really?" Jenni grinned at him. "Good for you!"

"I felt kinda guilty at first liking her. My wife died a year ago, so..." Bill shrugged. "You know what I mean."

Jenni actually didn't, but she nodded anyway. She felt no remorse about her relationship with Juan or any guilt. But then again, she had pretty much hated her husband.

"But I figure that in this world, you gotta just take your chance at happiness. So I got up the guts to do that. Besides, I guess we are all walking around with some survivor guilt. I feel it now. Looking at these people. I mean the fort hasn't been a cake walk, but we sure as hell had it better than these folks."

Jenni slowly ate, looking at the people around her. They were muted. Shadows. People powered down and living on what remained of their energy.

"This rumor about the Senator taking over the fort," Jenni started slowly as she stirred her meal.

"I bet it's real. It won't happen though. Can't. Notice how the high and mightys live up on the second floor? That shit won't work with us. I can't see it happening."

"The military though," Jenni said softly.

Bill sighed softly. "I know."

They fell into silence for a few minutes, eating slowly.

"Since coming here, I have been thinking a lot about the first day," Jenni said at last.

Bill looked at her curiously.

"My children died," Jenni said, her gaze straying to the playground where too-thin kids played with stifled energy. "I didn't fight to save my son Mikey. I just ran. I can't explain what I was thinking, I just ran. I wanted to get away, survive. I know that much. But I ended up outside of my house, with the front door closed and Mikey..."

Bill touched her hand gently, trying to soothe her.

"I heard him die, Bill. I heard it. I heard him screaming 'Mommy' and I didn't go back in." There she had said it. Admitted it. She had admitted it to herself and someone else. It felt like something large, inky, and horrible broke inside her.

"There is nothing you could have done," Bill said softly.

Jenni tried hard not to cry as she ran her hand over her long hair. "I know that, but I didn't even try. I didn't know what was even happening, but when I heard those horrible noises, I didn't move. I just stood there." She looked around at the people, noting that Amy sat nearby with her children eating. "How can I possibly ever make up for that?'

"You've gone out and rescued people. You've done a lot."

Jenni sighed, wiping a tear away. "I just...Bill, maybe this is survivor's guilt, but sometimes, especially now, I feel I should be the one who died."

Bill enfolded her in a big bear hug, holding her tightly. "Jenni, you're a good girl. You've done lots of brave things. Just because you didn't act the way you wished you had that doesn't make you a bad person. Hell, it's damn lucky any of us are alive. It all went to shit so fast."

Jenni snuggled into Bill's warm shoulder and whispered back, "I just feel so guilty."

"Well, don't. You got a fine boy waiting for you back at the fort and Juan loves you something awful. We'll get the hell out of here and get these people to a good life. You deserve it as much as anyone." Bill gave her a gruff kiss on the cheek and let her go.

Jenni forced a smile, looking around. "I even feel kinda guilty for having been at the fort and not here."

Bill frowned at her. "Jenni, stop that."

Jenni pouted at him then said, "Seriously, Bill. What if I was supposed to die that day? What does that say about my life now?"

"That you got a second chance." Bill shook his head. "Or maybe you were supposed to survive that day so you could help rescue all these people."

Jenni considered this. "You think so?" Her dream returned vividly to her mind.

"Why not? If destiny...fate...whatever has anything to do with our lives, then maybe this is what you were supposed to live to do."

Thinking back on her dream about Lydia, Jenni remembered what she had said about choices made and not made. She was Catholic. She believed in things greater than herself. She believed in the mysteries of the spiritual, therefore, she truly believed Lydia had come to her.

Lydia had said she would soon be afraid and she was now very afraid. She could feel the great clock of fate ticking downward. She knew soon she would face a difficult choice. She hoped she would make the right one and that she would get back to Juan and Jason.

"I guess you're right. I mean...I made the choice to leave home at seventeen and move in with my grandma. I made the choice to work at Pizza Hut where I met Lloyd. I was married and pregnant with Mikey at eighteen. Was a friendless trophy wife for years. And then it all went to hell. I screamed. Katie found me...then...It's kinda like all these choices I made just..." Jenni waved her hand. "They landed me here."

"To save these folks maybe." Bill shrugged. "Kinda weird seeing all that coming together, huh?"

"I just hope we can get these people to a better life," Jenni said with a sigh.

"We just got the military and zombies standing in our way," Bill decided. "Piece of cake."

As they finished eating, they heard the sound of the helicopter returning. Its shadow filled the food court as it flew over the enormous skylight, then it settled down somewhere beyond the mall's walls.

Jenni stood up to turn in her bowl and spoon to the cleanup crew. She saw movement out of the corner of her eye. Turning, Jenni saw the handsome black soldier walking in with a few other people. The bowl and spoon clattered to the floor when she saw Katie and Travis among them.

"Katie!"

Jenni pushed past people and rushed toward her friend. Katie saw her, called out her name and pulled away from Travis. Like some stupid movie, they ran to each other and flung their arms around each other. Katie squeezed her so tight Jenni could hardly breathe. Pressing kisses to her best friend's cheek, Jenni felt her tears falling down her face, hot and fierce.

Then Travis was there, hugging her tight, kissing her cheek while Bill bear hugged Katie and lifted her off the ground. They fell into a sort of four-way hug, tears and laughter spilling out of all of them.

"Juan, how is he?" Jenni asked.

"He's fine," Travis answered with a grin

Jenni started to sob with relief as Travis kissed her forehead firmly.

"What are you doing here?" she demanded. "It sucks here!"

Katie slid her hand gently over Jenni's cheek, smiling at her softly. "We came to take you guys home."

"And everyone else here," Travis added.

"We're game," Bill exclaimed. "Tell us what to do!"

Jenni became aware of Kevin and the other soldiers watching them and felt a little uncomfortable.

"They're with us," Katie assured Jenni, drawing her close again.

Jenni snuggled into her best friend's arms, trusting her. For the first time since she entered the mall, she felt a sense of hope.

2. The Spider and the Fly

Those around him would make decisions, Lydia had said, and it could lead to their death.

Travis sat solemnly beside Katie in the food court as they waited for Kevin to return with the Senator. Lydia's words echoed in his mind as he gently stroked the back of his wife's neck. Her decision to come to the mall had terrified him, but somehow he knew the moment he had read her father's letter that she would come here. One of the things he loved about Katie was her strength. He had to respect that no matter how difficult.

She looked at him with her clear, beautiful green eyes and smiled at him reassuringly. He smiled back at her and kissed her temple.

Jenni sat on the other side of Katie. Their fingers were intertwined as they sat hip to hip, watching the escalator Kevin had taken to the upper floor. Travis was relieved to see that Jenni and Bill were still alive. Not that he didn't mourn the passing of Roger and Felix, but in this world it was hard to not feel relieved when those closest to you survived.

Behind them the waterfall rumbled and roared. The rushing of the water sounded comforting. Kevin had briefly explained that the waterfall was constantly recycling its own water. It was their reserve water supply. The mall was on rationed water because a recon mission over the water treatment plant showed severe damage to the facility. There was uncertainty as to how long water would continue to flow or even if it was pure. Soon after the survivors had arrived at the mall, half the children and elderly died from a high fever and flu-like symptoms. All the water given to the people in the mall was now boiled before it was passed out. Even bathing was limited.

Kevin had also solved the mystery of the power at the fort never going down. Evidently a crew was manning the power station with the mall running regular supplies out to them. It was a reminder that the fort was not as cut off as they had originally thought.

The people of the mall kept stealing looks at them. Others just stared openly. Though several people seemed to be working hard at mopping, he noted they were actually spending more time watching them.

The light spilling through the enormous skylight above was somewhat comforting. All the mall doorways were blacked out. Travis supposed it was to keep the people from seeing the hordes of zombies outside. He had been horrified when he had seen the sheer number. How the soldiers had kept them at bay so long was beyond him. As the helicopter had swung over the mall, he had felt his chest tighten with fear. He had gripped Katie's hand even tighter.

He madly loved her and their baby growing in her womb. They were his life and he realized he would do anything to protect them. Yet, here they were, at the mall, and his rationale not to fight with Katie over her decision was based on his dream about Lydia.

He wasn't sure if it was the wisest thing to put stock in a dream about a ghost, but somehow he believed it had revealed a vital truth.

"It's so rough here," Jenni said to Katie. "There was no hope before Bill and I told them about the fort. FEMA just abandoned them at the rescue center and the Senator is a total bitch."

"Yeah, I know. I've met her more than once. She plays the political game very well, but after three glasses of wine, she made it pretty clear how bigoted she can be. Of course, that was back when she was just a city council member. She gave me hell over Lydia," Katie answered. "She had a real issue with 'special rights' for gays as she put it. She couldn't see that we just wanted the same rights as everyone else."

"She's a total bigot. She makes the Mexicans go and do chores outside. See that guy over there. His name is Miguel. He told me that she said in English in front of him that the Mexicans shouldn't get any assistance since they are not American citizens. The Major General overruled her since the Mexicans do chores too, but then she stuck them outside. She's such an idiot. She didn't realize Miguel is Texas born and speaks fluent English. She treats all the Hispanics like border jumpers." Jenni made a face and shook her head. "Like even that should make a difference."

Bill leaned in. "Nothing here is right. It's a hellhole."

Katie sighed. "I wish Dad would come down. I want to see he is doing okay."

"I'm sure he will come see you as soon as he hears you are here," Travis assured her.

Katie smiled anxiously. "I know, I just want to see him."

At the top of the escalator a throng of suited men and a woman appeared. Everyone was in drab colors except the Senator who was dressed in a bright red coatdress. Her blond hair fluffed around her head. She descended with a large smile on her face. Travis noted that the woman was wearing diamonds in her ears and they flashed as she moved.

Slowly, he stood up, Katie rising as well. Jenni reluctantly stood, but Bill remained seated.

"Welcome to the Madison Mall Rescue Center," the Senator said. She walked up to them, extending her hand. "I'm Senator Paige Brightman."

"Travis Buchanan and my wife, Katie," Travis answered, shaking her hand briefly. It felt dry and cold.

"Katie?" The Senator raised a thin eyebrow. "Katie Kiel?" She laughed a bright, amused smile. "I see you came back to the other side of the fence."

Travis could literally feel Katie's cold anger rising like a wave.

"My wife died the first day," Katie answered tersely.

"Oh, I see. I'm sorry," the Senator answered in a tone that Travis pegged as false. She looked toward Travis and gave him a wink. "But you found a strapping handsome man I see."

He could see Katie's eyes glittering with anger and unexpected tears. He took her hand gently to soothe her.

"And I was lucky enough to find a wonderful woman who has a heart open enough to love without discrimination," Travis responded.

The Senator raised both eyebrows and laughed. "Or there just weren't any other lesbians around, huh?"

"My personal life is not at issue here, Senator," Katie said coldly.

"No, no, it's not. But it is a shame about Lydia. She was one of the best interior designers in Texas."

Travis tightened his grip on Katie's hand to keep her from punching the Senator.

A tall man, with white hair and an imposing face, pushed through the Senator's entourage closely followed by Kevin. Silently, without a word, he shoved the Senator aside and gathered Katie up into his arms.

"Dad," Katie whispered. The tears that had threatened to spill before now streamed down her face. "Dad."

The white haired man, who Travis now realized was Bruce Kiel, kissed Katie's cheek and held her tightly. "Katie-girl, it's so good to see you." Despite his very intimidating exterior, the man was weeping.

"Dad, I can't believe you're here," Katie said in a happy voice and kissed his cheek.

"I'm so sorry about Lydia, baby," Bruce said.

"I know, Dad," Katie answered. She reached out to grab Travis' arm. "I want you to meet Travis, Dad. He's my husband now."

There are moments you wonder about. Where will you find your life mate? How will you know it's her? How will you feel when you meet her family? Jenni, his sort of sister in law, had been hard enough to deal with at times, but when Bruce Kiel fastened ice blue eyes on Travis it scared him almost shitless. Then the stern man smiled, took his hand and pumped it in a handshake.

"Good to meet you, son," Bruce said in his deep voice. "If Katie chose you, you have to be one helluva person. She's a connoisseur of the best people."

"It is a pleasure to meet you and find out that you survived," Travis answered, feeling a bit overwhelmed.

"And see, she's having a baby!" Jenni couldn't keep out of it any longer and patted Katie's swelling belly.

Bruce grinned and put his hand gently on his daughter's stomach. "I'm thrilled, Katie."

His wife's smile was rapturous. Travis felt pleased and awkward at the same time to be in the presence of her father and what remained of her former life. He suddenly felt nervous about how he compared to Lydia and wondered what Bruce thought of him.

"Not to interrupt such a wonderful family reunion," the Senator said in her Texas drawl, "but there are certain matters of great importance to be discussed."

Bruce looked toward Kevin. The black man slightly inclined his head and stepped closer to Travis.

"Okay. Where should we all talk? My daughter is here, so let's get to it."

A crowd of people were now gathering and the Senator gave then her best campaign smile. "Why don't we go upstairs to my office. The Major General is waiting for us."

Travis watched Kevin anxiously. There was tension in the other man's face and Travis could feel his own nerves twitching. The time was growing near.

"Very well," Katie said. "Let's get this over with."

"Agreed," the Senator agreed. "Let's go into my office."

"..said the spider to the fly," Jenni whispered from behind Travis and a chill flowed down his back.

3. Showdown

As Katie walked up the frozen escalator, she could feel the eyes of the hundred or so people gathered in the corridor below staring up at her. The irony of the rescue center being a mall made her smile slightly. And of course, Kevin was a black hero. Romero would be proud.

That she was a blond, pregnant woman was also amusing to her. But unlike the heroine of Dawn of the Dead, she was a former prosecutor that had no issue stepping up to the plate. She would not stand by and wait for the men to make the difficult choices. Add in that she was bisexual and she was pretty much blowing the stereotype.

She loved that.

Katie could see the strain in Travis' face and knew he was worried sick. Every time she looked at him, his gaze seemed to wrap around her protectively. She loved him and he loved her. That gave her strength. Strangely, Lydia being brought up by the Senator had given her strength as well. The memory of her wife made her feel more determined and strong. There was no way she was going to let the Senator enslave these people. They deserved a chance to have a good life. A chance Lydia never had.

She caught sight of her own reflection in a mirror set into the side of a storefront. She saw that her jaw was set and her gaze determined. Her blond curls fell in a tumble to her shoulders and her swollen belly rounded out her green sweater. She looked flushed and strong. That made her smile a bit more.

Entering the office behind the Senator, she saw a military man seated behind the desk. He vacated his spot to the Senator and Katie remembered that Kevin had pegged this man as someone who had joined the military to enhance his political resume. The Senator took her seat as her smarmy campaign manager took up his place behind her chair.

Kevin entered and sat down in a chair, his expression strained. Jenni and Bill had wanted to come as well, but only Travis had been allowed to accompany her. Her Dad also was allowed into the meeting. He gave her an encouraging smile as he sat next to Kevin. Travis leaned back against the closed door, his arms folded over his chest, his gaze encouraging.

The office was small, but not at all cozy. She took a breath, readying herself.

The Senator crossed her legs and rested her folded hands on her lap. "Let us get down to business. I take it you are speaking for the fort, Katie?"

"Consider me their ambassador," she answered.

"Very well, ambassador. We will be relocating to the fort immediately. I expect for you to have the Governor's Suite ready for us," the Senator started. "I want a meeting with the fort's former leadership for an in-depth debriefing within an hour of my arrival."

Katie arched her eyebrow. " I see."

"You all will then be instructed in our plans for the fort and be given directions on how we will go about establishing the fort as a supply depot to the President's enclave known as Central. Each and every person will be expected to do their part in our plan to create a strong, working force."

"I see." Katie repeated, raising her other eyebrow.

"We will expect full cooperation on all levels. The Major General will oversee all security matters with the assistance of the First Lieutenant. I would also like an armed escort dispatched to check on my sister, Blanche Mann, at her estate. Unless she is already in your fort." The Senator tilted her head. "Is she?"

"She was," Katie answered. "Until she shot a man and killed two others. Now, she is most likely staggering through the countryside."

"What?" The Senator rose sharply to her feet.

"Oh, and about your plans," Katie said blithely. "Fold them five ways and shove them up your ass." She heard her Dad and husband laugh at this and her smile grew larger. Diplomacy be damned. She was pissed off.

"Excuse me?" The Senator looked shocked to be spoken to in such a way. She probably was since she was accustomed to people kissing her ass.

"We are not giving up the fort. I'm here to inform you that the people of Madison Mall are welcome there. We are more than willing to take them in. We have enough supplies to last until summer and hopefully by then we will be growing our own food. Now, if you want to come as well, you will need to realize we are working hard on building a community based on respect of the individual and what each can contribute to our society."

"What the hell are you talking about?" The Senator looked confused and glanced sharply toward her campaign manager. Raleigh looked just as shocked as she did.

"We are determined to give people a chance to have a good life. If they don't agree with the concepts of hard work, loyalty, and the basic ideals of the US Constitution, they can leave."

"You will not tell me how to live my life," the Senator snapped.

"Oh, but you can tell us?"

"I am an elected official. That is my job! To make the hard decisions that you cannot," the Senator retorted. She came around the desk in a streak of red.

Katie didn't back up as she was sure the Senator expected her to, but crossed her arms under her breasts. She could feel the curve of her belly under them and felt even stronger.

"I am in charge here! I make the hard choices for the people!"

"You see, that is where you are mistaken. You're supposed to represent the people who elected you and help them by not hampering their lives. And that is what you want to do. Kevin showed us your plans. You call people assets! Breeders! You estimate how many of us can die and not be considered a liability to your plans."

The Senator shot a venomous look at Kevin. "You were supposed to convince them to turn over the fort."

Kevin stood up slowly. "I went and told them your plans so they wouldn't."

"Excuse me?" The Senator looked completely shocked.

"First Lieutenant Reynolds, how dare you defy a direct order?" The Major General rose to his feet heavily, looking furious.

"Easily. I realized it meant making the people surviving in this mall into slaves." Kevin stood with his chin up, his eyes blazing.

"Slaves?" The Senator barked a sharp, sarcastic laugh. "They are the future of this country! They need to be guided firmly and not left to their own devices or else we are going to be doomed."

"Our fort is much better off than this mall, Senator. We are just common people trying to survive in this new world and make a life for ourselves," Katie retorted.

"And doing a better job at it than we are," Kevin added.

"How long before your people fall into chaos without proper and experienced leadership? Let's be frank here. You have no clue what you are doing and you will need me to guide you. The civilians of this country have proven they can barely take care of themselves. Why do you think there are so many social programs to assist them? They have no idea how to make good, solid choices for themselves." The Senator's voice had gone very quiet and persuasive. It was the voice she was famous for during debates.

"Bullshit," Katie answered angrily. So much for her persuasive prosecutor approach. "You are completely underestimating the people who helped build this country."

"You will turn over the fort per the orders of the President of the United States," the Major General said in a firm voice.

Bruce Kiel shook his head. "There is no more United States. Don't you see that? It's fallen and all that remains are pockets of survivors that will do what they must to survive. Some will become animals but others will rise above. You've been making choices for everyone here and now it's time for us to start making choices for ourselves."

"If people want to stay here, then they can. But we are offering them a chance to come to the fort," Katie continued. "If you want to stay here, that is your choice. But you can come with us. You will just be one of many. You will have to find a way to make yourself useful and that doesn't mean trying to tell the rest of us what to do out of a false sense of superiority."

The Senator laughed and shook her head. "You are completely delusional. You actually think those sheep out there will follow you? I have proven myself as a leader of this State. I am an elected official. I know damn well how to lead people who are unable to even lead themselves."

Her campaign manager was wincing. Katie thought it was rather amusing. She supposed he still tended to think about popularity polls and campaign rhetoric.

"I think you're wrong. I know you're wrong. And I know this ridiculous plan you have to establish a totalitarian form of government is utter bullshit and doomed to fail."

"Government and the law bring order to the people. Without us they don't know how to think or act for themselves. Only the educated and the powerful truly understand the full dynamics of what it takes to run a society."

Katie shook her head. It shocked her to realize the Senator fully believed what she was saying. "You know what. I'm not here to debate politics. I'm here to tell you how it is. We are not turning over the fort and we are not going to follow your orders. Your rule is over. And we are leaving with whoever wants to go with us."

"My men will not follow you into mutiny, First Lieutenant," the Major General said, pushing out his chin, trying to look fierce. His eyes strayed to the woman who promised him power and guidance. His weakness was evident.

"They will and they are," Kevin answered. "We're done here and frankly, sir, you are disgrace to the uniform you wear. The minute you fell into bed with this woman you lost your right to order any of us."

The Senator's mouth opened in shock. "Well, I never-'"

"Oh, please," Katie said with the roll of her eyes.

"The worst thing I ever did was turn over the mall to you. I should have trusted myself. I learned my lesson. I'm leaving and taking these people and my men with me," Kevin said in a firm voice.

"There is no room for debate on this," Travis added. "We're taking these people home."

"We're done here," Katie said firmly. "We're leaving in the morning. We'll spend the rest of the evening organizing the people for the airlift. You are welcome, despite your bitchiness, to join us. But if you do, remember, you will be just another member of our little fort."

The Senator leaned back against her desk, smirking. "We'll see."

Turning around, Katie looked at her father, Travis and Kevin. The three men were all looking quite serious, but Kevin slightly smiled at her.

"Paige, you just can't let them do this," the Major General said in a low voice.

"Try to stop us," Katie answered.

Travis opened the door, and they left without a backward glance.

Chapter 18

1. The Last Hours

The afternoon was harder work than any of them had fully anticipated. Kevin made the announcement over the intercom system that anyone wanting to move to the fort and have a new way of life was to line up in the food court to be registered for the airlift. A few people had laughed when they heard Valerie's voice whisper: "And tell them the Senator won't be in charge." Kevin had then hastily added that sentiment.

The line had formed immediately. Jenni and Katie had found themselves scrambling to get organized.

Families were to register in one notebook. Elderly singles in another. Orphans in another. Singles in the last.

Jenni carefully translated for the immigrants that were confused and promised them that they were not going to be reduced to non-citizens. Meanwhile, Katie kept assuring the elderly that they would be taken care of and the helicopter ride wouldn't be all that bad.

"Child, after nearly having to run from those damn zombies, that helicopter will be like a ride to heaven," Ethel had assured her.

Travis and Kevin spoke with the soldiers that filed in from outside to make sure their allegiance was known. Most of them were relieved at the prospect of something more stable than the mall. They were weary and rundown. They had been keeping the zombies at bay for months with no chance of relief or to mourn all that they had lost. It had been hard and some men and women had broken. There were five soldiers that had disappeared over the last few months. It was tempting to try to make a break for it and try to make it home. But the zombie threat was all too real beyond the walls and too much of a risk if you were in your right mind.

But then again, who was truly in their right mind anymore?

"Jenni, I really do wanna make sure my kids and I get on the same helicopter, okay?" Amy's face was drawn with concern as she sat to write down her name and those of her kids. "Losing their Daddy like they did was so hard and I don't want them to think they're alone."

Jenni looked up to see a little boy with thick, straight bangs staring at her with the biggest chocolate brown eyes she had ever seen. She couldn't help but smile. The boy's older sisters were both blondes with eyes the color of the morning sea. All three were holding hands and the oldest girl, around eight, was holding her mother's shirt firmly in one hand.

"Don't worry. We want to make sure to keep families together if we can," Jenni assured her.

Amy scrunched up her face and sighed. "Just so hard, Jenni. Having faith again. After all that went down at the civic center and here."

Jenni leaned toward Amy and took her hand gently. "It'll be okay. I promise. Your kids are gonna get a good life. Okay? And somewhere far from here."

Amy forced a smile and clutched Jenni's hand. "Okay. I believe you."

With a smile, Jenni reached out and ruffled the little boy's hair. "You're going to have a big adventure tomorrow."

He just stared at her, blinking those huge dark eyes.

"He doesn't talk no more. Not since his Daddy died," Amy said softly.

Jenni sighed. "I understand. It's not easy." She thought of her own kids and brushed her hair back from her face, trying to regain her composure.

Amy stood and gathered her kids around her. "Thanks for doing this, Jenni. We needed it. Bad."

"Guadalupe Garcia," the old Mexican woman said to Katie. She wielded her cane like a sword. "Let the puta stay here and die."

With a laugh, Katie wrote down the woman's name. "Well, she can come along if she promises to behave."

Mumbling in Spanish, the old woman gave Katie a hard stare.

"Not that I think she will come along," Katie assured her.

"She won't give up control. She'll do something. That is her way. She's not a good person," Guadalupe said firmly.

"I know," Katie said softly. "I know."

The announcement from the Senator came about an hour before dinner.

"I realize that many of you have chosen to depart for the fort. This is understandable since you are desperate to escape the zombie scourge and the conditions here have not been easy. But what you need to consider is that you may be exchanging one haven you are not completely happy with for one that is in a worse condition. The reason why I want to take over the fort is to ensure that all the surviving citizens of this great State and this great Country are given a fair and equal chance to fulfill their patriotic duty. To ensure that all the citizens of this mall and the fort have strong and capable leadership in the coming years. I have worked hard for this State and its people. I am an experienced and strong leader. I believe in this country and its people. I know that this has been a rough time for all of us, but help me appeal to the fledgling leaders of the fort and help them see that true leadership will be best for all of us. I am in contact with the President and what remains of our government. They care about what happens to you and they have assured me that they will do all they can to assist us once we are at the fort."

"So why aren't they helping us now," Guadalupe said loudly, waving her cane at the nearest speaker

A few people laughed as the Senator's voice droned on.

"...together, unified, we can withstand all that comes against us. Do not give up hope. America will rise again and the President and the remains of the government are dedicated to helping you."

More laughter.

Jenni rolled her eyes.

Bill just shook his head.

"Come stand with me. Come to the top floor and let the leaders of the fort see that you want a strong, powerful new home. To be part of the rebuilding of America and the great state of Texas. Come, join me, and let's begin a new world together."

There were murmurs from the people crowded down on the first floor. A few people made jokes, others looked serious. No one seemed anxious to join the Senator.

"I think this is a pretty good answer," Katie said after ten minutes and still no one had attempted to go upstairs.

Travis just looked somber, his arms folded across his chest. He could see soldiers on the second floor, patrolling the escalators. It was still uncertain if those men would do anything to hinder them. Kevin had explained to him that the Senator had made grandiose promises to all the soldiers. A few were still holding on. It was hard to let go of the hope that somehow you would find your family and friends alive. Travis understood that far too well. Beyond that, some people found it hard to give up their faith in the old institutions. It was hard for some people to stop believing in their superiors.

At around eight PM, Kevin finally decided to see if the Senator had reconsidered joining them peacefully or if she was going to stay behind. He and Valerie started up the escalator, both of them bone weary and just wanting the day to be over.

"She won't come with us,' Valerie said softly. "She's too proud."

"It doesn't seem right somehow to just leave them here," Kevin answered, his eyes on the men at the top of the escalator.

"I have no problem leaving her here," Valerie assured him. She looked back over the people in the mall. There was excitement in their voices and people were carefully packing just one bag to take with them to the fort. "She'll just fuck things up at the fort."

They were almost to the top when one of the National Guardsmen came into view. He was from East Texas and determined to get there, one way or the other. Snapping off his weapon's safety, he aimed at Kevin and Valerie.

"Go back down," he said firmly.

"We're just coming to ask the Senator to come with us," Kevin answered.

"You made your choice. Now go back down," the man repeated.

"Ben," Valerie said softly.

"I said go back down. I have no problem shooting either one of you."

Kevin could see from the look in the man's eye that he meant it.

"Okay," he said softly. "Okay." Turning, he calmly walked back down the moving stairs to the main floor, Valerie close at his side.

"Told you," Valerie said.

"Yeah, I know." Kevin sighed. "We did our best."

* * * * *

Katie and Jenni shoved Jenni and Bill's cots into the corner of the store and set about inflating an air mattress for Katie and Travis to sleep on.

"I can't wait to get back to Juan tomorrow," Jenni said as she fluffed a pillow.

"Sorry you have to wait until tomorrow." Katie frowned as she sat on the air mattress, tucking her hair behind her ears. "But with the fuel being limited and all that."

"I understand. Hell, I'm not too happy about you and Travis being here tonight. It sucks here," Jenni flopped onto her cot and tucked her hands behind her neck.

"It feels a lot different from the fort," Katie conceded.

"It was worse before the people began to have hopes about the fort. It was very gloomy. Everyone just waiting around for something bad to happen." Jenni rubbed the tip of her nose and exhaled. "The atmosphere is a lot more claustrophobic. It feels like the first day never ended here."

"Yeah. That's it. That is the feeling." Katie looked around the store. "That is exactly how it feels. Like we should be out on the road running away from the city."

"About to find Ralph and Nerit at the gun store." Jenni rolled onto her side. "Do you have any regrets about the first day?"

Katie returned her gaze to Jenni's face, nodding. "Oh, yeah. Two actually. I just don't like talking about it. It seems fruitless. Useless."

"You don't have to tell me," Jenni assured her, reaching out to touch her hand.

"I really haven't told this to anyone. I haven't even thought about it too much." Katie rubbed her shoulder as she searched for words. "The morning it all went to hell, I was getting into my car. Lydia and I had just kissed goodbye and she was drinking her morning coffee. We were talking about our plans for the night and we noticed, through the trees and bushes lining our front yard, that our neighbor was stumbling up the walk to his front door. He was always getting trashed with his business buddies and coming home in the morning. We saw him fall over a bush then get up and start banging on the huge plate glass window they had in the front of their house. We laughed about it and I told Lydia I'd see her later. I drove off."

Jenni's mouth formed an "o" as she understood what Katie was telling her. "The neighbor..."

"I think she went over to see if he was okay. I saw him when I went home after being attacked. He was attacking the mail man, too." Katie shoved her hair back from her face, holding her head, her eyes unfocused as she remembered the painful moment. "That is my second regret. I didn't kill the zombie Lydia had become. I didn't give her peace."

Gripping Katie's hand tightly, Jenni kissed her fingers. "I think you gave her more peace than you know. I think she's okay. In fact, I dreamed about her a few nights ago."

Katie arched an eyebrow. "Really?"

"Yeah, she was telling me that I had to make some hard choices soon."

Jenni didn't think Katie's eyes could widen anymore than they were. "Really?"

"Yeah, why?"

"Travis dreamed about her and she said something really similar."

This didn't surprise Jenni. She was now convinced that she was fulfilling her destiny in a way she did not understand. The mall had forced her to face some terrible demons from her past, but now she had laid them to rest. She couldn't live with guilt or regret or fear. Fear had stolen too many precious opportunities from her as it was. She now realized that what she had been running from was exactly what she needed to confront. For the first time since the zombies rose, she felt sane. She felt solid inside of her own mind. No, she was not the Jenni that existed before she married that wife-abusing asshole, but she also wasn't the abused housewife anymore. She wasn't even the loca zombie killer, trying to get revenge against the dead for the death of her family. Strangely, she now realized after a few days in the mall that she was more than the sum total of her life's heartbreaks and torments. Looking into the faces of the people around her, she accepted that she was stronger than she ever realized and the choices she made had to be her own. She could no longer let life just sweep her along.

"What is it, Jenni? You look odd."

"I'm okay. Probably better than I have been in a long time," Jenni answered. "I figured a lot out while here. Seeing what could have been, pondering what could have happened. I've been in loca mode so much since it all went down, I don't think it ever hit me that maybe I am still alive because my life is important in some way I don't understand." She fingered the rosary around her neck. Juan's mother had given it to her before she had left for the hospital. "Do you ever feel that way?"

Katie smiled slightly. "I always felt I was supposed to save you. That it was my destiny. Or maybe just a way to keep me focused so I would survive that first day."

"My grandmother always told me that God had a plan for everyone's life. I don't think I really believed her until now. But then again, I don't think the world was supposed to die. I don't think that was God, but man. I think we did it."

"Probably." Katie twirled her wedding ring around her finger thoughtfully. "Lydia was a Buddhist. I was raised Methodist. We didn't get into a lot of spiritual talks, but we did agree that this life is precious and that we need to do our best, be our best in this lifetime. When I saw she was dead, I felt so lost. And then I heard you scream. And there you were. I could save you. And by saving you, I saved myself."

Jenni took Katie's hands gently in her own. "We're saving these people tomorrow and in a way I think we're saving ourselves. We're making a new world for all of us."

"It won't be easy," Katie reminded her.

"Nah, but it will be the right thing." Jenni grinned and kissed her friend's hands again. Pressing her cheek against Katie's palms, she closed her eyes, sighing. "I like that. Doing the right thing."

Katie smiled down at her. "It's the only thing we can do."

Pulling away and lying down on her cot, Jenni sighed with contentment. "I can't wait to see Juan tomorrow. I want him to see I'm okay now. No more fear. No more regrets. I'm okay now." The thought of telling him those words made her smile. "Tomorrow will be a beautiful day."

* * * * *

Outside, the moon rose. The pale white light flowed over the undead gathered around the mall, smashing their hands against the once white wall now a mottled black and dark red. Inside, the moonlight poured through the mall skylights washing over the sleeping forms of the people tucked away inside.

2. Exit the Wickedest Woman in Texas

In the gray dawn, the Senator and her people quietly walked down the employee staircase to the floor below. One of her guards swung the double doors open and she stepped out in front of the blacked out doors that were the main entrance of the mall. She stood at the pinnacle of the top of the "A" shape of the mall and smiled to herself.

"Sure about this?" Raleigh asked.

"Very sure," she answered.

The Major General was awkwardly absent, but she had explained he had second thoughts and had chosen to remain behind. In reality, they had fallen into a horrible row and she had shot him through the head without a second thought. She didn't have time for his bullshit.

The painted blackened door swung open and the low moan of the zombies beyond the wall filled her ears for a moment. One of her men entered, looking flushed and anxious.

"Okay, the guards are neutralized. We got two trucks pulled from the side parking lot. I don't think we were spotted."

"Good," the Senator said with a smile. "Well done."

"We should pull the guards in," the soldier continued. "So they won't get killed."

"Excellent point. Pull them inside," the Senator responded with a big smile.

Raleigh was fidgeting, staring down the darkened mall corridor toward the silent stores where the people slept. "If we blow the front gate..."

"The zombies can't get in. And besides, the two sides are blocked off. It'll be fine," the Senator assured him.

The mall parking lot was a trapezoid with the main entrance at the narrowest end. This gate had never been a major concern since the gate was solid metal and locked securely. The three gates in the parking lot behind the mall were more of a concern because they were wrought iron and had to be fortified with vehicles and heavily barricaded. The two narrow side parking lots had been blocked off as a preventative measure in case of a breach. It was thought they should try to keep the zombies contained on one side of the mall and escape through the other. Transports had been parked along the side of the mall in the front. Buses and transports and regular cars were on the other. All the gates were wired with explosives. Additional explosives had been tossed out on a line and their triggers were next to the interior of the gate. The idea was to blow the gate then the explosives out in the crowd of zombie to clear a path.

"I would really hate for these people to end up dead," Raleigh said after a beat.

"I didn't know you were such a bleeding heart," the Senator teased him lightly. She watched as her men dragged in the unconscious guards from the main gate and laid them on the floor.

"Just none of this feels right," Raleigh decided. He shook his head, gazing at the guards.

"They made their choice," the Senator said, her eyes hard. "In one month we would have been out of food and the water is contaminated. Without the fort there is no point in us staying here."

"There should have been another way. This seems too risky."

"Do you want to go to Central or not? Or do you want to go to the fort and be led by the hicks?"

Raleigh frowned, then shook his head. "I just want us out of here."

"We'll get control of the fort. At some point they'll be begging Central for help and we'll have to go and save them."

"Yeah. Yeah. You're right." He looked around nervously, his hands shaking slightly.

She always thought he was way too skittish. He was good at the campaign, but he liked to be apart from the process, ensconced in his privileged world. He hated dealing with the people that were behind his carefully monitored statistics and polls. The Senator didn't care much for the people either. She was in politics for two reasons: power and the knowledge that the peons really didn't know how the hell to take care of themselves. Without the government, she knew they would fall into chaos.

Mistakes had been made here. That was true. But she learned from her mistakes and she would move on. Once at Central, she would make sure the President understood her giving nature and her determination to stand with him and rebuild America.

"Ma'am, you ready?"

She flashed her perfect beautiful smile at the soldier in front of her. "Yes, sir. I am."

He opened the door for her and she walked out to the waiting truck.

* * * * *

"You're here for a reason," Lydia's voice whispered.

Katie forced her eyes open.

Her dead wife sat on the floor next to the air bed she was sharing with Travis.

"Lydia?" Katie sat up, the mattress rippling like a wave under her.

"Hello, darling."

"Lydia!" Katie stumbled to her knees and flung her arms around her wife. She could feel the softness of Lydia's curves beneath the long black jersey dress and her long dangling earrings tickled Katie's cheek. "I'm so sorry! I'm so sorry. I didn't make it home in time!"

Lydia drew back and kissed Katie softly. "It's all right, Katie. I promise."

"I'm so sorry." As Lydia gently wiped her tears away, Katie gazed at her, pleading with her gaze for forgiveness.

"Katie, it's all right. I'm not trapped in that body. I promise. And my death...I barely recall it. But, darling, listen to me. Listen carefully. There isn't much time now."

Katie blinked, her hands resting on Lydia's shoulders. "What is it? I'm listening."

"You came here for a reason," Lydia started.

"To save these people," Katie answered.

"No. For another reason. You don't know what it is yet, but you will when the time comes." Lydia's expression was filled with sadness.

"Lydia, you're scaring me. I don't understand."

"When the time comes, you will know what to do."

"What do you mean? Why are you telling me this?" Katie's brow furrowed. Fear welled up inside her.

"Because, you will give the one you love the gift you never gave me," Lydia answered .

Katie woke up with a start. Travis was deeply asleep beside her, his back to her. Shivering, she pressed herself up against him, her hand seeking out his. Her heart was thundering in her chest and she was terrified. Her gaze swept over the people in the boutique. Everyone was sleeping despite the excitement of the coming exodus from the mall.

Finally, she forced her eyes to close, her arm snaking around Travis' waist. She clung to him, her heart still beating hard in her chest. He rolled onto his back in his sleep, his face tranquil. Snuggling into his side, she stared at his profile, trying to calm herself. It had been wonderful to dream of Lydia, but her words had shaken Katie.

It may have been a dream, but she felt strongly that Lydia warned her. She did not want to even think about something terrible happening to Travis.

Beyond her husband, she could see Jenni curled up in a ball on the cot next to them, snoring softly. Her friend's black hair fell around her pale face. Jenni looked like Snow White with her white skin and raven hair. Her red sweater set off her looks beautifully.

Closing her eyes, her heart still thudding in her ears, she tried to sleep.

* * * * *

The gate slid open soundlessly and the explosive detonated with a loud thump. Flames erupted, setting the zombies near the gate on fire. They staggered back, setting more zombies on fire and a small stampede followed as the primitive fear of fire sent the undead scrambling backwards. The secondary explosives, that had been tossed out on a line, also exploded, setting more zombies on fire. The two trucks roared out of the gate and down the street, crunching burning zombies under the tire treads.

The Senator looked out her window at the mall and the burning zombies.

"I hope the doors hold," Raleigh said softly.

"I'm sure they will," the Senator answered.

The trucks roared into the gray dawn.

3. The Floodgates Open

Thomas jerked his head up when he heard a distant thud. The zombies at the wall were instantly whipped up into a frenzy. Some of them stumbled toward the sound, while others quieted down and continued to stare at the barricades and moan.

"Did you hear that?" he asked the soldier next to him.

The young private with the shocking red hair tilted his head. "Yeah. What the hell was that?"

They both looked toward the direction of the noise. The mall rose up in front of them, imposing and silent with its blacked out doors.

Thomas looked over the huge back parking lot with its many vehicles and National Guard helicopters. "Something is wrong."

* * * * *

The first zombies staggered cautiously past the remains of their burning comrades and into the wide drive in front of the mall. Huge white letters over the front doors read "Madison Mall," but none of the zombies looked up. They staggered to the front doors and began to claw at them. Some instinct deep in their reptilian brain told them that food lay beyond the doors.

Struggling to get to the doors, the zombies jostled each other, their masticated limbs sometimes breaking off. Pushing and shoving, the first wave of the zombie horde struggled to get to the doors.

The doors did not give, but blocked the dead outside securely. Desperate for food, the zombies clawed and pounded on the doors.

In the melee, one zombie stumbled into the bright blue button sticking out from the side of the door. The white outline of a person in a wheelchair was on the button. Long ago, in the first days of the mall, all the doors had been secured and the key copies were used by the guards on duty. But someone had forgotten the handicap door. It had stood unlocked all this time.

Now, the button was pushed.

The handicap door opened silently.

Several zombies immediately lurched through the opening and into the mall corridor beyond.

* * * * *

Poor Robert. He lived his life in obscurity. No one ever noticed him. No one seemed to ever see him. He had nothing to set him apart. He would never be known for anything special.

Even his death that morning would never be noted as the first causality in the mall.

He was dragged down on his way to the bathroom. So blinded by sleep, he had not even noticed the decaying man stumbling toward him.

Poor Robert; he was even robbed of a zombie afterlife. So thoroughly devoured, even his brain was plucked from his head.

* * * * *

The zombies filled the first two stores and set about devouring the sleeping people. The first few people died silently, they were killed so quickly.

Then the screams began.

Soon the entire Left Corridor was filled with people running and screaming, trying to escape the dead still pouring through the handicap door.

"They're in!"

"Zombies!"

"Run!"

Chaos descended.

* * * * *

Thomas reached the back doors and pulled them open in time to hear distant screams. Turning toward Arnold, he said in a horrified voice, "Get the trucks ready!" then raced inside.

* * * * *

Valerie dove off her cot and grabbed her gun and flack jacket. She could barely see, but she struggled to wake up. Located halfway down the Left Corridor, she stumbled into the mall to see zombies down at the far end greedily devouring people. In front of the oncoming zombies, terrified people were running her way. More soldiers appeared out of side stores.

"Stupid puta bitch," Guadalupe hissed as she was wheeled past Valerie in her wheelchair by a teenage boy running at top speed. "She did this!"

Valerie motioned to the other soldiers and they began shoving cots and anything else they could use as a barricade out into the corridor to slow down the zombies.

Thankfully, they were not running zombies. Sadly, the newly fallen dead were keeping them distracted as the zombies greedily stuffed their ruined mouths. Their hunkered forms further slowed the onslaught of zombies pushing into the mall.

Then, slowly, some of the zombies rose.

Valerie opened fire.

* * * * *

Martin wasn't known for thinking ahead. He heard the screams and the gunfire from the other side of the mall and ran to the nearest exit.

Desperate to get out, he pushed on one of the doors and found it unlocked thanks to the Senator. With relief, he opened it and immediately had his throat torn out. The zombie tried to bend down to eat Martin, but the undead throng pushed him over then trampled him. Soon the Right Corridor began to fill with the undead.

* * * * *

Arnold was breathing heavily from running around the parking lot and turning on the trucks when the first of the people from the mall ran out into the parking lot. Behind him the helicopters were already rising to try to help defend the mall.

"Get to the trucks," Arnold ordered. He pointed to the nearest ones. "Just get in!"

People ran past him, women, men, and children. All of them were screaming with terror.

Inside gunfire continued.

The soldiers assigned to the escape vehicles leaped into the driver's seats and began to rev up the engines of the big trucks and buses.

Arnold turned to see Guadalupe being shoved down the ramp toward the parking lot by a teenage boy. She looked terrified and was gripping the armrests of her chair tightly. Arnold wondered briefly if it was because of the zombies or the breakneck speed at which the boy was pushing her.

* * * * *

The crush of people running down the Right Corridor slowed them down and more and more fell to the zombies. In the Left Corridor, people were making it out to the back parking lot as the soldiers kept firing into the zombie throng. The dead zombies tripped up their stumbling comrades, but the horde just kept coming.

* * * * *

A soldier, defending the fleeing people in the Right Corridor was dragged down three minutes after the initial breach. He pulled the pin on the phosphorous grenade he had clutched in his hand and the explosion resounded through the entire mall. The resulting fire engulfed the surrounding zombies. In their desperation to escape the fire as their primal fear overwhelmed them, the zombies staggered into stores and set cots, blankets and clothes on fire. Soon black smoke began to fill the Right Corridor.

* * * * *

In the midst of the chaos, Travis, Katie, and Jenni fought their way out of their store to get out into the Right Corridor. Smoke and fire made the going rough. People were in a panic and shoving and pushing each other. Travis held tight to Katie's hand as he pulled her through the throng. Katie had a tight hold of Jenni's hand. The three of them were swept along in a crowd of people as the zombies stumbled out of the smoke behind them.

Chapter 19

1. Trapped

J enni held tight to Katie's hand as they made their way down the mall corridor. She felt she was being crushed from all sides and she could barely hold onto Katie's hand.

Smoke was rising to the ceiling and was blessedly not overwhelming yet.

"Jenni! Jenni!" a voice called out.

Jenni whipped around to see Amy's terrified face staring desperately after her. She was struggling to maneuver through the crowd, her three children in her arms. No one around her was even trying to help and Jenni kept losing sight of her.

"Keep moving!" Jenni called out to her.

The corridor widened as they passed the corridor that cut the mall in half and led to the food court. Jenni was shoved so hard into the wall by a man trying to escape, she lost her grip on Katie's hand and almost fell. She managed to keep on her feet and looked up to see Katie's horrified expression as she was swept forward by the crowd.

"Jenni!"

Jenni looked back to see the zombies were gaining on the last of the crowd. Gritting her teeth, she struggled to move on.

* * * * *

The first of the crowd in the Right Corridor hit the back doors only to find them locked. The blacked out countenance was unforgiving as they banged on the doors and tried desperately to open them. Behind them, people shoved forward, trying hard to get out. A few people were literally smashed to death against the doors by the push of a hundred people behind them. Others were trampled.

Precious minutes were lost as the crowd surged, cried out, and fought at the locked doors. Finally, people retreated leaving the dead victims of the chaos lying before the doors.

* * * * *

Travis heard the shouts of "The doors are locked!" and immediately turned back. Skirting the crowd and keeping close to the wall, he managed to get to the food court corridor. Dragging Katie behind him, he ran toward the other side of the mall. Other people began to follow his example and soon they were running down the hall toward the food court.

"Jenni! Jenni! Travis, I lost Jenni!" Katie pulled on his hand, trying to turn back.

"We can't go back! Keep moving, Katie. She'll catch up!" Travis kept pulling Katie after him, determined to save his wife and their unborn child. Lydia said choices were to be made and, dammit, his choice was for his family to live.

* * * * *

Katie ran behind her husband, his hand holding hers so tightly, she was sure he was breaking a few bones. As she ran, she kept looking around for Jenni, but could not find her. Her stomach clenched tightly as she whipped her head about, looking around desperately.

Fear hit, harsh and strangling, and she fought to keep her senses.

The gunfire, fire, smoke, and screams only made her blood pump harder.

* * * * *

Jenni reached the corridor to the food court and struggled to press her way through the crowd. She was at the back of the throng of people and the smoke was beginning to affect her vision.

Looking back she could see the zombies still dragging people down. But they weren't taking their time to completely consume their victims anymore. They were taking a few bites, then lunging toward their fleeing prey.

Out of the black smoke, two tiny figures emerged near her. Amy's daughter banged into her hip and Jenni swept her up into her arms. Then Amy's son gripped Jenni's hand.

"Where's your Mom?"

The little boy pointed.

The smoke parted as Jenni looked back. Amy struggling with a zombie that had grabbed hold of her from behind. Her elbow was up under its chin and she was trying to push it back away from her throat. Her eight-year-old daughter, Margie, was still holding onto her mother's shirt.

"Margie, run!" Amy screamed at her daughter, but the little girl kept held on.

"Oh, my God," Jenni gasped, unsure of what to do. The kids holding on to her were sobbing for their mother.

As the other zombies neared, Amy made a choice. She turned, grabbed her daughter, and threw her toward the Jenni.

"Run, Margie run! Go with Jenni!" Amy screamed, then the zombies dragged her down.

Jenni screamed in horror, then surged forward, reaching for Margie. She managed to grab the girl's hair and yank her back away from the zombies. The little girl was shrieking. Clutching Amy's children to her,

Jenni pressed forward into the crowd. She fought harder, pushing her way through the crowd with renewed vigor.

*****

Kevin and Valerie fell back as the zombies continued to swarm the Left Corridor. They were fighting with six other soldiers, but overwhelming numbers of zombies were filling the mall. Kevin ordered them to fall back to a candy kiosk just as the first running zombies appeared. Literally racing past the barricaded soldiers, they dove into the last of the fleeing people from the Left Corridor and began tearing them apart right in front of the doors to the parking lot.

Thomas began firing at them and Kevin motioned for the soldiers to run into the corridor that lead to the food court.

"We'll exit through the Right Corridor!"

More sprinting zombies appeared.

The soldiers turned and ran.

The only thing that saved them was that the new zombies, ravenously hungry, dove onto the already dying victims to feast.

*****

Greta swung her helicopter low for the third time, trying to blow the zombies off their feet as they struggled to get into the mall. Cursing that her helicopter was for rescue and transport only, she wished she had a nice bomb or machine gun.

Below her, the zombies stumbled and fell beneath the wash of the helicopters. But they just kept coming.

*****

Travis reached the food court and its thundering waterfall just as Kevin and his men did.

"We have to go out the Right Corridor," Kevin ordered.

"It's blocked!" Travis exclaimed in frustration.

"What?"

"We couldn't get out!"

The two men stared at each other in shock, then looked back and forth. Smoke was wafting in from the Right Corridor.

"Fuck, we're trapped, " Valerie exclaimed.

*****

Jenni and the children were some of the last people to escape the Right Corridor. The fire finally overcame the zombies and began to spread along the walls. It was a food kiosk that finally saved those fleeing. The fire hit it and the oils used to make donuts ignited. The fireball flattened zombies and set them on fire. The flames burned hot and fierce, pushing back the zombies and stopping their pursuit of the people escaping into the food court.

2. Fall to Grace

"Where the hell do we go?"

Travis' question hung in the air as Kevin's eyes strayed to the maintenance stairway that snaked up the side of the building toward the skylight overhead. Pointing to metal stairway, Kevin said, "We go up."

"To the roof?"

"A fire escape goes down to the parking lot from the roof," Kevin answered. "It's the only way out now."

"Then we don't have a choice," Katie said. "They'll be here soon."

"Go! Move!" Valerie started to shout, motioning people to the staircase.

"Bette, open that door up there," Kevin ordered a blond soldier nearby.

With a nod, Bette ran up before the people, climbing three stories to the door at the very top.

Thomas ran ahead of her and swung open the gate at the bottom. The jumble of old, young, men, women, and children poured up the stairs.

Valerie tossed chairs and tables into the corridor leading to the Left Corridor. The zombies tended to not pay attention to anything but their victims and were easily tripped. Thomas joined her as more and more people lined up to ascend the stairs.

"Katie, let's go," Travis said firmly, pulling her toward the stairs.

"But Jenni," Katie protested. "We need to find her!"

Travis turned to his wife and she could see the anguish in his eyes. "Katie, I love you and you know I care about Jenni, but we need to get out of here now! Think of the baby."

Katie nodded and, tears streaming down her face, she let him guide her into line.

"Target the fast zombies first," Kevin ordered as the five soldiers took up position, looking down the corridor. It was strewn with chairs, tables, and potted plants.

"Where the fuck did the fast ones come from?" Thomas yelled angrily. "They all slowed down. Why are they fast again?"

"They're the fresh ones," Kevin answered grimly.

"Oh, shit," Thomas said in an agonized tone.

Kevin didn't even want to think of how many fresh zombies there might be.

The people fleeing the Right Corridor were down to a trickle. Some had been overcome by the smoke or badly burned by the explosion. Finally the last survivors stumbled out of the smoke. It was Jenni with the children. Half-carrying and half pulling the children, she saw the line of people ascending the metal staircase crawling up the wall and hurried toward it.

The first of the running zombies appeared from the Left Corridor. Running at full speed, they howled with hunger.

"Fire!"

The soldiers opened fire, their bullets slicing through the air to impact with the heads of the runners. The zombies were eliminated one by one, several of them managing to make it close enough to trip over the tables and chairs. But they, too, were cut down.

"Running low on ammo," Valerie said to Kevin.

Kevin looked up to see that the majority of the people were now on the stairs. He caught sight of Jenni with three small children stumbling into the last part of the line.

"We keep them covered until they are up the stairs," Kevin instructed in a somber tone.

The soldiers all grimly nodded and looked back down the corridor.

The stumbling, slow dead were moving in one great wave toward them.

"Watch for the fast ones," Kevin instructed.

Valerie grimaced, reloading her weapon.

Katie was nearly halfway up the stairs when she looked down to see Jenni pushing the children onto the first steps of the staircase.

"Travis, she made it!"

"Thank God," Travis exclaimed, continuing to climb while holding his wife's hand.

Jenni pushed Margie up onto the stairs. She heard the gunfire and turned. The zombies had reached the food court and were lunging toward the soldiers. The soldiers backed slowly toward the staircase, attempting to defend those on the stairs.

Why she looked up, she would never know. But Jenni did and saw a single black bird flying over the skylight. She flashed on Juan being shot and all that followed. And she understood.

"Keep going," she told Margie, setting the two younger children on the stairs. "Get your brother and sister out of here!"

Jenni then turned and ran down the stairs. Running up behind Thomas, she grabbed his revolver from his holster.

"Hey!"

She ran past him toward the zombies.

The shambling corpses could not follow the people on the stairs. Amy had given her life for her children. They would live. Katie and Travis were going to have a baby and be a family. They would live.

This was her time. Her choice. Her decision.

"Hey, fuckers!" Jenni waved her arms. "You stupid gawddamn muthafuckin' zombies, c'mere!" Then she screamed at them and waved her arms desperately. "Look at me, you fuckers! C'mon, you fuckin' cannibals. Prime rib Jenni right here! Come get me!"

"What the fuck is she doing?" Kevin exclaimed as the woman danced terrifyingly close to the slowly advancing zombies.

Valerie looked up at the people on the stairs and the little kids trying to climb and understood.

"The right thing," she answered, running after Jenni. "Hey stinkbags, follow us!"

"Oh, shit. Dammit! I don't want to die," Thomas growled, but ran after the women.

Kevin was about to follow when he felt a tug on his hand. Looking down he saw a little girl Jenni had shoved up the stairs looking up at him.

"Mister, we need to go get my Mom," she said.

"Shit!" He snatched up the girl and ran to the stairs.

The last soldier, William, hesitated, then he too followed Jenni. "Awwww, hell..."

The four of them teased, taunted and lured the zombies after them and away from the staircase. Low on ammunition, they held their fire, moving ahead of the mob, keeping them away from the stairs.

Jenni screamed at the things, screaming her hate, screaming her joy, screaming her fucking lungs off. In that moment, she knew she was doing exactly the right thing. Glancing briefly up at the stairs, she could see Katie and Travis near the top and Kevin pulling the children up in the rear.

"Hey, you stupid shits, come get me, you stupid muthafuckas," Jenni shouted with glee.

Their grisly faces and clawed hands reached for her, grasping at empty air as she danced away from them.

"C'mon fuckers!"

She was moving back toward the waterfall. In her head was a half-formed plan to circle the waterfall and head up the stairs.

It was then the zombies from the Right Corridor made their appearance. Though delayed, the sprinklers had come on, quenching most of the fire. The zombies now filed into the food court behind Jenni and the soldiers.

They were now completely surrounded.

"Shit," William shouted, beginning to fire.

Jenni whirled around as the dead began to fill the space around her. "Oh, hell," she said sadly, but calmly.

William went down first, screaming, firing into the crowd of zombies. Thomas began to laugh hysterically and kept firing into the oncoming onslaught until he too submitted.

Jenni looked to her left and saw the waterfall rising above her. To her surprise, she saw a narrow staircase cutting up through the rocks.

Without hesitation, she began to ascend the fake stone facade away from the zombies below.

Valerie started to follow, but was cut off so suddenly by a runner zombie. She staggered backwards and was instantly grabbed from behind. Without a second thought, she lifted her revolver to her temple and fired.

Jenni climbed, moving quickly. Behind her, the zombies moaned and wailed. They struggled to push their way up behind her.

Glancing toward the staircase she could see Katie looking toward her, screaming her name. Kevin was almost to the top with the children.

Looking over her shoulder, Jenni saw the zombies climbing after her. Lifting the revolver, she fired off a few shots, watching with satisfaction as their disgustingly rotted heads exploded. Reaching the top of the waterfall, she stood on the edge next to the rushing water. Her gaze swept over the food court and was horrified to see all the dead looking up at her, their hands reaching toward her figure.

Even above the roar of the water, Jenni could hear Katie's voice screaming her name.

I've done the right thing, she thought as she saw Kevin push the children through the doorway to the roof.

The zombies had yet to go even near the staircase.

She was eerily calm. Looking down, she wondered how deep the water was. Maybe she could dive into it and swim to the other side. Maybe she would have enough time to climb the staircase and escape onto the roof.

Maybe.

A growl behind Jenni startled her. Turning, she saw Amy step onto the platform. Raising her gun, Jenni fired at her zombified friend.

The gun clicked empty.

Amy lunged forward and her teeth snapped shut.

Horrified, Jenni rapidly drew her hand back, but she felt her skin tear.

"Oh, shit," she said as pain erupted in her hand.

Amy chewed Jenni's flesh, then lunged forward again for another taste.

Jenni brought the gun down hard on Amy's head, so hard she felt the skull crack. A surge of anger hit her and she brought it down again. Screaming in rage, she slammed the gun into the zombie's head until Amy's skull splintered and shattered.

With rage, fierce and hot, Jenni reached into Amy's head and ripped chunks of her brain out and threw it out over the zombie horde below her. Amy's corpse slid to the ground in silence, truly dead.

Exhaling, Jenni stood over the dead body, tears on her face. As quickly as the rage had hit, it was gone.

I made the right choice, she thought again. Bending down, she washed her hands off in the rushing water, watching it turn red with her blood.

Looking toward Katie and Kevin, she could see them waving at her to jump into the pool of water below. They didn't understand, she realized.

She slowly stood and raised her arm to show them her hand. Blood, hot with her life, trailed down her arm.

"No!" Katie's shout echoed throughout the mall even over the roar of the water and the cries of the dead.

Tears filled her eyes as she saw Katie turn to Kevin and saw him hand Katie his rifle.

She kept her hand up as her victory salute. She had done the right thing. There had been no running away this time. She had faced the monsters and she had saved people she loved. There was no fear anymore. Just joy. She had won.

The zombies were coming up the narrow staircase but they didn't matter anymore.

I love you, Juan. I love you, Jason. I love you, Benji. I love you, Mikey. I love you, Katie.

Katie raised the rifle.

Yes, I did the right thing. This is how it should be. Absolution is good. I can face God and myself once more. I saved the children. I saved those people. I saved the ones I loved.

The zombies were so close now.

Jenni smiled a beautiful, intense smile as peace filled her and tears fell down her cheeks. She clutched her hand tightly over her head, the blood pouring more fiercely.

"It's been one helluva ride," she whispered to Katie.

Jenni saw the flash at the end of the rifle. It was bright and brilliant. It just didn't flash. It exploded out toward her. A brilliant white pure light. It was warm and beautiful and it filled her senses. The smell of death disappeared, the pain disappeared as all she felt was love.

Her body fell in silence from the top of the waterfall, just out of reach of the clutching hands of the zombies as they breached the top. As she fell, her leg hooked onto a rock for a second, twisting her around so she slid down onto a maintenance ledge hidden by the falling water. There she rested in the cold water, out of reach of the zombies forever.

If the ones who loved her could seen her, they would have seen that her silent form was laying face up, the tiny hole in her forehead covered by her long black hair. Her raven locks floated around her head like a halo as the blood she had sacrificed slowly turned the water around her red.

What would have given them true comfort was this:

On her face was a happy, satisfied smile.

3. Beyond the Light

Juan woke slowly. His eyes flickered open and he took a deep breath. Something felt different. Wrong. The gray morning light filled his bedroom in the makeshift clinic in the hotel. The light felt cold.

"Hey," Jenni's voice said as she slipped into view.

"Jenni," he whispered, tears unexpectedly filling his eyes.

"Hey, baby." She sat down next to his bed. Her long dark hair was soaked with water and fell across her brow and face.

"Why are you wet?" he asked as her hand took his. She felt so cold and damp.

"You know me. A total klutz." She waved her hand, grinning.

"You were kidnapped."

His mind felt jumbled and confused. He tried to focus on her, but her form seemed blurred around the edges by the morning light streaming around her.

"I know and it totally sucked. We got stuck in this awful mall and there was this bitch of a Senator and it was just bad." Jenni rolled her eyes. "A mall. Can you believe it? Ugh. So annoying."

"But you're here now," Juan said with relief. "Oh, Jenni, I was so worried."

"Juan, you should know me by now. Nothing, not even death could keep me from coming to see you," she said with a laugh.

Her kiss was soft and wonderful and he touched her wet hair lovingly.

"Loca, I missed you."

"I missed you," Jenni whispered, her smile beautiful and loving.

"You're hurt," he said with concern, looking at her hand.

"You know me. I do crazy shit sometimes," she giggled. She tucked her hand out of sight and winked.

"Are you okay?" he asked worriedly. He was sure they wouldn't let her into the fort if she were infected.

"Yeah, I'm fine now. I promise."

"But you're so wet." Something didn't feel right and he struggled to decipher what was bothering him.

"You make me wet, baby," she teased.

"Loca, I'm shot and you're beat up and you're thinking about sex," Juan teased right back.

"Uh-huh. Well, mostly thinking about how much I love you," Jenni said in a more somber tone.

"I love you. I promised myself that I would ask you to marry me when you got back. This really isn't all that romantic, but..."

Jenni kissed him again, then gazed deeply into his eyes. "In my heart, we were always married."

Juan smiled softly and tried to focus on her, but it seemed so hard. "You're getting me wet, Loca."

"I know. I have to go now anyway and you need to sleep."

"Loca," Juan gasped, suddenly feeling very emotional. "Loca, I love you."

She stood up, her hand holding his. She felt so cold and wet. He was worried about her.

"And I love you."

To his chagrin, sleep pulled at his eyes and he felt himself fading into slumber. "Jenni, be with me."

"I always will be," Jenni assured him.

As his eyes flickered close, the light behind Jenni seemed to brighten.

"Jenni," he whispered desperately as he finally understood.

She was engulfed in the light, but her voice whispered, "I love you."

And then he was asleep.

Chapter 20

1. Exodus

Trembling, Katie lowered the rifle. Tears, hot and angry, flowed down her cheeks as she watched Jenni's body fall. She choked back sobs as Jenni's body caught on the edge of the waterfall, then fell into a hidden spot behind the water. The zombies pursuing Jenni began to tumble into the pool below, thrashing around. Jenni's body remained hidden behind the waterfall out of the reach of the dead, her blood turning the flowing water red.

"Katie, we need to go," Travis said in a firm voice. He stood on the other side of the doorway waiting for her. His hand reached out to her. "Katie, you did the right thing for her, but now it is time to go."

She couldn't tear her gaze away from the food court filled with zombies. Several groups were feasting on the fallen soldiers while others fought to get to the top of the waterfall only to fall into the waters below.

"Katie," Kevin said softly. He reached for his weapon. "She's at peace. They can't even reach her."

Gulping down her sobs, she looked toward Travis, her eyes filled with tears. "I did the right thing."

"Yes, you did," Travis answered her in a soft, yet firm voice. "And now it's time to go."

Handing Kevin the rifle, she moved through the doorway onto the roof. The helicopters were trying hard to lure the zombies from the back gate and the sound of engines revving filled the air. People were still panicking as they were herded by the surviving soldiers toward the waiting vehicles.

Sobs of despair, screams of terror, and cries of desperation filled the air.

It was chaos.

Travis and Kevin grabbed Katie's arms and guided her across the roof to the fire escape. It was rickety and frightening, but she moved as fast as she could. Her body was trembling so hard, her teeth were chattering. She had no idea where Bill or her father was.

And Jenni was dead.

She had to bite her tongue to keep from screaming.

Jenni was dead because she had killed her, but it had been the right thing to do. Lydia had told her the truth. This is what she was supposed to do, but it did not make it any easier.

Bette rushed the children Jenni had saved to the nearby vehicles as

Travis ran with Katie across the parking lot. People scrambled to get into trucks or buses that weren't already filled. Kevin ran to the lead truck as Arnold motioned Katie and Travis to another one.

"We're almost out of here," Travis exclaimed. "We're going to be okay."

Nothing could be okay. Jenni was dead. But Katie ran with him, her hand slick with sweat.

The back of the National Guard truck was full of people, so the driver shouted at them to get into the cab. It was so far off the ground, it was hard for Katie to get in. Her stomach felt awkward and heavy as she tried to heave herself up into the cab. Travis grabbed her hips and helped her in, then climbed in next to her. The seat was horribly uncomfortable, but Katie squirmed until it felt better.

Black smoke billowed out of the mall. The helicopters continued to try to corral the zombies away from one of the gates, taking turns gliding over the crowd of zombies as one brave soldier hung out the side waving.

Travis' hand held Katie's firmly. Already bruises were showing on her flesh from where he had gripped her so tightly during their escape. He gazed down at her hand. She could see his concern, but the physical pain was nothing compared to her broken heart.

Arnold motioned to the drivers. Slowly, the buses and trucks began to move forward. Soon, they were moving in a huge circle around the parking lot building speed for their departure. The redheaded soldier dove into a big Ford truck just as the gate blew wide open. Immediately, the secondary bombs went off.

Katie realized Arnold must have triggered them.

Fire and smoke filled the street outside the mall as the first truck barreled out of the parking lot at a quick clip. One by one, the trucks, both military and civilian, and several metro buses and one school bus, roared out into the town of Madison.

Overhead the helicopters swooped in an attempt to distract the zombie throng. The mall doors shattered from the heat of the fire within, and burning zombies staggered out into the abandoned parking lot as the last bus rolled out.

Katie held onto the dash for dear life as the truck roared through the town. Zombies rushed them, but the vehicles smashed them or hurled them into the nearby buildings. Their salvation from being overwhelmed was that most of the zombie crowd outside the mall had managed to find its way inside the structure. That meant fewer zombies in the street, therefore, their escape was not as fraught with danger as it could have been.

At last, the convoy broke free of the city limits and climbed into the countryside.

Left behind, the zombies staggered, hands outstretched in desperate hunger, toward the escaping vehicles. Slowly, they began to walk determinedly after them.

The driver of the truck Katie and Travis were in looked very grim. When the radio cackled, he picked it up with a shaking hand.

"We're clear," he reported in.

Katie sank into Travis' arms. He kissed her brow, rubbing her shoulders. She cried as the truck rumbled on.

A few minutes later the word came over the radio. All the vehicles that had left the parking lot were accounted for.

The survivors of Madison Mall, overwhelmed by the morning events, rode into the hills toward their new home.

2. Long Road Through Hell

The sky was gray and low as the convoy wound through the barren hills away from Madison. The country road swerved and dove through the hills, the cracks in the asphalt already thick with gnarled weeds. The juniper and cedar trees stretched twisted limbs up toward the sky.

Staring out the window, watching the bare trees slide by, Katie wondered if the trees were praying for those in the convoy to get back to the fort safely. Her bible school days had instilled a lot of verses in her head and she remembered one about trees praying or dancing or something when no one else had a voice. She certainly felt like she could not utter a word without sobbing. She rubbed her brow and snuggled deeper into Travis' arms as she watched the landscape slipping past the window.

The convoy had taken a long roundabout way to make sure that any zombies trying to follow from Madison would end up wandering in a direction opposite of the fort. Now the convoy was maneuvering through back roads that led them past long dead farmhouses and ranches.

Occasionally, a zombie struggled toward the convoy from one of the long abandoned structures. They seemed pitiful in their slowness. In the first days they had been so fast but now they were so slow Katie was sure that they could be easily circumvented as long as there weren't that many.

Of course, the mall had flooded with them.

She closed her eyes and fresh tears slipped down her cheeks.

Travis tenderly wiped a tear away and stroked her hair.

There had been so many zombies it had been overwhelming. Running with Travis' and Jenni's hands clutched in her own had been the most terrifying event of her life. The moans and screams of the dead and living had been a mind shattering cacophony. Then the most horrible moment had come. Jenni's hand had slipped from her own.

As long as she lived, she would never forget the despair that filled her when Jenni's fingers slid so easily from her grip.

Of course, she would never forget what followed either.

Katie remembered looking down from the stairs and seeing the sea of dead looking up at Jenni. For a crazed second, she thought Jenni could maybe jump into the water and somehow make it to the stairs. But then that fast zombie had barreled up the stairs that led up the side of the waterfall, pushing aside the slower ones. Katie remembered that horrible moment when she had watched Jenni swing the gun at the zombie and it had been empty. She hadn't breathed as she watched Jenni bash the zombie's brains out with her gun then fling its brains across the crowd below. Foolishly, Katie had thought Jenni was safe. But as she watched Jenni wash her hands, dread had overwhelmed her. Then Jenni had raised her hand and shown the bloody gash on her hand and Katie had known the terrible truth: Jenni was dead.

All that followed...taking the gun from Kevin...sighting Jenni through the scope...pulling the trigger...was just a ritual for the dead. As Jenni stood there, her hand over her head, smiling, triumphant over the undead growling and moaning below her, Katie had understood as well as Jenni that it was over.

And then she had pulled the trigger...

Thankfully, Jenni's body had fallen where the zombies would never reach her.

Katie wiped another tear away.

Lydia had been right. She had been at the mall for more than just a confrontation with the Senator. She had gone there to lay Jenni to rest. Katie had thought her destiny was something totally other than what it had turned out to be. Yes, she had stood up against the Senator, but in the end, she had freed Jenni from Lydia's fate. She had also laid her to rest in a way she never could do for Lydia.

"Fuck!" The driver swore, breaking her out of her dark thoughts.

The driver of their enormous truck pulled hard on the heavy steering wheel, tossing them to the side in the big cab. Katie looked up to see the truck in front of them swerving wildly. Reaching out with her hand, she tried to brace herself as their truck shimmied, then caught the road. It began to pass the truck in distress.

The tarp covering the back of the truck opened and a young boy appeared. His face covered in blood, his mouth open in a scream, he reached toward them. Then someone inside pulled him back inside.

"They're infected," Katie gasped. She wasn't sure if the boy was already turned or a victim, but her pulse was beating rapidly.

"We didn't have a chance to check everyone before we left," Travis said bitterly.

The road was winding around a hill and a sharp incline led down into the tree line. As they watched in horror, the truck swerved off the road into the trees, shattering branches and slender trees before hitting the thick trunk of an enormous oak. People began to pour out of the back, bloodied and screaming. Horribly, it was hard to tell if they were turned or infected.

The truck Katie and Travis was in kept moving.

The sound of gunfire erupted. Katie looked into the side mirror to see the soldiers in a Ford Truck riding behind them opening fire on the people rushing up toward the road.

"They're taking care of it," the truck driver assured her.

Katie looked at his grim expression then returned her gaze to the tiny mirror reflecting the horror behind them. She saw two of the soldiers hurtling something into the back of the crashed truck, then there were two loud bangs.

"Grenades," the driver said softly.

Travis sighed and pulled Katie back into his arms. Kissing her brow, he whispered, "We'll get home soon and put this day far behind us."

Katie nodded mutely. She still wasn't sure her father or Bill was alive. She knew Jenni was dead and now so were all the people in that truck. All those poor people who thought they were saved were now dead.

Travis gently stroked her stomach and her hand intertwined with his. They stared into each others eyes, then kissed, holding each other close.

* * * * *

Kevin slid out of the truck and landed hard on his feet. He felt bone weary and numb. Motioning to a Dodge Ram full of soldiers, he stood in the road watching the convoy come to a slow stop. The road was straddled between two wide fields, so it would be easy to see if any of the zombies came their way.

Bette was the first one to him, her face pinched and tired. "What's up?"

"We lost a truck back there. We need to search the rest of the vehicles for infected. We need to go vehicle to vehicle," Kevin instructed.

"And if they're infected?" Arnold asked.

Kevin sighed, rubbing the back of his head with one hand. He looked over the faces of the eight soldiers gathered around him. "We have no choice. Bette, check our people out first."

For several tense minutes, there was silence as each man and woman was thoroughly searched for any bites by Bette. Cleared, they moved out.

Kevin hesitated, swore, then followed. If he expected his people to do the shit job, then he better damn well be willing to do it himself.

The first truck was his own. People were helped down and it was laid out simply to them. One woman hesitated then held out her arm, showing a clear bite. Those around her immediately drew back and the woman began to cry.

"I'm sorry," she whispered. "I'm sorry."

Startled that someone in his own truck was infected, Kevin took a deep breath. "It's okay, ma'am. Just step over there."

"I'm really sorry," she said again. "I wanted to say something, but it doesn't really hurt. Maybe..." She stopped then broke into sobs.

Bette carefully led her over to the side of the road and the woman sat down on the ground crying.

"Anyone else?" Kevin asked.

No one volunteered, so the soldiers slowly began their inspections. To everyone's relief, no one else was infected.

Moving on to the next truck, it was the same story. People were allowed to volunteer information then were searched. No one protested. Everyone gave in with sad smiles and hollow eyes. They were all tired and hungry and terrified. To everyone's relief, no one was infected.

Several trucks and buses were empty of infected and Kevin began to hope. They had already lost so many people he just didn't feel he could deal with too much more death. He was so tired and weary he just wanted to sleep for a very long time. Well, after a hot shower and a good meal that was.

Behind him, he could hear the infected woman still crying. One of his men walked over to stand behind her. It was a hard sight to look at, so he avoided it.

The people from a bus were given the all clear and piled back in. Many looked at him with desperate eyes, looking for some sort of reassurance. He forced a smile he did not feel and several looked relieved.

Moving on to the next truck, he saw Travis drop to the ground then reach up to help his wife down out of the cab. Bette and two other soldiers quickly examined them and the driver and gave the clear sign to Kevin. They moved to the back of the truck to unload the passengers. Kevin strode up to the couple and sighed.

"Good to see you're safe and sound," Kevin said in a low voice.

Travis looked over at the crying infected woman, then back at Kevin. "I wish everyone was."

"Yeah. But she probably won't be the only one," Kevin answered with a sad sigh.

Travis agreed silently with a grim look on his face.

"We have to do this. We can't risk the fort."

"Doesn't make it any easier, does it?" Travis reached out and patted Kevin's shoulder. "I'm sorry about your friends back in the mall. They were brave."

"So was your friend," Kevin said with a slight smile. "One helluva a feisty one, wasn't she?"

"You have no idea," Travis answered with a bittersweet laugh. "No idea."

Katie was holding onto Travis tightly and she even smiled at this comment. She looked exhausted. On impulse, Kevin reached out and tucked her hair back from her face.

"You did the right thing," he said, slightly embarrassed.

"That doesn't make it any easier."

"I understand," Kevin assured her.

"Katie!"

Kevin looked up to see Bruce Kiel heading toward them. His wrist was heavily bandaged. Kevin felt his heart sink.

"Dad! No! Dad!" Katie was instantly on the edge of hysterics and rushed toward her father.

"Katie!" Travis dove after her, catching her about the waist. "Katie, no!"

"It's okay, baby," Bruce called out to her, his expression agonized. "It's okay. Please don't cry."

"Oh, Dad, no. Please, God, no."

"Oh, shit," Kevin groaned. He rubbed his brow and looked back at the woman who was now silent. Either she was accepting her inevitable death or—

The woman lurched to her feet and whirled around on the guard. He was ready and shot her point blank in the head.

The people in the parked vehicles cried out in horror as Kevin closed his eyes.

Fuck. Could this get any worse?

"Dad," Katie exclaimed. "Please, not you!"

"I'm not sure it's a bite," Bruce said, his voice shaking. "I punched a few of them while escaping, but I also had to climb through a broken window to get out of a store."

"Let's see it," Bette ordered.

Bruce began to unwind what looked like bandages made of a shirtsleeve. Slowly, the bloody cloth fell away to reveal a bad wound. Bette took his hand and leaned down to look at the gash.

Katie was sobbing, clinging to Travis, her body shaking. Travis looked pale as he tried to calm her.

Bette sighed then wrapped up the wound. "There is glass in the wound, but there are clear teeth indentations."

With shivering breath, Bruce closed his eyes and tersely nodded. "I understand."

"This can't be happening!" Katie's legs buckled, but Travis managed to hold her up.

Kevin lowered his head, feeling sick of it all.

A soldier stepped up beside Bruce and pushed him gently toward the side of the road.

Opening his eyes, he looked at his daughter and gave her a smile. "It's okay, Katie-girl. It is. I promise. I got to see you again," he said, walking past her.

Katie reached out toward him, but her father shook his head.

"Bruce, I'm sorry." Travis' tone was full of grief.

"I'm not. I got to see you and my daughter. I got to feel my grandchild moving in my daughter's belly. I got to say goodbye." Bruce had tears in his eyes. "I love you Katie-girl. I love you and I'm proud of you. I'm damn happy you're going to be a mother and you're going to have a good life."

"Dad, I love you. I love you so much," Katie said passionately. Her nose was running and her eyes were nearly swollen shut.

Bruce blew his daughter a kiss, then stood on the side of the road with his head down. Katie held onto her husband, weeping, unable to go to her father.

"This day can't get much worse," Kevin whispered to Bette.

But it did. By the time every truck and bus was searched, seven people stood next to the side of the road. Four men from ages sixteen to maybe sixty stood in the cold wind, shivering from either the cold or the infection spreading through their bodies. Three were women. One was around eighteen the other two in their forties. The eighteen-year-old was having spasms by the time the search was done. Kevin was sure she was on the verge of turning.

"I'm sorry," he said as he walked down the line of infected. "You're infected. You have two choices. We leave you here and you turn. Or, we can put you out of your misery and save you from the fate of the rest of the world. I know it doesn't seem fair and it's not, but in the end none of us have any choice."

"I'll do it myself," the girl said through chattering teeth.

Kevin looked at her, then at the soldier standing behind the her. The soldier nodded. Sadly, Kevin handed the girl his revolver.

People in the buses and trucks behind him were watching. The soldiers had tried to make the people look away, but he knew there was something innately human in not being able tear their eyes away from the drama.

The girl's breathing was getting shallow, her eyes milky. Kevin could tell it would be any minute now. He took a step back and looked at the soldier behind the girl. Slowly, he saw the rifle being raised as the soldier stepped to one side to avoid the coming gunshot.

The girl looked at Kevin and whispered in a voice that was barely human, "Take my Mom to the fort." Then she shoved the gun in her mouth and, without hesitation, pulled the trigger.

The spray of blood splattered the others. One infected man screamed and ran into the pasture.

"Let him go," Kevin ordered. "He made his choice."

"I can't do it myself," one of the women said, her eyes flicking to the dead girl at her feet. "I can't."

Kevin hesitated, not willing to ask anything more of his men. It was one thing to shoot a zombie, another a person even if they were infected.

"I'll do it," Bette said softly.

"Bette, I-"

Bette came up behind the woman and shot her. It was so quick the shot made Kevin jump.

"Me, too," a man said. "Me, too."

Kevin looked into Bette's green eyes and saw a tear. He moved to stop her, but she had already fired.

The boy turned and ran.

"I can't," the last woman whispered. She also turned and ran.

Bruce reached down for the gun at the dead girl's side. He was very slow in his movements. When he took the gun, he shivered. "I don't want to ask you to do what I can do myself," he said in a trembling voice.

Kevin rubbed his brow and nodded, pressing his lips tightly together.

"You did a good job, son. Just some of us were a little slow. And a little foolish," Bruce said with a sigh.

Kevin looked back at Katie and Travis quickly. Travis had Katie's face tucked into his neck as her body shook with emotion.

"Katie, I love you. Travis, take care of her. I got to say goodbye and that makes this all worth it."

"Dad," Katie called out. "I love you."

"I love you, too. Take care, y'all." Bruce lifted the gun and pressed it to his temple.

The gunshot made Kevin jump even though he knew it was coming.

"Let's go," Bette said softly, her hand resting on his arm.

"One of them is coming back," a younger soldier named Kabuto said. "And the other one is eating that first runner."

Kevin looked up to see one of the infected running back. She wasn't human anymore.

A shot rang out, then another. Then silence ruled the world again.

"Let's go home," Kevin said at last, wiping his tears away.

3. Home

The sparkling Christmas lights were the first thing many of the evacuees saw as the convoy crested the hill and sped down toward the fort. Despite the gloomy cold, drizzly weather, the lights seemed very bright, twinkling in the grayness of the day.

Amy's children, huddled together in a metro bus, stared with wide, shell-shocked eyes at the lights. Margie leaned over and whispered to her brother and sister, "Maybe Christmas is here."

To Guadalupe, the lights were a welcome sight. She broke down crying, her gnarled hand, aching with arthritis cupping her forehead. It was almost too much for the old woman to bear. Those around her reached out to lay comforting hands on her.

On one of the lead trucks, Bette sat in silence, watching the lights with sad, weary eyes. Tired to the core of her being, she just wanted to be somewhere safe and warm. Despite being a nurse, who tried to heal the sick, she had been an executioner. Yet, it made sense to quickly destroy the thing that could infect so many others. She was just so tired. Exhausted, she rested her head back on the seat and watched the twinkling lights grow blurry through her tears.

As the gates opened to let the trucks in one at a time, the convoy fell into silence. No zombies attacked as they waited. Overhead, the helicopters hovered watchfully.

As Katie and Travis' truck passed through into the complex, Katie broke down sobbing, her hands covering her face. Travis gently stroked her neck and back, whispering softly to her. But they both felt the emptiness that could never be replaced.

Jenni was gone.

Bruce was gone.

Kevin turned his eyes up toward the wall when his truck entered. He saw the tall, older Israeli woman watching with keen eyes. They shared a moment where their gazes touched and something unspoken passed between them. She nodded, then his truck turned into the garage and she was gone.

As the survivors began to pour into the courtyard, that was once the construction site, the citizens of the fort rushed to greet them.

There were moments of sheer joy as family members were reunited.

Friends who had not seen each other in years wept as they embraced.

The weary soldiers found themselves hugged and kissed by strangers.

The Reverend found lost members of his flock and wept as they greeted him.

Unexpected reunions filled the dreary day with cries of happiness that were mingled with tears of sadness. There was joy and there was heartbreak, but it was human and it was real.

Finally, the last truck rolled in. A beleaguered man, his hair messed and his face drawn, trudged through the crowd to the redheaded woman staring at him with disbelief.

With infinite gentleness, Bill put his arms around Katarina and kissed her lightly, then said, "I need a beer."

Chapter 21

1. Moments

"**W**e must remember that our loved ones have moved on to a place where there is no fear or pain. It is we, who are left behind, who feel fear and pain. We must take comfort that their suffering is over and the salvation to our fears is to love one another and live the best life we can in honor of their memory," the Reverend's voice intoned, comforting his former parishioners as they gathered around him for prayer.

Katie moved past him, her legs feeling heavy and leaden. Her Travis walked behind her, resting his hands on her shoulders. She felt dizzy, tired, and her body was aching. Her hand pressed protectively against the swell of her stomach as she walked toward the hotel.

People from the fort flowed past her as they hurried to greet the newcomers. As one man moved aside to let her pass, Jason came into view, standing very still. Beside him, Jack pressed to his side. Shelley stood behind him, her face pale. Katie felt her heart break as she looked into the boy's eyes and his image blurred as fresh tears filled her eyes.

Blinking the tears free from her lashes, she saw Jason duck his head down, his bangs falling over his brow. His hand lifted to his face as Jack began to whine, pawing at the boy's knee.

"Jason," Katie managed to say before he flung himself into her arms. His body violently shaking, he buried his face in her neck as he cried. Clutching him tightly, she whispered, "I'm so sorry."

The teenager sobbed desperately, his body sinking downward. Travis wrapped his arms around both of them and pulled Jason firmly against him. "We're here, Jason. We're here."

"Mom! Mom! Mom!" Jason's voice was a screech of pain.

Katie kissed his brow and clung to both of them.

Shelley wrapped one arm hesitantly around Katie and Katie reached out to pull the girl into a four-way embrace. Jack squeezed between their legs and began to howl.

* * * * *

Nerit held out her hand to Kevin as he stopped next to her. She stood near the entrance to the hotel watching Travis and Katie trying to comfort the distraught Jason. The cries of pain said it all. Jenni was gone. She felt the sting of pain in her own heart and her eyes grew moist. As Kevin took her hand, she looked at him and gave him a tight smile.

Glancing over his shoulder, he saw what was happening and sighed.

"Jenni didn't make it, did she?"

Kevin ran a hand over his cropped hair. "Things went very wrong."

"That is what Greta said when she called us," Nerit said.

"Jenni died saving people. They didn't get her though. Katie released her before that."

"Good," Nerit answered with relief. "Good."

Three little kids wandered up to them. The two younger children were clutching the eldest girl's skirt so tight, the girl's Wonder Woman underpants were visible.

"Is it Christmas here?" the oldest girl asked.

Nerit blinked, surprised.

The little girl pointed to the Christmas lights strung up along the walls.

Nerit hesitated, then said with a soft smile, "I think a piece of Christmas is still here."

Kevin looked down at the kids and his face was full of pain. 'Yes, I'm sure it is here."

"Okay, cause Santa forgot about us at the mall..."

Behind them, voices rose in soft song.

"Praise God from whom all blessings flow..."

* * * * *

Rosie was in a feverish rush to get a lunch on the table for the newcomers. Fresh biscuits, golden and hot, came out of the oven and made the kitchen smell wonderful. Wiping her hands off on a towel, she moved to check on the fried chicken. She had decided to break out the rest of the frozen chicken to feed the new people. They needed good food from the sight of them.

"Hey, Rosie," Calhoun's voice called from the doorway. He looked mummy with his head heavily bandaged.

"What is it, Ernest," Rosie answered.

"Your Mama is out in the lobby. And, that old Amazon hit me with her cane."

Rosie looked up startled. "What?"

"Your Mama, Guadalupe, hit me with her derned cane," Calhoun repeated and began to saunter not too casually toward the biscuits.

Waving metal tongs at him, her expression was one of disbelief. "My Mama can't be alive. She went to the hospital for a checkup on the first day. Hospitals were death traps"

"Well, she's alive," Calhoun answered, trying to make a dive for the biscuits.

Rosie smacked him, and he grunted as he managed to snag one. She hesitated, then handed the tongs to one of her helpers. "Don't let him get another one."

Calhoun shoved the entire biscuit in his mouth and grinned at her as he dove for another.

Rushing into the hallway, she made her way through the growing throng of very smelly people to the lobby. The thought of her nearly hundred year old mother being alive was too much of a long shot to even hope for, but when she entered the lobby, she saw the hunched up old woman sitting in a wheelchair banging on the check in counter.

"I want a room with a view with no zombies!"

Rosie never made it to her mother. She passed out.

Guadalupe turned around as people cried out, surprised to see her daughter slumped in the arms of several people. "Dios mio! My baby is alive!" Motioning to the gangly teenager who was pushing her around, she began to cry.

When Rosie woke up, her mother was patting her face with a gnarled hand. "Mama!"

"Just tell me one thing," her mother said. "Is Juan alive?"

"Yes, Mama, yes!"

The old woman grinned as she fell back in her wheelchair and clutched her hands to her chest. "Thank you, Jesus, Mary and Joseph!"

Rosie wrapped her arms around her mother and together they wept with relief.

* * * * *

The dining room had never been so full. People were crowded in, eating feverishly, some laughing, some still crying, but the food was good. The Reverend blessed the meal and some people wept at his words.

It was a hard morning. So much death and so much sadness.

The mother of a girl named Kimberly sat in silence staring at her food as she remembered her brave daughter kissing her goodbye before taking her own life on the side of the road. Next to her, the only member left of her family, her youngest son, began to eat with relish. Looking up, the mother saw faces both new and old and with sadness in her heart, she began to try to eat. Kimberly would have wanted her to eat and go on.

Bette sat with some of the survivors and a few fort residents. She ate the biscuit on her plate slowly, picking off pieces, relishing the flavor. Across from her, a pretty Hispanic girl kept giving her furtive glances.

Finally, Bette put out her hand and said, "Bette."

The younger woman looked up at her, smiling shyly. "My name is Linda."

There was something startling and intense in the other woman's gaze. Nervously, Bette continued to eat, but the heaviness inside felt a little lighter every time she caught the other woman looking at her.

Three little kids sat in silence, eating their food hungrily, at a table of strangers none of them knew. Occasionally, one of them would point at something in the room and they would all whisper together. No one really noticed the little ones; they were so quiet. But if they had listened, they would have realized the children were looking at the leftover Christmas decorations that no one had felt like climbing a ladder to get down.

Bill and Katarina ate together, holding hands under the table, giving each other furtive looks. Despite the pain they felt around them, they were in their own little bubble of happiness. Bill was home and they were together. What exactly that meant, they weren't sure yet. But it felt good and it felt right.

Kevin and Nerit sat down together and ate in silence. As the dinner continued and people began to relax and laughter could be heard breaking out. Tears came to Kevin's eyes. Overwhelmed, he put down his fork and began to cry. His wide shoulders shuddered as he openly wept. All he had worked so hard to accomplish had failed in the end. So many had died. And yet, some still lived. They were safe, so perhaps he had not entirely failed. He wept because his soul was tired and he felt crushed by the remains of the burden that was no longer his.

Nerit reached out and touched his shoulder. Then another man reached out and touched him. Slowly, people began to move around his table, reaching out to him, touching him, whispers of "Thank you""You did well""Good job" filled his ears. He looked up to see people smiling at him and he stood up on shaky legs.

"I wish I had done more. I wish everyone had made it. I'm so sorry," he whispered.

Someone took his hand and hugged him, then another person and another. Soon, he was being pulled and guided gently through the room, people embracing him, kissing his cheek, thanking him, crying with him.

In the end, Nerit was there, her hand held out to him. He took it and she helped him from the room. She took him to her room and he lay down on her bed that smelled of lavender and sage.

"Sleep," she told him.

He covered his face, feeling like a child.

"Your job is done. Now you can sleep," she repeated.

Nodding, he closed his eyes and he felt her cool fingers rest on his forehead. He was certain he would never be able to sleep. But he did.

He did not wake up for two days.

* * * * *

Katie slipped into Juan's room and found his mother and Guadalupe in the room with him. A strangely familiar teenager sat in a chair looking bored.

"Katie," Juan said emotionally. He reached out to her and she took his hand quickly. She let herself be drawn down into a tight hug. Juan's scraggly beard scratched her cheek when he kissed it.

"Juan, I came as soon as I could," she said as she sat next to him.

"I know. I know. Have you met my grandma yet?"

Katie smiled at Guadalupe and reached out to the older woman. "We met."

Guadalupe returned her smile. "We hung out at the mall together, right chica?"

"We certainly did," Katie answered, and looked back at Juan. She could feel tears threatening her already. "Juan, about Jenni..."

"I already know," Juan said quickly.

"Who..."

"Jenni. She came to me," Juan answered.

Rosie dabbed at her eyes. "He told me about his dream, but I thought maybe it was just a nightmare, but now..."

"She came to you in a dream?" Katie blinked.

"I don't think it was a dream. I saw her. I felt her. She was wet and her hand was hurt. At first I thought she was just home, but then I realized..." Juan faltered and his voice grew hoarse as he continued. "I realized she was telling me goodbye."

Fresh tears filled Katie's eyes as she clung to Juan's hand. "She fell into water. But away from where they could get to her. They didn't touch her. And she's not one of them."

Juan sighed with relief and covered his eyes, trying to compose himself. "Did you, Katie? You..you...did..it?"

Katie nodded. "I did."

Juan drew her down into a tight hug again. "Thank you, Katie...thank you..."

* * * * *

"I dreamed of my Mom," Jason whispered to Travis in a slurred voice.

Startled, Travis looked up to see the boy had opened his eyes. Considering how strong the sedative was that Charlotte gave him, Travis was surprised to see Jason was awake. Next to him, on the bed, Jack continued to sleep, his tail wagging slightly.

"I saw my Mom. She's okay," Jason whispered in a hoarse voice. "She's okay." The boys eyes slowly closed and he was asleep.

Next to him, Jack let out a contented sigh.

Travis looked cautiously around the room. He felt foolish, but whispered softly, "Hey, Jenni. Don't go too far. We still need you."

If the ghost was truly in the room, he wasn't sure, but Travis felt better saying the words. He sat back in his chair, took a deep breath, and closed his eyes.

"Stay close, Jenni. Stay close."

* * * * *

Peggy finished checking in another survivor from the mall and rubbed her eyes. The line was getting shorter and people were getting settled. Soon she would be able to relax and eat the dinner that was cooling on the table behind her.

Looking up, she didn't see anyone in front of the check-in counter, but the people that appeared next in line were staring with blank looks on their faces.

"Next," she said again.

No one moved forward.

Then a small hand reached up over the counter and waved.

Peering over the counter, Peggy saw three kids looking up at her. "Oh, there you are. But where are your Mommy and Daddy."

"They got eated up," the oldest girl said.

The two younger kids nodded solemnly in agreement.

Peggy didn't know what to say.

"We need a room," the oldest girl continued.

"Well, we can't just put you in a room by yourself," Peggy answered.

"Do we have to go outside with the zombies?" The little girl looked terrified.

"Oh, no no. I meant...well, come around the desk. You need to have a room with an adult taking care of you."

Obediently, the children came around the desk and stared at her. Feeling flustered, Peggy gazed at the little darlings pondering what to do with them. It was too late in the day to try to find someone else. They'd have to stay with her.

"Okay, well, you can stay with me and my little boy. I'm sure he will enjoy the company."

The three kids kept staring at her with their shell-shocked expressions. Finally, the oldest girl said. "Is Christmas in your house?"

* * * * *

Katie stood up and slowly stretched. Juan was finally asleep and Rosie was snoring in her chair. Looking over at Guadalupe, she saw that the old woman was still praying the rosary. The teenage boy was looking at a magazine. Katie blinked, then leaned toward him slowly, studying his face.

The boy slowly looked up at her. "What do you want?"

"Who are you?"

The boy blinked. "Uh....why?"

Katie suddenly recognized him and gasped. "Oh, my God. You are that kid from the convenience store that we kept telling about the zombies and you wouldn't believe us!"

The boy hunched his shoulders, then said, "Yeah, so what?'

"What are you doing with Guadalupe?"

"He's a good boy," Guadalupe assured Katie. "He came with the soldiers to the rescue center and he always pushes my chair around."

Katie shook her head in amazement. "Oh, my God! The last time I saw him he was running from the zombies."

"I run fast. I got away. The soldiers picked me up and Guadalupe is like my grandma now. She's pretty cool." The boy shrugged his shoulders again.

Katie was in shock, but it was a pleasant one. "Well, I'm glad that you've been helping her."

With a slight laugh, she walked to the door and looked back at the boy again. Somehow, seeing him alive made her feel better. The world wasn't completely filled with death and it was a small comfort she would embrace.

* * * * *

Curtis stretched his legs and moved out of the communication center to see Linda walking down the hall.

"Hey, Linda," he said with a sheepish grin.

"Hey, Curtis," she answered with a smile.

"I hear that disco night is still on for Friday. We still going together?" Curtis asked.

Linda chewed her bottom lip. "Yeah, I think so."

She looked hesitant and it made Curtis nervous. They had been fooling around for a few weeks, but she always seemed a little elusive whenever he tried to get her to commit to anything.

"Okay, well we can dance and stuff," he said.

"Yeah. That will be fun."

The blond soldier named Bette moved down the hall toward them. Curtis had been told by Nerit that Bette would be coming to update the communication center so they could start monitoring official channels as well. She was very pretty with her short hair and large blue-green eyes.

"Hi," Bette said when she saw both of them.

Linda turned and gave Bette a wide grin. "Hi again."

"I'm supposed to help a Curtis," Bette said slowly.

"That's me," Curtis said, drawing himself up and trying to look official.

"Great. Then I'm in the right place."

Curtis' eyes narrowed as the two women looked at each other in a way he wasn't sure how to take. They seemed to share a secret, but he knew that was impossible. They couldn't have but just met.

"See you around," Linda said, and Curtis wasn't sure who she meant.

"See you," Curtis said quickly.

Bette just smiled at Linda, then turned to him. "Let's get started."

* * * * *

As Calhoun danced alone under the stars hours later, the fort slumbered. The old man danced a wild jig of glee as he ignored the throbbing of his head and the pain in his side. He was jubilant and he was celebrating.

The Amazon Bitch Queen had been dethroned and the fort still stood.

It was a night to rejoice.

And so he danced....

Chapter 22

1. I-35

"That's a helluva lot of zombies," Raleigh said in an oddly terrified yet awed voice.

Beside him, the Senator frowned she set her hands on her hips.

Beyond the copse of trees, that they were hiding within, was a dry and scrubby swathe of field that led down to the strangled interstate below. Vehicles of every size and description formed a tangled necklace of battered metal and glass. Standing among the ruins were thousands of softly moaning zombies. It didn't take a genius to figure out that the fleeing traffic of nearly every city and town along I-35 had become a buffet of fresh meat for the newly risen dead in the first days.

The large silent National Guard truck beside them was a small consolation facing such danger.

I-35 cut across Texas dividing the East from the West. It connected major and minor Texas cities together like a chain from Laredo through San Antonio, Austin, and Waco, before branching off to Fort Worth and Dallas and then continuing on up into Oklahoma. If they wanted to get to East Texas, they were going to have to find a way over the massive thoroughfare that was clogged mile after mile after mile.

"They're just standing there," Raleigh said, mystified by this. "Why do they just stand there?"

"They haven't seen fresh meat yet," Ruben, the soldier, answered him. "If they see us, they'll be moving like ants toward a picnic."

"We can't get across. We need to go back," a young black soldier His name was Lewis and he looked as terrified as the rest of them were trying hard to pretend they were not.

Ben, the soldier in charge and a native of East Texas, looked grimly determined. "I think we can barrel across and get onto the farm road."

"I don't see much of a weak spot," Lewis decided.

"I got family over yonder. We're going across," Ben said firmly.

The Senator looked toward him. "How?" Her expression was grim, all traces of her usual false bravado erased. She was facing the reality of the situation and she didn't like it. Her plans had seemed so easy when they had been formulating in her mind. It was a simple plan: show up at Central, present all the information on the fort, get the support of Central's firepower and take over the fort.

"First truck will gun it and hit that point right there. Those are just small cars. We can shove through. Second truck will then follow. We can do this," Ben declared. "We can do this."

"They'll follow," Raleigh pointed out. "Which is exactly what Central doesn't want."

"Fuck Central," Ben snapped.

The Senator was silent, her thin lips pursed together. The collagen that once plumped her lips was long gone and they were once more a tight little line on her face. She was furious at Central for placing her in this situation. After she had informed Central that the terrorists from the fort had sabotaged the mall, she had been receiving only vague responses to her request for assistance. She had been convinced they would send air transport for her and her men once Central understood her position. Instead, she had been told to find safe lodgings and hold tight.

There was no damn way she was just going to hold tight.

Of course none of this would have happened if Kevin hadn't betrayed her. Something had gone wrong with the military in the last few years. Everyone had seen it coming. Maybe it was the endless "nation building" in other countries with high casualty rates among the enlisted that had slowly eroded the blind allegiance soldiers once had in their superiors. She had met with strong resistance from the soldiers in the mall over and over again when she spoke of military action against the fort. It was clear they were loathe to move against the civilians. It had infuriated her to no end. The world had been a place of chaos before all this and now it was worse. When soldiers talked back and refused orders, it only proved to her that the government should have done more to control them before the world had gone to hell.

"Let's do it," the Senator finally said.

"We can reach Nacogdoches by nightfall," Ben assured her.

"Very well," she responded, walking back to her truck. She could hear Raleigh close behind her and she could feel his fear. She could smell it.

Ben and his men climbed into their truck as she, Raleigh, and Ruben rejoined the four men that were in theirs.

There had been a few losses along the way. Though they had avoided Fort Worth, they had run into trouble in one of the small towns on its outskirts. It was sheer luck they had made it through the rabid town at all. A few men had perished, but the Senator couldn't remember their names.

Ben's truck moved out of the line of trees and hit the narrow dirt road that cut through the field and led to the highway. Squeezed between Ruben, the driver, and Raleigh, the Senator gripped the dash tightly and concentrated straight ahead.

She knew Ben was half-crazed at the idea of reaching his family. She could see it in his eyes. That was why he was so perfect to lead them. He would do anything to make this happen.

The truck in front of them picked up speed and began to barrel down toward the highway, a plume of dirt spraying behind it. The zombies on the highway seemed to all turn at the same time to watch the speeding vehicle rushing toward them. Together, they began a determined march toward it. Hands outstretched, they moaned and bellowed.

"Catch up!" The Senator's voice sounded strained. "We're too far back!"

Ruben swore, but the truck sped up.

Raleigh looked terrified. "It's going to push through and we're going to get stuck in the breach. We're not going to make it!"

Ben's truck reached the edge of the field and roared up the short embankment. It sailed onto the shoulder of the highway so quickly, the whole truck seemed to be airborne. It hit the small cars like a torpedo and the screech of twisting metal filled the air.

No one could ever be certain what the huge truck hit, but one side of it suddenly pivoted upwards. For a moment, it kept moving forward cars being shoved away from it, then it began a horrible roll to one side.

"Turn! Turn! Turn! Turn! Turn!" Raleigh screamed.

Ruben whipped the wheel about in response to the Senator's command and the second truck slid around on the dry grass and dirt of the field.

Zombies were flooding toward the capsized truck, but others were now moving determinedly toward the second. Gunshots could be heard going off as the moans of the zombies grew louder.

The Senator fell into Raleigh as the truck made its steep turn. Ruben managed to keep control and the vehicle roared back up the incline toward the tree line.

No one spoke for at least ten minutes as I-35 vanished from the view of the side mirrors along with the determined crowd of undead stalking after the truck.

Finally, Raleigh said, "Now what?"

There was silence.

No one had an answer.

2. The Seasons Ends

It was inevitable that the fort would feel different after the new arrivals were settled. Suddenly there were a lot more new faces as people wandered around looking lost. Some new arrivals slept for days. Others were almost hyper-awake, afraid to go to sleep and wake up back at the mall. It wasn't unusual to see the newcomers walking down Main Street staring in awe at the buildings. The Saturday matinee of Star Wars was greeted with emotional sobs from some of the new people in the audience.

It was easy to understand that the people from the mall had given up all hope. Only the deep desire to survive had kept them going in the difficult conditions of their former haven. Now they had a refuge that felt a lot like the old world that had seemed so distant for so long. It was amazing to be in a safe place. A place where children could ride their bikes down the street and old folks sat in the sun talking about the good ol'days.

The rest of the week was about settling in and helping people find their niche. The soldiers from the mall seemed relieved to finally be able to do their job. They joined the guard ranks and began daily sweeps outside the wall. Construction began on another courtyard that would house the four helicopters.

The fort found itself once more evolving. Life moved on.

* * * * *

Katie was too tired to help settle the new citizens of the fort. She felt guilt, but after losing Jenni and her father, she just wanted to sleep. Travis stayed with her the first day, but he could not stand not doing anything and returned to work.

She nestled down in the bed, covered up in blankets, and slept. To her dismay, she didn't dream of Jenni. To her relief she didn't dream of the mall. She did dream of Lydia. She was having a picnic with Travis and Lydia. She sat in the bright sunlight holding her baby as they laughed and told stories as she played with her baby's toes. The day had been beautiful in her dream. The Texas sky seemed endless and majestic. A part of her had been terrified that something was going to go horribly wrong and destroy the tranquil scene, but it ended when she woke up to Travis lightly kissing her lips.

"You were smiling in your sleep," he said as he slid into bed with her.

She curled up against him and held him tightly. "I had a good dream. No zombies. No death."

"A very good dream then," he decided.

Her fingers played with the curls falling over his brow and he nestled into her arms. "I wish I would dream about Jenni. Juan and Jason did, but...I look for her in my dreams but never find her."

"You will," Travis promised. "Maybe she has nothing to say yet to you. You know Jenni. She's probably distracted watching over Jason and Juan and expects me to take care of you."

"True, but I miss her."

Travis kissed her brow softly. "I miss her, too. She was amazingly brave."

"Or stupid."

"She did the right thing. We both know it." Travis hesitated, then said in a gentler tone. "You did the right thing."

"I know. I know! But I just hate that she isn't here anymore. I miss her. I really thought she'd be here for the birth of our baby. I thought she'd be able to give me Mommy advice."

"Well, the one thing about Jenni is that she always made choices with her heart. She always did what she felt she had to do," Travis reminded Katie. "And that was one of the things that made her lovable even when you wanted to kick her ass for some of the stuff she pulled."

"Yeah. I know. She could be exasperating." She felt the tears welling up and she choked back a sob. "But I loved her."

With gentleness that was soothing, Travis stroked Katie's hair as he gazed into her eyes. "She loved you, Katie. You guys had a strong bond. It's still there. Don't forget that."

Katie wiped her tears away and tucked her head under his chin. "I know. I know. But it still hurts and I still miss her."

* * * * *

Nerit was on watch on the wall when Kevin finally reappeared from his long slumber. Blinking in the bright sunlight, he stood rather shakily, a peanut butter sandwich in one hand, looking out over the town.

"It's real," he said with relief.

Nerit smiled at him. "Yes and you're home."

Kevin smiled slightly as he looked down over the town and saw people from the mall moving about, living their lives once more. "It feels great."

* * * * *

Disco Night was a huge success. The Southern Baptists sat it out, but most of the people showed up in the ballroom. There was plenty of laughter, plenty of beer, and lots of dancing.

Kevin got on the dance floor with Nerit while Bill and Katarina attempted to remember the moves from the old days. Curtis followed Linda around and managed to get her to dance once or twice. Guadalupe and Old Man Watkins sat together, laughing as they watched the kids dance.

Katie sat most of the night in a comfortable chair, enjoying conversations with new friends and old. She didn't feel like dancing. She had always danced with Jenni at these socials and it felt odd to not have her best friend around.

After awhile, Travis stole Nerit away from Kevin and twirled her around.

The music pounded and thumped and kept people on the dance floor. It was a good night.

After coming off the dance floor, Kevin sat next to Katie. He had danced with quite a few of the ladies. He was popular with the mall women and the fort women thought him quite handsome. It was good to just sit down for a few and enjoy the music. He joined Katie in watching Travis dance with Charlotte. They didn't really speak, but smiled at each other often. Now that their battle weariness had worn off after their long slumber, they were left with just a dull numbness that was slowly ebbing away. They were both slowly coming back to life.

"Strange," Kevin finally said.

"What?"

"I didn't think Bette was gay," he said, then shrugged.

Katie looked out on the dance floor to see Bette and Linda dancing together. Many women were dancing together. It wasn't that unusual, but the amazing sparks flying between Bette and Linda were undeniable.

"I didn't think Linda was either and my radar is pretty good," Katie answered, then shrugged.

"It's like they say...love knows no bounds," Kevin decided.

Out of the corner of her eye, Katie caught sight of Curtis pushing through the crowd toward the exit. His expression said it all. He had seen the sparks as well. She sighed and looked back at the two women. It was always good to see new love, but sad to see hopes of love crushed.

Finally, Kevin turned to Katie and held out his hand. "Want to dance?" She hesitated, then nodded. "Why not? I have to start sometime."

It was almost like a sign when one of Gloria Gaynor's hits came on. Katie knew it was one of Jenni's favorites. With a slight smile, she started to move to the music, Kevin leading the way. Trying to follow his steps, she laughed when she tripped and about four people moved to catch her.

"I'm fine," she assured them, then began to move again.

Someone had rigged up a disco ball over the dance floor made out of foil and tiny lights danced over them like little fairies. She found herself laughing as Kevin showed off his fancy dance moves with mastery that would make John Travolta jealous. Soon he was twirling her around with an expertise that she found exhilarating. He was so great, he made her look good. With the music pulsating, they danced through the crowd, laughing and having a good time.

What made it more special was that every time Kevin twirled Katie around, for a moment, she would see Jenni dancing nearby. She could never look at Jenni straight on, but when she was whirled about, she could see Jenni's flying black hair as she strutted her stuff to Gloria Gaynor's "I Will Survive."

As the song ended, Katie hugged Kevin tightly. It may have been a mirage, but it had been a comfort to imagine Jenni near her. "Thank you, Kevin."

"Life's too short not to dance," Kevin answered with a small smile.

"I'll try to remember that."

Walking back to her seat, Katie still felt the absence off her father and Jenni, but she also saw the faces of those that remained behind. Her husband, Nerit, Peggy, Bill, Katarina, and all the others who were now dear friends. Even smelly Calhoun dancing in one corner with his dogs at his feet was a welcome sight.

Travis collapsed into a chair beside her and flashed his boyish grin. Katie grabbed his hand and pressed a kiss to his lips.

"You okay?"

"Not yet, but I will be," she answered.

Travis gathered her into his arms and she laid her head against his chest.

Chapter 23

1. Happy Anniversary

"Can't believe it's March already," Peggy huffed.

Stacey looked up from the ledger she was studying and lifted her eyebrows. "It is?"

"It's been one month since the new people arrived. It was the first part of February." Peggy was busy making a homemade calendar on the back of a used piece of paper.

"We missed Valentine's Day," Stacey said in awe. "Wow."

"I bet the men didn't mind that," Peggy grumbled.

"I guess we've all been so busy, we all forgot." Stacey marked off a few items on her ledger then reached for the next form in her pile. "Strange. Zombies rise and we're still doing paperwork."

Lenore knocked lightly on the door to the office where Peggy and Stacey were working. "I'm heading out to help the shopping crew. I took twenty more bolts. They're looking low."

Stacey reached out and Lenore handed her a slip of paper. "I'll let Jason and his crew know they need to make more."

"Thanks."

"How are you doing, Lenore?" Peggy began to number her calendar.

"A girl can only cry so much over a boy," Lenore answered.

"Gotcha." Peggy looked up at Lenore. "That handsome Kevin Reynolds is single."

"You do realize that just because you put a black woman and a black man in the same room, it don't mean they're gonna hook up right?" Lenore scowled.

"I was just saying-"

"Crazy ass white people," Lenore rolled her eyes.

"You'd make cute babies," Stacey offered helpfully.

Lenore just growled and stalked off.

"What got into her?" Peggy arched an eyebrow.

Stacey shrugged and updated her ledger again. "We're getting low on sweet peas."

"We're getting low on everything. Hopefully, all this damn shopping in town will help." Peggy finished her calendar and circled the present date. "Well, I'll be damned."

"What is it?"

"It's been a year. Today." Peggy laid a trembling hand over her heart. "It's been a year ago today since it all went down into zombie hell."

240

"Should we tell people?" Stacey's face had drained of blood beneath her ever present tan.

"I don't know. Would it do any good?" Peggy looked down at the calendar again. "It seems so much longer."

"It's Spring, too." Stacey sat back in her chair, her fingers playing with the tip of her ponytail.

"A year." Peggy thought of all that had happened and was amazed. "A year."

2. Spring Shopping

The house was at least seventy years old. The paint was peeling off the front porch and the screen door hung limply from the one hinge keeping it in place. Spring had brought fresh blooms to the plants nestled in pots in the window boxes and along the front path. Fresh green blades of grass were pressing up through the cracks in the walk up to the house.

Heavy boots moved slowly and almost silently up the sidewalk. Six figures garbed in camouflage headed toward the house. Each soldier moved with agility that comes with endless hours of training and experience. All of them wore heavy gloves, helmets and imposing gas masks. Speaking only with hand signals, they moved smoothly up to the front door.

Two soldiers peered in through the front windows then signaled to the leader. He nodded and made a motion. Another soldier immediately kicked in the front door.

They flowed into the house, moving swiftly, their weapons held ready.

The living room was devoid of life. A dog lay near the front door. It was emaciated and long dead. It had never made it out of the house. Moving on, they cleared the dining room then a kitchen. Every door was opened, with soldiers at the ready.

Finally, they began down the narrow hallway to the bedrooms. The leader motioned to everyone to be as silent as possible. The first bedroom door opened on a neat room with everything in its place. The closet door was opened, the bed checked under, but nothing stirred. The next room was more chaotic and there were signs of a struggle. But again, nothing lurched out of the shadows.

The next room was also a bedroom and a corpse lay near the door. Its head was bashed in and a heavy lamp lay nearby, the base of it caked with dried blood. Again, the room was quickly checked and then one last door remained.

One soldier leaned over and gently turned the knob. The door swung open and revealed a narrow little bathroom. A woman stood in the shower. She growled and lunged forward, but one hand was tied firmly to the shower head by a towel and she struggled to get free. Either she had tied herself to the shower before she died or someone else had done it. Snapping her teeth at them, she again lunged forward, but only managed to trip and slide downward. Trying to get up, she pulled hard on her restrained arm. Bones cracked and ligaments snapped and it was clear she would pull free of her arm to get to them.

One soldier moved forward and shot her in the head.

It was over.

The house was secured.

"It's clear. Get the shoppers in here," Kevin's voice said from within one of the gas masks.

* * * * *

The door of the moving truck slid up and a soldier motioned to the men and women huddled inside.

Pulling off her mask, Bette said, "The house is clear and the perimeter is secure. Get in and get out as fast as possible."

The Shoppers began to jump down, carrying boxes and storage bins. They hurried into the house as soldiers stood on watch, weapons at the ready. The Shoppers would clear the house of all useful items then return to the truck. It was a dangerous job, but they were getting better at getting in and out before the undead population turned out in force.

Linda jumped down last and squeezed Bette's shoulder. "I get scared every time you go in."

"I worry about you, too," Bette said with a shy grin. "Now, hurry. Let's get this shopping done so we can go home."

"It's a date," Linda said with a wink, then hurried away with her basket in her hand.

Nearby, a stumbling zombie was taken down with a single shot to the head.

Shopping day was always a bitch.

3. Out With The Old

The first bulldozer tore into the old house with frightening ease. The old structure quivered then began to slide off its foundation, folding in on itself in a splintering splendor. From high above, Nerit watched from the Eagle's Nest. It was actually a suite in the hotel set aside for overseeing the demolition of the rest of the town. Someone had named it the Eagle's Nest and it had stuck.

Standing on the long balcony, she watched through binoculars as bulldozers destroyed the block designated for demolition this morning. The Shoppers had come and gone, taking all that was left of use in the houses. The structure's usefulness in this new world was over and would be destroyed.

There had been relatively low appearances of zombies. Considering all that had occurred since the first day, it was pretty much safe to speculate that most of the town's resident zombies were now dead. There had been a danger of zombies still trapped in the houses, but those had also been few and far between. Broken windows and splintered doors told of their escapes.

The residents of the fort had always known the town would be destroyed at some point. It had been inevitable. Now that the winter was becoming a fading memory and their stores were depleted by the influx of newcomers, tempers were flaring more often now.

Personal relationships were never easy and the honeymoon was over. The greatest deterrent to anyone trying to cause drama was the thought of ending up outside the walls. After the exile of Shane and Philip and their fate and the fiasco with Blanche, people kept things as civil as possible. It wasn't easy with a diverse group from just about every background.

The small group of Baptists were not pleased with certain developments in the fort. The special nights of dancing and drinking were heavily protested. The Reverend had tried to calm them, but they had turned on him for siding with the "heathens." Mary, the leader of the Baptist Coalition, petitioned for a room to be set aside for a new Baptist church. This has been granted and now there were two churches running in the fort.

Nerit was disappointed, but she did not attend either one of the services so it was really not her concern.

One of the smallest groups in the fort was the Hindu population. They were industrious, but often set apart. Nerit knew they were struggling to fit in. One of the older Indian women had cried when the Shoppers returned with bags of saris and cholis. It had been hard for her to try to adapt to wearing Western clothing.

Despite the growth of the fort population, things were running more smoothly. New extensions were being built as were more defensive traps. Maybe it was the beauty of dawning spring, but people seemed less restless than they had during winter and more willing to help out.

What had brought on the need for the demolition of the town was the foray to the National Guard in a town 120 miles away. It had been used as a rescue station until it had been overrun. Like many rescue stations, it had tried to help those who were mauled or bitten. Of course, this led to rapid infection within the compound. It had been overrun within hours. Two of the helicopters were from that base.

The soldiers had been relieved to move into the roles of protectors and not prison guards at the fort. They helped train their civilian counterparts under the watchful eye of Nerit, creating an even more effective force. Like Kevin, they were all smitten with Nerit. One of the younger men called her the hottest old lady ever when she showed off her sniping skills. But her knowledge went only so far and they were able to go beyond that point and continue the training of the civilian volunteers. One of the first things that was decided was that the civilians needed more protection when they ventured out of the fort. This resulted in a flyover of the National Guard Base. Supplies were needed and it was decided to risk it.

To Greta's surprise, not one creature was moving in the base when her helicopter flew over. There was no sign of any zombies inside or around the surrounding area. After several more recon flights, it was decided that the military would go in. It was one of the most terrifying moments in the fort history. But all the soldiers had returned with two helicopters full of additional equipment and weapons. They had found a few zombies inside the buildings, but they were slow and easily put down. The massive crowds of zombies they anticipated were not found.

"Migrating," Travis had said softly when he heard the news. "They're migrating."

"You know how they follow the living. Maybe someone was stupid enough to drive by or try to get in," Katie had offered up.

"The west gate was down. Twisted and bent like a great force went through it," Kevin had answered. "My bet is that the zombies all pushed against it until it went down and then they were free."

"Which direction are they going then?" Katie had asked.

"My guess? North. We didn't see anything between here and the National Guard."

"But they could come this way. Or another large group like that," Nerit had pointed out. "If they are not staying put and migrating, as Travis put it, then we could end up seeing a mass gathering of zombies coming our way."

"Shit," Katie had whispered.

It was then that they decided to do everything possible to secure the fort from a large invading body of the undead. The fort had already been constructed with the idea of a possible breach. There were strong, reinforced gates for every section. But if a large enough group of zombies came up against the fort walls...

"How's it going?" Travis' voice asked from behind her.

Nerit turned and gave him a tight smile. "So far, no trouble."

Travis gripped the railing and leaned against it staring out toward the bulldozers. A good three blocks were now demolished. "Damn shame."

"The old things are useless to us now," Nerit answered. "And we need to be able to see anything that approaches the fort."

"I wonder if we'll ever live in houses again," Travis pondered. "Go to the grocery store. Drive to a movie."

"In time, perhaps. But most likely not you or me. But your children's children, maybe."

Travis nodded with a grim expression etched on his face. "But we can hope. And plan. And try to make it happen."

"Yes," Nerit agreed. "We are pioneers in a new world. Frightening, isn't it? We were so used to the old. Unchallenged. So spoiled. Now we are back to hunting and gathering."

Below them several large trucks were heading back into town. The hunters had gone out for meat. The cattle population had dropped during the winter in the neighboring ranches, but the deer population seemed to be up. A group of men were now seeing to the care of the cattle. Once the herd was healthy again, beef would be back on the table. But until then, venison was the meat of choice.

"At least we got big guns and ammo," Travis said after a beat then winked at her.

Nerit laughed. "Yes, at least we have that."

They both looked out over the town as another house crashed to the ground. Birds were singing in the trees. Wildflowers covered the hills. The sky was bright blue with enormous fluffy white clouds gliding overhead.

Below them, the bulldozers continued to reshape the old world into the new.

Chapter 24

1. Regrets

"Go! Go! Go!"

Raleigh stumbled as he fled down the access corridor. His teeth snapped hard together and he immediately tasted blood. His hands caught onto a cart shoved up against the wall and he steadied himself, then kept running. He could see Charlie up ahead with the Senator. The soldier had a tight grip on her upper arm and despite her cries that he was hurting her, Charlie kept shoving, pulling and yanking her along.

Glancing behind him, he could see the dark face of Ruben glaring at him as he snarled at him to keep moving. Beyond Ruben, in the dim, sickly light, the undead followed. They were moaning and reaching out for the living, their slow, yet determined stride frightening in its relentlessness.

Ahead, Charlie reached the outside door and hesitated.

Raleigh stumbled on, barely able to catch his breath. The ammo was low so he knew Ruben wouldn't start firing unless he absolutely had to. The moans and stench of the dead were making his skin crawl. He turned to see Ruben shove some old chairs over, trying to block the dead.

"Just go," Ruben barked at Charlie over his shoulder.

With the sharp nod of his head, Charlie shoved the outside door open. Almost immediately gray hands shoved in toward them.

The Senator began screaming as Charlie opened fire, precious ammunition splattering the brains of those creatures trying to reach them. Then Charlie and the Senator were through the door and Raleigh, despite his terrible fear, followed.

Blinking in the harsh sunlight, Raleigh tried to rid his eyes of the temporary blindness that instantly fell on him. Stumbling over the dead bodies near the door, he started to follow Charlie and the Senator. They had been holed up in the theater for days. He felt dizzy and knew that all the sugar in the movie theater candy he had consumed was affecting him. He had to keep moving. It was almost comical how he reached into his pocket, pulled out a bag of M & M's and poured most of them into his mouth.

Ruben grabbed him from behind and shoved him down the alleyway. The moans of the undead echoed all around them.

Ahead of them, the Senator was cussing at Charlie, telling him not to be so rough. Charlie, to Raleigh's great satisfaction, was not listening.

The four of them, the last survivors of the second truck from the mall, stumbled into the street of the small town, and stood on unsteady legs, uncertain of what to do next. Their previous truck had broken down in this small town and they had to run for it when they were besieged by a mob of the undead. The theater had been their shelter until the front doors had given away.

A few vehicles stood in the street, empty of life. Some had flat tires now. The sun would soon bleach them of color and the elements would begin to slowly corrode them.

Nearby, a gas station stood silent. In the shade next to it was a brand new truck. The paper license plate was long faded, but it had been new when all of this had began.

"Go," Ruben ordered.

The four of them hurried down the street, the soldiers holding onto the arms of the civilians. The undead were at least a block away, slowly moving toward them. They had a little time. Thankfully, the zombies were very slow now. But if the humans did not move swiftly and intelligently, that slow moving mob would find them and then...

Raleigh felt sick and wanted to throw up, but he kept chewing the chocolate in his mouth. For the billionth time he cursed himself for staying with the Senator. He should have gone to the fort. He should have taken a knock to his fucking pride and joined the rednecks of the area in making a new life. Instead, he was on the run with the Senator, barely keeping alive.

"Keep moving," Ruben ordered as zombies appeared far down the street. "Just keep moving."

Raleigh had been stupid and he knew it. He had been so flattered by the Senator's pursuit of his skills as a campaign manager he had disregarded so much about her. Of course, her brother-in-law's money had boosted his confidence that he could shape her into a real political threat. It hadn't been easy. She was a bigot, an elitist and tended to not think before she spoke. She was a person of grandiose ideas with very little concept of how to execute them. People not in her own social circle tended to be disregarded. But he had worked damn hard on her. His whole team had managed to get her elected despite her stupid comment that she liked "brown people" when she was trying to impress the Hispanic vote.

What annoyed him the most was that he had known the Central idea was bullshit. He had sat in on her conversations. He had listened to everything said on the other side, but it was clear she never really understood what was truly happening. She had colored every conversation with her own point of view. She had been so intent on getting to Central, she didn't seem to understand that Central was barely existing. That is why they had been so desperate to establish supply lines to other survivor enclaves.

Why the hell had he gone with her?

It had been his desire to somehow make it to a better place than that damn mall. He should have realized that was the fort.

Looking around, he knew how terrible a mistake he had made.

The dead were coming.

Charlie moved swiftly to the truck and checked the doors. One was unlocked and he opened it swiftly. There was no key inside. Shoving the Senator in, he said, "If we're lucky, the guy is inside the store."

Ruben motioned to Raleigh to get into the truck and he willingly obeyed. Then the two soldiers disappeared around the corner.

"How did we get stuck with complete morons?" the Senator huffed. Her usual bouffant hair was flat and her face was clean of makeup. She began to search the truck, feeling under the seats, looking desperately for a key.

Raleigh joined her, uncertain of where to look, but scrounging around anyway. He could hear the moans getting louder.

"They're coming," he whispered.

"I know, moron," she snapped.

Raleigh opened up the armrest and was startled to see the car keys. He pulled them out and looked at the Senator in shock.

"At least you can do something right." She grabbed them from him and turned on the truck. With the ease of any rich soccer mom, she pulled the truck around to the front of the gas station and honked.

The two startled soldiers rushed out. They had been inside systematically killing the four zombies inside then looking through their pockets for keys.

"Get in," she ordered, sliding into the center of the seat.

Charlie slid in behind the wheel while Ruben moved around to the other side of the truck. Already the fit was tight and Raleigh tried to make himself as small as possible.

"Get out and let him in first," the Senator ordered.

Raleigh hesitated, then obeyed. His eyes flicked to the horde coming closer and closer.

Ruben slid in and pushed himself up tight to the Senator. Raleigh began to climb in when he saw the Senator smile then slam her foot down on Charlie's as she shifted gears. The truck lurched forward, knocking Raleigh to the side.

He never realized how close the undead were until he saw one reaching down for him. He really should have gone with the others from the fort. He really should have...

Inside the truck, Ruben shouted, "What the fuck?"

"We needed a distraction," the Senator answered, leaning across Ruben's lap to shut the door.

Shakily, Charlie continued driving, trying not to look at his mirrors.

"You are one cold-hearted bitch," Ruben declared angrily.

"I could have driven off with him and left you," the Senator answered coolly. "Remember that."

Behind them, the zombies feasted. Ruben averted his eyes from the mirrors and looked down at the M & M wrapper on the floor. He wondered if Raleigh tasted like chocolate.

2. When All is New

Everything had changed. Nothing was the same.

Katie jogged down Main Street, her pony tail swinging back and forth behind her head like a pendulum.

Overhead a helicopter was veering off toward the north. It was probably running some field workers out to a nearby ranch the fort was attempting to secure. Or maybe going to the farm. Or maybe taking someone to check on the water station. Or maybe it was just refueling at the nearby airstrip.

Helicopters...

Who would have thought the fort would have helicopters back when they were just trying to survive. Jenni had joked about a handsome black leading man and helicopters when they were first on the road. She had been full of Romero film facts and tossed them out as if they were the zombie bible.

Katie's eyes suddenly stung and she tried not to think of Jenni in her pink bathrobe riding shotgun beside her in that old white pickup.

Jogging around the corner she saw Nerit taking a calm stroll down the street. Her hands were tucked into her pockets and she looked more relaxed than Katie had ever seen her. Of course, with the influx of soldiers into the fort, Nerit's job had become easier. Beside Nerit ambled her old hunting dog and Katie smiled at them as she jogged past.

How different Nerit was from the first time she saw her on the roof of Ralph's Hunting store. The long braid was gone now. She had a younger hairdo, cut short and sassy to her shoulders. Ken had insisted on it along with the rinse that took the yellow caste from her silver locks. Nerit looked younger now and more at peace.

Katie almost felt resentful of Nerit moving on past Ralph. Of course, she had moved on past Lydia. Even her father's death was muted now. She had assumed he was dead for months and to be given a chance to talk to him, share with him her new life, and say goodbye had been a gift.

But it was hard to let go of Jenni.

They had saved each other in so many ways so many times. In her heart she knew Jenni had done the right thing that day and so had she. It was only right that she fired the bullet that rescued Jenni from death at the hands of the zombies. But it still hurt.

Swinging around another corner, she jogged along the interior of the wall. Above her, on a sturdy platform were Jason and some of the other teenagers. They were busy building a catapult. Even Jack was up on the platform, leashed in case he tried anything crazy like diving over the wall at a zombie.

Jason seemed better lately. Stronger. He had wept for days, but even through his tears, he kept saying that he knew his Mom was all right. He had seen her in a dream and knew she had come to comfort him. It was all right. Soon, he had crawled out of bed and started drawing defensive weapon schematics for the fort.

He was moving on...

With a small frown, she ran under the platform and then turned down another street. Bill came into view wearing his new police uniform. The police force for the fort was now five former police officers. They all wore matching uniforms when on duty. Though crime was not a common occurrence in the fort, they did have to deal with a small load of petty theft, occasional fights, and sadly, domestic disputes. Since the council had made it clear that any major crime would result in immediate expulsion from the fort, those inclined toward crime were kept in check. There was a strong fear of what lay beyond the hills.

"Hey, Bill," Katie called out as she jogged toward him.

"Hey, Katie. How you feeling," he answered with a grin. He looked kind of handsome in his uniform. The fresh glow of his newfound love with Katarina also made him more attractive.

"Good. Just getting my morning jog in before chores," she answered. Running up to him, she kept moving, but managed to give him a quick hug.

"Tell your husband the poker game is at eight tonight," Bill said. I plan to demolish him, Juan and Eric."

"Okay. Will do," she answered, laughing.

As she passed by the theater she caught sight of Linda and Bette holding hands and staring up at an old poster someone had tacked up announcing the premiere of Jaws. The bloom of their brand new love affair was still fresh and beautiful. Of course, there were naysayers. There was a group of fundamentalists, mostly Southern Baptists, who had a strong issue with the miniscule gay population in the fort.

And then there was Curtis.

Curtis was never happy anymore. Never smiled. Never did much of anything other than sit in the communication center or patrol the streets with Bill. He avoided social gatherings that would put him near Linda. Curtis' total breakdown after Linda hooked up with Bette was heartbreaking. It was just a damn shame that he had to be hurt because Linda found someone to truly love.

Of course, moving on in this world was important.

But how could she let Jenni go? Their life together seemed unfinished.

Kevin and Travis came into view as she headed back toward the hotel. They were standing up on the wall with Eric. Talking animatedly, they were obviously planning more expansions. They were all smiling. Kevin clapped Travis on the shoulder and they both laughed. It made Katie smile a little, but it hurt at the same time.

Jenni was gone...

Kevin was just as powerful a presence as Jenni in the fort. At times, Katie resented it. But he was very nice and she liked him very much.

But sometimes she wanted to scream at him. "Why are you here and she's not?"

But she knew the answer and it wasn't Kevin's fault.

Tears were now hot and heavy in her eyes and she fought them.

Running through the gates into the old construction site, she saw Juan in one corner. He wasn't allowed to do any of the heavy work. He was still healing, but he had managed to get permission to build a small garden as a memorial to Jenni and others who had died. Already he had the area roped off and was busy breaking the ground. Bags of rich soil and fertilizer sat nearby. Behind him was a statue of the Virgin Mary resting against the wall, ready to be erected at some point.

Slowly, she came to a stop near him, slowly stretching out her limbs. Her baby bump was a little bit of an issue, but she was learning to work with it.

How could she have gained and yet lost so much in just a year? She had been shocked when Peggy had told her a whole year had passed since the first day.

Standing with her hands resting on her swollen belly, she looked toward Juan. His ponytail was falling into his face and he kept flipping it back. He seemed intent on not looking up and slowly Katie realized he was crying as he worked.

Refusing to cry, refusing the release it might bring her, she walked determinedly into the fort.

She wasn't ready yet. She couldn't do it. Despite the changes in the world around her she couldn't let go of Jenni. Not yet.

She just couldn't.

3. While You Were Sleeping

Walking light-footed across the floor, Ruben moved toward Charlie. The younger man was seated in a window, hunting rifle slung across his lap, staring down over the darkened street. They were holed up in a small town museum and night was settling firmly over the land. Only the full moon gave any light to the room.

Behind them the Senator was fast asleep on a World War II cot in a recreation of a bunker. She was snoring loudly.

"Charlie," Ruben said softly, barely a whisper.

Charlie looked at him slowly. The boy's face was pinched and a little gray. The food they had salvaged two days before had been bad. They were all a little shaky still.

"Wazzup?"

Ruben crouched down next to the nineteen year old. He had eight years on the boy, but he felt old and fatherly toward the younger man.

"Time to go," he whispered.

Charlie looked slowly toward the Senator, then back at Ruben. "Gonna wake her?"

"No." The word was said softly, firmly and with conviction.

"Okay," Charlie answered, slowly sliding off the windowsill. He stood on still shaky legs and took a deep breath. "Is it right? To leave her?" His voice was soft, but the emotion was thick.

"I listened in on her last conversation with Central," Ruben said oh so quietly. "Everything she's been saying is bullshit. They aren't telling her to find a safe location for pickup. They're telling her they ain't gonna get us."

Charlie pressed his lips firmly together and in the moonlight his eyes glistened with tears. He was an East Texas bayou boy. All he wanted to do was get home to the swamps. Ruben was from south San Antonio. He wanted to go home, too, but he knew that there was nothing left. Central had given Charlie hope and Ruben had just killed it. He felt like a shit doing it, but they had made enough mistakes.

"We left those people in the mall..." Charlie whispered, his voice catching. "We saw the smoke. But we kept going..."

"I know. We fucked up," Ruben said softly.

Charlie lowered his eyes, then nodded. "Yeah."

"Look, kid, we stay with her, we die. You saw what she did to Raleigh. She'll do it to us. We're her fucking bodyguards. She doesn't give a shit about us," Ruben said firmly.

Charlie sighed, then picked up his backpack very quietly. "I know. I just wanted to go home."

Ruben nodded and grabbed the boy firmly by the back of the neck and pressed his forehead to the boy's. Behind them the Senator snored loudly. "I'm gonna get you to a safe place. I promise."

"The fort?"

Ruben sighed. "No. We fucked up like the devil and we're cast out of paradise. We gotta find another place."

The younger man looked fragile in the light. Like a ten year old. He reminded Ruben of his younger brother and it hurt like hell.

Without another word, they crept across the floor, careful not to make noise, then stealthily down the stairs. The zombie infestation was minimal in this town, but they carefully looked out the windows before unbolting the door. Stepping out into the cool spring air, they moved toward the truck.

A zombie lurched out from the shadows, uttering a low moan startling both of them. Its rotting hands reached for them as its yellowed teeth champed together. Ruben stepped forward it and firmly cold-cocked it with his rifle. It fell to the ground, still moaning. Ruben brought the rifle butt down again and silenced the fiend.

Charlie slipped into the driver's seat of the truck and flung his bag in the back. It held a few possessions, but mostly ammo for the hunting rifle he had picked up a few towns back.

Ruben also slid into the truck and shut the passenger door.

"Where are we going?"

Ruben stared down the silent street. A few zombies staggered through the gloom, washed gray by the moonlight.

"West."

Charlie nodded. "Okay."

The truck roared to life and moved down the road a block before the headlights flipped on. It moved faster, zombies bouncing off its grill, then it turned a corner and was gone.

Meanwhile, the Senator snored on.

Chapter 25

1. A Beautiful Day Gone Wrong

Travis glanced out of the helicopter window down into the lush hill country and slightly smiled. It was beautiful now that spring was fully spread over the land. Trees were radiant in their coats of leaves and the wild grass flowed like rich green water over the hills. Cows ambled down country roads while deer frolicked among the overgrown orchards. A few horses were racing across a field with wild glee, free of human restraints.

"Beautiful, huh?" Kevin grinned over at him. "A gorgeous April day."

Travis nodded and adjusted his headset slightly. It was uncomfortable but it was the only way to hear anyone above the roar of the helicopter. "I wish Katie could see it. That the world is still alive."

"She will. Things are getting better for all of us," Kevin answered.

It had been weeks since the last zombie had been seen around the fort. Of course this didn't stop the constant reinforcement of the walls or the defensive traps being put in place. Catapults were up on the walls now, giving the fort a medieval feel. Large bins were full of all sorts of heavy trash to lob at any invading zombie horde. The walls were higher now and topped with razor wire. The new areas were being reinforced.

Everyone, including children, were being given regular training to defend themselves. Someone nicknamed the fort "Sparta." After seeing a five year old spearing a zombie dummy over and over again, it somehow seemed appropriate.

What a bizarre world to bring a child into, yet, they had to move on. Live on.

"I know that," Travis said after a long moment. "I know things are better. But it's hard not to look back and mourn all that we have lost."

"How is Katie doing about Jenni?"

"She won't talk about her anymore. She's doing great with the pregnancy and we're fine. Jenni is a topic we can't address at all." Travis rubbed his chin and sighed. "I miss Jenni, too, but they were out there on their own for awhile and that really bonded them. Katie is taking her loss very, very hard."

Kevin's expression was sad and understanding. "Yeah. After awhile you feel you can't lose anymore or you'll lose yourself."

Thinking of Katie and her radiant smile, Travis silently agreed. He couldn't imagine a world without her. The feel of her soft hair, the kiss of her lips. In every way he completely adored her. If he lost her...

It killed him to see Juan working so slowly, but so diligently on his small memorial garden for Jenni. Juan was not only in physical pain, but he was emotionally hurting in a way Travis could only imagine. Yet, what Travis imagined was so painful, he couldn't fathom what the reality must be like. Juan had to live that reality.

Juan joined them for the Thursday night poker games, but he seemed a muted version of himself. He still laughed and joked, but his expression was haunted. Rosie told Travis that Juan just needed to find something to live for. Maybe that little garden was it. At least, for now.

Slowly, the helicopter banked over the ranch the fort had reclaimed and Travis caught sight of the cowboys riding their horses alongside the herd of cows. They were moving them to a reinforced pasture surrounded by a new high fence.

"This is really amazing. We're really doing it. Building the new world," Travis said in awe.

"Yep," Kevin grinned. "We are."

"As long as-"

"Don't jinx it, man!" Kevin gripped his arm and gave him a stern glare. "Don't say anything to jinx it. Just enjoy it."

Travis laughed, then inclined his head. "You're right. You're right."

The helicopter finished its pass and headed back toward the fort on the hill.

2. Daddy One

It started slowly as all love stories do.

It started with one lone man working long hours on a small garden in a corner of what had been a construction site. Day by day, he toiled slowly and painfully. His long curly ponytail fell over one shoulder as he worked and he rarely looked up as people strolled by.

Silence is what he craved and silence is what he received. Everyone seemed afraid to talk to him and he was relieved. He didn't want to talk about her.

His Jenni.

His loca.

His heart and his love.

So he toiled on the memorial garden, the last thing he could give her.

True love comes slowly, they say.

In Jenni's case it had hit him so hard he had never seen it coming. Just one day it was there and it was good. He had relished every moment with her. In his mind's eye he could see her laughing until she fell over in a heap or dancing with wild abandon to some horrible song. Then there were the quiet times when she lay in his arms and her smile made this life beautiful and good.

Now she was gone and he could find no beauty around him. Everything was gray and dark.

So he was planting flowers for her. Something beautiful to remind him of her beauty.

When he had started his little endeavor, Charlotte's strict rules ringing in his ears, he had felt he would never love again.

He was wrong.

Working hard one morning, a shadow fell over him. He did not look up. Most of the time he was working with tears in his eyes and he did not want to reveal them to anyone. This time was no different. He did not look up.

"Whatcha doing?"

"Planting a memorial garden."

Standard reply. Standard neutral voice.

"What does that mean?"

The voice was tiny. Female.

"It's for those who died. To remember them."

"Oh." A long pause. Then, "My Mommy and Daddy died."

Hesitating, he looked up slowly.

A blond girl around eight or nine years old stood above him. Her long blond hair trailed around her face and her eyes were so dark and vivid, they reminded him of Jenni. Holding tight to the girl's t-shirt was a little boy around four or five and another girl maybe around six. The little boy had masses of dark hair and big chestnut brown eyes. The second girl was blond with clear blue eyes.

It was the three children Jenni had given her life for.

Juan had been avoiding them for weeks now. He had seen them wandering through the fort, always looking a bit lost, three little waifs. Peggy tried hard to take care of them, but the three children did not speak to her or anyone else. The oldest occasionally would ask a question, but mostly they drifted through the fort like tiny ghosts.

Juan didn't know what to say. At times, he could barely stand to look at the three children. He almost hated them. They were alive because Jenni had died.

The little boy leaned down and began to gently run his fingers through the earth at the base of the freshly planted violets.

"I have a lot of work to do," Juan finally said.

"Can we help?" the oldest one asked.

"No, no. I don't think so."

The middle child, her lips pursed, gently ran her fingers over the features of the face of the Virgin Mary statue. "She's pretty."

Juan felt a sense of panic coming over him.

The oldest girl squatted down and began to dig another hole. A whole tray of flowers were waiting to be planted. They had been salvaged from yards around town by Linda and Bette for him.

"We used to do this with our Mommy," she said finally.

Juan felt a lump in his throat and fought not to cry.

The children clustered around him, already finding things to do. The middle child began lay bits of pink granite in a little row along the walkway Juan had already laid down. People had been writing the names of their deceased family members on each stone. The oldest girl began to work at planting the next batch of flowers while the little boy diligently helped.

Unable to speak for fear of crying, Juan let them be and kept to his work. Their tiny presences made him angry. Jenni had died to save them. They were here because she was gone.

"What is your name?" the little boy asked in a hushed, raspy voice.

As far as Juan knew, this was the first time the boy had said anything to anyone.

"Juan," he managed.

"One," the little boy said with satisfaction.

"No. Juan."

"One," the boy said with a small smile.

Juan started to correct him and then thought differently. The boy was talking and that had to be important.

Despite his agony, despite his pain, he let them be. To his surprise they were good little workers. When he came out the next day to work, they were waiting for him. He hesitated, not sure if he could deal with their presence another day, but finally he relented to their tiny smiles.

They worked hard around him, sweating, getting dirty, talking in hushed voices, but they were determined to help. A few people came by and tried to get the children to talk, but they refrained, drawing close to Juan as if seeking his protection.

Once more, he felt angry and wanted to scream at them and make them flee, but he couldn't.

So they worked on together.

Every morning he found them waiting for him. Peggy would make sure they had breakfast and had work clothes on, but otherwise left them to Juan's supervision. They called him One and would ask him countless questions about the garden, but when others would speak to them, they fell silent.

Slowly, his anger faded and he began to enjoy their company. The garden began to look lush and beautiful with its red brick walkways edged with pink granite and the plethora of blooming flowers.

"I like bluebonnets," the oldest girl, Margie, told Juan and tickled his nose with one.

"And why is that?"

"Cause they're pretty," she answered with a laugh and rolled her eyes. Juan just smiled.

He began to have lunch with them and then breakfast. They began to laugh and tell him stories. Every night when they went inside to be with Peggy and her son, they would hug him and give him kisses on his cheeks. The pain slowly lessened inside and he found himself smiling.

One morning, as a helicopter ascended into the sky, he found himself seated in the completed garden. The bench beneath him was cool and the breeze was fresh. The three little ones came and sat on the bench across from him, all three smiling.

"We decided that you are now our new daddy," the oldest informed him.

The other two nodded, smiling wide happy smiles.

Flustered, Juan said, "You did? Why?"

"The lady with the black hair told us," the eldest answered.

The other two nodded.

"Which lady?" He already knew the answer in his heart.

"The lady from the mall. The nice lady who took care of us after Mommy got..." the girl hesitated. "You know."

"When did she tell you this?"

"Last night. In our dreams," the little boy answered. "She's pretty."

This was so like Jenni. She was making sure the kids were fine and that he was, too. He laughed, tears in his eyes, and whispered, "Oh, Loca..."

Then the kids were leaping on him, hugging him, kissing him and he held them tight.

"Daddy One! Daddy One," they chanted.

Juan felt the shadow of pain lift from him and he threw back his head and laughed. He was so full of love he felt as if it must be bursting out of him. He leaped to his feet and danced around with glee, the kids dangling off of him.

Somewhere, he knew Jenni was smiling down on them.

3. The Wickedest Woman in Texas Returns

Patting her hair once more, the Senator regarded her image in the mirror. Armed with a teasing comb and the best hairspray on the market, she had manipulated her blond hair into a bubble of perfectly coiffed golden locks. Spritzing more hairspray onto her bouffant, she closed her heavily made up eyes, complete with false eyelashes, and enjoyed the fragrance of the spray as it fell in tiny drops over her hair and face.

Opening her eyes again, she studied her reflection in the soft, white glow of the chandelier over her head and smiled. It was her best smile. Her trademark. The pearly white freshly scrubbed teeth glistened between her bright pink lips. Perfect.

Tilting her head, she fastened diamond and pearl earrings to her ears as the tranquil sounds of Frank Sinatra wafted in from the intercom.

At least Blanche had the decency to keep some good music in her old mansion.

Walking away from the vanity, she studied herself in the full length gilded mirror in Blanche's enormous closet and turned one way then the other. The dark pink suit looked perfect and the gold sling back heels were very nice. Her nails on her fingertips and toes were freshly polished.

Nearly three weeks ago she had awakened to utter silence in that dank old museum and realized the chickenshits had run off without her. Sitting up she had studied the room while listening for sounds of any undead in the building. At least the assholes had been decent enough to shut the door behind them.

"Fuckers," she had hissed, then reached down and picked up her hunting rifle.

Now it was propped on a chair behind her. She had used it a few times since that day. After making sure that the idiots had really run off without her, she had slipped off the safety, slung her bag with the portable radio inside it over one shoulder, and walked into the morning air. Comfortable with the hunting rifle, she was a Texas girl after all, she had taken a deep breath as she walked to steady her nerves. If she remembered correctly, she had downed about five zombies before commandeering a truck standing empty in the middle of the road with the keys still in the ignition. It had taken a few tries to get the engine to turn over. She knew she had been lucky on that point. The zombies banging on the windows had been damned determined.

"Oh, shit," she now muttered and fussed with the collar of the jacket.

The last few weeks had been hard. She had even cried once or twice. She hated not being able to fix her hair and makeup. Worse yet, forced to eat convenience store junk food, she had often been sick to her stomach. Sticking to back roads, she had slowly found her way back here to Blanche's mansion.

When she had driven up, she had found the front door open and dried bits of bone and flesh on the doorstep. No zombies had been around and she had stepped inside and shut the door behind her. Quickly searching the house, she found nothing dead and smelly to greet her.

The water had been on, but there had been no electricity. Checking the breaker box, she had seen that the main one had flipped. In a few seconds, the mansion was lit up and the air conditioning switched on.

What had been even nicer, was that on her way to the mansion she had found a car stalled off the side of the road, full of supplies. It looked like someone had been fully stocked and making a run for safety then their car had broken down. Since there was something disgusting and dead on the doorstep, she wondered if that was the driver. Or maybe, Blanche.

Oh, well.

Going over to Blanche's dresser, she pulled on a nice string of pearls and studied her reflection in another mirror.

Yes, much better.

Frowning as the sound of zombies moaning seemed to grow louder, she walked over and turned up the music. She really had no time to deal with them and they were definitely not getting in past the heavy doors and reinforced glass.

Feeling pleased with herself, she went downstairs and into the kitchen. Her dinner of rosemary chicken was just about done and she inhaled the rich fragrance. Shooting that little shit's head off had been fun, but eating it would be so much better. There was quite a few wild chickens now and she didn't think she'd be starving any time soon. Pouring herself a glass of wine, she leaned against the counter and watched the decaying remains of what looked like a Mexican field worker bang on the kitchen window. She knew there was no way he was getting in, so she lifted her glass and toasted him.

Stupid spics. Even dead they were annoying.

For a moment she missed Raleigh chiding her for her "bias." Well, he was gone, that little annoying faggot, and she was still here.

Now that a few days had passed and she was feeling more sure of herself, her thoughts were once more turning to the fort. Slowly, she was making plans. Plans that would restore her to where she needed to be.

Smiling, she turned her back on the moaning zombie and sipped her wine.

4. The March of the Dead

Rune slept in the hunter blind he had discovered off a back road. His parked bike was right next to the trap door and his hand grenades were in the bag next to him. The ramshackle wood blind was sturdy enough for his temporary needs, but the canvas roof was torn and not much protection from the wind and light rain. He was huddled up against the wall, snoring lightly when he was awakened by a simple touch on his knee.

Waking up with a start, he drew his Glock and aimed it at the figure kneeling next to him. The trap door was still shut and how the stranger next to him had entered the blind was a mystery.

"Don't move," he ordered.

There was no zombie moan in response. The dark figure didn't even move.

With his other hand, he lifted his Maglite flashlight and flicked it on.

A pretty face with huge dark eyes was illuminated by the harsh white light.

"Jenni!"

"Hey, Rune."

Rune lowered his gun slowly, his hand beginning to tremble. He swallowed hard, then said, "Sorry."

She rolled her shoulders under her red sweater. Her dark hair framed her face. "I'm okay with it."

"You go out good?"

"Hell, yeah! I went out in style! I saved a bunch of people I love. It was good. I'm proud of how I went out!" Jenni grinned with satisfaction.

"Good for you. You went out a warrior. Good for you," Rune commended her proudly. It was a damn shame she had crossed over, but he has always thought she was something special.

He began to reholster his Glock, but she held out her hand, her smile fading.

"Don't. You need that. In fact, you need to get moving," Jenni urged him.

"Shit. What's going on?"

"They're coming out of the east. They started walking this way a few weeks ago. They've grown in number. You have to warn the fort."

"Damn, Jenni, that don't sound good!"

"You need to go now." Jenni was beginning to blur around the edges.

Rune fought to keep his teeth from chattering as the air around him grew colder. That she had appeared so realistically was impressive, but she was drawing all the energy from the air around him.

"I'm going," he answered.

Jenni didn't even answer. She was simply gone.

Whipping the trap door open, Rune dropped his motorcycle bags down onto the ground next the bike. It looked clear under the blind. Heaving his bag of grenades onto his shoulder, he swung his legs down over the ladder.

Faint moans made his skin crawl.

A gray, badly chewed hand reached out to grip his boot. A badly mutilated head missing large portions of its scalp and hair, drew close to his ankle, the rancid mouth of the zombie opening wide. Rune shot it and it fell away.

"Where the fuck were you?"

He kept his gun securely in one hand and dropped to the ground. He swung around in a circle and didn't see anymore dead things near him. Working quickly, he secured the motorcycle bags onto the bike. A few figures were struggling out of the trees off to his right. They moved slowly, but when they saw him their moans grew louder. The answering moans of what sounded like thousands of zombies made Runes' bowels heave.

Swinging his leg over his bike, he quickly gunned the engine. He didn't want to do it, but he turned on the headlight anyway. The bright light washed over the countless zombies filling hillside and valley.

"Shit!"

Pulling around, Rune raced the bike up the path, away from the shambling dead. His heart was beating fast in his chest and the Glock felt slippery in his moist hand. A few zombies were moving through the brush and reached out for him as he zoomed by. None were close enough to snag him, but their stench was rancid.

The night was full of the moans of the dead and Rune prayed hard as he made his way up the dirt path. He couldn't go as fast as he liked and the path was nearly overgrown in a few sections.

He was beginning to fear he was lost when he saw Jenni standing near the path. The light sluiced right through her as she urgently pointed he should swerve to his left. It was not the way from which he had originally come from, but he obeyed. The new path led him up a hill away and was not easy going. Another rider may not have been able to traverse the terrain, but he managed to reach the top, breaking through a line of trees around a stately old house.

Looking behind him, the moonlight illuminated the countless zombies filling the world below. His original path would have led him straight into them. Jenni had saved him.

Yanking on his gloves and helmet, he looked around and saw a long drive leading down to a country road. It was clear of the undead.

Feeling like Paul Revere, he gunned the engine and roared off toward the fort. Too bad he wasn't wasn't going to get to deliver the same message. Instead, he was going to have to tell them the zombies were coming.

5. The Long March Into The West

For weeks the undead had been making a long trek toward the west of Texas.

It had all begun when a handful of zombies ignored the unexpected feast in a military truck trying to break through I-35 and wandered after an escaping truck lumbering up a hill. The fifteen zombies had walked determinedly after the truck, stumbling and struggling over miles of fields and roads.

The original fifteen swelled in number as they walked through the south side of Fort Worth, then dead towns and farms. Some were caught in fences and languished there until the crows plucked out their eyes and vultures ate their flesh. Others toppled off overpasses onto the streets below, their heads cracking open and rendering them finally, truly dead.

A tornado blew through their ranks one dark stormy night, sucking a large chunk of their numbers into the air and pulling them apart. In the aftermath, bits of the undead littered a swath of countryside a mile long.

Months of rot, decay and exposure had slowed the undead down. Sometimes they would find the living and bombard their havens until they either broke in or moved on.

Slowly, resolutely, the undead wandered into the west toward the fort.

Chapter 26

1. The Dead Are Coming

R une was impressed by the changes in the fort as he drove up the country road. It looked more like a fort than ever before. "They have catapults," he murmured, impressed. They would need them.

A lot of the outskirts of the town had been razzed to the ground. The debris was gone and Rune bet the people in the fort were using it as building supplies or weapons. The road he traveled on had new roadsigns. They were clear directions on how to safely approach the fort. Rune noted some nasty looking traps along the way. The zombies couldn't read or think, so he could see how the traps could be very effective.

When he finally reached the gated entrance, he was immediately let in by the guards who recognized him. He was exhausted and hungry, but he needed to let the fort leaders know what was going on. Ken and Lenore were the ones who began to check him out for bites and it was good to see familiar faces.

"Can you let the Big Boss and Nerit know I need to speak to them right away?" Rune asked Lenore.

"Sure thing," she answered and pulled out her walkie-talkie.

"Is Dale still around? And Maddie?"

"Yeah, they're still here," Ken answered, his smile brightening at the mention of Dale. "It's been kinda rough since you left. A lot of people died. But a lot of people also came to join us."

"Fort grew in other ways, too." Rune motioned with his head toward an outgoing helicopter.

"You have no idea," Ken answered.

"Go on in, Rune. They'll meet you in Travis' office," Lenore instructed.

"Thanks. See you guys around."

Despite all the changes to the fort, Rune found his way back into the old familiar territory of the hotel. There were definitely new people around and when Maddie spotted him, he got an enormous hug. Politely disengaging from her, he hurried past Peggy and Eric discussing something about the front doors. Bill and Curtis greeted him as they exited the communication center and Dale gave him thumbs up from where he was playing with some little kids.

It was strange to be among the living after being around the dead for so long. But what was even stranger was the disconcerting lack of ghosts.

Before, the fort had seemed full of spirits. Now, he didn't sense any. But then again, the deadlands had been strangely quiet of spirits as well. Something had changed. Some event had allowed the spirits to start moving on again. Maybe it was the fort. Or something else. But the energy around him was changing.

Travis greeted him warmly when he entered the office. "Hey, Rune. Good to have you back."

"Good to be here. Nerit, like your hair. Looks good." He shook both their hands and Nerit looked pleased with the mention of her new hairstyle.

"What do you have to tell us, Rune? Lenore made it sound urgent." Travis sat on the edge of his desk as Nerit took a chair.

Rune remained standing and crossed his arms over his chest. "Well, it must have been my tone. I've been riding most of last night and today trying to get here. I need to warn you about something big."

His smile fading, Travis said, "Go on."

"I woke up last night. Got woke up last night. Jenni was there. She told me that I needed to come warn you. Needed to get moving."

"Jenni?"

"Yeah," Rune answered, then exhaled as he shrugged. "I see the dead."

"How do you know she's dead?" Nerit tilted her head.

"Because I saw her last night in the hunters blind where I was sleeping. She was a spirit. She's dead. And she told me that there is a whole mess of zombies heading this way. She told me to get my own ass moving. Sure enough, I saw a mess of zombies like I've never seen coming out of the valley."

Travis looked at Nerit, his expression troubled, and obviously unsure of what to say.

"If you think I'm nuts for thinking I saw Jenni, I get that. But you gotta go check it out for yourselves. I saw some helicopters out there. Send one of them."

"We need to check it out, Travis." Nerit stood up slowly. "We have to see if what he is saying is accurate."

"They're heading straight for the fort. It will take them a lot longer to get here cause they're going over every hill, through every forest, every pasture along the way. But they're coming." Rune would have felt resentful if not for the fact he was used to people doubting his abilities. He probably shouldn't have mentioned Jenni.

"We'll send one of the helicopters and check it out," Travis assured him. "Welcome back, Rune."

"And I did see Jenni," Rune declared. "I did."

"I don't doubt it. The dead don't seem to stay dead in this world anymore." Travis smiled ruefully. "Let's talk to Kevin, Nerit, and get this ball rolling."

Satisfied, Rune finally let himself relax and fell into a nearby chair. With relief, he listened to Nerit calling for the helicopter pilot and someone named Kevin. He would tell them where to look, then find a hot plate of food, and a place to sleep.

Despite the terror of the night before and the coming dangers, Rune was glad to be back at the fort. It was like coming home.

2. Family Life

Juan wasn't real sure he could deal with this.

It was almost too much.

His stomach was clenched in a tight little ball and his heart felt fluttery. He felt dizzy for a moment.

Slowly, he lowered the tiny pink panties with the bows on them into the dresser drawer.

Jack lay on the bed next to the trash bags full of clothes and toys Juan was unpacking. The dog was trying to edge his way toward a stuffed bear. Jack was doing his best innocent look while being very sneaky.

"My bear," Juan's new son said to the dog and grabbed the teddy bear.

Jack whined and looked as pathetic as possible.

The kids were moving into the suite he had shared with Jenni and Jason. It had been a sad little home for him and Jason and the ever-faithful Jack, but now it was filled with laughter and loud little voices. Jason sat on the bed opposite him, smiling from beneath his thick bangs, as Margie talked his head off. Holly, the middle child, was busy stuffing her toys into the shelf in the side table, talking to each one as she transferred them to their new home.

"Bad dog," the little boy chided Jack.

"Troy, don't be mean to Jack," Margie scolded her brother, then went on talking to Jason in her rapid, little-girl speak.

I'm a father, Juan thought. I have four kids. And a dog. How did this happen?

Oh..yeah...

Jenni.

With a wry smile he folded up some tiny jeans and placed them in the drawer. Troy leaned over and pressed his forehead to Jack's brow and was given a sloppy lick in response. Troy laughed and crawled onto the bed and promptly tackled the dog. The tussle that ensued had Juan half-annoyed, half-amused as he tried to get the clothes tucked away.

A knock on the door startled all of them and Holly screamed, "I'll get it!" and ran out of the room.

A minute later, Travis walked in behind the little one, looking confused.

"Uh, you have kids," Travis said to Juan and eyed his friend thoughtfully.

"Yes, yes, I do. I took over custody from Peggy," Juan said with a sheepish, yet proud grin.

"Daddy One," Troy said and pointed at Juan. He was now lying on the bed cuddling his teddy bear and using Jack as a pillow.

Travis chuckled and sat down on the edge of the bed. "Well, fatherhood suits you. You beat me to the punch."

"Yeah," Juan said with a grin. "Weird how that happened. But it's good. It feels right." He looked down at the little Spider-man shirt in his hands. "Peggy did a good job trying to take care of them, but they feel like mine. It felt like it was time to bring them home."

Travis smiled and nodded. "I think I understand."

Juan relaxed a little and tucked more clothes into a second drawer. "You have that look. That something is up."

Travis sighed and rubbed his brow. "We need you at a meeting in thirty minutes. I didn't realize you had such a huge life change and I hate to bug you right now, but this is urgent."

"About the stinky people?" Holly asked as she leaned against the bed and played with a battered Barbie.

"Yeah, the stinky people," Travis answered.

"I don't like them," Troy said in a soft voice.

"They killed our mom and dad," Margie added.

"They killed a lot of people," Travis said softly. "But we need Daddy One to come help us make plans to get rid of them."

Margie was frowning and Juan leaned over and kissed the top of her head. She was the little worrier. "It's okay. I'll come back soon. Jason, can you watch them?"

"Sure," Jason answered with a typical teenager shrug. "I can do that...Daddy One." He smirked a little and Juan lightly tousled his hair.

"Make sure they get down to dinner and that they don't feed Jack too many cookies." He sounded like a Dad. Wow.

Jack gave him a reproachful look and Juan grinned.

"Dog farts in the middle of the night are no fun, Jack," Juan informed the dog, who whined a little in response.

Kneeling down, Juan let himself be engulfed by little arms and kissed the kids one by one. Standing, he felt his throat tighten with emotion.

Jason stood up and gave him a quick, light hug, then flopped onto the bed next to Jack. "Don't worry about the kiddies. I got it covered, Dad."

Juan felt tears in his eyes. He joined Travis at the doorway into the room and together they walked across the living room.

"Daddy One, eh?"

"I blame Jenni," Juan answered.

Travis grinned and opened the door to the hall. "Ornery beyond the grave, ain't she?"

Juan laughed as he headed down the hall. "That's our Loca."

3. Grasping Shadows

The sun was still blazing hot outside when Katie drew the curtains and turned down the air conditioner. She felt tired after her morning walk and decided to lay down again. At eight months pregnant, she was too big to run anymore.

Laying down on the bed in the cool darkness, Katie tried not to think of the latest news from Rune and the recon mission Travis was sending.

Her eyes easily closed and sleep fell over her immediately.

She dreamed of her mother...

"...Katie, of course you love your best friend. She is your best friend. Just because you love her doesn't mean you have to kiss her. You're just confused..."

"But, Mom, I'm in love with her. I need you to understand," her teenage voice answered.

"Don't be foolish, Katie-girl," her mother chided.

Agitated, she fought the dream away, not wanting to remember her mother's unrelenting refusal to accept her for who she was. The dream wavered then Lydia sat at the kitchen table as her mother fussed with dinner.

"...and this is simply ridiculous. Women do not marry women," her mother was saying to Lydia.

"Sit down, Katie," Lydia's sweet voice said as she patted the chair next to her.

Katie moved into the dream and took the seat next to her dead wife. Her dream mother continued to cook, filling the room with fragrant, delicious aromas.

"You look lost," Lydia decided, and gently swept Katie's hair back from her face.

"I was looking for Jenni," Katie answered glumly. "I never see her in my dreams."

"I know, honey." Lydia smiled sweetly. She reached out and squeezed her hand. "It's not time yet."

Katie's mother turned, saw their clasped hands, and quickly turned back to the stove.

"I miss her, Lydia. So much. She's my best friend," Katie whispered emotionally, tears in her eyes. "I need her here. I am so afraid. I don't have you or her here to help me through this. I feel so emotional over the baby and so lost. Travis tries, but he doesn't understand how this feels."

Katie pressed her hand to her stomach.

Lydia fastened her gaze firmly to Katie's face and said, "Katie, look at me."

With tears glittering on the edges of her eyes, Katie obeyed.

"You're going to be okay. You're going to be fine. Travis will take good care of you and the baby. But you need to be careful. Things are about to become very, very difficult. Very dangerous."

"I can't deal with anymore loss," Katie whispered.

"I know, honey. I know. But you need to listen to me. You've always been strong. You've always been confident. Trust your instincts. Do what you know is right and don't back down."

"I need Jenni," Katie insisted, her hands trembling.

"You know, Jenni," Lydia said with a smile. "She'll be there when you need her. She won't let you down. But until then, you need to be strong and listen to your instincts. Do what you know is right."

Lydia looked up sharply toward the door, then back at Katie. "I need to go now. Remember what I said." Standing, she kissed Katie gently on the forehead and smoothed her hair before fading away.

Katie's eyes opened to see a sliver of sunlight had found its way through the closed curtains and was drawing a line of glowing light over the floor. The motes of dust swirling in the beam danced like little fairies and she smiled to herself. For some reason, Jenni felt very close in that moment.

The door opened and she rolled over to see Travis slip into the room. For a brief moment she saw Juan outside the door.

"What's wrong?" she asked.

Travis hesitated, then slid onto the bed. "Recon came back with photos."

"It's not good, is it?"

"No. It's not."

Katie rolled over and lay on his lap, her arms around him.

"You don't seem surprised."

"Lydia warned me."

"Oh," Travis answered, his fingers lightly brushing her shoulder. He seemed uncertain of what to say.

"I never dream of Jenni," Katie said finally. "Just Lydia." Pulling herself up, she kissed his lips lightly.

Travis stroked her hair and said, "I'm sure you will dream of Jenni."

"She's come to Juan and Jason and now Rune. Why not me?" Katie couldn't help the hurt from leaking into her voice.

Travis rubbed her cheek and looked thoughtful. "Maybe it's just not time yet."

Katie pouted then let out a heavy sigh. "Lydia told me that, too. You two conspiring behind my back?" Sliding off the bed, she tried not to feel put out.

With a laugh, her husband stood up and laid his hands on her shoulders and turned her around. "Katie, your spouses got to stick together. You're kinda tough to handle at times."

Katie made a face at him, then laughed a little. "Fine, okay." She shook free of her hurt feelings and forced herself to concentrate on the moment at hand. "So the recon wasn't good."

"Nope. It's not. We're meeting in about five minutes. We need you there."

"Does everyone in the fort know yet?"

"Not yet. We're getting the core group together to come up with strategies on how to handle telling the fort populace." A shadow of fear flickered over Travis' features and he looked haunted. His hand rested lightly on her belly and he kissed her forehead.

"Oh, shit. That bad, huh?" Katie felt her throat tighten and her pulse quicken.

"Yeah," Travis answered. "Yeah."

Katie rubbed her suddenly wet palms against her jeans and headed to the door. Travis opened the door for her and she looked out to see Juan gazing back at her. His forehead was covered in a light sheen of sweat and he looked pale under his tan.

"Shit."

"Yeah," Juan answered.

Travis shut the door behind them leaving the room empty save for the stream of sunlight glowing brightly in the darkened room. Then the curtain shifted and the light was gone, leaving the room empty and cold.

4. Facing the Truth

"What we are looking at is at least fifteen thousand zombies heading straight our way," Nerit said as the photos were slid across the table one by one.

"Possibly up to twenty thousand," Kevin added.

Travis frowned as he studied one, then passed it on to his wife. "Where did they come from?"

Greta shrugged. "Who knows? They're just there. Moving straight toward us. Rune was right."

Curtis and Bill studied the photos side by side as Katarina sat down sharply and looked rather ill.

Eric sighed softly, also looking a bit pale. "Could it be the people from the National Guard rescue center? Wouldn't that be from the right direction?"

"It was completely empty when we went there for supplies," Greta noted, then shrugged again. "But why'd they leave?"

"Who knows what got them started in this direction," Katie said with a sigh. She sat down slowly in a chair next to the table and her hand pressed firmly against her belly. "We know that once they get started in a direction it's hard to deter them." Travis kissed the top of her head softly and rubbed her back. She leaned back into him, trying to find comfort, but not truly finding it.

"Will the walls hold them back?" Bill asked abruptly.

Juan shifted his weight from foot to foot, his arms crossed against his chest, his brow furrowed, then finally shrugged. "I can't say."

"That's not very damn reassuring," Curtis snapped. His young face was flushed with emotion and his brow was beaded in sweat.

"Yeah, well, we have been building pretty damn fast. We haven't been sitting down and estimating how much stress those walls could take. Up until now we only had to hold off a couple hundred of those things."

Looking calm, thoughtful, but a tiny bit pale, Eric nodded. Dressed in a white shirt and navy trousers, he looked as casual as it got for him. "We haven't done any stress tests at this point—" he started.

"Well we better hurry the hell up and figure it out," Curtis wailed, flinging out his hand dramatically. "'Cause they're fucking coming."

"The outer wall is new," Travis said. "That would be our major concern. I have more faith in the older walls inside,."

"We could always fall back to the inner areas," Kevin suggested.

"Less to protect," Nerit agreed. "And the walls are thicker around the hotel and entry lock."

"We're talking like we're going to get overrun," was the soft comment from Bill.

The stress in the room was growing more and more palpable. Katie's fingers found Travis hand and she held him.

"It has always been a possibility," Eric answered calmly.

"Why are you such a gawddamn Vulcan about this?" Curtis nearly screamed. He backed away from the table and the photos, his eyes wide, terrified, the drops of sweat on his face rolling down to his chin.

"Curtis, calm down," Bill said softly, holding out one hand. "Just calm down."

Running his hand over his hair, Curtis backed all the way into the corner of the room, shaking his head. "We're going to get overrun, I knew it, I knew this bullshit would happen when we brought in all those people from the mall."

"This has nothing to do with the mall," Nerit said sharply. "The direction these zombies are coming from indicate they came most likely from the National Guard base or from Fort Worth or Dallas."

"And it doesn't do any good to panic," Eric pointed out.

"But people are gonna panic," Peggy's quivering voice said from the corner. She was smoking a cigarette and her hand was trembling. "Fuck, I'm panicking. That's a damn lot of zombies. More than we've ever seen out in these here parts. And if I'm panicking you know everyone else out there is going to panic, too."

"Then we have a plan in place to deal with all of this before we take it to the general population," Travis said, his voice raw, but firm.

"I agree. We have been working hard to get fire traps up, the catapults and all sorts of other defensive weapons rigged. We can take a good chunk down before they ever hit the wall," Kevin added.

"We plan carefully, then tell the people," Nerit agreed.

"Yeah, well how fucking long do we have, Nerit? How long before they are at our fucking wall moaning and screaming for our guts? Huh? How gawdamn fucking long," Curtis screamed.

"Eight days," Greta said. "At the least, eight days."

"How do you know that?"

The hysterical note in Curtis' voice was sharp and desperate and Bill reached out to calm his fellow officer. Curtis avoided him and glared intently at Greta.

"Number of miles divided by their walking speed. Rough estimate," Greta said regarding him coolly.

"So we plan. Today. All day if we have to, how we are going to deal with this," Travis said.

Eric nodded solemnly. "Agreed. Before we terrify the rest of the people."

"They're going to be terrified anyway," Peggy scoffed.

"Let's try to give them less to be terrified of then," Kevin said with a small smile in her direction.

Juan shook his head, his curls bouncing. "This is not going to be easy. Getting rid of that many of the dead. We're talking a total siege."

"We'll deal with it," Nerit said firmly. "We have no other choice."

Katie's fingers were trembling in Travis' grip and he leaned over and kissed her cheek gently.

Juan rubbed his brow and whispered, "We got kids and kids on the way. We gotta do this. We can't afford to lose all we fucking gained."

"Then we do this," Nerit said again. "We deal with it."

Kevin sat down at the table, his expression pensive but determined. "Then let's do it."

With that declaration, Eric rolled out the schematic of the fort and they began to plan. All except one. Curtis slipped out and ran down the hall. He did not stop until he reached the roof of city hall and it was there that he sobbed until he collapsed.

No one came to soothe him.

Chapter 27

1. Judgment Day

Travis had never been so scared in his life. He had faced many terrifying events in the last year, but this had to be the worst.

The entire dining room was crammed with the residents of the fort. They were crowded around tables, lined up against the walls, filling up the aisles, their voices a loud rumble in the large room. No one knew, except a small handful, what the meeting was about and the room was filled with old and young and a small herd of dogs sitting around Calhoun.

The Reverend had brought in the PA system from his brand new church on Main Street and Travis tapped the microphone lightly. The thick booming sound that filled the room made everyone look up sharply.

He swallowed hard and glanced at Katie. She graced him with a slight, but encouraging smile. The tension in her face made him want to hug her, but he had a job to do. As Mayor he had ended up the spokesman for the council and now he stood before an anxious group of people staring up at him intently.

"Okay, let's get started," he said, his amplified voice startling him. He cleared his throat again, then took a deep breath. "Well, as you know, we've been working to make this a safe place for all of us. I want to thank everyone for their hard work out in the gardens, the fields, the ranch and on construction. And, oh yeah, the grub patrol. Last nights biscuits were awesome."

There was a smattering of applause and Rosie smiled at him from where she sat with Juan, his children and her mother, Guadalupe.

"But, that's not why we're here. We're here for another reason and not a good one." He flinched as people began to look frightened. Katie's hand rested on his arm and she gave it an encouraging squeeze.

"What's going on, Travis?" someone yelled from the back of the room.

Other voices chimed as the faces in the crowd grew grave with concern.

"I'm going to be straight with you. Things have taken a turn for the worse," Travis said.

"And it ain't the toilet paper supply running low again," Peggy drawled, folding her arms grumpily across her chest.

This drew a bit of laughter and broke a little of the tension.

"No, no, not the toilet paper running low. It's...we got a large group of zombies heading this way. And not in the numbers we've seen before. It's around fifteen to twenty thousand zombies."

There was complete silence and it felt as if no one in the room drew a breath for a few minutes, then suddenly the room exploded into sound. People were on their feet, some were crying, others shouting, children clutched their parents tightly with fright, and Calhoun's little pack of dogs started barking wildly.

Travis held up his hands. "Please, calm down! Calm down! We do have plans on how to handle it!" Despite the microphone, he felt as if his voice was small and inaudible to the panicking people.

"Plans? Plans? What kinda of plans!"

"Are the walls going to hold them back?"

"We need to leave!"

Voices mingled as they fought for dominance.

"Please, listen up! Please!" Travis could hear the firmness in his voice getting hard and angry. "I need you to fucking listen up!"

"There are children in here," a woman snapped.

"Then listen up!"

"Please listen to the man," the Reverend called out. "Please listen before you let fear overwhelm you."

There was much grumbling, but the din slowly lowered in volume.

"We have plans," Travis repeated. "Solid plans. We will need volunteers to implement them, but if we work together we can do this."

"Like what sort of plans?" an older black woman shouted.

"We need to change the direction of the mob or at least get a lot of them moving away from us. Zombies tend to follow after humans. They get going in one direction and stay that course until they find their prey. The helicopters have tried to buzz the crowd and get them to peel off, but it's not working. So we're going to use the Durangos from the dealership about fifty miles from here."

The cries of dissent began again, but he kept talking over them.

"We'll send out trucks with fully armed drivers and one passenger. Their role is to try to lure the zombies off track. We've mapped out how we want to do this and we already have a few volunteers. We need to split off as many as we can from the main group before they reach our area."

"And what about the ones that do reach us?"

"Eric's been working on estimating the amount of stress the walls can take. The safest area in the entire fort is the original wall around the hotel. But we will defend the entire area. We've been working on fire straps, catapults, barbed traps and a variety of other ways to decimate any undead ranks heading our way. We have firearms and we have crossbows. But we're going to try to divert as many as we can and thin their ranks out on the outer edges of the town before they even reach us."

The murmur in the room grew louder as people began to talk among themselves.

Katie's hand was gentle on his arm as she moved closer to him. He draped his arm around her shoulders and squeezed her into his side. He was as afraid as everyone else, but there was no real choice. They had to defend their home.

"It's suicide to go out in those trucks," someone shouted.

"It's volunteer only," Travis answered.

"And if no one volunteers?"

"I do," Bette said, standing up, her expression grim. "I'll go."

Linda instantly stood up next to her and took her girlfriend's hand. "I'll go with her."

"Count me in," Bill said, and beside him Curtis scowled angrily.

"Me, too," a man shouted from the back.

A few more voices called out and the dissenter sat back down.

It was then Mary West stood up. She was in her fifties, one of the last of the survivors to be rescued and brought to the fort before the evacuation of the mall. A dour woman with a pinched mouth, she was the leading voice of the Baptist Coalition (as they liked to call themselves).

Travis felt his pulse quicken slightly as she stood up and he acknowledged her with a brief nod of his head.

"We understand your plans, Travis. But they are for naught. The sin of this fort has offended God and He will strike you down. As He passed judgment on the earth, He will pass judgment on this fort."

The nodding heads around her and "amens" made Travis feel cold inside.

"I think many of us feel God has brought us all here to begin anew," the Reverend responded quickly. "That He has shown us grace in our time of need."

Mary's tight little smile had no mirth or kindness to it. "You would think that. You have fallen away, Pastor, and your congregation is full of fornicators, idolaters, and homosexuals."

"Hey," Ken cried out, jumping to his feet. "Hey, I'm a Christian, too!"

Lenore's hand came up to draw Ken down, but he shrugged her hand away.

"A homosexual cannot be a Christian," Mary responded coolly.

"I love Jesus," Ken shouted. "I read the Bible. You can't tell me that I'm not a Christian!"

This time Dale took hold of him and sat him down, whispering to him.

Katie's fingers were icy on his arm and Travis kissed her brow softly to reassure her.

"An unrepentant sinner cannot enter the Kingdom of Heaven," Mary answered in her smirking manner. "But this fort will fall because you have let sin run rampant in its walls." She pointed abruptly at Bette and Linda who sat nearby. "Lesbians and gays in open displays of affection." She pointed at Travis and Katie. "Children out of wedlock."

"Hey, we're married," Katie protested.

With a cold look at the Reverend, Mary answered, "Are you really? By a holy man of God?"

"Oh, that is going too far," Juan said, standing up sharply. Margie was holding tight to his hand and glaring at Mary. "Just because we may not believe as you do-"

"Catholics worshiping idols and putting them up in a garden for reasons of idolatry," Mary droned on.

"That is a tribute to those who fell," Juan shouted. "It's Jesus' mother, Mary, for God's sake."

"Taking the Lord's name in vain. Is it no wonder that God has sent down this horde of demons to destroy your fort?"

Around Mary there were confirmations of "amen" and bobbing heads.

Travis felt sick to his stomach and he took a breath to steady his temper.

Voices were now rising in anger and frustration. People were arguing and it was quickly devolving into something very nasty.

"If we die, you die with us," Ken shouted angrily.

"We must repent and throw out the fornicators, adulterers, idolaters and homosexuals, then God will deliver us." Mary raised her chin, her confidence impressive, yet terrifying.

And to Travis' dismay more than thirty people stood up in unison to stand with her.

2. Trouble in Paradise

Horrified silence filled the room after Mary's words stopped reverberating. Those who stood beside her looked resolute and hard. To Travis' dismay, the family they had rescued thanks to the Reverend stood with Mary. The young father and mother, who had kept their entire family alive beyond incredible odds, stood with Mary and her cohorts, looking just as angry and firm as she did.

"Look, I don't agree with gay people or what they do. I think it's wrong. Not of God in anyway," Peggy said loudly. "I think it's a sin just like you."

Travis felt Katie's hand tighten on his and he looked sharply at Peggy, his gut clenching with anger at her betrayal.

"But I don't believe in putting anyone outside these walls just because we don't like what they do!" Peggy's voice trembled with her emotion and her eyes were full of tears. "Death is outside those walls and we're all safe in here. Even if we don't all agree on what is right and what is wrong, we all got a right to live!"

"God's judgment is on this fort. Sin fills its halls with gambling, alcohol, dancing, fornicators, adulterers, homosexuals and false prophets!" Mary looked sharply at the Reverend. "You're leading them astray!"

"God is a God of love, not hate!" The Reverend rose to his feet. "You have no right to put words of hate in His mouth."

Mary's face was full of cold fury. "Jesus will judge you harshly for leading His people astray."

"Well," Bill's big booming voice rang out as he stood up. He adjusted his belt around his beer belly and fastened his eyes on Mary. "As a good Southern Baptist boy, son of a minister, and former summer missionary to Mexico, I gotta say I don't remember Jesus saying anything about being so damn hateful."

"You're a fornicator and a man with a serpent's tongue," Mary shot back.

Katarina stood up abruptly behind Bill, her face as red as her hair. "Bill and I have never had sex! We're waiting until we get married! You have no right to say that! You don't even know us! I was raised Baptist, too!"

Nerit rose smoothly from her chair and gently took Katarina's hand to calm her.

"Harlot," Mary snapped and her imposing husband behind her added, "I saw them kissing with tongues. Disgusting whore."

"That is enough," Travis said loudly into the microphone. It hissed and sputtered for a moment.

Travis felt fiercely angry and his face felt like stone. His eyes were so hot in their sockets he felt as if they would explode into flames. Everything he and the others had fought for was being torn apart.

"You have no right to judge anyone here. Didn't Jesus say judge not least ye be judged?" His voice was firm and clipped.

Mary lifted her chin a little and her eyes narrowed. "A sinner needs correction."

"Jesus said to love one another," someone called out. "He said to love!"

"Lucifer himself used the scripture to his purposes," Mary hissed.

"Is that where you learned it from?" Ken asked smartly.

There was laughter throughout the room.

"We will not stay and be slaughtered with the sinners!"

"Then leave," a voice called out.

It was Kevin. He looked as fierce as Travis felt.

"Then take your followers and leave," Kevin repeated. "We're not going to hold you here like the Senator held us hostage. Just go."

"Agreed," Nerit said from nearby.

"God has passed judgment on this fort and you must repent," Mary repeated, but she was losing her fire as more and more people were standing up and voicing their opinions. Some were quoting scripture right back at her, others were just angry.

The small Hindu population sat together in silence, their discomfort clear. A few of the old-timers of the town reached over and patted their shoulders, reassuring them.

"Most of us here would call ourselves Christian," Eric said abruptly. "Whether we are Catholic or Protestant, we all believe in the message of Christ. Even those of us here who are not Christian but of other faiths or no faith at all deserve to be loved as Jesus commanded. So if you want to hate, then hate somewhere else. Personally, I am done with you."

"Your sin will be your downfall," Mary shrieked. Her eyes seemed too wide and her voice was harsh.

"Then it's our choice. What is yours?" Travis asked firmly. "Are you staying or going?"

Mary clenched her hands at her side. Around her, the followers that had made their stand with her looked uncertain and looked to her anxiously.

"We will not stay and bear the judgment of the fornicators, idolaters, and pagans."

"Fine then," Bill said. "I bet we could give them some supplies and a few vehicles, couldn't we?"

"I don't see why not," Nerit said in her ever so calm voice.

"Any objections?" Travis asked. He felt a little calmer now that most of the fort had sided against the extremists.

No one raised their hand.

"Then we will be leaving immediately," Mary said firmly.

Her tall, imposing husband nodded his head grimly and motioned to the others to leave. Slowly, the thirty or so people filed out of the room.

"We have seen the enemy," Eric whispered, moving closer to Travis.

"Yeah," Travis whispered back. "Yeah."

It took a few minutes for things to settle down. Slowly, some sort of calm returned. Juan kissed his kids and moved up to help set up the large maps and plans they had prepared. He looked pale and grim.

Travis returned his gaze to the people staring up at him and took a deep breath. "The fort is about life. It's about a new beginning. It's about building a new world out of the old. It's about not making the same mistakes of the past. We may not always get along or share the same opinions about things like religion or ethics or what have you, but we gotta respect one another or we're going to rot away at our core and end up destroying everything we have now. And what we got is a chance to fight for what is ours and to keep growing stronger. I am not a perfect man. I am...yeah...a sinner. I fall short of the mark a lot. But I believe in a God that will honor those who work hard to do what is best for everyone. I think He...or She...whatever you believe God is...has been helping us along. I'm not a highly religious man, I admit to that, but I believe in the goodness of the human heart and the integrity of the human spirit. And I think God does, too."

Tears stung his eyes as he finished and he took a deep breath as applause filled his ears. A few black women shouted, "Preach it!" A few old fogies said, "Amen."

"So let's get to planning and doing and let the good Lord lead us on," Travis said.

He caught sight of a few women waving their rosaries at him and the Hindu people smiled at him. The lone Muslim gave him a thumbs up and the one person from Mary's group who had chosen to stay behind gave him a firm, stern nod. Beside him Katie was smiling proudly and he felt himself blushing.

"I'm going to turn this over to Kevin now," Travis said and stepped back. He felt relieved to some degree and smiled over at Eric, who nodded with approval.

Juan held up the first poster board and Kevin stepped forward. "Now, this is what we have to do..."

3. The Unexpected Guest

Nerit felt bone weary as she entered her small hotel room that she now considered her home. Her old dog was asleep next to the bed, snoring loudly. He was sleeping more and more in his old age and she didn't blame him.

Kevin lingered in the doorway, watching her with some concern. She favored her leg as she walked now that she was out of view of the fort populace. She always made sure that no one could see how much her arthritic hip hurt her. It was important to her that people see her as indestructible, to trust her and her abilities.

"We should get you some medicine for that," Kevin said after a beat.

"Hospitals aren't safe," Nerit answered as she sat down in the large recliner tucked into the corner of the room and slowly exhaled.

Leaning against the open door, Kevin shook his head at her. "You're a bull-headed woman."

"Yes, I am." Nerit smiled.

Her old dog woke up and tottered over to her and laid his head on her knee. Scratching him behind the ears, Nerit slowly relaxed into the chair.

"Makes it hard to take care of you."

"You know you don't have to watch over me."

"I know, but it makes me feel better," Kevin answered. His eyes were concerned and she appreciated it despite herself. "Think the fort took the news well?"

"As well as could be expected," Nerit answered.

Kevin took a step into her room and the door shut behind him. With a solemn look on his face, he walked over and sat on the ottoman near her feet. "We need to talk about something important."

"All right," Nerit answered, waiting.

"If they get in, if there is no hope, if we can't get out," Kevin started.

"You have a plan."

"Yes, explosives set in the ballroom."

"All right. If you want, I can detonate them. I will take care of it," Nerit answered. She gazed at him solemnly and sincerely. She would kill their friends and family to keep them from the brutal death the undead gave so ferociously.

Kevin sighed. "No one can know about the explosives."

"Agreed. Just make sure that you wire it up with enough explosive to destroy the ballroom and everyone in it. Make it a fast death."

Kevin rubbed his brow. "I hope it doesn't come to that. All of us retreating to the ballroom just to face death by explosion."

"Of course not. Neither do I," Nerit answered softly.

"I would hate to think that I brought all those people here just to die." Kevin sighed wearily. "I really thought we were safe here."

"We are. For now. We just need to make sure things stay safe," Nerit answered. "At least we don't have to worry about the Vigilante on top of all of this."

"The Vigilante was the Senator's sister, right?"

"Yes. And good riddance to her." Nerit ran her hand slowly over her hair. "We just need to keep focused on the course we have determined."

Kevin nodded silently, then stood up, leaned over and kissed her cheek. "Good night, Nerit."

"Good night, Kevin," Nerit answered, patting his cheek softly.

She watched him walk out, his shoulders slumped with heavy emotions, and door shut behind him. Running a hand over her shortened hair, she exhaled slowly as she reached for her pack of cigarettes. With a small grunt, she stood up, moved to the window, and pulled the curtains back. The window slid open and she sat down on the wood chair she had placed next to the window so she could relax, look at the stars, and smoke. She had one of the rooms without a fancy balcony.

Lighting up, she felt her sore muscles protesting as she tried to relax. Exhaling slowly, she rested her forehead against her hand and looked down into the silent courtyard below.

"Strange things happening since the dead all stood up," Ralph's voice said.

Looking up, Nerit saw her deceased husband sitting in her recliner, his hand stroking the Tucker's floppy ears.

"Ralph," she gasped.

"Things are all messed up now. Nothing like it was. Nothing quite right no more."

"Ralph!"

"The dividing line is all blurred. Crossing over ain't hard. Getting easier. For now." Ralph smiled slightly at her. "You look real pretty, Nerit. I like yer hair."

"Ralph, why are you here?" she whispered.

With his crooked little smile, he said, "Came to take you home with me."

"Ralph, no!" She stood up sharply, the cigarette falling from her hand. She immediately reached down and grabbed it, her back screaming in pain. "Ralph, I have too much to do here! Please, no! Ralph, no!"

Slowly standing up, Ralph held out one hand. "Honey, I know. You're a good woman. Good soldier. You have done a good job avoiding death. You were supposed to go when I did, but you're too damn stubborn."

For the first time in her life, Nerit felt afraid of her husband. "Ralph, please, I have so much to do here. Ralph, please."

He reached out and took her arms in his hands and he held her gently. He felt like real flesh and blood, but she knew he could not be. "I know, I know. But you're sicker than you think, Nerit. You got the bone cancer. That's why you're hurting so bad."

Nerit held onto her husband, feeling the roughness of his shirt in her hands and his bony arms under it. "Ralph, if you can ask, for me, please...."

Kissing her cheek, Ralph held her tight. Nerit felt tears sliding down her cheeks as her dog whined at her feet.

"I miss you, Nerit. Is it so bad to have peace?"

"But I won't, Ralph. I won't! Knowing that these people need me. For who I am, for what I am, I won't have peace unless I help them. Tell Him that for me." She drew back to gaze into her dead husband's warm, loving eyes. "Please."

"I love you, Nerit," Ralph whispered, kissing her brow softly.

Nerit felt something in her head pop. It was a soft, delicate feeling, as if someone had switched something off. Then she was falling, slipping from Ralph's hands.

She thought one more time, "No, not now" then the world faded into comforting black.

* * * * *

Kevin had just started to open his hotel room door when he had the strong urge to return to Nerit's room. He couldn't explain the feeling in that moment nor would he in the future when he looked back on that horrible night. But it was so strong, he ran to her room. When he reached her door, he heard the sound of something being overturned and the mournful wail of her dog.

Without a second thought, Kevin kicked in the door and rushed in. His worst fear was made real at the sight of Nerit lying on the floor, the floor lamp overturned beside her. The old dog was licking her face and whining loudly. A cigarette lay smoldering on the carpet.

Kevin immediately grabbed the cigarette and tossed it into the nearby ashtray then knelt beside Nerit. She looked very frail as she lay on the floor, but also very young. The lines were smoothed from her countenance and her hair looked gold, not silver, in the light. Touching her wrist, he felt for her pulse and couldn't find one. Tears brimming, he touched her neck. Maybe it was wishful thinking, but he thought he felt a faint pulse.

Picking up her surprisingly heavy form, he rushed toward the door whispering fervent prayers all the way.

4. Faith

Travis walked briskly through the lobby of the hotel. The meeting had gone well enough. People were signing up as volunteers for a variety of tasks, some life threatening, some not and there seemed to be a strong sense of determination to defeat the oncoming undead army.

Of course, in the midst of all the planning, the Baptist Coalition was getting ready to leave.

Bill walked toward him and motioned for him to hold up. Travis stopped in his tracks, his hands tucked into the pockets of his jeans. Bill drew near, looking a tad breathless.

"Okay, got them set up in the extra short bus. Got extra fuel in the back and just about anything I could think of that they might need short term. Long term, they are on their own."

"Did you give them something to siphon gas out of cars?" Travis asked.

"Sure did and loaded them up with mostly MREs. Gave them hunting rifles for protection and some spears."

"Sounds good," Travis decided, crossing his arms over his chest. "Is that young family still going with them?"

"Yeah," Bill answered sadly. "Yeah, they are. Can't change their mind. Father keeps saying that if they stay their kids will surely die. If they go, God will show them the way."

"Let's hope He does," Travis answered grimly.

"They're leaving tonight," Bill added. "I tried to get them to stay until morning, but they just want to go. It's like they think God's about to hurl lightning bolts down on us."

"Wasn't that Zeus, not Jesus?" Travis said with a wry smile.

"You know how Fundies are," Bill responded. "Hellfire and brimstone, God is gonna getcha."

"Yeah, unfortunately, yeah," he sighed.

Mary walked up to join them. Her blue skirt and pale blouse were heavily starched and very neat. Her hair was swept into a chignon on top of her head and Travis thought she looked a little like Peggy from King of the Hill in that moment.

"We're leaving now, Travis. I felt it best to give you one more chance to repent your sins and do what is right. Cleanse the fort and return to godly ways," she said.

Her towering beanpole of a husband stood behind her looking rather fierce.

"If that means casting out the people you consider undesirable, I think I'll stay with my sinner ways," Travis answered.

Mary's face darkened. "A proud heart belongs to the fool," she responded tersely.

"Yeah," Travis said significantly, looking at her pointedly. "It does."

The elevator doors slid open behind them and Travis paled as he saw Kevin stumble out with Nerit in his arms.

"No," Katie exclaimed from nearby as Bill instantly rushed forward.

"God is already striking down the sinners," Mary said to her husband with a vindictive gleam in her eye and a smug smile.

"Get the hell out of the fort," Travis snarled at her before rushing to where people were gathering around Kevin as he carried Nerit toward the clinic.

"What happened to her?" Katie asked as she kept pace with Kevin's heavy footfalls.

"I don't know. I found her on the floor of her room," Kevin answered, tears gleaming in his eyes.

"Is she...is she.." Bill's voice cracked.

"I think I felt a pulse. I'm not sure," Kevin responded in a voice thick with emotion.

Travis moved ahead of the small throng and flung open the clinic door to let them in. Bette looked up from where she sat reading a book. She was the night shift nurse for the week.

"Oh, shit!"

Bette was instantly at their side, guiding Kevin with a hand on his arm. Switching into full nurse mode, she quickly began to check Nerit's vitals even before she was completely on the bed.

Travis stood next to Katie, his arms crossed over his chest, swallowing hard.

"Is she...Is she..." Bill whispered again.

"I have a pulse," Bette answered. "Barely." Then she shooed them out the door. "Get Charlotte," she said, then shut the door on them.

"I'll get her," Peggy said.

"Oh, God, we can't lose Nerit, too!" Katie exclaimed.

Travis reached out and gently guided her into his arms. He held Katie close, feeling her body trembling.

Kevin sank into a chair in the waiting room and buried his face in his hands.

"She can't die," Bill said after a moment of excruciating silence. "She just can't. We need her. She's vital."

The clinic door swung open and Charlotte raced in followed by Belinda. The two woman rushed into the examination room where Nerit was and when that door was briefly open, Travis caught sight of Nerit's pale unmoving form.

Katie was pale and gently dabbing her eyes with her shirt sleeve. Being pregnant, her hormones tended to get the best of her, but she was trying to remain calm.

The Reverend entered, his Bible clutched in one hand, his expression bewildered and frightened. "They're saying Nerit is in here dying."

"She can't die," Bill repeated.

Kevin looked up at the older gentlemen and sighed. "Her pulse was barely there. She felt so heavy in my arms."

The Reverend looked down, his eyes glimmering with sudden tears. "I will pray."

Outside the door Curtis' voice screamed shrilly, "Get the fuck out of here! Get out!"

"You will all be struck down as she has been! All of you! Consumed by sin you will be consumed," Mary shouted back.

"Get them out of here," Travis said to Bill, his voice raspy. "Get them the hell out of here!"

Bill looked up then over his shoulder, as if becoming aware of the commotion outside. "Oh, yeah. Okay."

"Fucking get out of here now!" Curtis sounded as though he was about to break.

Bill stood up, adjusted his uniform, then headed out.

Silently, the Reverend sat down, his hands clutching the Bible.

"Sorry, Reverend," Travis finally said. "I didn't mean to swear in front of you."

"It's all right. These are hard times."

Kevin looked toward the door that Nerit lay behind. His expression was shadowed by pain. "I didn't know what to do when I found her," he said in a low voice.

"You did the right thing bringing her here," the Reverend assured him.

Katie looked grim. "This can't be happening. It can't be."

"It is and we must do what we can to support her during this time," the Reverend answered her.

Katie reached down to the Reverend. He took her hand then Kevin's.

Travis slowly stepped into the circle and took Katie and Kevin's hands. The four of them stood in silence for a moment, then the Reverend's voice, full of warmth and faith began, "Dear Heavenly Father, be with us now in this most terrible hour of despair and rest your hand upon your child and our dear friend, Nerit. Bring her comfort in this time and heal her body..."

5. Where The Dead Are

Juan slowly crept into his hotel suite, hoping not to wake the children, but instead found them in their pajamas gathered around his grandmother, Guadalupe and his mother, Rosie.

"Hi, Daddy One," Holly said with a somber expression on her face.

"Why are you children still up?"

"Praying for Nerit," Margie answered, her hair falling around her face. Her small hand swept it back, but it promptly fell back into her face.

"She's sick," Troy added.

"How is she, Dad?" Jason looked at him through his bangs.

"Yes, how is she?" Guadalupe asked.

He saw the rosaries clutched in their hands and those of the children.

"Coma. They don't know why. Charlotte says she's stable, but in critical condition. Her life signs are not very strong." He sat down on the sofa and Holly and Troy promptly crawled onto his lap. He cuddled them close and sighed into Holly's hair.

"We're praying and asking Daddy God to make her well," Margie assured him.

"And Jesus, too," Holly added.

"And his Mom," Troy said in a soft voice. "I didn't know we could pray to Jesus' Mom. Can we pray to my Mom, too?"

"I am sure your Mama hears your every word," Guadalupe assured Troy.

"Does she?" Troy looked at Juan expecting the truth of him.

Juan thought of Jenni appearing to him after her death and nodded. "Yes, I know she does."

* * * * *

"We got zombies!" Katarina swung her rifle around and aimed down toward the edge of the lighted area in front of the west wall of the fort.

Two zombies staggered into view, staring up at her with lidless eyes. One slowly reached its hand up toward her while the other moved slowly toward the wall.

"Shit, already?" Bill peered down and took aim. The reaching zombie's head exploded almost in time with the one about to reach the wall.

"Check in. We had zombies on the west side," Katarina called into her headset.

"I'm watching the fucking Baptists circling around trying to figure out where the hell they are gonna go. Do they count?" Calhoun's voice answered her. "Oh, yeah...East Wall reporting in."

"South Wall reporting in. No sign of zombies."

"North Wall reporting in. No go this way," Lenore's voice answered.

Katarina nodded and looked toward Bill, tears in her eyes. "Oh, God, my heart is beating so fast I can barely stand it. How the hell am I going to feel when all those zombies show up?"

"You're just spooked because of Nerit, honey," Bill assured her.

"Look at me! I'm shaking! I don't do this, Bill. I don't freak out," Katarina said, running her trembling hand through her hair.

He kissed her cheek softly and held her tight against him. "It's okay, honey. It will be okay."

Chapter 28

1. Goodbyes

urtis watched through squinted eyes as the shiny new Durangos were having last minute checks done. He stood on the platform that straddled the wall between the hotel courtyard and the entry gates.

It was two days after Nerit's collapse and she was no closer to life or death in that time. She seemed suspended between the two worlds and the Reverend was holding an around the clock prayer vigil for her.

Nervously, Curtis shifted from foot to foot, his hands tucked into the pockets of his trousers. Glancing over his shoulder at the back entrance of the hotel, he saw several of the volunteers saying emotional farewells to their loved ones.

Linda and Bette came out together, Bette walking in front dressed in Army fatigues. Linda wore hunting clothes and her hair was pulled back in a ponytail. To his disgust, they were holding hands. As they neared him, he took a breath and boldly stepped in front of them. Bette looked surprised, but Linda already looked annoyed.

"Linda, I would like just a moment of your time," he said softly. He tried very hard not to glare at Bette.

"I don't know, Curtis," she said.

"It's okay, hon. You take care of this," Bette said, giving Linda's hand a squeeze then walked on.

Linda put her hands on her hips and looked at him intently. "What is it Curtis?"

"Look, I...uh...know I fucked up...somehow...somewhere...you know...with you," he stuttered, trying to remember his well rehearsed speech.

"We were never together, Curtis. We were fuck buddies," Linda answered tersely.

He winced, but plunged on with his pre-planned speech, "But you're going out on a dangerous mission. You could die. I just don't want, you know, bad blood between us."

Linda sighed deeply and folded her arms over the breasts he had loved to touch so much. She looked away from him, then said, "Okay, that's true. I don't want bad blood either. Look, I just wasn't clear enough with you. I needed you to relieve all that stress. I thought you understood. That it was just sex."

Curtis felt his temper rising and felt his face flushing, but he curled his hands up tight and tried not to scream at her that she was a dirty whore. "Linda, I love you."

She took in a deep breath and exhaled very slowly. "Curtis, I'm sorry. I just don't feel that way toward you."

"I did something wrong. I know that. I know I'm young and not wise in the ways of women," he said in a voice that was becoming increasingly heated. "I know I do not fully know how to satisfy a woman yet. But if you had just given me time-"

"Curtis, the sex was fine. It was what I needed at that time. I was not looking for a relationship. I didn't want that. Bette just happened. I've never been with a girl before. Ever. It's been all new to me. But I love her. I'm sorry that hurts you. But if we can just be friends and let our past go, Curtis, that would make me so happy." Linda was close to tears and looked at him with trembling lips. "I really don't want bad blood between us."

Hurtful, angry words danced on the tip of his tongue, but he swallowed them away, nodding slowly. "Okay, okay." Forcing a smile, he said, "Friendship is good." In his mind though, he saw the two of them, tangled up, naked, sweating, touching each other, kissing each other and he wanted to hurt them both so badly he felt pain in his gut. "I can live with friendship."

For the first time in awhile, Linda smiled at him. She leaned over and kissed his cheek. "Thank you, Curtis. That makes me feel good."

He kissed her awkwardly on the cheek, tasting her skin, and hating her as much as he loved her.

Linda walked on toward the woman that she now let touch her breasts and the other places Curtis had considered his. He felt himself grow hotter and more flushed.

"Hey, Curtis, ready to go?" Greta asked from beside him.

He started, his sheepish grin wiping away the tension in his young, handsome face. "Sure. Yeah. I'm ready."

Greta nodded. "Great! Let's go zombie hunting."

* * * * *

"You die, I kick your ass," Lenore told Ken firmly.

"Okay. Do it now," he said, presenting his rear.

Smacking it, she gave him her sternest look. 'You shouldn't go out without me."

Dale tattooed and intense, stood nearby. "I'll take care of your boyfriend."

"He's not my boyfriend."

"I'm her girlfriend," Ken said, putting on his best flaming gay routine.

Lenore growled at him and he pulled on one of her braids. Reluctantly, she smiled and they embraced tightly. "Take care, you crazy faggot."

"Will and can do! Dale will protect me, won't you?"

Dale just grunted, grinned, and donned his sunglasses.

"I love it when he does that," Ken whispered to Lenore.

"He's straight," Lenore chided him softly.

"For now!" Ken then heaved his rifle over one shoulder and jauntily strode over to Dale. "Let's be off, my good man."

"I'm gonna punch him," Dale said with a grin.

"Get in line," Lenore answered and sulked.

* * * * *

Katarina read over the map and the notes from their briefing. She looked nervous, but was keeping it in check. Bill looked down at his boots and sighed. His beer belly was smaller now and he didn't huff when he ran. He was becoming a fit man who was dating a younger woman. And here he was running off to lead a zombie parade. He wasn't sure whether he was brave or a damn fool.

"I think I have this memorized now," Katarina decided.

"You better. That's our asses," Bill answered her gruffly. He heaved himself up into the fancy Durango and adjusted the seat.

Katarina slammed the passenger door shut. Like everyone else on the mission dubbed "Operation Distract" she was in hunting clothes. Only a few volunteer soldiers were in their old army camouflage.

"I got it. I promise. Just do what I say."

"Oh, God, is that what our marriage will be like?" he kidded her.

She took him seriously for a split second, then laughed and smacked his arm. "Oh, you."

Ahead of them Bette and Linda shared one last kiss. Behind them Ken was tapping out some obscure song on the car horn.

Dale shouted, "Lesbians kissing, oh yeah! A good day to die!"

Maddie smacked Dale's cheek playfully then gave him a big hug. Dale lifted the older woman off the ground, hugging her tight, and kissing her cheek. She was his surrogate Mom and tears were running down her cheeks. Rune and Dale clasped hands, exchanging last words, then Dale slid into the Durango's passenger seat. Rune gently led Maddie away as the older woman wept with worry.

Juan stood nearby watching with Travis and Katie. He noted that the vehicles were ready and motioned to the gate operator. The gates began to whine open.

"Here we go." Bill gripped the steering wheel tightly, trying not to let his nerves get to him.

"Yeah."

They both took deep breaths.

"I wonder what twenty thousand zombies look like," Katarina finally said.

"Dunno, honey," Bill answered. "But we're about to find out."

2. Facing Death

The sun burned brightly in the sky above as the helicopter flew low over the three Durangos speeding down the old farm road. Already nature was taking advantage of the fall of Man. Crabgrass spread tendrils across the unused road as weeds poked through the asphalt. The elements were eating away at the structures along the road as the foliage around them rose up and shrouded them in leafy robes.

It made Curtis feel despair about their situation. How easily humankind was being erased from the face of the earth.

"Almost there," Greta's voice said in his headset.

Shifting in his seat, Curtis looked ahead, but saw no sign of the mobs of undead. "I don't see them."

"We estimate that they are about fifteen miles in front of us at this point," Kevin's voice answered him. "Bring the Durangos to a stop."

Curtis looked into the back of the helicopter where Kevin sat flipping through a sheath of papers on a clipboard. The man's forehead was beaded with sweat. These were his plans that everyone had agreed on and he had insisted on flying out with Greta to run strategy from the air. Curtis resented him to no end. Kevin was not one of them. He was one of the others. An interloper. Just one more person to complicate things and make it hard at the fort.

With a curt nod, he sat back in his chair and looked down at the Durangos now idling on the road below. Linda was down there with that slut. It ate at him that Linda was a volunteer, but at the same time whatever happened, she deserved it. He had hoped that she would see the light. That he was the one for her and that she needed to be with him. But that hope felt futile every time he saw the two women together. The Southern Baptists had that right. It was just not natural.

If only he could go back to the old days, sitting at the station house, flipping through the latest catalog detailing the best in prisoner restraints, watching Linda deliver the mail every morning. Those were the days.

"Bette," Kevin's voice said in his headset once more.

"I'm here," Bette answered.

Curtis could feel the hesitation in Kevin before his voice said, "You have a go."

"Roger that," Bette answered.

Curtis looked down to see the Durango that Linda was in began to move down the road, while the other two remained in position. The windows of the departing window rolled down and the two women stuck out their hands to wave and give the thumbs up.

Curtis felt his stomach slowly roll over, but his jaw set. Looking down at his map, he readied his pen. Time to go to work.

* * * * *

Bette closed her window as she drove on, a grin on her face, her blond hair sticking up around her head at odd angles. Grabbing Linda's hand, she kissed it and winked at her.

"Let's do this!"

"Woot!" Linda shouted out the closing window on her side.

"Scared?"

"Shitless."

"Me, too." Bette donned a very worn dark green cap. "I swear my insides are quivering."

Linda pushed up the brim of her beat up cowboy hat and exhaled slowly. "I think my stomach exploded."

Reaching out, Bette snagged her hand and squeezed. "You didn't have to come,"she said softly.

Linda looked at Bette very intently. "Oh, yes. I did. Where you go, I go."

Tears flashed into Bette's eyes as she pressed a string of kisses to Linda's knuckles. I'm lucky to be with you."

"Let's hope your luck keeps up," Linda answered, her voice trembling with emotion.

Bette crossed her fingers on both hands and pushed her foot down on the accelerator. Above them, the helicopter swooped ahead, the wind from its enormous blades buffeting the SUV. Linda swallowed hard next and reached for her water bottle.

"It's okay, babe," Bette assured her. "It's okay."

"I've never been so scared in my life," Linda answered, then gulped down her water.

"I know. I know."

"We have a problem," Greta's voice cackled through the CB radio tucked into the dashboard.

Linda snagged the mouthpiece. "What do you mean?"

"They're not where they are supposed to be," Kevin answered, his voice surprisingly calm. "Slow down now."

Bette immediately began to slow the Durango, her foot pressing down steadily on the brake. The Durango breached the top of the hill they were ascending and both women gasped.

Moving resolutely toward them was a multitude of undead. They filled the road and spilled over into the countryside. They slogged relentlessly forward with mindless determination.

The plan had been simple. Sit at the crossroads of another farm road until the undead came into view. Lure them onto the side road and keep ahead of them, drawing as many away as possible. Diverting the dead to the west seemed the best plan. They would eventually hit the desert where hopefully the elements would destroy them.

The first zombies were already to the crossroads. Maybe ten or fifteen, but they were stumbling along the center of the road.

"Babe, take a breath," Bette said.

Linda gasped, not realizing she had been holding her breath. She felt unable to breathe, blink or even move.

"Babe, take a breath," Bette said again. "We can do this."

Linda forced air into her lungs, then lifted the mouthpiece to her lips. "Bette says we can do this."

Above them, Curtis and Kevin were talking quickly between each other, looking for an alternate route, looking for another viable option, but this intersection had been a major part of their plan.

After a minute, which seemed more like an hour, Kevin's voice said, "Okay. Go for it. Be careful."

"I feel like Thelma and Louise," Linda whispered.

"We'll have a happy ending," Bette assured her.

They quickly kissed before Bette shifted gears and floored the Durango. It sped down the hill and toward the intersection at a fast clip. The zombies slowly became aware of the vehicle and almost in unison, they raised their arms and began to moan loudly.

"We're going to have to slow down as I take the curve," Bette said in a quivering voice. "Don't freak."

"Okay," Linda answered. She was transfixed by the sight of thousands of mangled creatures reaching toward them. Usually she was in a vehicle racing away from these things, not toward them.

The deer guard caught the first few zombies and flipped them out of the way as they neared the intersection. Bette slowed down only enough to keep control of the vehicle. The wall of gray, mottled creatures seemed to rise up before them like a nightmare. A few of the undead managed to strike out at the Durango, their rotting hands leaving smears of gunk on the windows.

More zombies moved onto the side road to cross it on their trek and the Durango plowed through them as it gained speed. Linda let out a small scream as the Durango slammed through a small knot of undead, sending the creatures flying in all directions. Bette fought the wheel, but kept on the road, her expression grim.

The Durango sped past the cluster of zombies at the crossroads and Bette fought her instincts to flee and slowed it down enough to keep the zombies interested. Twisting around in her seat, Linda looked back toward the creatures now stumbling after them.

"They're following," she whispered, both terrified and jubilant.

Then the runners appeared.

3. Running with the Dead

"We have runners!" Greta's voice was so sharp and loud in their headsets that Curtis yelped.

Kevin scrambled to the window and looked down. "Shit! Where the hell did they come from?"

"They're gaining fast," Curtis answered.

"Ed," Kevin said, motioning to the grizzled old hunter seated near the door.

"Got it," Ed answered.

The old geezer double checked his harness, then slid the door open. Wind buffeted them and Kevin pressed his clipboard tightly to his chest. Flipping off the safety on his rifle, Ed took aim as Greta swung the helicopter down low for him to get a good shot.

"What do I do?" Bette's voice was crackling over the radio as Linda screamed, "Runners! Runners!"

"Go! Go! Go!" Kevin answered firmly. "Gun it!"

Below them, the runners were now racing alongside the Durango, smashing their hands against the SUV, howling with hunger. There were at least thirty of them.

The Durango lurched forward in response to Kevin's order, leaving the shambling dead behind, but still being pursued by the shrieking runners.

* * * * *

"Babe, calm down," Bette said firmly.

Linda was fighting her panic with all her might, but she couldn't help the trembling of her hands. She gulped, twisting around in her chair to look out the back window. The runners were keeping pace. The road was winding and Bette couldn't risk going too fast for fear of flipping them.

A disgusting, bloody figure kept pace beside the Durango. Its mouth was open as it screamed. The entire lower half of its face had been torn away and its gaping maw was the stuff of nightmares. Its head suddenly exploded and it fell, tumbling along the roadside, before it landed in a bush.

"They're shooting them," Linda said, feeling the knot in her chest lessen.

Bette didn't answer as she concentrated on the winding road ahead and kept a diligent eye on the throng behind them. As the Durango began to take a long slowly arcing curve, Bette's eyes widened as a large portion of the zombies merely ran into the field, ignoring the road.

"They're going to head us off," Bette gasped. "Greta! Greta! They're going to head us off!"

"I've got you covered," Greta answered.

The helicopter began to zoom as low as possible over the zombies in the field, buffeting the running creatures from above. A few fell, but the more persistent, less mutilated ones, kept their breathtaking sped toward the road. Linda wasn't sure how many fell from the wind drafts or the sniper shots from above, but quite a few of the zombies fell into the deep grass, disappearing from view.

"Shit! Shit! Shit!" Bette's knuckles went white as she held firmly to the steering wheel as the first of the runners reached the road ahead of her and charged them.

Linda grabbed hold of the handhold over the door and braced herself.

The Durango slammed into the zombies and there was a sickening lurch to one side as something caught in one of the wheel wells. Bette regained control and the undead were tossed away from the front of the truck like chaff in the wind. Some of them were still smart enough or something akin to that to dart out of the way then leap onto the side of the Durango, hooking their gnarled fingers around the luggage rack.

Linda screamed as one snarled at her through her window and began to beat his free hand against the window with all his might.

More zombies leaped onto the road and managed to avoid being struck outright by the Durango. They, too, leaped onto the truck, holding on, even fighting with each other as they tried to get at the two women inside.

The banging of the bloodied fists and feet against the windows and doors had both women shaken. Trying hard to compensate for the extra weight as she drove on, Bette whispered a soft prayer.

The zombie pounding on Linda's window was getting more and more agitated, his blows seeming more fierce. Linda took a deep breath, raised her gun, flicked off the safety and placed her finger on the button to roll down the window.

"Babe," Bette said. "What are you doing?"

"I got it," Linda assured her.

She pushed the button. As the glass slid down, she shoved the gun through the gap and fired point blank into its face. The zombie dropped off the Durango and tumbled away into the ditch. But Linda had forgotten that the window would automatically scroll all the way down if she didn't stop it. When it kept rolling down, she panicked. Grey, bloodied, shredded arms began to thrust in the window at her and she began to scream.

From above, Curtis watched in fascinated horror as one zombie tried to climb into the Durango as others tore at it, trying to get in instead. The Durango abruptly swerved and for a long moment was airbourne before it slammed down into a field at an angle. It slid across the unplowed, hard ground, shedding zombies as it went, then hit a piece of equipment hidden in the wild grass and flipped completely over. It tumbled maybe two times before coming to a stop, zombie-free, but a mangled wreck.

"Dammit," Greta hissed. She swung the helicopter around, aiming for the runners pursuing the fallen vehicle.

"Look for survivors! Look for survivors!" Kevin's voice was harsh with emotion.

Curtis gave him a dark look over his shoulder.

The zombies were closing in on the Durango. The helicopter buzzed low over them as both Kevin and Ed fired at them.

Curtis saw the two women scramble out of a broken window and struggle across the field toward the tree line. He could see Linda's face was smeared with blood and Bette's arm was at an odd angle. He started to speak, but his voice caught in his throat.

"There they are," Kevin shouted.

Greta glanced down, nodded and tried to move in for a rescue. Four runners darted through the wake of the helicopter and toward the woman.

With looks of terror on their faces, Linda and Bette darted into the tree line.

"Look for them! Look for them!" Kevin grabbed Curtis and hauled him out of his chair, taking his place.

Curtis stumbled into the back of the helicopter and looked toward Ed. The old hunter was determinedly taking down as many of the zombies as possible. After a quick check of his safety line, Curtis moved to the open door and looked down. The wind buffeted him as he looked down into the trees below, looking for the two women. He realized that their army greens and hunting clothes had them camouflaged and he rubbed the side of his nose anxiously. Now that the helicopter was over the trees, it was harder to see the zombies. Beside him, Ed was swearing up a storm.

"I don't see them," Greta said, her voice stricken.

"Keep looking," Kevin answered.

The helicopter moved slowly over the forest as the zombies continued into the trees. Suddenly, Curtis caught sight of the women. In a small clearing was a broken down tin and wood structure. It had probably been a makeshift barn at one time. The women had climbed up onto its rusted metal roof and were huddled under the overhang of the second roof that covered the barn loft. They had probably climbed up on something then kicked it away, he figured, but it was apparent that the women were trapped. The fastest of the runners were now in the clearing, looking around with hawk-like movements for their prey. He could see both women curled against each other, trying to keep out of view of the zombies below. But by doing so, they were also keeping out of view of those above. Curtis was barely catching glimpses of them from between the tree branches.

"Do you see them?" Kevin's voice was strained. "Does anyone see them?"

The helicopter began to drift away from the clearing and the barn. Curtis stared down through the trees to where he knew the two women were hiding. The zombies were clustered in the clearing, looking around, sensing the fresh meat. It would probably not take too much for them to bring down that barn and rip apart the two women.

"Anyone see them?" Kevin's voice was persistent, eating away at Curtis' resolve.

"I see nothing," Greta answered dismally.

"I ain't got em," Ed answered. "No sign."

Curtis wanted Bette gone, but not Linda. Then again, Bette had corrupted Linda, hadn't she? They were lesbian whores. Sinners. Just like Mary had said.

"Curtis, do you see them?"

Curtis opened his mouth, hesitated, then said, "No, no I don't."

The sounds of the helicopter roared around them as the humans fell into silence.

"Zombies see something," Greta said suddenly. She pulled the stick to the left and banked around. "They see something!"

Kevin appeared beside Curtis, looking down. The zombies in the clearing now were banging on the barn and it was shaking under the assault. A pale hand darted out from beneath the overhang and waved at the helicopter, then a frightened bloodied face looked up at them.

"We got them!"

There was a mad scramble for the rescue line and safety harness as Kevin began barking orders for Greta to get her closer to the women. Slowly, the safety harness drifted down toward the barn.

The zombies were in a frenzy now, the old structure shaking apart. Curtis hunched down by the open doorway and watched, feeling cold and disconnected from those around him.

Linda reached out and hooked the safety harness and Curtis watched the two women struggle to get it on her. He could imagine Bette telling Linda, "You first." He saw their heads draw together in what he knew was a kiss, then Bette signaled for them to hoist Linda up.

As Linda swung over the heads of the zombies, they leaped at her, forgetting the barn temporarily. Curtis watched Linda's bloodied upturned face as she was pulled up to safety. He loved how her brown hair swam in the wind around her face. He imagined touching it.

Then Linda was being pulled into the helicopter and struggling out of the harness.

"Hurry! Hurry!" Linda didn't even acknowledge him, but clung to safety straps just inside the doorway to watch the harness descend to Bette. "Her arm is broken! She made me come first."

4. The Restless Dead

The zombies returned to shaking the barn, pieces of it breaking off. It was beginning to list to one side and Bette was holding on for dear life with her one good arm.

"Bring it back up," Kevin ordered, and the harness was drawn back up.

"No! No! Don't leave her," Linda screamed at him. "No!"

"I'm not," Kevin answered, shrugging into the harness and securing it. Then he pushed out of the helicopter as Ed lowered him down.

Again, the zombies paid attention to the food dangling over their heads and not at the woman clinging to the roof of the barn. Curtis looked toward Linda and saw her gaze was firmly fastened on Bette.

Kevin reached Bette, his feet just barely out of reach of the zombies leaping up at him. Stretching out his hand, he motioned to her. Struggling to stand, Bette reached out with her good hand. Several zombies hit the barn again, with such force, it knocked Bette off balance and she lurched forward.

Kevin barely grabbed her arm as the zombies below grabbed her booted feet. Twisting and kicking, Bette struggled to break free. Kevin's hands tightened their grip and he hooked his legs around her waist and pulled her up as hard as he could. But still the zombies held on.

Curtis could see that both of them were screaming. Beside him Linda's cries of fear were ear shattering. Yet he couldn't bring himself to care. He hoped the bitch died.

"Fuck this," Greta said, pulling the big bird upwards.

* * * * *

Bette screamed as the zombies held onto her legs. She felt like she was being pulled in two. Kevin had such a tight grip on her, she could barely breathe. She kicked and twisted hard and finally managed to get free of most of the gripping hands.

Swinging upward, Kevin and Bette dangled over the barn as one lone zombie held firmly to Bette's foot. It was a woman in a house dress and to Bette's horror, it began to pull itself upwards. Its drawn back black lips and toothy grimace made Bette scream with sheer terror. The tiny blond tried to push the creature off with her other foot. The abnormally fast creature grabbed it and began to draw itself toward her exposed shin. The accident had torn Bette's pant leg and her skin was a tasty lure for the gaping maw of the zombie.

Both her legs trapped by the creature, Bette struggled, but not so much as to have Kevin lose his grip. The zombie's teeth gnashed together as it drew closer to her flesh. The young woman could not tear her eyes from the zombie as it strained to reach her tender skin.

Bette felt Kevin let go of her with one arm and she screamed in terror as she felt as if she was about to drop. The zombies head exploded as Kevin shot it. The creature's fingers went slack and it tumbled to the ground.

Pulling her up, Kevin held her as Bette sobbed with pain and relief.

* * * * *

Curtis watched the scene with cold detachment, but he put a smile on his face when Kevin and Bette fell into a heap inside the helicopter. Linda shoved everyone aside and gathered Bette up into her arms..

"I promised you a happy ending, babe," Bette shouted to Linda and pressed a fervent kiss to her lips.

"Are you bit?" Curtis asked, hoping she was.

"No, no! The car accident banged us up," Linda answered.

"Gotta check," Ed said, then did just that.

Curtis almost hoped Bette or Linda or both were bitten. Instead, Ed nodded that they were okay and the women cried with relief.

"Now what?" Greta asked as she swung the copter around.

Below a long steady stream of zombies were stumbling past the field and the destroyed Durango toward the west.

Kevin fell into the seat next to her and donned his headset.

"Now, what?" she repeated.

Kevin hesitated, then said, "Signal the next Durango for phase two."

Chapter 29

1. Hordes

D ale and Ken had sat in silence in their Durango listening to the drama unfold. Neither one of them had dared to interfere or make suggestions as they had heard the desperate voices over the cackling of the radio. Once or twice they had each uttered 'shit' or 'dammit,' but otherwise had been silent.

When the word came through that Linda and Bette were safe, Ken let out a sigh of relief and collapsed against the dashboard. "Oh, God, I was praying so hard I thought my head would explode."

"Well, at least they didn't get ate," Dale decided. "Guess that proves the Baptists wrong, eh? The hot lesbians live to kiss another day."

"You're really sick, you know," Ken chided flirtatiously.

"Yeah, I know," Dale answered, winking. "And that's why you like me."

Ken blushed deeply.

* * * * *

In Bill and Katarina's Durango, they too had listened in silence, their fingers intertwined. It was far too easy to imagine themselves in the place of the two women. The thought of losing each other was too much to bear.

At last, when they knew that the women were rescued, they hugged each other tightly.

"I love you, Bill," Katarina whispered.

"I love you, Kit-Kat," he answered, giving her a gruff kiss.

"Durango Two, prepare to depart," Kevin's voice said through the radio static.

"That's us, honey," Bill said, kissing her one more time. He ran his hand over her long red braid then sat back in the driver's seat and steadied his nerves. Shifting into drive, he looked up at the helicopter drifting into view. "Let's hope it goes better for us."

"I'm praying something awfully fierce," Katarina answered softly. "But if it's our time, I just pray that the Good Lord gives us time to do what we need to."

With sadness in his eyes, Bill nodded.

"Durango Two, depart," Kevin said.

* * * * *

"We almost lost Bette and Linda," Travis said to Katie and Juan as they entered the communication center. "But they're okay."

"Shit," Juan uttered. "How?"

"Runners. Sounds like they ended up with more than they expected and there were some miscalculations. They're on the helicopter now. A little battered, but okay." Travis ran his hands over his hair and then rubbed his face. "They're okay."

"And they got a lot of zombies to go off in the right direction away from us," Peggy added from her post before the radios. "So that's good."

"So the plan is working." Katie sat down in a chair and ran her hand gently over her large stomach.

"So far," Travis agreed.

"Shit,"Juan said again. He was perched on the edge of a table. "I told my crazy ass cousin not to go."

"You couldn't stop her from going with Bette," Katie reminded him.

"Yeah, I know," Juan answered. He sighed and rubbed his day old stubble. "Who's the bait now?"

"Bill and Katarina," Peggy replied. One of her well-manicured hands rested against the ear piece of her headset. "They just got the word to move ahead."

Katie silently reached out to Travis and he took her hand. Giving her a small encouraging smile, he squeezed her fingers.

"Bill knows those roads. He'll be fine," Travis assured her.

Katie gave him a hopeful, yet solemn look.

* * * * *

Don't scream don't scream don't scream don't scream don't sceam...Katarina's mantra repeated in her head in rapid succession.

The Durango idled at the next crossroads waiting for the lumbering zombies to grow closer. There were so many of the hungry dead. They clogged up the road, filled the ditches and extended into the trees. Despite the air conditioner being set to recycle the air in the Durango, the stench was growing unbearable.

Thousands of outstretched hands reached toward their vehicle as the zombies marched toward them. They were gray and somewhat blackened by the sun. Their bristled hair stood up around their heads in the humidity and heat. Their clothes were almost unrecognizable as they clung to their decomposing flesh.

Men and women, young and old, shambled toward them. There were no signs of runners and that was a relief.

"Dear God, Bill, one is in a wheelchair," Katarina gasped.

A terribly eaten zombie was rolling its way down the road. It was being

300

swept along by the other bodies around it.

Bill arched his neck to see, then began to laugh his huge bellowing chuckle. "Shit, babe, don't that beat all."

A tiny little boy, a cap still on his head, baseball bat in one hand, his cherubic face somehow still cute in death, reached the Durango and banged on the door with his fist. Katarina leaned over into the backseat to look down at him. In another time, this little guy could be any little leaguer banging on his Mom's SUV after a hard game. But this child didn't whine or smile, it hissed and growled.

The boy began to hit the Durango with his baseball bat.

"Time to go," Katarina said.

Bill watched as more zombies came within a few feet of the Durango. "I agree."

Slowly, the Durango moved forward onto the side road that would head into the west and away from the fort.

Almost in unison, the zombies turned to follow, the little boy dragging his baseball bat on the asphalt.

* * * * *

"So why are lesbians hot but gay men aren't to you Neanderthal straight men?" Ken asked. He felt contrary. He sat in the passenger seat, arms across his chest, staring out the window.

"Uh, cause women are hot," Dale answered.

"I have it on good authority that I'm hot," Ken responded. "By many many women and men."

"Eh," was all Dale said, then shrugged. He was grinning. He enjoyed giving Ken a hard time.

"I'm so not eh. I am anything but eh. I am a good and solid hunk of a man. Before I came out of the closet I had so many women after me, I was a stud." Ken frowned at Dale. "A total stud after I came out as well. It is not my freaking fault the world died and did not provide an adequate pool of gay men for me."

"I'm sure there are guys in the fort who are gay but aren't out," Dale answered.

"Really?"

"Yeah, I'm pretty sure of it. My money is that you're not the only Nancy boy."

Ken sighed. "Well, they're so deep in the closet I can't find them."

"It'll happen. When the time is right," Dale assured him.

"Are you sure you're not gay?" Ken arched an eyebrow at him.

"Yep. Tried it...kinda...once. Well, actually I thought she was a girl. She was a guy."

"Real Crying Gamish, huh?"

"Yeah," Dale nodded. "She was damn hot, too. Until you know...that."

"You brute! You turned her down over that?"

"Hey, I tried. I just couldn't." Dale looked at Ken very solemnly. "I did try. I really did. I just..."

Ken let out a soft sigh. "I know. I feel the same way about girls. Love Lenore. She's my girl. If she were a guy, maybe she'd be my groove thing, but..."

"Sometimes love ain't enough," Dale sighed. "But at least I got laid last night."

"Did not!"

"Oh, yeah. Sure did!"

"Who? Tell!"

"Peggy."

"No!"

"Yep."

"She's a dirty whore!" Ken frowned, clearly jealous.

"Oh, yeah," Dale answered with satisfaction.

"No fair! I didn't get laid! I'm laidless. No fair!"

Suddenly, Dale reached out and grabbed Ken's shoulder.

"Okay, if you insist!" Ken joked, then saw the look on Dale's face. Turning, Ken gasped as he saw a horde of zombies emerging from the trees next to them.

"They shouldn't be here!" Dale grabbed the radio. "We got hundreds of zombies at our location. A massive horde. Do you read me?"

In a panic, Ken hit the Lock button and the doors all locked.

"Repeat that," Kevin's voice answered.

"We got zombies," Dale answered, then muttered, "Oh, shit" and tossed the mouthpiece to Ken. Shifting gears, the Durango lurched forward as the zombies began to encircle it. The vehicle smashed into a few undead then rolled down the street out of their grasp.

"Zombies everywhere. Coming out of the trees on both sides of us. Oh, shit, and up the road. I thought you got them to turn to the west," Ken screamed into the radio.

"Pull back," Kevin ordered. "We must have missed some in the recon."

"I should say so," Ken snapped back. "Because, brotha, they are all over the freaking place."

Dale shifted gears again and began to turn the big vehicle around. The narrow road didn't allow a full u-turn, so he had to back up to readjust the angle again.

"We are totally surrounded! This is not good," Ken shouted into the radio.

Dale backed up to readjust one more time when the wave of zombies hit the truck in full force. It was an unrelenting wall of flesh, bone and decay that pushed in with such force, the Durango rocked. Moaning, desperate faces filled the windows as claw-like hands scrabbled at the doors.

"Fuck," Ken whispered into the mouthpiece, then dropped it.

The moans of the hungry zombies was deafening.

Dale reversed and tried to back up but it was as if the truck was trying to push its way through a brick wall. The zombies barely yielded and the press against the truck from all sides continued.

"Dale," Ken said softly.

"I know," Dale answered.

The Durango was now being pushed across the road, despite Dale's attempts to floor it. There was too much pressure coming against the vehicle from the enormous wave of zombies coming up through the forest. Sliding sideways, the truck protested as the metal groaned against the constant assault. Ken screamed as a zombie's body pressed against his window began to pop and split apart like a ripe melon.

"Shit, oh, shit," Ken whispered. He heard Kevin's voice demanding to know their status, but he ignored it. Dale was cussing so colorfully Ken would have been impressed if he wasn't so damn scared.

Then the truck was pushed over into the ditch on the side of the road. The undead in the ditch were squashed beneath the truck, but more took their place beating and pushing against the Durango. The two men inside ended up lying on the driver's side windows, staring up at the zombies swarming on top of the capsized vehicle.

"We're not gonna make it, are we?" Ken asked, his voice catching.

"Nope," Dale answered.

They both watched in horrible fascination as one of the zombies began to beat against the window with a rock. Cracks slowly began to spread across the glass.

"Nope. We're not, Ken."

"Oh, God," Ken whispered, covering his mouth in horror.

Dale pulled the smaller man into his arms and cradled Ken's head against his chest. "It's okay, Ken."

Ken sobbed softly into his chest.. "Lenore is going to kill me."

"At least you know someone loved you," Dale consoled him.

"Yeah," Ken whispered as the glass shattered and rained down around them. "Yeah. I do."

"Ready to go?"

Ken watched Dale flick the safety off his pistol. Pressing his lips tightly together, he nodded.

"I'll do it for both of us."

Ken nodded fervently, unable to speak anymore.

Dale kissed Ken's forehead gently as he brought up his gun. "Sleep tight, Ken," he said, and fired.

Ignoring the bits of brain and blood splattered over him, Dale wrapped his arm tightly around Ken's shoulders and took a deep breath.

"I'm right behind you, buddy."

Just as the first of the zombies fell into the truck on top of them, Dale pushed the gun into his mouth and fired.

2. The Helpless Living

Despite everything going on in the outside world in the deadlands, Katie fell asleep on the couch in the communication center. She had felt drained all morning. When she had laid down on the sofa, she hadn't expected to fall asleep, but she had.

She awoke to someone crying out.

It was Travis she saw first, his face strained and tears in his eyes. Peggy sat at the communication hub sobbing loudly, her hands over her face.

"What happened?" Katie asked in a hoarse voice.

"Ken and Dale..." Travis' voice broke. "We think they're gone."

"No," Katie whispered.

Peggy wiped her tears on the bottom of her t-shirt and again pressed down the button on the microphone in front of her. "Dale, Ken, please respond. What is your status?"

Only cackling static responded.

"What happened?"

"They said zombies came out of the forest and surrounded them. It sounded like they were trying to drive away then the line went silent," Travis answered.

"Oh, God," Katie exclaimed.

"What's worse is that they hadn't left the departure point. Which means the zombies are further ahead than we thought," Travis said in a hollow voice.

Juan stepped into the room. "We're taking off in the other helicopter. I'll let you know what we find."

"Be careful out there," Travis answered.

Peggy continued to try to raise the two missing men.

"I will be," Juan assured him, then was gone.

Katie sat up slowly and curled up on the sofa, tears. Her arms folded over her belly as though to shield her unborn child from all this terror. The loss of life in the last few months was staggering. How much more could they endure?

"I wish Nerit was here," Peggy said through her sobs. "I wish she was here. She'd know what to do. No offense, Travis, but she would."

Travis nodded grimly. "I know. But we need to keep doing our best. Once we know what is going on out there, we'll figure out the next step."

Peggy wiped her tears away again and turned back to the communication center. "Come in, Dale. Come in, Ken. What is your status? Repeat, what is your status?"

* * * * *

"Keep going, Bill," Kevin said into his headset. "You've got them following you and that's what we need. Keep an eye on your gas gauge and keep right at the speed where you are now."

"Can't say I feel too comfortable right now," Bill's voice answered.

Kevin looked down at the bright cherry red Durango and the mass of gray, decaying people following behind it. "I know, Bill. But you're doing a good job."

Next to Kevin, Bette sat trembling from pain as Linda did her best to set her arm and bandage it. Curtis was a hunched figure in the passenger seat up front. Ed sat grimly with his rifle at the ready watching the horde of zombies below.

The tension was unbearable. They had all heard Ken's hysterical voice. There was a very good chance that Dale and Ken were gone.

As the news came in that the second helicopter was now in the air and going to check out the situation, Kevin looked down at the Durango and the following parade of the dead.

The situation was beginning to feel helpless.

3. The Pied Piper of the Living Dead

Katarina looked into the side mirror of the Durango to see her sunburned face gazing back at her from beneath her cowboy hat. Her sunglasses hid eyes that she knew must be wide with fear. Her gaze slipped slightly to one side and the undead stumbling behind the Durango came into view.

The creatures were so determined they had actually increased in speed. Bill had to push down on the accelerator just a bit to keep ahead of the flesh eating mob.

Twisting around in her chair, she looked out the back window at the massive crowd of zombies trailing them. Her stomach heaved again and she tried hard not to vomit. Her fear was so powerful, she was trembling. She had lost any semblance of calm quite some time ago. Her teeth were chattering and Bill kept touching her to reassure her. She was sure Nerit would be sorely disappointed in her. But this was different from being a sniper. Not since the first day had she seen the dead so close, and beyond that, so many.

Behind the walls, even the makeshift walls from the first days, she had felt safe whenever she had faced a large mass of zombies. She had faith in those walls. But out here on the country roads, there were no walls. Just endless road, trees, shrub and the unwavering dead. And out here, despite the helicopter overhead, it was just she and Bill. Bill, who loved her. She loved him so much that she was terrified of what could happen to him. Yes, she was terrified of possibly dying under the snapping, tearing jaws of the undead, but Bill...

"Bill, how much longer?"

"About ten more minutes," Bill answered. He was sweating profusely because of the unrelenting glare of sunlight through the windshield.

Katarina could feel sweat trickling between her breasts and she rubbed the top of her nose. Drops of tears and sweat dripped from her fingers.

"Ken and Dale are dead," she said softly. She still couldn't fully fathom that her two friends were gone.

"We don't know that," Bill answered.

"You and I both know it, Bill. You heard what was on the CB!"

"We can't give up hope, Kit-Kat," Bill answered determinedly. "We just can't."

Katarina shook her head. "We gotta get out of here, Bill." Just looking at him made her even more afraid. She touched his shoulder lovingly. His fingers covered hers.

"We'll be out of here soon enough, baby."

Katarina watched the undead with a growing sense of dread and horror. Her stomach rolled again. "Please, Bill, let's just go."

"We gotta make sure that the fort is safe," Bill answered.

"Bill, we need to leave now!" Her voice cracked as she screamed and the sound startled her.

Bill didn't look at her, but kept driving. He was smart not to take his eyes off the road. Just around the curve was an overturned semi-truck.

"Shit," he whispered.

There was barely any room to edge around the truck and Bill swore as he slowed down to maneuver around it. He grabbed the CB mouthpiece. "We got an obstruction in the road. We're going around."

There was loud static, then a voice said, "We're moving up to rendezvous."

"Don't slow down," Katarina hissed.

She gripped her head in agony and turned away from the view behind them, unable to watch the horde getting ever closer as the Durango slowed down to cautiously creep around the overturned semi.

"Bill," she whispered. "I'm so afraid."

"Baby, you're going to be okay."

"But if anything happens to you, I can't bear it."

"Kit-Kat, if anything happens to you, I can't bear it. I can't. We're going to be okay. We'll get around this truck, then we'll be fine." Bill risked letting go of the steering wheel so he could grip her hand and kiss it.

It was then that the driver of the truck made his appearance. Darting out from behind the truck, he struck the window with a wrench held tightly in one hand.

Reacting on pure impulse, Bill jerked the wheel and the Durango clipped the guardrail then bounced off to hit the edge of the back of the semi-truck. Fighting to gain control of the wheel, Bill swore. Katarina fell back into the back seat headfirst.

"Bill, there's a--"

Greta's voice over the CB was cut off as the Durango plowed into the station wagon directly behind the semi. The rending of metal and the scream of the tires filled their ears, then Bill and Katarina were tossed about inside the Durango as it flipped over and slid down the street.

"Get out! Get out!" Bill shouted,

Katarina scrambled for the door, shoved it open, and climbed out. Tumbling out onto the road from the overturned vehicle, she dared to look back. The horde of zombies was beginning to come into view behind the semi. Bill climbed out behind her. His forehead was gashed and he wiped the blood from his face as he looked back toward the zombies.

What he saw that Katarina did not was that the accident had freed the rest of the undead family inside the station wagon. They were scrambling out of the ruins of their car, decayed and wretched, and fiercely hungry.

"Kit-Kat, run!"

She turned and ran. Pulling his gun from his holster, Bill was obviously in pain as he ran after her. Katarina ran as fast as she could on her banged up legs. Meanwhile, the freed family and the semi-truck driver moved with a swiftness that was terrifying. They weren't runners, but they were fast enough.

Out of the corner of his eye, Bill saw something lurch up off the side of the road and reach for Katarina as she ran. Without a second thought, he tackled the thing. He crashed into the brush, the thing under him hissing and growling as it snapped its teeth at him.

Katarina started to turn, but Bill's voice urged her keep running. She heard a gun shot and felt a sense of relief.

"Keep going," Bill shouted.

The helicopter slowly descended in front of her like some great bird. She sucked air into her burning lungs through bruised lips and ran toward it.

"Keep running, honey!" Bill urged her, more gunshots sounding behind her.

The helicopter came down to hover over the road. Katarina forced her body to move those last few steps and she collapsed into Kevin's arms. He swung her up into the safety of the bird. Turning around she saw that Bill was not running toward the helicopter, but firing into the quickly advancing crowd.

"Bill! Run! Bill!"

"He's bit," Kevin's ragged voice said in her ear.

"No! No! Bill, run!"

Bill turned and smiled at her in that special way that made her heart beat faster. Giving a short wave with a badly mangled hand, he turned back to firing into the advancing horde of undead.

Katarina felt her heart lurch in her chest as she was pulled backwards from the door by gentle hands.

"No! No! We're getting married! No!" She kicked and fought to get away, but Linda and Curtis held her firmly back from the door.

Ed moved to the doorway as the helicopter lifted up and took aim with his rifle.

"Ed, please, don't! We're getting married! Bill just fell! We had an accident! He's not bit!"

The gun fired once.

Kevin and Ed both averted their eyes as Ed lowered the gun and the helicopter swung about.

"No," Katarina said again weakly. "No! You don't understand. We're getting married."

4. Open Doorways

The sound of the helicopter's enormous blades slicing at the sky filled her ears as Katarina lay sobbing on the floor beside Bette and Linda. The two women were trying to comfort her, but there was no comfort to be gained. Her insides felt like they'd been torn out. Katarina felt like throwing herself from the helicopter and joining Bill.

Through her blurred vision, she could see Ed, Curtis and Kevin speaking. Beyond them, in the cockpit, Greta was flying the huge beast, whisking them to safety. Another figure appeared, sliding out of the seat beside Greta. The big, lumbering form of Bill moved past the three men talking softly together and moved with absolutely no grace to where she lay.

Mesmerized by her fuzzy vision, she didn't dare move or blink her eyes for fear of him vanishing.

Slowly, he knelt down next to her and took her hand gently in his. "I need you to know something before I go on, baby."

"Bill," she whispered, more tears filling her vision.

He shifted his weight and sat next to her on the floor. "When Doreen died there was nothing I could do but watch that cancer eat her up from the inside out. I sat on the Internet at night looking for alternatives, trying to find that magic cure for her. She was a spry thing but the cancer was too mean, too fast. It ate her up and when she died, she was so sad she had lost that battle. She had been so determined to win. If I could have taken her place, I would have. I would have given my life to save her."

Katarina didn't dare blink, but her eyes were so full of tears she could barely see him.

"Today, that thing came at you out of the brush and I didn't think twice. I knew I could die right then and there, but I knew you would get away. I knew it! Don't get me wrong, I tried hard not to get bit, but it got my hand pretty bad. I'd rather be going home with you than moving on. But I had a chance with you that I never had with Doreen. And I took it. And I'm glad for it."

"Bill," she whispered again.

"It's okay," Bette whispered, smoothing her hair back. "He's at peace now."

"She's right, Kit-Kat," Bill assured his bride-to-be. "I'm at peace because you're alive. The fort needs you and you need them. You keep them strong and sure as the battle rages. You can do this. I know it. I've been damn lucky in my life to love two strong women. You keep strong, Kit-Kat. I love you."

"Bill," she whispered again. The tears slipped out of her eyes and his blurred image vanished. All that was before her was an empty space on the floor.

Sobbing anew, she covered her face with her hands, his presence still close to her. Bette and Linda leaned over her, trying to soothe her, stroking her hair and back.

"Oh, Bill," she cried again as she fully realized the depths of his love for her. Without a doubt, his last act in his life was to show her how much he loved her.

* * * * *

The door slid open and Kevin leaped out of the helicopter followed closely by Ed. Katarina appeared next, her face and eyes swollen, her expression grim. Linda helped Bette out, Ed joining her to lift her down.

Charlotte arrived with a wheelchair to take Bette to the clinic to set her arm. The Reverend moved forward to greet each person, whispering a soft prayer of thanks as he touched each one. When he reached Katarina, he held her in his arms and wept with her.

Travis reached out to Kevin and they clasped hands tightly. They stood in silence, their expressions tormented, then walked on together.

"How does it look?" Kevin finally asked.

"You guys peeled off at least half of the undead. They're on a steady trek away from here. What remains has slowed down slightly. Some are still turning back and following the others into the west. I think we confused them."

"Dale and Ken?"

Travis shook his head grimly.

"Shit," Kevin sighed.

Travis looked back to where Katarina was talking to the Reverend. "Losing Bill is one of the hardest hits this fort as ever taken. Everyone is important, but Bill…"

"I know what you're saying," Kevin responded with a weary sigh. "Damn, it feels good to know we got a good portion of the zombies diverted, but losing Bill and the others doesn't make it feel like much of a victory."

As they walked through the different gates to get into the old construction site, the two men found themselves lapsing into silence. The people on the street gave them wide berth at the sight of their stooped shoulders and somber expressions. The word had spread quickly about the deaths that had occurred in the world beyond the walls.

They reached Juan's memorial garden and found Katie sitting on a bench with Lenore. The big, black girl was crying silently, clutching a bright pink teddy bear. Peggy sat nearby dabbing at her eyes and smoking a cigarette. Maddie sat beside Rune, eyes closed, tears staining her face. Rune had his head down, his arm around Maddie's shoulders, grief etched into his posture.

"This is just the beginning of it," Kevin said somberly.

"I know," Travis answered.

Both of the men hesitated at the edge of the garden, feeling as if they were about to enter sacred ground. Above them the second helicopter was coming in.

"We did the right thing," Travis said finally. "We've diverted half of them today."

Kevin nodded. "Doesn't make it feel any better though, does it?"

"No. No it doesn't," Travis agreed.

Katarina came up behind them with the Reverend, her soft cries breaking both men's hearts. They turned as she drew near and she forced a smile.

"He died like he wanted to," she assured them.

Travis hugged her first and kissed her cheek. He could feel the deep shudders inside her body and it broke his heart. She turned to Kevin and hugged him, too.

Katie came, kissed Katarina's cheek, and drew her into the garden. For a brief moment, Travis took Katie's hand and they exchanged a deep, sorrowful look. The Reverend joined the mourners and took a seat, his Bible clutched in his hands.

"Dale was a good guy," Peggy said.

"He was, Peggy," Travis agreed.

Peggy nodded and dabbed at her eyes with her damp Kleenex again. Travis and Kevin moved on.

"I didn't know," Kevin said finally. "About Dale and Peggy."

"I think it was new," Travis said. "Poor Peggy. Poor Ken and Dale."

They reached the doorway to the hotel and both men looked up. It seemed unconquerable and strong, but they could not depend on that impression.

"Let's get to work," Travis said, walking into the hotel.

Kevin followed.

Chapter 30

1. The Fine Line

The room was dark except for a small Sponge Bob night light tucked into a wall socket across the room. Kevin sat at her side, his hand tucked under her long, pale hand. It felt slightly cool to his touch and he pressed his other hand on top of it to warm it.

Nerit looked younger with her hair falling gracefully alongside her face. Her strong features were not what someone would call beautiful, but perhaps elegant. Kevin wondered what she had looked like as a young Israeli sniper.

It was nearly midnight and the fort was very quiet. The day had drained everyone. It was hard to find one dry eye in the entire fort. Dale, Ken and Bill were men who left an impression. The chapel had been overflowing with people trying to attend an impromptu memorial service.

Meanwhile, the meeting in the manager's office had been crazy. Calhoun had crashed it, bearing his camera like a samurai sword. A few other concerned citizens had forced their way in as well. It had been a tense event with quite a few raised voices.

The recon mission with Juan had showed just how successful they had been in their attempt to draw off the zombies. The two trucks had directed a majority of the zombies traveling along the road toward West Texas. That had been the good news.

The bad news had been a large swarm of zombies that were trekking through the wild and nowhere near a road. A segment of this group had swarmed the Durango with Ken and Dale inside. Some of those zombies were still standing in the road around the Durango. Another portion had drifted off toward the West. Another faction was traveling down the road.

Despite the success of the mission to direct the zombies away from the fort, the loss of life had been high. Since most of the zombies were off the roads at this point, it was determined not to send anymore Durangos out.

"We're going to have to fight them on the outskirts of town. We control this area. There are too many variables out on those roads that we cannot control," Travis had said.

"The secret government is controlling the clones, I tell you," Calhoun had declared immediately. "They are trying to wipe us out cause we won't obey their stupid laws."

Kevin smiled slightly at the memory and looked toward Nerit's peaceful face. "You should have been there, Nerit. Calhoun was in top form."

"And how the hell do you expect to fight off that many zombies on our territory?" one of the concerned citizens had shouted back.

That question actually led to some positive planning. Kevin had been amazed by the plans organized by a man named Roger and a bunch of teenagers. Evidently the science teacher, who had perished on a mission, had worked with the kids on some very creative ideas to defend the fort. It was Juan's adopted son, Jason, who had laid out the plans for the adults. Kevin had been impressed.

Calhoun had to be his weird self. He repeatedly sniffed Jason, declaring, "He is possessed by his dead mother, Jenni! Her wisdom from beyond the grave is guiding him!"

His odd declaration worked in their favor, because Calhoun then shut up and stared enraptured at the teenager.

In the end, the meeting had terrified everyone with the truth of the oncoming dead, but had calmed everyone when the plans to defend the fort were laid out.

It would take a lot of hard work to pull it off, but it was doable. How effective it would be was yet to be seen.

"It is never easy to face death. Even when you have laid out plans so perfect in composition you cannot believe they will fail," a voice said behind Kevin, jarring him from his memories.

He turned in his chair to see a young woman standing next to the bricked up window. She had long blond hair that was braided over one shoulder and was wearing a uniform he did not immediately recognize until he saw the Israeli flag. Tall, lean, and elegant despite her intense stare, she was striking to gaze upon.

"Nerit," Kevin whispered.

Stepping toward him, he saw the sniper rifle slung over one of her shoulders.

"The truth of any war is that you must plan for any eventuality. You must be persistent in trying to tear apart your own strategies. You must anticipate all possibilities and be prepared to immediately adapt." The young woman ignored the form on the bed and sat next to him, her keen gaze resting on his face. "You must know your enemy and never underestimate him."

"The enemy is dead, Nerit. They are us, dead and gone, but still up and moving around. You know this," Kevin answered. "They don't think. They just do."

"You are underestimating them."

"I'm not. Nerit, they're dead."

"You're underestimating them," she repeated.

"They don't think," Kevin persisted.

"Again, you are underestimating them. Three men died today. You almost lost three others." Her gaze was so intense it was almost unbearable.

Kevin took a deep breath and looked at the old woman in her bed then to the woman seated next to him. He could see the similarity between them.

"Are you dead?" he finally asked.

"If I am and I am sitting here talking to you, then consider the capabilities of those who are dead and out there."

"But they don't think, Nerit," he insisted. "They just kill and eat."

"A force drives them," Nerit answered. "A basic need to eat. That is instinct. It is overwhelming. And that instinct makes them cunning whether or not you wish to believe it."

"There is no way those things are smart, Nerit"

"Cunning. A small child is cunning when it wants a cookie in a jar. It just does what it has to to get to the jar on the counter. It moves on instinct, does what it must."

Kevin stared at the young woman's face all the while holding the old woman's hand. "I see what you are saying."

"Desperation can create the most deadly of foes," Nerit said.

Letting go of the old woman's hand he reached out and grasped that of the younger. He could feel the similarity between the hands even though the older woman's knuckles were thicker. The young version of Nerit stared intently back at him.

"We need you," Kevin said. "You can't just leave us."

"I obey my God. I will do as He says," Nerit answered.

Kevin had not expected this answer for some reason. Nerit had never come across as especially religious in anyway.

"We're all praying that you wake up," Kevin whispered. "We're lost without you."

The young woman's hands encircled his and she leaned toward him. "You are all stronger than you realize. I am just a soldier who has more experience than you. All of you are capable of great things. Today, Bill, Dale and Ken did great things whether they realized it or not."

"I need you back," Kevin said, his voice breaking. Tears filled his eyes. "I need you back, Nerit. You make me feel less alone in this world. Less afraid. I stand next to you and I feel strong."

Nerit's young face smiled at him softly. "Have faith in yourself, Kevin. You did good things at the mall. You saved so many."

"So many died..."

"So many lived. Trust yourself. Trust what you have learned. Trust Travis and the others. You are all strong."

"Please wake up, Nerit. Wake up," he insisted.

"Are you listening to me?"

"Yes. Yes. I am."

She reached out and her hand gripped his chin. Leaning very close to him, her eyes seemed to burn with light. "Then you must understand that you must go on and win this battle. The fort must survive and this world must go on. This is Eden and the snake attacks from without. Do not let it in."

Kevin struggled to speak, then he nodded. "I won't let it in. I will go on."

Nerit smiled and dropped her hand. "Do not give into despair now, Kevin. It is not the time nor the place." She slid to her feet and Kevin rose with her.

"Nerit," he said, taking her arm.

"Shh," Nerit answered.

"I just want to say-"

"Shh," she said again and laid a finger on his lips.

Kevin pulled her close and stared into those brilliant eyes. "Nerit, if only-"

He woke up with a start. The hand resting in his felt too cool to his touch and he panicked. Sleepily, he searched for Nerit's pulse. Tears filled his eyes as he tried to find it, his fingers trembling.

"Nerit, please, don't go," he whispered fervently to the older woman resting on her bed.

Then he found it. That steady, faint little pulse in her wrist.

"Oh, God," he whispered and fell back in his chair.

Before him, Nerit slept on.

2. The Winds of War

"Bring it in! Keep moving," Juan called out as the fort gates yawned open to let in more supplies.

For the last two days large trucks with heavily armed contingents had been raiding every supply store within a hundred miles in the opposite direction of the zombie horde. The fort seemed to be bursting at the seams with all the new stacks of wood, cement bags, razor wire and various other building materials.

Outside the walls, small Bobcat construction vehicles were busy clearing away the last of the brush from around the fort. In the distance large bulldozers stacked the remains of houses and trees into high barriers.

Volunteer workers toiled endlessly outside the fort on a variety of traps. Large signs were posted all around the fort, directing people as to where not to go.

As one of the trucks rumbled past Juan, his cousin, Linda, leaped down off the back and walked over to him. She had been persistent about going out on the salvaging runs despite the protests of her family.

"How's it going out there?"

"Couple of zombies. Nothing major," Linda answered Juan.

Juan nodded, his cowboy hat perched far back on his head. "Mom was going nuts with you being out there again. Bette didn't seem too happy either."

"Can't stop working just cause of the other day," Linda answered crossly.

"Yeah, I know." Juan sighed, shrugging. "You know Mom. And Grandma ain't much better."

"I gotta do what I gotta do. Your Jenni knew that, too."

"How do I have so many damn bullheaded women around me?"

"Sheer luck," Linda answered with a wry grin.

A huge military truck rolled in crammed full of more razor wire and other supplies.

"Bette doing better?"

"Her arm is seriously messed up. They aren't sure how much use she'll have when it heals." Linda tucked her hands into the back pockets of her jeans and furrowed her brow. "And things feel weird now with us. I dunno why. I just..."

Juan looked down at her, his arms crossed over his chest. "What do you mean?"

"I dunno" Linda shrugged. "Like I keep feeling I should have died back there and now when I'm around Bette it feels fucked up. I love her. But it's like..."

Juan reached out and gently rubbed her shoulder. "It's okay, Linda. It was rough out there."

"Lenore and I are the only survivors of the run to the hospital, Juan," Linda said softly. "Felix, Dale, Ken, Bill, Roger, Jenni...all gone now. Only Lenore and I are still here."

Juan winced at the mention of the hospital run. It had saved his life, but he had lost Jenni because of it. "Linda, that is just how this fucked up world works. Don't let it get you down."

"Hey, I got no regrets about going there. That medicine and stuff is helping a lot of people. It helped you. But it freaks me out. I seriously feel I should have died out there." Linda's gaze was intense.

"Is that why you keep going out there?"

"Yeah." Linda admitted. "Yeah."

"Zombie in the hold!"

Juan and Linda's heads both jerked up. The inner gate was still closed. Above them on the walls, two people were trying to aim at something down in the holding area.

Running up the stairs, Juan reached back to grip her hand and despite herself, Linda felt comforted by it. Reaching the top, they looked down to see a woman in a red sweater moving swiftly around the truck, banging on it with slim hands. Long black hair obscured her face, but her growls revealed her true nature.

"She dropped off the back of the truck when it got into the lock," one of the guards shouted.

"Put her down," someone shouted.

Juan felt like he couldn't breathe. Something about the figure reminded him of Jenni. The sweater, the long dark hair, the slim build. Beside him, Linda squeezed his hand.

"It's not her. Katie put her down. It's not her," Linda's voice whispered.

A sniper finally got a good shot and the creature's head exploded, then it fell back. Despite the shot through its forehead, its face was still reasonably intact. It bore no resemblance to Jenni whatsoever.

"It's okay," Linda said once more.

Juan nodded slowly then turned and took his cousin into his arms and held her tight. "We're both okay. You're supposed to be here. Don't think about being dead. You got Bette. Don't forget that. It's okay."

They clung to each other as the all-clear signal was given. The large inner doors opened and the truck rolled on leaving the dead zombie alone in the lock.

3. Family Way

It was sheer chaos in the suite. Three little kids were scampering around screaming and laughing as they were chased around by Juan. Troy was only in his undies while Margie was in her nightgown with her hair soaking wet. Holly was half-way into her pajamas sporting the topless look.

"Okay, now be nice to Daddy One and do what I say," Juan ordered.

Margie managed a feat worthy of an Olympic gymnast to get over the sofa and looked at him. "No!"

Holly and Troy stopped on the other side of the sofa and laughed like little hyenas.

Juan frowned and put on his most authoritative voice. "Get your PJs on or you are all in big trouble."

The three hellions looked at each other, then took off running again, laughing like the evil little fiends they were.

Clutching Holly's top in one hand, Juan pursued them, finding it damn hard to catch the little ones. Troy was especially good at evasive maneuvers. Juan couldn't help but think he'd make a great football player.

Despite his frustration with them, he knew most of this was them craving his attention. He had been gone all day working on the fort defenses and when he had come home, his beleaguered mother and grandmother had quickly dumped the kids off on him.

"They need their father. We're done," Rosie had said as she rolled her mother to out of the room. With that he had been on his own with the little terrors.

"Holly! Freeze!"

To his surprise she froze in her tracks, giving him her big-eyed look of surprise. Slowly, he approached her, holding her pajama top in his grip, readying to put it over her head. Just when he got close, she took off again.

"Dammit!"

"You said a bad word!" Troy popped up from behind the recliner. "I'm gonna tell."

"Yeah? Who are you going to tell?" Juan asked.

"God," Troy responded.

Well, Juan thought, at least Troy didn't waste time with the middleman, but went straight to the top.

The door opened behind him and he turned to see Jason walk in. Covered in dirt and grime and reeking of gasoline, the teenager shut the door, then leaned back against it.

"Is there hot water left?" Jason asked eying Margie's soaking wet hair.

"Hey, kid," Juan said, ignoring the little scamps rushing around him, trying to egg him into a game of catch again.

"Hi, Dad," Jason answered. He disengaged from the door and walked over to hug Juan. He was stopped by the trio of terror leaping on him. Clinging to him like monkeys, the three began to talk his head off and Jason slowly smiled from beneath his long hair.

Juan walked slowly toward the kids. "You're just in time for the nightly roundup."

"Yeah?" Jason looked down at the little ones yammering away at him, then grabbed all three of them up in his arms.

Massive squeals of delight followed. Juan managed to snag Holly and get her top over her head.

"Ha!" Juan chucked her onto the sofa. "Stay there or no cookies tomorrow."

Holly immediately froze and sat wide-eyed in false innocence.

Grabbing a towel off a stool, he wrapped it around Margie's hair and knotted it on top of her head. Tossing her onto to the sofa, he muttered the same threat and was rewarded with another frozen child.

Troy tried the squirm and kick maneuver but Jason reduced him to giggles by tickling him. Juan somehow managed to get his pajamas on despite all the wrestling. Then Troy was also chucked onto the sofa and joined his sisters.

"Now! In this family, we behave. Or no cookies," Juan said.

Jack looked up from where he was trying to sleep on the recliner with a look of horror in his doggy eyes.

"Understood?" Juan asked.

The little heads nodded, then Holly yawned.

"Okay, now to bed. And no more horsing around," Juan said firmly.

Forming a short line, the kids all came up to kiss and hug him and Jason, then trekked to their bedroom pretending to be the best little kids he'd ever seen.

"And I better not hear any talking in there," Juan added.

Jason giggled and sat down at the bar. Popping open a can of soda, he yawned long and hard.

"Hard work out there today, huh?"

"Yeah. Got the fire traps set though. Had some trouble at first, but we sorted it out. Had a zombie creep up on us and try to bite Calhoun's arm, but his jacket didn't let the bite go through. Got a shitty ass bruise though. It must have been in some rubble from a house or something. It was weird."

Juan sat at the bar and rubbed his brow. "We got a lot of stuff rigged up, too. Not too sure about the tar and cement traps, but we gotta try. I think the tiger traps will do okay until they fill up."

"It's all crazy, you know. I keep thinking about Mom coming and saving me from that camp and now I'm here. The world seemed so small then. And now... it's still small, but it feels bigger. I dunno I have been feeling like we're not just fighting for us but for the world." Jason sighed and rested his chin on his hand.

"There is a lot at stake. We can't pretend there isn't, ya know. We just gotta buckle down and do what we can. And next time we'll be better prepared and ready to deal with all of this." Juan rubbed Jason's shoulder gently. "You're doing a good job, Jason. I'm proud of you."

Jason looked toward him in surprise, then slowly smiled. "Thanks, Dad. That means a lot."

"All of this has been a lot for a kid your age. But you're not a kid anymore, Jason, you're a man and I'm damn proud of you."

Jason grinned even more. "Yeah, well, I kinda had to grow up fast." He looked toward the partially open door behind which the three kids were tucked into their beds. "I don't want them to lose their innocence. They should get to be kids."

With a sigh, Juan nodded. "Yeah. I know. But we're all changed now. All of this bullshit with the zombies has changed everyone."

"What is bullshit?" a small voice said from behind the recliner.

"Holly, get to bed," Juan ordered without turning around.

With a little giggle, the little girl ducked back into her room.

Jason and Juan looked at each other before bursting into laughter.

* * * * *

Travis rubbed his face, feeling the stubble scrubbing at his palms. With a sigh, he drank more of lukewarm coffee. Standing outside the hotel, he looked up at the perimeter wall. Catapults, mounted crossbows, and other inventive weapons decorated the top.

Nearby, Curtis and Linda were in a deep conversation. He was trying not to pay attention, but Linda was obviously crying. Curtis looked close to it as well. It was easy to figure out what was going on. The police officer had been sulking ever since Linda and Bette had become a couple.

"Look," Linda's voice raised in the warm night air. "There is no going back. Okay? Maybe if Bette hadn't shown up maybe things would be different. But she is here and in my life, so let it be! Let it go! I can't do this anymore!"

The few people still working on the defenses nearby all pretended not to hear her words. They also tried not to watch her run into the hotel or notice Curtis' stricken expression.

Travis looked away. Sipping his coffee once more, he started up the stairs to check on the defenses at the gated entrance.

* * * * *

Katie stirred in her sleep. The room she shared with Travis was dark except for some light seeping through the curtains from the security lights on the perimeter wall. Exhausted from the day, she had taken a hot bath and gone to bed.

In her mind's eye, she saw visions of her future baby, her father, Travis and even her long dead mother. She dreamed of playing in a field of flowers with her family and making a wreath to put around Travis' neck. It was a pleasant dream and she smiled in her sleep.

In her dream, she looked up to see the meadow that led up to the walls of the fort, standing strong and proud over the countryside. It gleamed golden and she lifted her hand to wave to the people on the walls. Then suddenly she was standing on the wall looking down at her family in the field below.

Slowly, the sky darkened and night came.

Worriedly, she strained to see her family, but it was so dark she could not see. Then, out of the darkness, came the moans of thousands of zombies.

Waking with a start, Katie pressed her hand to chest to feel the rapid beat of her frightened heart. A knock on the door made her jump and she slid her hands through her hair.

"Okay, calm down," she whispered. Sliding out of the bed, she moved slowly toward the door. Her stomach felt heavy and she cupped her hands under it as she walked.

"Hello?"

"Katie, it's Curtis," a very sad voice called out.

Opening the door, she peered out to see the young man's swollen and tear-stained face.

"Curtis, are you okay?"

"I need to talk to you, okay? I need advice."

"Okay, come in," she said.

"No. No. Not here. I need fresh air. I'm just..." He shook his head. "I can't talk about it here. Meet me up on the wall on the corner of Morris and Main in like fifteen minutes?"

He looked so sad and pathetic, Katie couldn't refuse. "Okay. I'll get dressed and meet you there."

"Okay," he said with a sigh. "Just don't tell anyone okay? I'm way embarrassed about what is happening and I don't want people talking."

Katie nodded. "Okay, hon. I understand."

Curtis tucked his hands into pockets and lowered his red face. "Thanks, Katie. You're a good woman."

"Thanks, Curtis. I'll see you in fifteen."

"Okay." He looked at her sheepishly, then walked away, his head down.

With a sigh, she shut the door and rubbed her eyes. She was exhausted but sleep would have to wait.

4. The Last Night

Travis unlocked the door to the room he shared with Katie and stepped in as stealthily as possible. He had seen how weary his wife had been at dinner and he wanted to make sure not to wake her. He was surprised to see her up and shrugging into t-shirt.

"Babe, what are you doing up?"

Pulling the shirt down so her face popped into view, Katie groaned. "Curtis came by. He looked like shit. He says he needs to talk so I told him I'd meet him in a few minutes at the corner of Morris and Main."

Slightly frowning, Travis moved toward her. He admired her long legs and smiled at the swell of her belly above her bikini underwear. She leaned over to reach for her jeans and he gently stopped her.

"You're exhausted. You have dark circles under your eyes and, honey, your eyes are bloodshot as hell."

Leaning against him, Katie sighed and tucked her hands into the small of his back. "He just looked so upset. I felt so bad for him. I know things have been rough on him with Bill dying and Linda not being with him."

Kissing the top of her head, Travis sighed softly. He laid his cheek on her soft hair and closed his eyes, enjoying the feel of her in his arms. As tired as he was, he could stand here forever holding her. "I'll go talk to him."

"Travis, you're tired, too," Katie protested. She gazed up at him in a way that made him feel as if he could fight a million zombies and win.

"I would love nothing more than to lie down next to you and feel you in my arms as we sleep, but you're right. Curtis is having a rough time right now. I think Bill may have been the closest thing he had to a best friend and he's gone now. I saw the last fight between him and Linda. It was harsh." Travis gently pushed her down on the bed. "So you sleep and I'll go see if I can offer him some brotherly advice."

Katie started to refuse, then sighed as she lay back on the bed. One hand draped over her pregnant tummy, she gazed up at him sleepily. "Okay, okay, I won't fight you. I'm too tired anyway."

Lifting her legs up onto the bed, Travis leaned over and kissed her belly, then her lips. "I'll be back soon. I'll take a shower, then climb into bed. We'll have a few hours of nice cozy sleep."

"Yum," Katie whispered. "That sounds wonderful."

Travis smiled slowly. "You're wonderful."

Running her hand lightly down the side of his face, she smiled. "Hurry back."

"I will." Travis leaned down and kissed her lips softly. "Love you."

"Love you," Katie answered drowsily.

"Always and forever," Travis added.

She snuggled into her pillow. "Send Curtis my love."

"I will."

After one last kiss on her brow, he straightened the covers around her then moved toward the door. A quick, sudden chill flowed over his body and he froze. He literally felt the hair on his head stand up on end. Turning quickly, he saw Katie already asleep in their bed, the lamp next to the bed illuminating her hair into a halo. Rubbing his hand over his chest, he could feel his heart beating a little faster and he swallowed hard. He had no idea what had just happened to him, but it frightened him.

Taking a deep breath once more, he opened the door and stepped out.

* * * * *

It had been awhile since justice had been dealt out at the fort. A long time. In those months, the Vigilante had watched and waited to see what the so called leaders of the fort would do or say.

The Vigilante had not been very satisfied. It had been hard to withhold the hand of justice, but the time had come once more. The Vigilante would deal out justice to those who were weak and a burden to the fort.

Yes, the time had come.

Walking down the hallway, the Vigilante hesitated before the communication center where Curtis could usually be found and looked in the glass window set in the door. Smiling, the vigilante studied Curtis' features. He had obviously been crying.

Curtis was weak.

But the Vigilante was strong.

It was time for justice.

5. Between Two Worlds

"I always loved to watch you sleep," Lydia's voice whispered.

Katie stirred slightly, her eyelashes fluttering, then she was still.

Lydia's apparition moved into the light next to the bed and stood silently. Her expression was full of love and yet it was sad. Slowly, she sat down on the edge of the bed and folded her long hands on her lap..

"The veil is so thin now I can almost touch you," she said softly. Slowly, she rested her almost corporeal hand on Katie's stomach. "I miss touching you so much."

Katie let out a soft sigh and rolled completely onto her back, her hand resting against her stomach.

"I love seeing you this way. In all our years together, I never saw you as a motherly woman. But seeing you like this now, it touches my heart so deeply. It makes me happy." Lydia smiled softly. "We had so many plans, you and I. Happy with our family of two. If none of this had happened, I never would have seen you as I do now. Full of life and glowing. A mother to be."

Lydia sat in silent repose, then laid her hand ever so gently on Katie's hand. "Strange how all that happened has been a curse, yet a gift. I miss you. I do, Katie. But you have moved on in away that makes me so proud. I love you and I want you to be happy. But I do fear for you. I have done all I can to help you and yours. And now..." Lydia sighed. "Now there is nothing more I can do. It's time for us to move on. All those still lingering between the two worlds. We've done what we can and now the world will change again. It is time for us to leave you to do what you must. After tonight, I will no longer return to you as I have. My time here is done."

Tears in her eyes, Lydia pressed a hand to her slim throat composing herself. "You are all standing on the brink of a new world. Whether the dead or the living rule will be decided. I know you think of yourselves as just survivors, but you are more than that. You are the new Eden. You are the new beginning. There are other enclaves of survivors, but none are as important as this one. This is the place that was chosen to give birth to a new world. The choices you make tomorrow will have ramifications far beyond what you understand or see."

Leaning down, Lydia kissed Katie's hand and pressed her cheek to her knuckles. Gazing into her face, she smiled softly. "We lived in a world that was black and white. Reality was so sharp and clear. We never realized how deep, wondrous and how frightening the roots of our world truly are. I've stood in the center of the veil and seen the world of your reality and the world of my new life. I have seen wonder and I have seen horrors. I have seen many possible futures and many possible pasts. But tomorrow is the one point in time that can change everything."

Rising up, Lydia straightened her long skirt, then tucked her hair back behind her delicate ears. Composing herself, she leaned over Katie one last time.

"I pray that you live. But if not..." Lydia gently touched Katie's cheek. "I will be waiting for you."

In her sleep, Katie sighed.

Leaning over, Lydia softly kissed Katie's lips. "I love you, Katie."

"Lydia," Katie whispered, her eyes slowly opening.

The room was empty.

Katie rolled over, tucking the pillow under her head. Feeling more alone than she had in a very long time, she closed her eyes and fell back to sleep.

Chapter 31

1. The Veil Falls

Travis walked up the stairs to the wall feeling weary in every way possible. The earlier storms had managed to dissipate the heat, but the humidity hung in the air making him feel sticky.

Looking around, he was a little discomforted by the fact Curtis had picked the most isolated area on the wall. Thinking about Katie standing out here with Curtis made him feel leery although he really wasn't sure why. He rubbed his chin and looked around thoughtfully.

This area of the wall was tucked between the hotel and another building across Main street. It was basically a dead end alleyway next to the huge wall that encircled the front of the hotel. It had been decided to leave access to the loading dock off the kitchens. The loading doors were heavily reinforced and they had added an additional entry with metal doors to thwart any breach. As another measure, a catapult had been built right next to the wall. It had a shorter range than the ones built along the wall and was intended to smash any zombies entering the alleyway leading up to the wall.

Looking to one side, Travis could see the the large pile of junk collected to load onto the catapult. It was mostly broken TVs and other large appliances. It was a very impressive stack. Strange how the most common household items could be transformed into weapons.

Standing in the warm night air, he was awed at how peaceful the world felt. After days of hard work and desperate planning, it seemed as if the world was enveloped in chaos. Yet here he stood feeling the comfort of the warm night. Nothing in the world made sense to him anymore other than Katie and the baby.

He heard a step on the catwalk and turned to see Curtis moving through the darkness toward him.

"Hey, Curtis," he said.

"Oh, Travis! Hi," the younger man said awkwardly. Looking around swiftly, Curtis shifted uncomfortably on his feet. "I..uh..."

"Katie's asleep, Curtis. She's real tired with all the hard work and the baby is tiring her out. I told her I would come out and offer you a sounding board. I know this is a really rough time for you."

Curtis looked extremely uncomfortable as he drew near. "Yeah. It is. I guess for everyone. I just--today was rough. I thought Katie could give me some good advice. I didn't know who else to go to. With Bill...you know..."

"I know," Travis answered. "It has hit all of us profoundly."

"Really?" Curtis said. "You seem not to be affected by too much going on around us."

Travis looked up sharply at the tone in Curtis' voice. It was an odd inflection on top of an odd comment. "Of course, I'm affected."

"Oh," Curtis answered. "I guess you're just good at hiding things. I'm, you know, just too emotional."

"We're just different people," Travis answered with a wry smile. "We just deal with things differently."

"Yeah," Curtis said slowly. " Yeah, we do."

* * * * *

Katie slept restlessly.

She dreamed of Lydia. She dreamed of the first days. She dreamed of the oncoming zombies. She dreamed of her child. She dreamed of Travis.

She dreamed of Jenni.

It was one of those horrible nightmares where you dream you wake up and the world is dark and frightening. In her dream, she sat up in the bed, the covers falling around her waist. Instinctively, she knew she was not alone and looked around the darkened room, trying to see into every shadow.

Her heart began to beat harder as she heard a soft noise near the corner of the blackened room. She stretched out her hand to turn on the lamp. Again she heard a noise, like a footstep or a shuffle, and her fingers strained to find the knob to turn on the lamp.

Breathing harshly, she leaned sideways off the bed, trying to find the lamp on the stand next to it. Desperate to fill the room with light, she groped blindly in the darkness as her heart beat harshly in her ears.

Her fingers found the tiny knob and she began to turn it just as something grabbed her wrist. With a scream of fright, she twisted the knob and light flooded the room.

Jenni stood over her, gripping her arm tightly, her dead eyes staring at her intently. Her sickly pale skin and dark hair were wet with water.

Katie screamed in terror...

...and woke up.

Jenni still leaned over her, holding her arm, staring down at her. Katie screamed again, this time with the terror of knowing she was awake.

The apparition of her friend screamed, too, letting go of her arm, jumping back and whirling around. Jenni's long black hair fanned out around her as she twisted this way and that as Katie continued to scream.

"What? What?" Jenni looked around the room with her large dark eyes. "What?"

"You! You...you...you...you're dead!"

"Oh, that! Oh, I know that."

"I dreamed you were a zombie!" Katie rambled from where she was curled up against the headboard staring at Jenni in shock and fear.

"Oh, God. I'm not!" She she did look very alive. Her skin was pale, but pink, her eyes dark and brilliant. Her long dark hair fell over her red sweater in silky long tresses. Laughing, she slid onto the bed. "You're such a stupid dork."

Katie blinked then swallowed hard. "You're dead," Katie repeated.

"Yeah. I know that." Jenni laughed. "It was so dramatic, wasn't it?"

"But you're here," Katie said, not blinking, just staring. "And this isn't a dream?"

"Not a dream. I'm here. Only for a short time. I've been saving up all my energy just to push through tonight. Not too easy to do." Jenni looked around the room, then back at Katie. "I've always been nearby, but I was waiting." Leaning over, she checked the clock, looked satisfied, and sat back.

"Jenni, oh, God, Jenni!" Katie suddenly realized she truly wasn't dreaming, She flung her arms around Jenni and felt flesh and blood in her grasp. Clutching her best friend tight, she burst into tears.

Laughing with joy, Jenni clutched her close, and kissed her cheek.

"You're here! You're here! I can feel you!" Katie was laughing and crying at the same time. She gripped Jenni's face between her hands and kissed her long and hard on the forehead. "Oh, my gawd, Jenni, you're here."

"I know! I am! Isn't it cool? Only for a little bit, but good to be here. And look at your tummy!"Jenni snuggled up to Katie, holding her tighter. "You look so good, Mama."

Katie sobbed with joy and clung to her best friend. "Oh, Jenni. I've missed you so much."

"It's okay, sweetie. I'm here now. I'm here to save you and Travis just like I promised." Jenni drew back and touched Katie's check very gently.

"What do you mean?" Katie demanded, hearing the seriousness in Jenni's tone.

Jenni glanced at the clock again, her fingers gripping Katie's hand. It was beginning to not feel as real as it first had. "It's almost time. Crap. I forgot what time was like. It's different on the other side where all time is the same: past, present, future." She sighed softly. "I thought I had more time."

"Jenni, what do you mean?"

"I'm here to save you and Travis," Jenni replied. "Cause if I don't, tonight you're both going to die."

* * * * *

"Everyone deals with stress differently," Travis said uneasily.

"Yeah, I know. I just, you know, being a cop and all, I just see how things are going seriously wrong and I want to set it right."

"I know what you mean." Travis watched Curtis thoughtfully.

"I see people doing shitty things to other people and I just want to tell them that they need to shape up and get with the program. This is the law. You gotta obey it. You know, I believe in order. But lately..." Curtis shook his head. "I can't even find order in my own damned life."

Tucking his hands into his jean pockets, Travis bobbed his head slowly. "Yeah, I know what you mean. We're all just doing our best."

"But people keep on dying, Travis, don't they?"

Measuring his words carefully, Travis answered, "This world is dominated by death, Curtis. The living got a rough time of it."

"Yeah, yeah," Curtis agreed. "But sometimes, you know, the living make it harder on the rest of the living."

Travis tried to keep his face neutral, but he felt his body beginning to tense.

"How many people are gonna die, Travis? I don't mean when those fucking zombies get here. But tonight? Tomorrow? The suicides haven't even started yet, you know? But they will. Bill warned me about them. Gawddamn lucky it ain't like those old zombie movies where you just die and you're a zombie else we'd be shit out of luck fast."

Standing in silence, Travis looked at the younger man, studying the policeman's tense posture and flushed face with growing anxiety. "We're doing what we can, Curtis."

"Yeah, yeah, we are. Right. Saving people. Bringing them here. Taking a fucking stand against religious people who just don't agree with us. But maybe they were right, Travis. Did you think of that? Your girl got all right and straight," Curtis laughed sarcastically. "But my girl went all queer when you got the mall folks here. They are corrupters and sinners! Do you even give a shit about that?"

"Linda and Bette-"

"And you say their names together like they fucking belong together. They don't! Linda, my Linda, was okay before those shitbags from the mall got here. And that nigger-"

"Hey!" Travis voice was harsh. "Don't go there."

Curtis glared evenly at Travis. "This is the country, city boy. We talk different out here though you may not like it. And why the hell is an outsider our leader anyway?"

"Curtis, I'm one of many who make decisions around-"

"You blew into town all fancy and handsome. All the girls got all crazy about you right away. Making a big deal out of you and your fancy ways. Then all this shit hits and you're the fucking king? If the Mayor wasn't such a pussy and rolled over for you, we may have had a little more fucking luck with keeping our fucking senses and taking care of our own before dragging every fucking faggot, raghead, nigger-"

The punch was hard, fierce, and caught Curtis in mid-sentence. It knocked him back a few feet and stunned him. Shrouded in shadows, the younger man slowly brought his hand up to his face, feeling the quickly swelling flesh beneath his fingers.

Trying to keep calm, Travis said softly, "You're freaking out, Curtis. You need to calm the hell down right now. I'll drag your ass down to the clinic and sedate you if I have to."

In the darkness, the younger man stood in silence then slowly, methodically stepped into the light. "Try it,"he said in a low whisper and a knife glittered in the starlight.

* * * * *

"What do you mean?" Katie demanded, her eyes widening. "Explain, Jenni!"

Jenni tilted her head, looking at the alarm clock. Grabbing it up, she studied the numbers then cocked her head again, as if remembering something. "Oh, fuck, I was always late when I was alive."

"Jenni, you're scaring me," Katie whispered.

"Get your jeans on!" Jenni flung them at Katie and whirled around, her long hair fanning out around her. "Shit, shit, shit! I got the time fucked up in my head. I was thinking of Nerit's time, not Travis'!"

Fumbling with her jeans, Katie struggled into them, nearly tripping as she tried to also shove her feet into her jogging shoes. "Jenni, you're scaring the hell out of me! What is going on?"

"Curtis is about to kill Travis! We have to hurry or he'll do it!" Jenni grabbed at Katie's hand. Their fingers did not touch, but passed through each other. "Oh, damn! I'm already fading!"

"Jenni, what do you mean Curtis will kill Travis?" Katie felt as if she couldn't breathe as she tied her shoes.

"Come with me! Hurry! I'm sorry, Katie. I got the times wrong!" Jenni waved at her best friend again, her body seeming not as solid as before. "C'mon! We have to save Travis!"

"What do you mean Nerit's time? Jenni, what is happening?" Katie raced after her friend throwing open the bedroom door that Jenni simply ran through. She followed Jenni into the hallway. "Jenni, what do you mean?"

* * * * *

"Nerit," a voice whispered softly.

Standing on the shores of the Red Sea, Nerit turned slowly. Raising her hand to shield her eyes, she looked for the source of the soft voice.

"Nerit, come to my voice," it came again softly.

Turning completely around, she looked into the horizon as the sun blazed down on her. Her long blond hair whipped around her face and she could feel the sand and salt tucked into the creases of her uniform and rubbing against her skin.

"Where are you?" she asked.

"Here. Come here." The voice was behind her on the waves.

Stepping into the water slowly, she felt disoriented and afraid. Behind her the wind howled.

"Come deeper into the water, Nerit," the voice called out again. "Come to my voice."

"Ralph?"

Now in water up to her waist, she felt the warm water lapping up around her hands as she held them out at her sides.

The howl of the wind was louder now, almost screaming in her ears.

"Don't look behind you, Nerit, just come here," Ralph's voice persisted.

Slowly, despite his words, Nerit turned. Behind her the shore was filled with the undead, screaming, howling, reaching toward her. A few were daring to enter the water behind her.

Then a hand reached out of the water, grabbed her and dragged her down into the salty depths.

In the tiny clinic room, Nerit's eyes opened from her nightmare. Her fingers trembling against her heaving chest, she tried to focus her eyes and take a deep breath. It hurt at first, then the pain in her chest lessened and she pressed her hand to her forehead.

The I.V. was an annoying pain in her wrist, but she ignored it as she caught sight of Kevin asleep in a chair near the door.

"Kevin?"

She was sure the voice in her dream had been Ralph, but now she wasn't so sure.

Slowly, Ralph stepped out of the shadows near the bed and sat down in the chair closest to her. He smiled softly at her and reached out to take the hand still clutching the bed covers.

"Nerit, you're okay. You're awake. It was hard to get you back. You were so far gone."

"Ralph," she whispered, laying her other hand over his. "I can feel your hand."

"Only for a little bit, hon," he answered, giving her a small smile.

"Am I dreaming?"

"No, hon. You're awake. Out of the coma. Lots of prayers were going up for you, you know," Ralph said with a wink.

"What's happening?" Nerit asked slowly, cautiously.

Looking sad, Ralph sighed and squeezed her hand. "What happens next is gonna be hard. Not to my liking. Probably not to yours. But how it is."

"Ralph, you're frightening me," Nerit whispered. She felt groggy and unsure of the world around her. The dreams of Israel had been so vivid they had felt real to her.

"Sometimes, Nerit, we gotta sacrifice ourselves for the greater good. We gotta do the hard job. The thing that hurts most." Ralph sighed softly. "Lots of prayers for you, like I said. Lots of fear here. Lots of need."

"Ralph, please, I know I have cancer, I know--" She dreaded that he was here to take her for good.

"Not no more, Nerit. It's gone. I wanted you home. With me." He looked so heartrendingly sad and Nerit squeezed his hand tightly. "But, you got an extension. You got more time. They need you here. They need who you are and what you can do. I even prayed myself for you to stay here."

"Ralph, I'll always love you and-" The sense of relief she felt was overwhelming. To not die of cancer, to fight on for the fort, it was all she wanted, yet; she felt so sad to not be with him.

"I know, Nerit. But your place is here. And this changes everything for the fort. Time is not set in stone. Some of us on the other side realized that. We saw it all: Past, Present, Future. We knew what could happen and we...we found a place in time to try to change how it comes out. Not saying it's going to turn out okay, but you guys got a better chance now."

"I don't understand, Ralph," Nerit said softly.

With a sad, weary sigh, her dead husband said, "There are points in time that the future hinges on. A moment when it can all go one way or the other. This is one of those times. Some of us have worked hard to see that this swings in a way that will let the living win."

Slowly, achingly, Nerit sat up. She could feel herself growing stronger in mind, body and spirit and her eyes became more sharply focused. "I see."

"I've seen two futures, Nerit. I hope, pray that..." He hesitated and slowly stood up. "I hope that the world lives on beyond tomorrow."

"Ralph," she said softly. She looked at him evenly. "Tell me what to do."

With a short nod of his head, Ralph said, "That's my girl. This is what you gotta do..."

* * * * *

"Curtis," Travis said in a low, soft voice. "You don't want to do this."

"No, actually I do." Curtis took one step forward. His young face was very calm, his eyes hard, and his jaw set. He was more self-assured, cockier than usual. He moved with confidence that made him only seem deadlier.

"What purpose will it serve to kill me?" Travis asked, watching the knife warily. His body was tense, ready to evade any attack. His heart was thundering in his ears.

"I'm not going to kill you, Travis. Just help you along." Curtis smiled slowly. "You know, originally, I wanted to ditch Katie over the wall. Let you see how it feels to lose the woman you love. But I am okay with this. You dying works fine."

The cold manner in which Curtis spoke of throwing his wife over the wall had Travis speechless with horror. He took a long breath to calm himself. He needed to think clearly, not emotionally. Stepping back, Travis could feel the catwalk sway slightly. Looking around him, he realized how perfectly isolated they were. Curtis had picked one of the best places in the entire fort for an attack.

"Who knows? Maybe your lesbo wife will hook up with Bette and return my girl to me. That could work. Maybe." Curtis moved forward in a slow relentless pace.

"Curtis, think about what you are saying. You're speaking about murder," Travis said in a measured voice. "You don't want to do this."

"Why not? I've done it before. I got rid of the people you wouldn't. I took care of the fort when you wouldn't. Yeah, yeah, you all blamed Blanche, but she was a stupid whore. I took care of this fort when you wouldn't. I did what was necessary!"

"You're the Vigilante," Travis said slowly, the shock of his words making him feel a little numb.

"Yeah, Travis, took you long enough. You're dumber than I thought." Curtis laughed. "You're all so busy just trying to be goody goody and make the world great by talking and talking, but I am the doer. I do what needs to be done." The young man's face was full of cold, raw anger. "I am the law around here, whether you want to admit it or not. I am the only real cop left standing around here. I took care of our people while you just talked and talked and talked."

"I'm not the only one making decisions around here," Travis started.

"No, you're not. But you got more influence than you deserve to have. You're an outsider, Travis. You don't belong here. But ever since you blew into town, everyone has acted like you're some great wonderful messiah. All the girls were blabbing on about you and all the guys wanting to be your buddy. But you ain't all that. You're a city slicker that came out here to play country. And your city slicker ways ain't doing us no damn good."

"So you killed all of them, huh? Ritchie, Jimmy, Phil, Shane..." Travis tried to push his shock away and focus on the moment.

"Shane and Phil may have been a mistake. I'll admit to that. I don't approve of men raping women. But now that I know she really was a

332

lesbian before she was with you, I see now that I may have gotten the wrong sinner."

Travis swallowed his anger and took a step back from the young man with the sharp knife. "You're afraid of what you don't understand."

"Oh, I understand plenty. Trust me, Travis. I can see very clearly that you have been letting in sinners that will destroy this fort." Curtis took a firm step toward him.

Trying to furtively examine his surroundings and figure a way past Curtis and out of the dead end the man was pushing him into, Travis decided that to keep Curtis talking was the best route. "Yeah, you seem to hate it that the people from the mall are here."

"The Baptists got that right. Crime went up when they got here. People got sick with the flu. Got more gay people and wetbacks to deal with. We were moving toward being a solid, Godly community until that happened."

"I guess you forgot our Reverend is black," Travis said with a slight smile. "Or is your bigotry arbitrary."

"Fuck you," Curtis hissed.

A low moan whispered through the night.

Both men froze.

The sound made both of them tense even more. Simultaneously, they looked over the wall to see a zombie staggering into the alley.

"Well, now that is perfect timing. Guess he heard the lunch bell," Curtis said with a grin.

Then he lunged at Travis.

* * * * *

Katie ran down the hallway, her feet pounding the floor in rhythm to her rapidly beating heart. She tried to keep the apparition of Jenni in view as her dead friend ran in front of her. Skidding around the corner, she almost ran into the Reverend as he stepped off the elevator.

"Katie, are you okay?" he asked worriedly as Katie pushed past him.

"We're fine," Jenni answered as she reappeared next to Katie and dragged the blond into the elevator.

The reverend's eyes grew wide just as the elevator doors shut cutting Katie off from his view.

Katie whirled around and tried to punch Jenni in the arm, but her hand went through her. "What is going on?"

"Crap. I'm losing it fast," Jenni pouted.

"Jenni!"

"Oh, Curtis is the freaking Vigilante and about to kill Travis,' Jenni answered. Frowning, she kept trying to touch Katie and failing.

"Oh, God!" Katie felt her chest tighten and she gripped Jenni's wrist tightly.

"I'm back!"

"Jenni, you have to help me save him! I can't lose him, too!"

"I know! That is why I'm here," Jenni poked Katie's forehead with one finger. She smiled as she managed to touch Katie.

"Jenni!"

"Okay, okay. They're on the wall where Curtis was going to meet you. Curtis was originally going to toss you over the wall as a punishment to Travis. Curtis is way sick in the head."

"Oh, God. He killed the other people. Curtis killed the other people!"

Jenni nodded. "Oh, yeah. He's twisted. He would have killed more, too, but me and the other ghosts worked hard to try to stop him."

"The other ghosts?"

"Lydia, Ralph, and some others." Jenni bounced on her heels as she waited for the elevator to hit the ground floor.

Katie blinked, not sure what to say, and looked toward the doors. She had to save Travis. To lose him would be too much to bear.

The doors slid open onto an empty lobby. Grabbing Katie's hand, Jenni pulled her from the elevator and across the lobby. Katie ran as fast as she could, desperation clouding her senses. Raw fear gripped her and she ran with her ghostly friend in a mad dash to save her husband.

* * * * *

Travis ducked under the first swipe of the knife and slammed into Curtis with his shoulder, knocking the attacker back. Curtis hit the catwalk on his back, the knife clutched tightly in his hand. He scrambled to get up.

Kicking at the younger man, Travis tried aimed for the wrist of the hand holding with the knife. Instead he hit Curtis' arm, enabling Curtis to grab onto Travis' leg with his other hand. Trying to keep his balance, Travis grabbed onto the rail next to him as the hungry moans of the zombie grew louder.

Getting some leverage, Curtis managed to get to his knees and drew the knife back to stab Travis.

With a grunt, Travis managed to twist away and staggered back a few feet as the knife cut through empty air.

"Curtis, think this over," Travis said in a firm voice. "You can't do this."

"Oh, cause you're so damn important?" Curtis laughed and began to close the gap between them.

Travis took another step back to find himself in the dead end. Sliding into a defensive posture, he readied himself for Curtis' attack.

Curtis drew back his hand and brought the knife down toward Travis. With a quick swipe of his arm, Travis defected Curtis' attack and shoved him back hard with both hands. Shocked, the younger man took several steps back.

"I've got a wife and a kid. I'm not going over this wall," Travis said firmly.

Below, the zombie watched them, moaning hungrily, its hands reaching up.

"Yes, you are," Curtis hissed through clenched teeth, then attacked again.

Again, Travis deflected the attack, shoving the younger man back, but Curtis grabbed onto his t-shirt and dragged Travis with him. Struggling with each other, off balance, and both desperate, they fell against the railing over the grasping hands of the zombie far below.

Managing to plant his elbow in Travis' throat, Curtis raised the knife over his head. "It's better for the fort this way," Curtis hissed.

"No!"

Katie slammed into Curtis full force, knocking him and Travis off their feet.

Travis had a moment of complete vertigo before he managed to grab the rail as his feet swung over his head and he toppled over the wall. His shoulder popped painfully as the full weight of his body jerked his arm and he almost lost his grip on the rail. Groaning, he reached up to grab the rail with his other hand. He could hear Curtis and Katie wrestling above him and the zombie moaning below.

"Katie, don't fight him! Get help," he called out to his wife.

Curtis appeared over him again.

"That's not going to happen," Curtis hissed.

The knife glittered as he brought it down to stab Travis' hand. Instinctively, Travis tried to jerk away, but only managed to lose his grip with his second hand. The blade sliced easily into the back of his hand and he cried out as he lost his grip and fell.

Despite the sheer terror of the moment, he remembered to tuck his body and roll as he hit the ground. The impact was jarring and he immediately tasted blood as he bit the inside of his mouth.

The moan of the zombie was near and he panicked as he struggled to his feet and tried to catch is breath. He sensed more than felt the creature. He struck out with one foot, catching the beast square in its torso and sending it falling to the ground.

Bracing himself against the wall, he looked around desperately for a weapon. To his relief he saw the knife glittering nearby. He moved swiftly to kick the zombie over as it tried to scramble to its feet. Travis darted to snatch up the knife.

"Travis!"

Above him, he could hear the struggle. He looked up to see Katie gazing down at him as Curtis grabbed her from behind.

"Katie, just run! Get help!" Forcing himself to look away from the top of the wall where his wife grappled with Curtis, he reached for the knife.

The low, hungry growl of the zombie made him spin around and he was surprised to see the creature so close. Its gnarled, gray hand reached out to grab him as its teeth snapped together. Circling around it quickly, Travis thanked God for its slowness. He shoved it over as hard as he could. It landed face down and began to claw at the ground. He gave wide berth to the zombie and snatched up the knife.

He fought the urge to look up and see how Katie was doing. He had to kill the zombie before he could even begin to figure out how to get back into the fort and help Katie. The thing was trying to get to its knees and he moved around it and kicked its hip as hard as he could, knocking it over. Disoriented, the thing writhed on the ground, then its dead eyes found him and it began to try to rise.

A scream from Katie made him look up and the creature grabbed his foot far faster than he would have expected. Its strength startled him and he found himself losing his balance and falling.

Concentrate, dammit, he thought to himself.

Shifting his body weight so he had leverage, he kicked the thing as hard as he could in the face with his boot heel. Its head bobbed back, but immediately, the thing reached for his foot, trying to grip it again. Kicking it again as hard as he could while shoving himself backward, he managed to get to his feet and away from the creature.

It began to try to rise and he rushed forward and planted his foot squarely on its brittle neck. He could feel it give way under his weight as he brought his left hand downward, the knife glittering, and rammed it into the creature's eye socket. He felt the mush inside give way as the thing continued to grab him. Its teeth champed just inches away from his hand as he leaned all his weight into the knife and felt the knife push further in. Working the knife back and forth, he finally felt the creature go limp.

Another scream made him look up. Katie dangled from the railing, her blond hair obscuring her face. Curtis was struggling with her, trying to pry her grip lose from the bar.

"Curtis, stop," Travis shouted angrily, rushing forward, but standing helplessly under his wife. He could see her legs kicking as she tried to get leverage, but she was dangling precariously.

Then it occurred to him that she might be safer with him than up there. "Katie, drop," he ordered, preparing to catch her.

Low moans from behind him, made his scalp crawl. Slowly, he turned. At least a dozen zombies were lumbering into the mouth of the alley.

"Don't drop, Katie!" His voice was harsh and full of fear.

Looking up, he saw her look down toward him, then toward the zombies.

He felt completely and utterly helpless.

* * * * *

Katie struck Curtis as hard as she could as Travis fell from view. Terror unfurled within her as she heard the low moan of the zombie below. Hissing with anger, she grabbed Curtis' shirt and tried to knee him. Stunned by her abrupt movement, he staggered back, but then he seized hold of her with shocking strength. His fingers dug fiercely into her wrists as she tried to draw back from him. Though her haze of fear, she could hear Travis calling out to her. She managed to look down and see him deflect the zombie's attack below.

Curtis whirled her around and shoved her hard against the rail. It was then she regained her senses enough to fight back. Twisting her wrists inward and down as she tucked her fists in, she broke his hold and shocked him. Shoving him hard with both hands, she saw him stagger back. Quickly she turned to see if Travis was okay. Below, her husband was shouting at her, but she barely heard him over the harsh beating of her own heart. Looking around, she tried to see what she could lower to him to pull him up.

"Travis," she called out.

He looked up at her just as Curtis grabbed her from behind.

"Katie, just run! Get help!"

Curtis lifted her up off her feet, his grip hard and suffocating around her chest. She kicked her feet and wiggled, trying to get away. Attempting to scream, she found she could not. Her breath was being cut off.

"You stupid little lesbo whore," Curtis hissed in her face. His features were so distorted he looked as unreal and corrupted as the thing trying to attack her husband below.

"Let me go," she managed, gasping for breath.

He tightened his grip and dragged her to the rail. "Don't worry. I will."

Katie's eyes widened as he lifted her up over the rail and let go of her. She managed to grab onto the bottom rail and hold on tight with both hands. Pulling herself up, she managed to hook her arm over the rail as her feet scrabbled against the wall.

Calmly, Curtis leaned over and began to try to dislodge her grip.

"Let go of me, you fucking bastard," she shouted at him.

"Katie, drop!" Travis' voice rose from below her.

She craned her neck and looked down toward him. Her husband was looking back toward the mouth of the alley and he took a step back toward the wall.

"Don't drop, Katie," he said in a stricken tone.

And then she saw the zombies in the alley making their way toward the man she loved.

"No! No!" She held on tighter, her feet fighting for purchase on the wall, as she looked up and saw Curtis smile. Leaning over her, he looked even more hellish as he tried to pry her hands loose. She managed to get her boot up onto the wall and began to push upwards, but he put his hands on her shoulders and shoved downwards.

"Fuck you!" she screamed.

"It's okay," Curtis whispered. "Really. It will be okay. Y'all will be together in the afterlife. You, Travis, the baby, your dead wife..."

"Go to hell," Katie spat at him.

"Looks like Travis is going first," Curtis answered, winking.

The moans were louder below and Katie screamed.

* * * * *

The elevator doors opened and Peggy blinked.

"What?"

Nerit walked briskly past her, sniper rifle slung over one arm, barrel pointed downwards, as she moved down the hall.

"Nerit?"

The old woman stopped and turned. Her gaze was steely and her face seemed younger somehow.

"You're...you..."

"I have a job to do," Nerit answered, walking on.

Peggy backed into the elevator slowly and then hit the button for the ground floor. She had to let the others know Nerit was up and around.

To her shock, she suddenly realized she was trembling and very afraid. She wondered if Nerit being up was a good omen or bad.

* * * * *

Nerit reached the room she was looking for and knocked. When there was no answer, she pulled her revolver and took a step back. She fired and a hole was punched very neatly through the door. Reaching through, she unlocked the door, pushed it open and entered.

The air in the room was stale and she rubbed the tip of her nose. This room had no balcony and she frowned. With a shrug, she shattered the window with the butt of her sniper rifle, the glass cascading around her like silvery rain. Grabbing the comforter off the bed, she shoved the musty thing over the window ledge, then dragged a chair over.

Carefully, she climbed onto the chair, then sat down on the ledge, the comforter keeping her safe from the broken glass. Tucking a strand of hair back from her face, she brought the rifle around and smiled slightly. It felt good and solid in her hands.

The wind howled around her as she perched in the window high above the fort below. Her eye became one with the scope and she looked down into her narrow world knowing exactly what she would see.

Travis came into view standing at the base of the wall. She quickly checked on the zombies and saw she still had time. Then her "eye" swept upwards and she saw Katie struggling with Curtis as she tried to hold onto the rail. Unfortunately, he was leaning over her in such a way Nerit could not get a clear shot without endangering Katie.

"One clear shot," she whispered softly, then realized it was a prayer. "I need one clear shot."

* * * * *

Juan wiped his brow with a kerchief and tucked it into his back pocket before reaching down to lift a concrete block up onto a cart. There were worries that one of the perimeter buildings needed reinforcement. A crew had been working on its back wall for most of the night.

"Juan! Juan! Where's Travis and Katie?" Peggy ran toward him, her eyes wide.

Looking around the large old construction site, he shrugged. "I haven't seen them for awhile. Why?"

"Nerit is up!"

"What?"

"I saw her come out of the elevator on the sixth floor. She looked great!" Peggy looked more lively than he had seen her in the days since Bill and Dale had died.

"Holy shit! I should have known that old woman was too tough to die," Juan declared.

"But the weird thing is she had her sniper rifle," Peggy continued. "And she looked deadly."

Juan's brow furrowed. "What the hell does that mean?"

"No clue."

The wind was loud, blowing hard off the hills and whistling through the fort. Juan turned to feel the air rush over his sweaty face. It felt soothing. Yet, he did not feel soothed.

"Shit, something is wrong, isn't it?"

He began to walk back toward the hotel feeling grim and afraid. Just then a bulldozer pulled across his way, hauling a load of stuff for a catapult. Forced to go around, he and Peggy ended up going along the old perimeter wall.

"Nothing feels right," Peggy said shortly. "You know, zombies coming!"

"Yeah, but Nerit being up and armed..." He shook his head as he walked. "Something is up."

It was then he heard Jenni's voice shout "Hey, fuckface" and the whole world changed.

Katie felt her grip slipping and Curtis was smiling madly down at her.

"It's okay, really. It's fine, let go." He kept saying to her.

She screamed again, but felt as if the wind tore it from her lips and dissipated it.

"You're going to die, Katie," Curtis whispered to her as he pried her fingers loose at last. He leaned far over her, shoving her back from the rail, her fingers of her other hand beginning to slip. "You're going to fall and die."

The moans of the zombies were closer now and Travis was swearing at Curtis, his voice full of despair.

"You're going to die, Katie, just like Jenni did. This is the end of your little Thelma and Louise story. No one can save you," he said softly.

"Hey, fuckface," Jenni's voice said sharply.

Katie caught sight of Jenni standing behind Curtis. She looked real. Solid. When Katie had reached the wall, Jenni had vanished. To see her again, Katie sobbed with relief.

Jerking around, Curtis saw Jenni and his expression was one of utter surprise.

"Why don't you try fucking with me, asshole?" Jenni taunted.

Abruptly letting go of Katie's hand, Curtis turned as he straightened.

"You're dead," Curtis exclaimed.

"So?"

Katie managed to hold onto the rail for a second with her other hand, but the sudden release of her weight by Curtis let gravity grab her and she half-slid, half-fell down the side of the wall.

Jenni's eyes flicked toward her friend's falling form, then she stared Curtis straight in the eye as he turned fully to face her.

"Bang," she said, and grinned.

"Wha-" he managed, then a hole was punched neatly through his brow above his left eye.

He fell slowly to her feet, crumpling like a puppet. Jenni looked up to the sixth floor window and waved to the woman perched there.

* * * * *

Juan reached the catwalk just in time to see Katie fall, Curtis turn toward Jenni, and then die at her feet. Startled, he could barely breathe as he stumbled toward the woman he loved.

Jenni waved to someone in the hotel, then turned to see him.

"Loca," he whispered.

"Hey, baby," she answered with a wide smile, then said, "Shit!"

And just like that, she swung her legs over the rail and dropped down below.

* * * * *

Travis lunged to catch her and Katie fell into his arms and sent them both sprawling. Immediately, they both scrambled to their feet to see the zombies moving ever closer to them. There were now maybe twenty moving slowly, but resolutely toward them. Behind those zombies, more staggered into the light in the street beyond. Their twisted, gnarled bodies were grotesque in their decay.

"They're early," Katie said.

"Yeah," Travis answered, holding her close. "Curtis?"

"I think Jenni has him covered."

Travis looked at her sharply. "Jenni? Huh?"

* * * * *

Nerit saw Jenni wave to her and she smiled briefly, then was on the move again. To get a clear shot of the zombies she had to be in a different location. The fire escape to her left would be perfect. Leaping off the chair, she ran across the room and out into the hallway.

* * * * *

Katie clung to Travis as they both began to shout at the top of their lungs for help. A form fell from above and they both ducked slightly as it landed near them.

It was Jenni. She landed on her feet and flipped her hair back from her face.

"Hey, Travis" she called out.

"Jenni," Travis whispered in shock.

With a grin, Jenni walked toward the zombies, her long hair flowing in the night wind. She sauntered up to the determined flesh eaters and her laughter drifted into the night.

"What the hell?" Travis managed.

"She's back...sorta...kinda," Katie answered.

* * * * *

Jenni's hair danced around her face as she smiled at the undead approaching her. She understood them now in a way she could not in life. They were desperately sad and terrible, but they were hunger personified and her friends were their chosen meal.

That was simply not acceptable. This was no place for pity or mercy.

"Hey fucktards, why don't you stop right there and wait for the nice sniper lady to shoot your heads off?" she said, then stepped into the midst of them.

The zombies stopped in mid-step. Slowly, they turned toward her, their hands grasping at her arms, face, and neck. The growled in confusion and hunger. They could not grab their delicious prey.

"Good zombies. Now. Bang."

The first zombie's head exploded.

* * * * *

Holding each other tight, Katie and Travis watched as Jenni walked into the center of the approaching zombies and they gathered around her, grabbing at her hungrily. From the wall, Juan and Peggy stood in shock and stared at the form of the woman in a red sweater, hands on her hips, standing the midst of the zombies as Nerit took them down one by one.

"Get the loading dock open and get them in," Juan said finally.

"The zombies," Peggy began to protest.

"She's got them," Juan answered in awe. "Loca's got them."

* * * * *

Anyone who saw it, could barely believe what they witnessed. Others, who were not there, did not believe it at all. But the woman in the red sweater with the long black hair held the zombies at bay as Nerit shot their heads off one by one.

The loading dock doors slid open and heavily armed fort personnel covered the distracted zombies as Katie and Travis ran to safety. The heavy doors clanged shut. Those gathered in the hotel windows and along the wall watched in awe as Jenni walked calmly over the downed monsters, pulling the remaining zombies along with her.

"Jenni!"

She turned at the sound of Juan's voice, her dark eyes smiling up at him. She lifted her hand and blew him a kiss as the zombies clustered around her.

More were coming now.

Jenni shoved a few out of her way as she walked, but none could grab her. They followed her relentlessly, moaning with aggravation.

As Jason and Jack joined the group on the wall, Jenni squatted down and looked at the ground.

"What is she doing?" Peggy asked.

"The explosives," Juan whispered.

"Go, Mom," Jason said softly, tears in his eyes.

Jenni activated the hidden dynamite under the dirt and blew the zombies to hell.

As the smoke cleared, nothing moved in the mouth of the alley or beyond.

And Jenni, once more, was gone.

Chapter 32

1. The Time of Choice

The lobby was packed with people as word of what had happened between Curtis, Travis, and Katie spread throughout the fort. Katie found herself huddled on a couch with Travis, sipping water and trying to keep her hands from shaking. She wasn't sure what had happened to Curtis' body, but a few people kept commenting they should throw him over the wall to the zombies.

Kevin sat nearby with Nerit. He looked utterly shocked that she was up, let alone looking so good.

"This is bullshit," a man declared.

Katie tilted her head to see Ed standing nearby.

"Sorry, folks, but I can't believe no shit about ghosts. Jenni is dead. End of story. Curtis may have been the Vigilante, but we broke fucking protocol opening the loading dock."

"Were we supposed to just leave them out there to die?" Peggy exclaimed.

"I'm just saying that this place is going to shit fast," Ed responded.

"I saw Jenni," Juan said sharply. "I saw her!"

"So did I," Peggy exclaimed. She was smoking up a storm and was shaking.

"Ghosts are bullshit and if this is what I can expect when the zombies get here, people busting protocol 'cause someone is in danger, I'm out of here," Ed said firmly.

"I saw ghosts, too," Katarina said from near the elevators. "I saw my Mama until Bill and I got engaged. After Bill died, I saw him."

Voices began to rise up, some agreeing with Ed.

"Ghosts? Give me a break."

"People are losing it."

"How many here saw a ghost tonight?" Nerit's voice broke through the murmuring.

Silence fell over the lobby, then slowly, nearly a third of the room raised their hands.

"So did I. I saw my dead husband. And he told me what Curtis was trying to do. I saw Jenni, too. Now, I may be an old woman, but that only means I've lived longer than most of you and I have seen things I cannot explain. The ghosts were here. They came to guide us. But they have all passed on now and it's up to us to deal with what happens next." Nerit's voice was firm and strong. It was a far departure from her frail appearance when she lay in a coma.

"C'mon," a voice said nearby. "That's a bunch of bull. You're sounding as crazed as those Baptists we threw out."

"Our leadership seems to be under a lot of stress," a familiar voice said. The former Mayor stood nearby. He wasn't doing very well health-wise and looked strained.

"I saw Jenni, too," Travis finally spoke up. "I saw her clear as day. I saw her turn back the zombies coming for me and my wife. If we have the dead walking the earth, why are ghosts so hard to believe in?"

"If your ghosts are real, why don't they just come and save us all?"

Katie couldn't see who all was talking now. The lobby was packed.

"They did what they could to give us a fair chance to fight back. But what happens next is up to us," Nerit said.

"So did they give you any assurances, huh? That we'll live?" Peggy asked this, her face quite pale.

"No. They did not." Nerit stood slowly and her presence seemed to push back those closest to her. "It is up to us if we win or lose. If we live or die."

"That side door was opened up," Ed said again. "After there was explicit orders to keep it closed."

"That was my call," Juan said. "To save Travis and Katie."

"No offense to them, but if we go around breaking all the rules for the popular folks, we're all gonna die," Ed continued.

Gretchen, former librarian and always an outspoken woman, stepped next to Ed. "He's right. We've all been following along behind the leaders of this fort. Doing what you said. Even when we disagreed because we all wanted this to work. But would that door have been opened for me?"

Angry murmurs grew loud until Nerit held up her hand. "Juan did what he felt was right. Whether you agree or not, the choice was made."

"You know, the Baptists hightailed it out of here talking about God's judgment. Now you're talking about ghosts. Anyone noticed that the gay people around here have kinda been dying?" a male voice called out from the back.

Bette looked sharply toward the person who spoke and Katie saw Linda take hold of her arm.

"You have no right," Lenore suddenly shouted. "No right to say that. Ken gave his life for all of us!"

The Reverend took hold of her arm and drew her back. Comforting her, he said, "Many have given their lives for all of us."

Travis stood up and towered over everyone. Katie held onto his hand and he rubbed her fingers gently with his thumb. "This isn't a time to fall apart."

"The ghosts came to warn us! To tell us to fight!" Katarina sounded close to hysterics. "Bill says the veil is thin and that is why he could come to me. He said we gotta fight and we can't lose."

"What the mighty hell is this damn veil?" It was the same man who had made the comment about the gay people. Katie finally recognized him as someone from the mall. His name was Art or something like that. He was a former councilman of another town.

"It's what lays between the physical realm and spiritual realm," a woman's voice said. It was Maddie Goode. "The veil is what keeps the worlds from bleeding over."

"Witch stuff, huh?"

"No, real stuff. Plus, a New Moon tonight. The veil is very, very thin." Goode lifted her tiny chin and looked defiantly at Art.

The Reverend cleared his throat. "God does send messengers. We must remember that."

"She's talking witch stuff," another woman said. "Everyone knows she's one of those Wiccans."

"Just because she's from another religion, does not mean her belief is not accurate in some form," Rune spoke up for Maddie.

She gave him a tight hug, but looked wary of the people glaring at her.

This comment did not sit well with many gathered in the lobby.

The long festering resentments were flowing to the surface very quickly. Friends and family members were arguing with each other. The stress was overwhelming. Everyone was on edge. Everyone was afraid.

"Maybe the Baptists had it right. Maybe it isn't safe here," Art said at last. "If we can't trust our leadership to look out for all of us."

"They've been excluding us a lot lately. They tossed out Blanche without a vote!" someone shouted from the back.

Travis winced and shook his head. "We made a choice at the time-"

"You cut us out of that decision," Ed said sharply.

Kevin moved to stand with Nerit. "Everyone standing here knows how hard it has been on those we voted into leadership roles. They've suffered losses just like the rest of us."

"Maybe looking out for our own best interests is the way to go," Ed decided at last.

"I don't understand where this is coming from," Travis protested. "This fort is doing damn good right now."

"A lot of us are tired of not feeling we have a choice about what goes on," Gretchen said. "No offense, Travis, but it's damn hard in this world to give our lives over to other people."

Ed nodded slowly. "Don't mean nothing personal. I may be a might angry, but I'm damn scared. What happens if something goes wrong out there and someone opens a gate or a door they shouldn't. I dunno if I can trust y'all"

Katarina looked at Ed, her expression was full of pain. "Bill died trying to protect this fort."

"I know that, Katarina. I know that. But...I don't like feeling like I'm not in control of my own life. Gimme a truck and some ammo. I'm more willing to take a chance out there on my own at this point."

Silence fell over the room. Then slowly people began to whisper among themselves. Katie could feel Travis' hand trembling and she knew he was hurt and trying to hold his temper. It was hard not to be trusted after all they had worked to achieve.

"Let them go," Eric said from near the front desk. "Let whoever wants to leave the fort take what they need and go."

"We can't hold them here," Kevin added.

"We need them here. Everyone has a role to play in the upcoming battle," Juan protested. "Everyone has assignments!"

"Some of us don't want to be here for it," a man near Juan snapped.

More voices rumbled through the vast room, disagreeing and agreeing.

"We can do it without them," Jason called out.

Jack immediately woofed in agreement.

Peggy stood smoking her cigarette, looking pale. Katie tried to reach out to her, but Peggy turned and walked away through the crowd.

"Very well. If you want to go while the going is good, go. We got extra vehicles out there. But you're on your own once you're gone," Travis finally said.

Ed nodded. "That's fair."

Nerit looked around the room thoughtfully. Katie noticed Kevin's hand was resting on her back in a gesture that seemed more for his comfort than for hers.

"If you are going, you must go tonight," Nerit finally said.

"Why is that?" Gretchen asked. There was an edge to her voice, but it sounded more like frustration than anger.

"The zombies arrive in the morning. At 9:20, the first zombies will cross over the first line."

"And how do you know this?" Art asked sharply.

"Ralph told me. The zombies arrive early. Tomorrow. The battle is tomorrow. If you're going to leave, you need to leave now," Nerit said in a firm, strong voice.

"And why are we supposed to believe this?" a voice Katie didn't recognize called out.

"Because she knows what she's talking about." Calhoun moved through the crowd. He looked haggard and held a tape recorder in his hand. "I've been taking care of the communication center, monitoring for alien transmissions. Got this instead." He held up a tape recorder and hit PLAY. "If anyone can hear us, we were trying to get back to the fort, but we can't get through. There are thousands of zombies near the junction of 16 and 1456. They're everywhere. We had to make a run for it. We're going to have to head back to the Baptist Encampment. Hello? Can you hear me? This is Milo and Susan. We were trying to head back but they're everywhere."

Katie tried to remember the junction they were talking about and realized quite quickly it was close to town.

"I gotcha," Calhoun's voice said on the tape. "You head back to the crazy Baptists and stay low. Make sure their demon-possessed leader don't do nothing stupid. We'll fight off the zombie clones and let you know when it's clear."

"Thanks, Calhoun. Just thought I 'd give ya heads up," the voice answered, then Calhoun hit STOP.

The silence was, as they say, deafening.

"We leave tonight then," Ed said.

"Can I go with you?" a voice called out.

It was Belinda. Juan's one time crush and Mike's widow. She pushed through the people to Ed's side. "I want to go, too."

Juan lowered his eyes and his mother squeezed his arm gently.

"Okay. You can come. Let's roll within the hour," Ed said.

Then the room was full of people arguing and crying.

Chaos filled the lobby and Katie put down her head and wept.

2. Sweet Sorrow

The paddock was full of people as Durangos were loaded up with carefully doled out ammunition and MREs. Jugs of water were rolled up to each vehicle and loaded. Bags of clothes and personal effects were tossed into the trucks. A small pink backpack full of toys was packed into a back seat.

Families gathered around departing members, in some cases still fighting bitterly, with others it was a tearful farewell.

Ed strode through the throng to his designated vehicle with Belinda in his wake. Gretchen stood nearby with a few other people and her gaze followed the old hunter. If she had designs on going with Ed, they were shot down by Belinda joining him. Ed's sons were already in the backseat arguing over something, holding their shotguns.

Travis and Juan leaned against a nearby pallet loaded with bricks watching sadly. Six vehicles were leaving. Twenty-three people in all.

A young woman picked up her six year old daughter and pushed her into the back seat of a nearby truck, buckling her in, while two men climbed into the front of the Durango. Travis remembered her name was Cindy and he smiled slightly at her as she gave him a sad look. Then, determinedly, she circled the vehicle and climbed in.

"They're probably all going to die," Juan said finally.

"Yeah, but it's their choice."

Ed saw to Belinda getting safely into his vehicle, then walked back to the two men. His grizzled face was worn and his eyes tired, but his jaw was set firmly. As he drew near, he thrust out his hand.

"Boys, it's been good," he said.

Travis didn't hesitate to take his hand and clasp it tightly. "We'll miss you."

"We did good here, but gotta move on," Ed said.

Travis gave Ed's hand one firm shake, then stepped back. Juan stepped forward to grip the older man's hand tightly.

"Take care, man," Juan said.

"I will. I'll take care of Belinda, too. This place has been good and bad for all of us. Hope you guys make it through tomorrow okay."

"We will," Travis said firmly. "We will."

Ed nodded once. "Good luck."

"Same to you," Juan answered.

With one more nod, Ed set his thin lips into a line and walked back to the Durango. Around him, other people followed his lead and climbed into their vehicles as well.

Juan lifted a walkie-talkie to his lips. "Clear?"

"All clear," a voice cackled back.

"Then open the gates," he ordered.

Travis exhaled slowly as the massive doors opened. Out of his peripheral vision, he saw Peggy sobbing as she watched Gretchen leave. A few people were still pleading with those in the Durangos to stay as the long line slowly began to roll out of the fort.

"This shit sucks," Juan finally muttered.

"Can't be helped," a voice said beside them.

They turned to see Rune standing near them.

"What do you mean?" Travis asked.

"Look, Dude, no offense, but you're still a city boy at heart and you don't quite get it at times. Texans stick together as long as there is a common enemy. That will get fucked up if two things happen: religion; or you feel you're at the mercy of someone else. Things go fine around here most of the time cause we got those dead folks trying to eat us. But right now, people are feeling mighty powerless and they're gonna either fight or run. Those folks...God bless 'em...they're running." Rune grinned, showing all his teeth. "Don't matter what they say. They're scared and they don't have no gawdamn control, so they're outta here. I say let em go." He turned and waved to the very last Durango leaving through the gate.

Travis shook his head. "Well. No point keeping them here anyway."

"They're a bunch of ingrates," Peggy said joining them. She was still crying and her face was swollen.

Juan watched as the gate begin to close. "Ed's freaking out about us opening the loading dock? Well, I'd be freaking worried that he'd pull something stupid like run away in the middle of it. Better now than later."

"Amen," Rune said. He then reached out to greet Calhoun as the old man approached.

"Okay, the pussies are gone and the real soldiers are left. So, I gotta know a few things real quick."

"What is it, Calhoun?" Travis smiled slightly at the sight of the older man. He was wearing some sort of weird hat with what looked like a miniature satellite dish on top. It was made out of foil and odds and ends.

"Is your wife going to have the Amazons come help us tomorrow?"

Travis grinned a little, then shook his head. "No, they're keeping put on Paradise Island."

Calhoun abruptly frowned.

Travis lifted his eyebrows realizing he said something wrong.

"They don't live on Paradise Island. Don't your wife tell you nothing?" With one last scornful look, Calhoun stalked off muttering about Amazons not helping out like decent women should.

"Oops," Juan laughed.

Travis shook his head again, looking bemused.

Manny Reyes, the former mayor, walked up slowly.

"Hey, Manny, how you doing?" Peggy asked, dabbing her eyes.

Juan gave him a pat on the shoulder. "Hey, Manny."

The man had not been seen often as he grew weaker and weaker. Charlotte believed he had severely blocked arteries. He was often pale and short of breath. He was taking aspirin, but it was hard on him without a proper diet for his heart or any way to remove the blockage that was slowly taking his life.

"I'm fine," Manny said in a breathy voice. "I came down to say goodbye to a few friends."

"Yeah," Travis said slowly. "Guess they didn't care for our leadership." He looked up at Manny cautiously, not sure if Manny took his removal from the mayor's office personally or not. The man had become ill nearly immediately after Travis and the council rose to power.

"Let me tell you something. It doesn't matter if they were happy or not. In the end, you can only do your best. People will agree with you. People will disagree with you. For every person who hates you, there is someone who loves you." Manny sat down on a box and rested his hands on his knees.

Rune nodded his head in agreement.

"Well, we're doing our best," Travis said after a beat. "I guess we gotta be okay with that."

"You do. And, the council has gotten things done I never could have. I never could have done all this or even thought of it." He waved a hand indicating the high walls and the fort in general, smiling slightly. "I know you guys did your best by us. Whether we make it through tomorrow or not, know that you have my support. You guys gave me one more good year of life."

Travis smiled at the man and took his words to heart. "I think we all got one more year of good life. Those things out there, they didn't get what we got. A chance to be happy despite it all going to hell."

Juan looked away emotionally. "We'll win this. We gotta. We don't have what we used to...a whole world to feel free in, but we got this fort and our families."

The old mayor inclined his head. "Worth fighting for, isn't it?"

"Damn straight," Rune declared.

"Do you think we can win?" Peggy looked at Travis, sniffling loudly.

"I think so. We're gonna try."

"But we don't know for sure, do we?"

"Peggy, I promise you, we will do our very best for everyone in this fort."

"I don't want to get eaten by those things. I don't want my boy to get eaten by those things. I want you to promise me we'll live through tomorrow," Peggy exclaimed, jabbing her finger into Travis' chest.

He gripped her arms firmly and looked down at her with compassion. "I promise you we will do our very best."

With an agonized cry, Peggy pulled away and ran off.

Manny gazed after her solemnly. "She's a good woman, but she's endured a lot. I hate to see her cry."

Juan crossed his arms and looked over the fort slowly. "We're ready as we can be. But I can't make no promises."

"None of us can, Juan," Travis decided. "None of us can."

"There's only one solution to it, man."

"What's that, Rune?"

"Kill the zombies," Rune answered, grinning.

* * * * *

That night, when Travis laid down to sleep for as many hours as he could, he wrapped his wife up in his arms, and held her tight. Katie, feeling his arms, rolled over and pressed her head to his chest to hear his heart beat. Between them was the swollen lump of her belly that housed their unborn child. After a few sweet kisses, they nestled down to try to sleep, content in each others arms.

In Juan's little abode, he stretched out on the sofa, his thoughts on

Jenni and the kids and all that had happened since the first day. He gnawed on his scarred thumbnail, the nervous habit somehow soothing. Jack padded out of Jason's bedroom to flop tiredly next to the sofa. Reaching down, Juan began to stroke the dog's head thoughtfully.

Nerit caught a few hours of sleep, then rose early to sit with Kevin on the city hall roof, sipping soda and looking over the defense plans. At one point, he reached over and took her hand and she squeezed it tight. They gazed at each other, not saying a word, then went back to the plans.

Calhoun and Jason worked deep into the night on the last minute wiring to some of the defenses.

Katarina fell asleep alone in her bed, clutching her rifle and wearing Bill's shirt.

Peggy silently watched her little boy, Cody, drink his chocolate milk laced with poison, then tucked him into his bed and kissed him one last time. She waited until he was gone, then with tears streaming down her face, rose and entered the bathroom. It was there she found her own personal peace at the end of a razor blade and faded from the world knowing that she and her child would never know the horror of the zombie armies against the walls or the agony of being eaten alive.

And then the sun rose...

Chapter 33

1. Final Exit of the Wickedest Woman in Texas

Politics was a fickle lover.

One moment you were the hero, the next the villain. But if you were clever, you could be the hero once again. The salvation to the masses. The public was immensely short-sighted with no memory to speak of. Even Nixon had been immortalized for his virtues when he had died.

The Senator tucked her hair up from her face with her hand. It had taken some hard work, but her bouffant was firmly in place. Studying her image in the mirror she felt a surge of pride. Her appearance was dignified and feminine but with a touch of strength. She had discarded her darker suits for a soft pink one with rose satin lapels. Her shoes were sensible and her jewelry was just the right level of gold and quartz to be perfectly understated yet elegant.

Fixing her cuffs, she nodded to herself.

This would be an excellent morning.

Her long days and nights alone in the house had given her time to think. She realized now her own failings. She had taken too strong of an approach back at the mall. People still could not appreciate a woman's strength. Instead of taking the strong, stately role she had worn at the mall, she should have taken the motherly approach. People were sheep, but they were stupid sheep stuck in stereotypes.

She reached into her coat and checked her gun one more time. The holster fit nicely and was hidden under her suit jacket. She had ransacked the house from top to bottom and had found the holster and the small .22 in one of the desk drawer. A rifle may seem a bit too masculine for her to wield when approaching the fort. The undead were a concern, but she was certain she could deal with them as long as she kept calm. They had slowed down significantly as time and the elements had taken their toll. The zombies were not the threat they had been in the early days. They were laughably easy to evade and kill as long as they were low in numbers. In the countryside, they were few and far between.

Picking up her small suitcase off the bed, she smiled, feeling her face stretch into the highly practiced gracious smile Raleigh had taught her to adopt. With a little laugh, she wondered what the little faggot was doing now. Probably wandering around half-eaten like the rest. Unless the undead had cracked his skull open like a boiled egg and eaten his brain.

After a blase shrug, she walked out of the bedroom and down the stairs to the front door. The truck she had arrived in waited outside. She had cleared out the zombies from around the house over the last few weeks. She stepped neatly over a few rotting bodies on her way to the truck. Once settled behind the wheel, she patted her suitcase and smiled.

It would be good to approach the fort with a motherly smile in place, her well-prepared speech spilling from her lips ringing out as though it was flowing from her heart. She would even let tears spring to her eyes. They would have pity on her and take her in. She would be humble and repentant before them.

Slowly, she would work her way back into their hearts and back to the top. But this time, oh, yes, this time, she would be Mother Teresa, the Virgin Mary, and Princess Diana all rolled into one. They would forgive her past and embrace her as one of their own. It would be only a matter of time before she ousted Travis and became the fort leader. Then, she would slowly, but surely make the fort believe in her special plans for them.

The drive toward the fort was boring. The sun was just barely rising and a scattered mist gave the impression of wandering ghosts flowing over the fields. She hummed to herself as she drove and couldn't help but smile.

Failure was not an option to her. She had taken a hard knock, but she knew how to recover. Lord knows if George Bush could win a second term in office way back when, she sure as hell could get her ass into the fort.

Cresting the hill, she looked down at the fort and gasped. The walls were a lot more extensive than she had remembered the photos showing and there seemed to be catapults mounted on top of buildings. A lot of the town had been demolished, but there was a no man's land leading up to the fort walls for a two block radius in every direction except for a large expanse before the hotel.

"Interesting," she said.

Pushing down on the accelerator, she drove the truck down the winding road until she was driving through the old demolished neighborhoods toward the east side of the town. Many of the roads were destroyed or barricaded with what looked like the remains of the old houses and buildings. It was like driving through a maze.

She never saw the hole the truck fell into, but one second it was cruising just fine, the next it was nose down in a huge hole in the ground. Luckily she had her seat belt on and only hit her forehead on the padded steering wheel, but the jolt made her scream. She hadn't even seen the hole and it was huge. How she had missed it, she couldn't imagine. Staring out the windshield she was eye level with the road. The truck was sputtering its last as steam rose from beneath the crumpled hood.

Getting out of the truck slowly, her heels sank into the mud gripping the front tires. The hole was about three feet deep and the mud immediately sucked her shoes off her feet. Panicked, she managed to grab her suitcase and fling it and herself onto the back end of the truck bed. She had to scramble, but she managed to climb in. Catching her breath, she looked down at the hole again to see what looked like a swatch of cloth painted like the road mushed up into the mud.

"A fucking trap," she muttered. Probably for outlaws. Cursing under her breath, she opened her suitcase and pulled out a fresh pair of shoes. Using a blouse to clean off her feet, she kept an eye on her surroundings. No undead fuckers were around here. Tucking her feet into the almost too tight black shoes, she forced herself to calm down. She would walk to the wall of the fort. It would be fine. She zipped up her suitcase and decided to leave it there. Someone could come back for it. It was a little pain getting the bullhorn she had found in Blanche's sports closet out of the cab, but she managed to lean in through the open doorway and snag it.

Maneuvering over the cab of the truck was difficult and she almost fell. Finally, she managed to leap from the top of it onto the street. A quick tuck of her blouse, fluff of her hair, and adjust of her jacket, and she was ready again. Taking a few deep breaths, she concentrated on reclaiming her earlier mood. That's right, she had to be positive and glowing. She had to be as genuine as possible to win over those behind the walls. She was sure she could do just that.

Walking briskly down the street, clutching the bullhorn, she kept her eyes on the corner. She would have to go around that corner, then down another block to draw near the wall. The windows and doors of all the buildings were boarded or bricked up, so she wasn't worried about anything lurching out at her.

She reached the intersection and took another breath.

This time she caught whiff of something bad. She spun around worriedly and spotted a dead body sprawled on the street nearby. It looked like someone in a police uniform and they were truly dead. Nothing to worry about there. She looked beyond the body down the long narrow street that seemed to swerve around toward the area where the hotel loomed. Again, she felt like she was in a maze.

Turning to face the wall, now a block down from her, she walked on. The sun was higher in the sky now and sweat began to trickle down the back of her neck. She shrugged her shoulders and felt a few beads of moisture slide down her spine. Ugh! She hated sweating.

Her foot hit something on the road and she stumbled forward in an unstoppable fall. She reached out to catch herself and heard a sharp mechanical clang. The ground was rushing up to meet her and she gasped.

She never hit the ground but was abruptly shoved back as what felt like an invisible truck hit her. Gasping, she found herself gazing at her hand lying on the ground a few feet away from her, the bullhorn still gripped tightly in it. Her mind sputtered as it tried to register what she was seeing and feeling. It was a cascade of information filling her brain and she could barely comprehend what was happening.

Her hand lay nearby, perfectly manicured, sliced off at the wrist. Her vision was blurred with a thick liquid flowing from her forehead. She tried to move, but she could not. She felt numb but beneath it was excruciating pain. It made no sense as her body tried to understand its state.

What her mind never understood as the Senator bled to death in a matter of seconds was that one of Jason's traps had gone off. It was razor wire carefully laid over a frame and rigged to springs. It shot up from its prone position when she had triggered it and locked into latches attached to metal pipes driven into the road. As it had snapped upright, the mesh had cut deeply into her body.

Arteries were sliced open and her blood flowed onto the street and slowly ran downhill past Curtis' body.

The Senator was still staring at her hand and trying to call for help when her eyes clouded over and death came for her. Her last thought was a panicked one.

They don't know I'm here, she thought. *They don't know--*

Then she was gone.

No one knew. Or would have cared.

2. When All That Is Left Is Goodbye

"So this is what the last day of your life feels like," Katie mused as she stood in the moving elevator waiting for the doors to open.

"Yep," Nerit answered from beside her.

"Pretty much," Travis said as he rubbed her back.

"Sucks, huh?" Juan gave her a slight smile.

"Feels..." Katie struggled for the word.

"Normal," Nerit offered.

"Boring," Travis decided.

"Annoying," Juan finished.

Katie laughed and turned to look at all three of them. "You're all twisted."

Travis grinned his goofy smile. "Yeah, but..."

"It's a good day to die," Kevin said from the corner of the elevator.

Katie flicked her gaze at him and shook her finger at him. "Oh, no! I'm not dying."

"Keeping it positive, huh, babe?"

"Or just annoyingly optimistic," Juan decided.

"Or she knows something you don't know," Nerit teased as the doors opened to the foyer off the ballroom.

It was crammed full of people leaving off their small children, the elderly and the disabled. It had been planned that anyone not involved in the battle would remain at the highest point in the fort. Despite the tension flowing through the room, the sounds were muted and tender. People held their loved ones one last time as they said goodbye.

Katie stepped out and to the side as the others filed out. Everyone was not only saying goodbye but eating breakfast tacos laid out on the buffet tables and drinking coffee. Jack came bounding up to her and she leaned down to hug him.

"Hey, boy," she whispered, and he licked her face. She flashed back on the old days on the road with Jenni, the dog tucked between them as they rode into the west in their beat up truck, and she smiled a sad smile. "Who thought we'd come this far, huh?"

Jack woofed at her, then took off to weave his way through the crowd back to Juan's four children. The kids were in the ballroom sitting around Juan's grandmother's wheelchair munching away on tacos.

"She gave me four kids," Juan said to Katie.

Looking toward him, she lifted an eyebrow. "Hmm?"

"Loca. She couldn't have anymore kids, but she found a way to give me four. Two boys, two girls." Juan grinned. "That woman had a way of getting her way, huh?"

Katie smiled with bitter sweetness. "Yes, she did."

Pulling her close, Juan held Katie, then kissed her cheek. "Thank you for bringing my Loca to me."

Tears sprang instantly into her eyes and she couldn't speak.

Juan seemed to understand and patted her cheek, then headed over to his kids.

Her husband drew near and smoothed her golden hair back from her eyes. Cupping her face, Travis kissed her lips, then pressed his forehead to hers. "We're going to make it."

Katie nodded vehemently. "Of course."

The elevator doors slid open behind them and an ungodly smell hit them. Wincing, Katie looked toward Calhoun, satellite dish hat intact, looming in the opening.

"Calhoun, what is--" Travis started to ask.

"One of the traps is disconnected on the east side," Calhoun exclaimed, waving his hands in front of him. "Gawddamn mind waves of the clones are disrupting my instruments and--"

"Cal, hold on," Nerit said from nearby around a mouthful of taco. "What do you mean--"

"I lost one of the traps. The controls are dead! Something got disconnected out there!"

"Shit," Kevin sputtered as he tried to talk and drink coffee at the same time.

"They're not arriving on the outskirts for another thirty minutes," Nerit said firmly.

"Sorry, Amazon lady, I don't trust your dead incubus of a husband!"

"Calhoun," Katie chided. "That wasn't nice."

"I don't trust these ghosts with their mysterious ways," Calhoun retorted. "Especially that crazy Mexican one. She was loca in real life and sure as loca in death."

"Better not let Juan hear you say that," Nerit said calmly.

"My trap has been disrupted by the evil brain waves of the clone hordes--" Calhoun then sputtered into a tirade that had half the people in the room gasping.

Small children were quickly ushered into the ballroom while some of the older teens looked impressed.

"We got thirty minutes, Calhoun. Let's do it," Rune said from nearby.

"Huh?" Calhoun blinked.

"Go out and fix it," Rune continued.

"Is it the razor wire trap?" Travis managed to grab a cup of coffee from a nearby tray.

"Nope. The fire one. And you know gawddamn well how important that one is."

"Shit," Kevin muttered again, trying to stuff an entire taco in his mouth.

"Let's do it, dude. I mean it. Let's go!" Rune was clad in his motorcycle leathers and looking ready for war. "C'mon, Calhoun. We can do this."

Calhoun looked uneasy for a second. "Okay. Let's do it."

With a grin, Rune gripped Calhoun's shoulder and dragged him back into the elevator. "It's a damn fine day to die," Rune assured Calhoun as the doors shut.

"I better monitor them," Keven decided.

"Good idea. I'll get Katarina out there," Nerit responded and took up position with Kevin to wait for the elevator to return.

Katie took a cup of coffee from a tray, then snagged the other half of Travis' breakfast taco. She felt strangely calm. Maybe it was the golden sunlight of the new day pouring through the windows or the light blue sky that seemed so welcoming, but it felt peaceful up here.

Greta appeared nearby already dressed in her uniform and looking ready to go. Her bird would be up in the air soon. Everything they had planned for was about to kick into gear and Katie had to believe it would work.

* * * * *

"...and then we shoot them in da head," Holly assured Juan.

"They're not getting in," Jason promised the little girl again.

"Nieta, the bad monsters will not get past the walls," Rosie assured her adopted granddaughter. "It's not going to happen."

"But if they do," Margie said in an ominous voice, "we will shoot them in da head."

"Shoot them in da head," Troy said firmly.

Juan couldn't help but laugh and leaned over to kiss his kids fondly. "It won't come to that. I promise."

Jack flopped down amongst them and Jason leaned over to rub the dog behind the ears. Troy flopped backwards to rest against the dog's stomach like a pillow.

It seemed like a regular moment for his family: his grandmother had drifted off to sleep in her wheelchair; his mother was fussing with the kid; the kids were ornery as ever; Jason was peering at everyone through his bangs; and the dog was trying to get something into his stomach. This was his family. The thought made him smile, but made his stomach lurch at the same time.

He would do anything to protect them. Jenni had made this happen. His loca. His crazy, freaky, probably partially insane girlfriend. God, he loved her and missed her. But she was at peace, he knew that, and knew her prayers were with him. He had lost her, but gained his children. His heart, he realized, was healed because of their love and need for him. A gift to him. Without their love, he would still be in mourning.

"I need to get going," Jason said as the other three kids prattled on.

Suddenly, the little family looked quite somber. Jason, like many of the teenagers from thirteen on up, was part of the fort's defenses.

"Give me a kiss, nieto," Rosie said throwing out her arms to him.

Jason stood up and moved into her arms and looked a little embarrassed by her tight hug and kiss. Juan rose to his feet as well and moved to hug his son tightly. Jason's arms came about him and they held each in an embrace that said more than words ever could.

"Me, too!" Margie leaped onto Jason. He laughed as he hugged the younger kids.

Juan took a step back, feeling tears threatening. Jason was his son. He loved him fiercely. He could not love him more if he had fathered him. The pride he felt in him was overwhelming and he fought for control.

Leaning over, Jason kissed the sleeping old woman that was his adopted great-grandmother, then strode away.

"He's a good boy," Rosie whispered.

"So am I!" Troy leaped into her arms to hug her.

Rosie laughed and hugged the little boy tightly. "Yes you are. Now kiss your Daddy One."

Juan could feel his control slipping, but he managed to not cry as the three kids kissed him and hugged him tight.

"Go kill the zombies," Margie ordered.

"I will," Juan promised.

"Shoot dem in da head," Holly instructed.

"I will," Juan answered.

"In da head," Troy repeated.

"In the head," Juan assured him.

Then he was walking away, his heart in his throat and his head spinning.

There was just no way about it. His children would not die today. They would not. There was simply no other choice but to win.

* * * * *

Kevin and Nerit stepped into the elevator and the doors closed behind them.

"Here," Kevin said softly, pressing a tiny metal box into her hand.

"The detonator?"

"I have one, too."

"We won't use them," Nerit assured him. "We'll win."

"But just in case."

"Of course."

Kevin shifted on his feet and looked at her steadily. "I want to say something. It's something I wanted to say since you woke up."

"I already know. You don't have to say it," Nerit responded quickly.

"Arnold once called you the sexiest old woman around, you know." Kevin said bashfully.

Nerit rolled her eyes, but looked amused.

"I think he was right." Kevin drew closer to her. "Nerit..."

"You deserve the right to find a new family. To rebuild just like everyone else once this is over. I can't give you that."

"But you feel it, too. If we were closer in age and met-"

"Yes," Nerit said simply. "But that is not the case, is it?"

Kevin nodded sadly, his green eyes staring deeply into hers. "I wish it was."

Nerit looked away and stared at the elevator door. "Me, too."

Just before the elevator reached their floor, Kevin pressed a firm, hard kiss to her cheek. To his delight, Nerit blushed.

The doors dinged then opened. Kevin stepped out onto this floor, waving at her.

Nodding once, she tucked the detonator into her jacket pocket and took a breath as the doors closed.

3. And The Clock Winds Down...

It was an odd moment. One of many, considering the last year. As Katie was staring out the window over the fort's defenses in front of the hotel, the ascending sun caught the glass. A flash of light blinded her instantly.

When her eyes cleared, she was driving the old white truck. Jenni sat next to her in jeans, a tank top and a cowboy hat with a good pair of knock off Fendi sunglasses perched on her nose. Jack sat between them, the hot wind ruffling his fur as it poured through the open windows. Beyond her was the desert, hot and fierce. Waves of heat rippled over the endless stretch of highway.

"Jenni," Katie whispered, confused, her fingers gripping the steering wheel.

"This could have been it. You know. Our future." Jenni grinned at her and turned her face into the scalding wind. "The desert."

The heat was amazing and the sun was unrelenting. Jack woofed beside them and licked at his paw.

"I thought about it," Katie confessed. "Before we found Nerit and Ralph."

"Me, too. Even after we found the fort. I thought about us and Jason just going away."

"You would still be alive if we had," Katie said after a beat. Tears were in her eyes again.

"Maybe," Jenni agreed. She leaned over the dog and kissed Katie's cheek and hugged her tight. "You miss me!"

"Well, yeah, you bitch. You went and died on me!"

Jenni laughed. "Yeah, but it was one kick ass exit."

"Oh, fuck you," Katie snapped, but couldn't help but smile.

"It was worth it! Everything was worth it!" Jenni grinned at her. Reaching out, she gripped Katie's wrist tightly and leaned toward her. "You know it, Katie. You know. Every moment was worth it. Every little tiny bit of it...all building up to this."

"Which is?"

"The beginning of everything new," Jenni said and winked. "Or the end of it all."

Katie rolled her eyes. "That is not encouraging."

"But every moment of happiness we had this year was that much sweeter because of every other horrible moment that we experienced. Admit it, Katie."

Katie gripped the steering wheel more firmly as she thought of all the loss, the pain, the death, but then of all the good moments. Dancing with Jenni, kissing Travis, her swelling belly, playing with Jack, hugging Juan's kids, learning how to two step....all of it. "Yeah. You're right."

"Totally worth it," Jenni said firmly.

The light caught her again, blinding her, then she blinked to see she was back in the hotel. Travis walked toward her as the sunlight streamed through the window. He drew near her and slid his hand behind her neck and pressed a lingering kiss to her forehead. Closing her eyes, she relished the moment and felt its sweetness fill her.

"I love you," Travis said softly.

"Yeah, well, good. I'm crazy about you, too," she said.

Ruffling her hair, he winked. "We'll be okay."

"I'm going to hold you to that."

Out of the throng of people eating breakfast Eric appeared, his brow furrowed. Close behind him was Stacey. She was crying. Pepe, their little dog, stared up at her sadly.

"What's up, Eric?" Travis asked.

"We have a situation," Eric answered. His expression was stricken and tears glimmered in his eyes. "Peggy's gone."

"What?" Their voices chorused. Travis and Katie glanced at each other briefly.

"Took herself and her kid out last night," Stacey sobbed.

"Define the whole took herself out part," Travis said. "Out of the fort?"

"You could say that. She poisoned the little guy and slit her wrists," Eric explained.

"Oh, Jesus," Katie murmured, raising her hand to her brow.

"Shit," Travis said. "Shit!" He shook his head in disbelief. "I knew she was scared, but not that scared."

"She's not the only one. We have about four more. At least two jumped over the wall...headfirst. Old Harris took himself out by hanging. Shea took himself with a shot to the head through a pillow." Eric sighed. "So a lower suicide count than we expected. I was really hoping there would be none."

"Peggy was going to run communications," Katie said softly.

"Gotta pull Yolanda to do it," Travis decided.

"She's not as experienced as Peggy," Katie pointed out.

"Without Curtis and Ken, she's the best we got," Travis answered.

"I'll find her," Stacey said, vanishing into the crowd, Pepe skittering along behind her.

Eric rubbed the bridge of his nose with one finger, shoved his glasses in place, then shook his head. "I better take another swing around the wall. We don't need fresh blood luring those things in." He hurried off.

From the sound of the crowd, people were finding out about the deaths. There were looks of dismay and a few tears. Word traveled fast in the fort. As Peggy would joke, "There were no secrets in a small Texas town. If you farted, everyone knew what you had for dinner."

"Oh, gawd, Peggy," Katie whispered softly.

"I'm sure she did what she thought was right for her and the kid."

Katie pressed her hand to his cheek. "They need to know there is hope. That we can do this. You and the Reverend need to speak to the fort before those things get here. Everyone needs it."

Travis started to protest, but already the Reverend was on his way to Travis through the crowd. As usual, Katie understood very well what was needed.

"Travis," the Reverend said drawing close. "The people are in despair. We need to rally them."

"I agree. Let's head down to communications," Travis said, kissing her cheek.

Both men moved toward the elevators.

With a sigh, Katie brushed her blond hair from her face and looked out over the desolate swath of land before the fort. In the distance were the edges of the ramshackle mounds that formed a wall around the fort. There was a massive opening right down the middle. It was the killing zone and huge fire traps were set to ignite in the gap.

Taking a deep breath, she thought of Jenni's words. She knew they were true, but all she could feel was her fear and her fingers trembling against the warming glass of the window.

Chapter 34

1. Time to Die

"Move it, Calhoun. They're coming and they're hungry," Rune said firmly. He seemed unfazed by the utter reek coming off the old crazy guy. He straddled his Harley and waited for Calhoun to slide on behind him.

Rune had ridden the makeshift elevator, which was a pallet lowered by a crane down to the ground outside the wall, holding his bike firmly to his side. Calhoun had ridden down behind him. The fire line was far from the wall and there was no way Rune was going to be caught without a quick getaway. He shifted the bag of grenades so it rested more firmly against his back. Today seemed like a good day to use them.

"I ain't as young as you, you long haired hippie," Calhoun muttered, managing to swing his old leg over the bike.

"I ain't a hippie, Cal. I'm a biker," Rune answered.

Calhoun's response was cut off with a shout as the bike lurched forward and roared over the rough terrain toward the fire line.

"Damn smart ass city folk. They should have started bulldozing those mounds in the middle and worked themselves out. Now we got a huge ass "v" with a big ol hole right where we should have our best defenses," Rune shouted into the wind.

"Nobody listens to me! I said that from the get go! But they wanted a kill zone! I got the inside information! I know how to deal with this stuff. Years and years of planning for the clone uprising."

"You may be a crazy old shithead, Cal, but you know what's going on in your own way," Rune's voice growled. "You're a mean old codger."

"Not as mean as Nerit," Calhoun pouted.

"No one is as mean as Nerit," Rune admitted as the bike came to standstill.

They were close to the open end of the high walls made of dirt, dead foliage, tree trunks and the remains of houses and buildings. Beyond the opening were the gas tanks half buried into the soil. Beyond that, the hill dipped downward. The wind was moving downhill and away from the fort. The smell was just barely noticeable. The smell of death.

Calhoun fell to his knees and began to dig up the device rigged to explode the fuel tanks. When he had tried to begin the start up sequence, there had been no response from the remote device. He knew the problem had to be right here, where it was set up to transmit and receives. Pulling out the huge metal box, he popped it open and began to examine it closely.

"What's wrong with it?" Rune asked.

"Don't know yet," Calhoun answered.

"Cause, you know, it's almost time," Rune stared out through the wide opening, arms folded across his chest.

"Yep. I know." He glared down into the device. "Gawddamn gremlins got into it. I knew it!" Calhoun beat the ground with one fist, then controlled himself and adjusted his satellite dish hat. "Okay, I need Jason."

"The kid?"

"Yeah, the kid! You know, our future leader. Our John Conner? Our freaking salvation! THAT ONE!"

"Take a chill pill, Cal. Calling the fort," Rune said, then took out his walkie-talkie.

"I don't need a chill pill," Calhoun muttered as he began to sort through the wires with his grubby fingers. "I need the freaking gremlins to stay out of my stuff."

"We need Jason down here, Peggy," Rune said, then listened to the static for a moment.

"Okay, I let him know," a voice said that was not Peggy.

"Hey, Yolanda. You pulling double shift?"

"Yeah, things not so good with Peggy."

"That sucks," Rune said, and didn't press it. He didn't want to know.

Calhoun rubbed his big nose and frowned. "Who's idea was it to blow up the gawddern fuel tanks?"

"Yours," Rune answered.

"Gawdammit! Why do people listen to me? I'm freaking nuts!"

"And that, sir, is why they listen to you," Rune informed him.

Calhoun began to laugh.

Despite the slowly strengthening stench of death, Rune threw back his head and laughed, too.

* * * * *

Jason made his way to the makeshift elevator and hoisted his tool bag onto his shoulder. Reggie, a big black guy, nodded to him and helped him onto the pallet platform. Reaching out, Jason took a firm grip on one of the thick cables.

"Ready?"

"Yeah," Jason answered.

Reggie signaled the crane operator and the pallet lifted with a sickening lurch and began to swing toward the edge of the wall.

With a sharp bark, Jack dodged around Reggie and leaped over the empty space between the rooftop and the pallet and landed with a sharp yelp. Jason reached down immediately and grabbed his collar. The pallet swung sharply and Jack slid across the wood. Holding tight, Jason felt the dog's weight shift back against him. Tucking Jack securely between his legs, Jason looked down at the startled dog.

"Damn dog. You were supposed to stay with the kids," Jason chided him.

Jack gave him a soulful look of apology, then looked out over the wide expanse before the fort. He growled low in his throat and his ears slid back.

"I know, boy, I know. They're coming," Jason whispered. "I know."

* * * * *

Rune looked down toward the angrily muttering old man. Calhoun was in a tizzy, obviously trying to figure out what was wrong. Rune leaned over and figured the dim lights on the lid of the metal box was a bad thing. Tilting his head, he looked out toward the gap.

"Smells worse than you now, Calhoun," he said.

"Soap is ungodly and unnatural. It poisons you slowly," Calhoun answered.

"Right," Rune looked back toward the fort to see the kid running down toward him with the big ol' German Shepherd at his side. "Here comes your help."

Calhoun glanced up to see Jason drawing close. "Good, cause those damn gremlins screwed this up royally. Worse than when the fairies stole all the wires out of my TV."

Jason rushed up and fell to his knees beside Calhoun. He immediately began to look through the wires as Jack stood guard beside him, growling low in his throat.

"You know," Rune drawled. "I always wanted to die a noble death."

Calhoun glanced over his shoulder. Beyond the gap, just coming up over the edge of the hill, was a lone zombie. It hesitated as it saw the fuel tanks, then saw what lay beyond and let out a mournful wail. It reached out its gnarled hands and began to limp forward.

"I think he's hungry," Calhoun decided.

"Well, boys. Time for me go do the hero thing and probably die. But let it be known to all survivors of the fort that I went out like a warrior!" Rune grinned his toothy grin and got onto his bike.

"What are you going to do?" Jason asked, his eyes huge with fear.

Rune shifted his bag around so he could reach in and grab the grenades easily. "Not sure yet, but it's gonna be wild."

With that the bike lurched forward toward the wide opening.

Jack began to bark fiercely as ten more zombies crested the hill and came into view.

Then twenty more.

The lone biker rode toward the undead with a gleeful shout that sounded like, "Time to rock and roll!"

* * * * *

As Rune barreled toward the zombies and Jason and Calhoun struggled to repair the detonation device, Yolanda sat nestled in the communication center listening to the various groups check in from all over the fort. She checked off the numbered groups one by one on the notepad in front of her, her full lips pursed slightly.

She knew what had happened to Peggy. She felt both very sad and very angry. Peggy had always been kind to her, but today, of all days, to leave them in the lurch pissed her off. Yolanda was supposed to be up on the wall with Lenore manning the huge crossbows, but instead she was trapped in the windowless communication center. She hated feeling disconnected from defending the fort even though she knew what she was doing was important. But dammit, she wasn't fully trained for this.

Scratching her head with the end of her pen, she sighed and responded to the last call in. She tried not to notice her stubby fingernails painted bright red. The black women of the fort had all cut off their fingernails and braided back their hair in a big party last night. It had been a rough thing to do. It may have seemed silly to some, but it had made them feel connected to their culture and their old lives to have their fancy nails and hair. But in the last week, they had decided to braid up their hair and cut their nails for safety reasons. A few of them had caught their nails on triggers during practice and their hair could be dangerous if the zombies managed to breach the walls.

In fact, everyone was under orders to have their hair up and pinned, just in case. Though she had noticed Rune had ignored this order and had worn his hair down at breakfast.

"Yoli, gotta create a distraction," Rune's voice cackled. "Something went wrong with the damn fire line. Cal and the kid are working on it.."

"What you talking about?" Yolanda snapped at him. "You're supposed to be-"

She heard him laugh, cutting her off. "Say boom, baby."

A second later, she heard a faint boom in the distance.

Travis and the Reverend entered just as she began demanding to know what the hell was going on.

"That crazy ass long haired biker boy is off doing some stupid shit," Yolanda informed Travis.

The tall man's eyebrow shot up and he glanced at the clock. "Shit! It's time. Sorry, Reverend" he quickly apologized for the profanity.

"No offense taken," the Reverend assured him.

"Rune, what the hell are you doing?" Travis asked, leaning over to talk into the microphone.

"Getting the zombies to move my way. The fire line has got probs and the kid and crazy old guy are working on it."

In the distance there was another boom.

"Don't worry about me. I got my bike and bag of grenades."

Over another channel Nerit's voice cackled to life, "Rune is making some sort of a crazy run to draw the zombies away from the fire line and Calhoun and Jason. Those explosions you hear are him lobbing grenades into the horde following him."

"We just got the word from him," Travis said to Nerit. "How's he doing from what you see?"

"He's got the first hundred or so walking straight for him and away from the opening," Nerit answered, then laughed. "Honestly, he looks pretty happy about it."

"He's a brave man," the Reverend decided.

"More like damn crazy," Yolanda muttered.

"We're going to say a few words before they breach the fire line," Travis said to Nerit. "Keep an eye on Calhoun and Jason. Pull them back in if it gets too close."

"Understood," came the reply.

"Yolanda, open up the speakers," Travis instructed and ignored her sour look. He picked up the microphone and was surprised at how slick his hand was. He almost dropped the microphone. Fear was slowly unfurling deep inside of him. For so long they had all lived with low-grade paranoia and fear it had become a part of them. Now those emotions were swelling as the dead approached.

The Reverend seemed to sense what was behind his hesitation and gently patted his shoulder. "You can do this, Travis."

Travis tried not to think of Katie up there on the wall ready to fight for their lives. He closed his eyes. Steadying his nerves with a silent prayer, he pressed the button and spoke.

"Good morning seems like the wrong thing to say," his voice boomed over the speakers scattered over the fort. "I don't think we've had a good morning for a damn long time. But...hell...good morning anyway."

Near the gate, Juan looked up from where he was busy doing the final tests on some of the traps. He slightly smiled at Travis' words and turned back to what he was doing. His long hair was pinned up on his head and he was wearing a cowboy hat. Nearby stood one of the bulldozers rigged up to fight the zombies. Spray painted along its side were the words "La Loca."

"But if we have to fight for our lives, I guess we couldn't ask for a prettier morning."

Travis' voice floated through the air as Lenore loaded up the giant crossbow perched high on the wall. She glanced toward the battered speaker near her and had to agree. The sky was brilliant this morning with the sun shining through beautiful white clouds sliding over the endless Texan sky.

"So this is it. What we all feared. But we can do this. We can fight and win. No matter how afraid you are, remember that we're in this together."

Old Man Watson in his wheelchair watched out a window as several men loaded up a catapult on the wall beneath it. Chetan, the Indian from Austin, was helping Jimmy Ray, a good ol' boy from East Texas and Jerome from Houston, lift the heavy pieces of junk onto the catapult. The shrapnel was going to be used against the zombies. The old man smiled with satisfaction and patted the rifle on his lap.

"I'm not much of a speaker, so I have no idea what to say except y'all are my family. I'm glad to know ya and I'm glad to stand with you today. And now a word from the Reverend."

Katie pulled on her gloves and smiled as she listened to her husband's words echoing around her. Looking up, she could see over the wide expanse in front of the hotel. The smell of decay was now floating on the wind and she pulled her kerchief over her nose. She could see the dark wave of the undead in the distance just beyond the fire line. It was such a beautiful day the sight of the zombies was like a sacrilege against nature. With a deep breath, she began to load up the giant crossbow.

There was the sound of the microphone being jostled as it was handed off and Katarina smiled slightly. She was perched on one of the highest points of the fort. Her sniper rifle rested comfortably in her arms as she tilted her head and closed one eye. Abruptly the undead filled her vision and she drew in a deep breath. The first zombie to swim into view was vile beyond belief. A large woman, half eaten, her womb torn open to reveal the fetus inside, its small limbs moving, came into sharp view. Katarina closed her eyes, steadied herself, then reopened her eyes and fired. The dead mother jerked once, then stumbled on, oblivious that the tiny form inside of her had stopped moving.

"This is the day that the Lord has made. Let us rejoice and be glad in it," the Reverend's voice boomed with smoothness and gentleness that Travis' did not have. It was like balm on the fevered minds of the inhabitants in the fort.

Kevin looked down at the map held under heavy plastic on the table before him and took a deep breath. Nerit stood next to him, her face calm as she gazed out toward the oncoming horde.

"Difficult words to embrace on a day such as this, but we must do just that. For this is the day the Lord has made for us to fight for our lives and the lives of those we love. This is our home, our fort, our safe haven. It has been called many things: the Fort, Eden, Sparta and a slew of other names. But it remains simply one thing to all of us: home. Our home. And, now, we face our greatest challenge as a family."

Kevin looked over at Nerit and she smiled slightly at him. He moved several red markers along the map as another explosion by Rune's grenades boomed in the distance.

"We have lost many friends, many family members, during this long plague of the dead. We have seen many atrocities at the hands of these creatures. Our beloved have fallen to their ranks and in some cases, joined their ranks."

Margie leaned against her new grandmother listening to the Reverend's voice as she played idly with the dry tangled hair of her doll. Her brother and sister weren't paying attention, but she understood the Reverend's words. She thought of her old Mommy and Daddy and of the nice lady with the black hair who had saved them. Kissing her doll, she pulled it close to her and hugged it like her grandmother was hugging her.

"But we must resolve ourselves to be strong. To stand firm. To not waver in the face of evil. It may wear the face of humanity, but it is corruption. We must remember this. They were once alive. They were us. But now, they are the undead. The enemy of life. Be strong and know that the battle you fight today is just and good in the sight of God."

Linda pulled back on the lever of the catapult she was manning and it groaned as it prepared to fire its heavy junkyard load. Her expression was full of rage and determination as she watched the zombies stumbling after Rune's motorcycle in the distance just beyond the high wall made of the town's ruins.

"Today we fight for our lives. We fight for the lives of our family and friends. We fight for our future. We fight for life itself. And it is a good and right thing."

* * * * *

Rune grinned as he brought the motorcycle to an abrupt halt. The zombies were stumbling along after him, moaning loudly, their stench overwhelming as they drew close. He was satisfied that he had drawn so many after his bike. In fact, it looked like most of the horde coming up the hill had altered direction to skim along the outer wall in the pursuit of him. The big bike rumbled between his legs as he drew another grenade and whistled loudly at the zombies.

Aggravated by the nearness of him, the zombies thrust out their decayed hands and let out moans of desperate hunger.

"Yep, damn good day to die," he said with a grin, and lobbed another grenade into the horde.

He gunned the bike and rode off in front of the mob. The grenade went off with a resounding explosion and peppered him with body parts.

Grinning, he lured the zombies on.

* * * * *

"Damn gremlins," Calhoun muttered as he fumbled with the wires.

Jason glanced back over his shoulder to see most of the zombies were stumbling past the opening a couple of hundred yards behind them. The dead didn't seem to notice them with all the noise Rune was making with the grenades.

"The gremlins probably took off when they saw Jack," Jason said, trying to calm Calhoun. He needed the old man's mind working on a solution, not freaking out over invisible opponents.

Jack barely glanced at Jason when he heard his name. He was poised to attack, his body rigid, his eyes narrowed at the undead. The boy had told him not to do anything and he was obeying for now. But if those smelly things came toward them, he was going to rip them to pieces.

"Yeah, gremlins hate dogs," Calhoun conceded. "Good old Jack here probably got them running for the hills."

"Yep," Jason assured the old guy and wondered if Calhoun even noticed the zombies. Nervously, he looked back toward the undead filing past the fire line. They were still unnoticed. Trying to concentrate, his trembling fingers moved methodically through the innards of the contraption he and Calhoun had built together.

"Jason," Calhoun whispered.

"Yeah?"

"The clones are here," the old man's voice trembled.

"I know," Jason answered and flipped through the wires and studied their connections.

Jack let out a low whimper.

"Well, uh. I think they noticed us."

Jason quickly looked over his shoulder to see one lone zombie staggering toward them. It was so badly decayed he wasn't sure if it was a woman or a man. Jack let out a low growl and looked to Jason, awaiting orders.

"It's still far away." Jason returned his gaze to the contraption. "Don't shoot it or the rest of them will come at us."

Calhoun drew his gun anyway. "I don't like the idea of those things having an all they can eat at the Calhoun buffet."

Jason moved so he could keep an eye on the lone zombie moving toward them and keep working. It was clear Calhoun's concentration was shot.

The zombie kept coming, its movements jerky and rigid. It was obviously hard for it to move.

Jason dug deeper into the box, his fingers tracing the wires carefully.

Jack growled angrily and woofed slightly.

Looking up, the teenager was startled to see the progress the zombie was making. Then, abruptly, it fell backwards and lay still. Calhoun scrambled forward and looked down at the thing.

"Right through the head! DAMN! That old woman is evil!"

Realizing the snipers had taken the zombie down, Jason felt safer and kept working. He could still see the zombies staggering past the entrance in the distance. The two humans and the dog had to be obscured from view from below. They were not drawing any attention. Another explosion in the distance sounded. Jason heard a catapult creaking as it unfurled its arm and tossed a load of microwaves and TVs into the crowd of zombies passing alongside the fort.

"That's not good," Calhoun decided, scuttling along the ground on his hands and knees.

"They're probably trying to keep them from getting Rune," Jason answered.

"Not that. That!"

Jason looked up once more. But this time his blood ran cold. Three zombies were running up the hill, pushing past the shambling ones and rushing straight toward them.

"Oh, shit!" Jason jumped to his feet and scrambled to get his gun out.

Calhoun took a shot and hit one of the runners in the shoulder, spinning it around. But it recovered immediately and kept rushing toward them.

Jack launched himself into the first runner and snagged its shoulder in his teeth. It went down under the momentum of the dog's leap and struggled to get free of the growling canine. As with all other zombies, it was not interested in animals. It only wanted to break away from the dog to get to the humans.

Another runner went down under a sniper shot. Jason managed to get his gun out and aimed it at the next one coming up fast on him. He saw puffs of dirt kick up around the zombie. Whoever was shooting from the fort was not Nerit. They were missing. The zombie screeched as it barreled toward him. Calhoun took another shot and missed. Jason could see the old man stagger back as the runner Jack was battling grabbed the old man's ankle.

Jason raised his gun and aimed at the zombie, but then it was on him. It took a swipe at his arm, its bloodied face seeming to streak toward him, and Jason ducked away. He felt the creature grip his long bangs and Jason spun around on his heels as he lost his balance. They both fell. The zombie's howling mouth was inches from his face. Jason barely managed to get his hand under the thing's chin and push upwards.

In the next instant, Jack was on the zombie, his jaws clamping down on the back of its neck and pulling it away from his master. The undead howling remains of the man tried to hold onto Jason, but Jack yanked hard and it slid off Jason.

Calhoun was nearby using the detonation device to bash the other runner's brains in.

"Calhoun, no!" Jason managed to utter, then heard a terrible sound. A steady beeping. "Jack! Let go of it! Come here!"

Jack whirled around and rushed toward the boy. The nearly decapitated runner pushed itself to its knees but then the sniper finally got the right shot and it fell over.

Calhoun looked at Jason startled, then up at the box. The light that had so determinedly not come on before was blinking red. Calhoun looked toward the fuel tanks then the boy. "This is not good."

"You triggered it," Jason shouted back. "We need to run. Now!"

Jason glanced toward the opening and saw zombies were now trudging toward them. They had finally been noticed and around fifty zombies were already past the fire line. He didn't say another word, but turned and ran.

Jack growled at the shambling zombies, then ran after his boy. The stinky old man threw down the metal box and began to run after them. He was bit slower because of his creaky old bones. Jack barked at him to hurry it up, darted back to urge the stinky man on, then ran back after the boy.

The teenager and the old man ran as hard as they could as the red light blinked faster and faster. They were halfway to the fort when the fuel tanks exploded. The blast blew them of their feet and hurled them to the ground as a gush of hot air, then flames filled the air.

On the fort wall, everyone hit the ground as the blast filled the morning sky. Fiery debris rained down as the roar of the explosion rang in the fort occupants' ears.

When the flames began to die down, zombies were burning, debris littered the wide expanse before the fort, and a boy, a dog, and an old man laid unmoving on the ground.

* * * * *

Katie lifted herself up off the floor and looked over the rail at the devastation the fire line had wrought. Zombies were burning, as was the makeshift outer wall. Many of the zombies had been blown into bits and others tossed back down the hill into the mob. Clutching the railing, she tried to see through the acrid smoke.

It took a moment for her to see that at least twenty zombies were still alive inside the fire line. Most of the zombies outside the fire line seemed to be in a panic and struggling to get away from the fire. The enormous crowd was peeling apart with zombies moving off in two different directions.

As the black smoke slithered over the ground below, Katie struggled to see Calhoun and Jason. She saw Jack first as he slowly stirred, then began to bark anxiously as zombies moved determinedly toward two fallen figures.

"Oh, shit!" Katie grabbed her walkie-talkie and pushed down the button. "Jason and Calhoun are in danger near my point. Someone kill those bastards!"

* * * * *

Katarina heard the call from her perch but she was nowhere near Katie's assigned position. At least she could take out the zombies that were in her range. As the staggering figures materialized out of the smoke, she took her shots.

* * * * *

"My boy!" Juan exclaimed, turning to rush to Jason's rescue.

One of the men assigned to his team grabbed him. "We got a job to do, man."

Juan tried to push past him but realized the truth of that statement.

"They'll save them, man."

With a breaking heart, Juan turned back to his duties. His shoulders ached from the tension and he felt tears in his eyes. He prayed to God someone would save his boy.

* * * * *

"Let the two lines that are flanking the fort go. I have a feeling they will keep going," Nerit ordered over her walkie-talkie. "Concentrate on anything that breaches the outer perimeter. Anything that moves into your hot zone, nail them."

"The outer ridge line is on fire. It's splitting the horde in half. That worked out better than we hoped." Kevin rapidly drew on the map, updating the battle.

"But the fire will die down and whatever is out there will come into the kill zone."

"We're ready."

* * * * *

Travis reached the wall just in time to see his wife about to slide onto the makeshift elevator. "Katie!"

"I need to get Jason!" She answered defensively. Her gun was already in her hand. "He's Jenni's boy. I have to."

Nearby, there were soft hisses as the sniper attempted to keep the zombies away from the two humans down on the ground. Jack's barking and growls sounded as he defended his fallen boy.

"You're pregnant. You are not going down there," Travis said firmly, swinging himself onto the elevator. He could see her jaw setting and he pointed a finger in her face. "Jenni wouldn't want you risking the baby."

"Dammit," she said, sighing as she conceded his point.

Travis grabbed her and kissed her firmly, then motioned for them to lower him. Drawing his gun, in one hand, he took a deep breath and almost choked on the acrid smoke. This day was already off to a great freaking start.

* * * * *

Jason came to slowly. Coughing on the thick smoke, he struggled to roll over. As he fell onto his back, a man lurched out of the smoke and fell to his knees. The dead gnarled face instantly moved to bury itself into his soft flesh. Jason raised the gun in his hand to the man's temple and fired.

The zombie fell over.

Blinking his eyes, Jason sat up. Jack hurtled out of the thick black wisps and nearly landed on him as he barked angrily into the smoke. Jason almost called out for Calhoun, then thought better of it. The zombies would find him faster if he called out. Holding onto Jack's collar, he pulled himself up to his feet and stood, feeling quite wobbly. Slowly, he realized he would look a lot like the zombies in his present battered condition. Jack would be his best defense against being wrongly identified. Leaning over he whispered to the dog, "Find Calhoun" and held on.

Jack looked up at him with his clear brown eyes and Jason could see the concern in their depths. Jack seemed to think this foolhardy, but obediently began to lead him slowly through the hot, acrid air and dark smoke.

A low moan near him made Jason jump and he twisted around. Jack growled low in his throat and Jason raised his gun in the direction of the moan. The stench of decaying burning flesh filled his nostrils and he stared into the smoke in terror.

A woman suddenly lurched out of the mist and Jason instinctively pulled the trigger. She fell back a few feet, snarled, then started forward again. He fired again, this time the bullet punching through her forehead. The zombie fell back without a sound.

He took a deep breath to try to steady his nerves and began to cough. A groan behind him startled him and he spun around in time to see a burned zombie right on him. It growled low as it seized his shoulders. Jack was instantly tearing at the creature as Jason brought the gun up and fired through the creature's head. Another one staggered toward him and he aimed at it.

Jack shoved hard into his legs, knocking him sideways just as the new zombie revealed himself to actually be a living Calhoun.

"Damn clones," Calhoun muttered as grabbed Jason's arm to help him up. "They're all around. We gotta back up toward the wall."

Together, the dog at their side, they moved toward the wall.

"Where is your gun?" Jason whispered.

"No clue. Got the living bejeezus knocked out of me by that explosion," Calhoun answered.

The dark smoke began to dissipate as the fires began to burn down. They moved a little faster as more and more figures materialized out of the haze.

"This ain't good, boy," Calhoun decided.

Another explosion near the opening made the zombies howl and more body parts rained down on them. The roar of a motorcycle filled their ears as Rune returned to the fort.

"That crazy hippie," Calhoun muttered as he grabbed Jason tight as the motorcycle drew close to them.

Rune looked a bit bedraggled and was covered in soot. His shotgun was across his lap and he motioned to them. "Get on."

Calhoun shoved Jason onto the bike, then managed to squeeze his skinny butt on. Jason grabbed hold of Rune as Calhoun grabbed hold of both of them. Jason wasn't sure what smelled worse: the zombies or Calhoun.

"Sorry, boy, you gotta run back," Rune said to Jack, then hauled ass toward the elevator at top speed. They dodged around zombies at a breathtaking speed.

Jason looked behind him to see Jack running as fast as he could with a big doggy grin on his face. He supposed a motorcycle was almost as good as a car when it came to chasing.

The smoky haze was continuing to clear. More zombies were pushing through the opening. The motorcycle reached the elevator just as Travis reached the ground.

"Rune!"

"Hey, dude. Wazzup?"

Travis helped Calhoun off the bike and onto the elevator. "Didn't know where you got off to."

"Got a lot of them moving out of town, then double-backed and got past the traps right when the tanks blew." Rune climbed off his motorcycle and lifted his shotgun calmly to blow the head off an approaching zombie. "Gotta leave you here, Charlain," he said to the bike and climbed onto the elevator. "Sorry, babe."

Jack caught up and leaped onto the elevator just as it began to lift.

Jason went down on his knees to hold onto the dog.

Travis and Rune began to calmly fire at anything that staggered out of the smoke as they were lifted back into the safety of the fort.

Just as they reached the top, a shift in the wind blew much of the smoke away from the fort. Jason looked over the wide expanse of land and saw that a lot of the zombies were moving off away from the town. The fire had spooked them. Once they were moving in one direction, they kept going.

What remained was a large number of zombies still approaching and moving into the kill zone.

"We're clear," Travis said as they reached the top of the wall as Katie grabbed up Jason to hug him.

"No one is bitten? Right?" Katie ran her hands over Jason's arms.

"No, we're good. Promise," Jason answered.

Calhoun reluctantly let Reggie check him for bites. "Damn things smell to high heaven, don't they?"

Reggie, trying hard not to smell the old man, nodded. 'Oh, yeah.

Katie watched anxiously as Travis and Rune were checked for bites. The moans of the zombies grew louder as they drew ever closer to the fort. Cleared of any bites, Travis kissed his wife as Rune heaved his bag of grenades over his shoulder.

"Time to get to work," Rune said.

Together, Travis and Katie looked out over the wide expanse of land before the fort. It was filled with the shambling dead.

"They're here," Travis whispered.

Within seconds the catapults began to creak and moan, then sling their heavy loads into the air and down on the zombies.

The war began...

Chapter 35

1. The War

I t is common knowledge that war is hell. But what is also not so well known is that war is surreal. Hyper-reality often mixes with moments of feeling oddly disconnected from reality. A sense of fragility wrapped up in a feeling of invincibility. Nothing about it makes sense. Nothing about it registers fully in the human senses.

The morning air was filled with the creaking of catapults showering the undead with their loads of discarded junk. The sharp twang of the massive crossbows was followed by the hissing whistle of twenty arrows splitting through the air in a gentle arch only to slam into the battered, mangled bodies of the dead. The sudden whoosh of the gas jets being activated out on the field below, then the loud bang as they ignited, was followed by the intense wail of the zombies on fire.

The smell was unbelievable. Charred flesh. Rotting flesh. Fire. Human sweat and fear.

From the massive crossbows to the catapults to the gunmen, everyone had a section of the area lying before the fort which they were responsible for. Target zones were erected along the wall with colored paint. If something crossed into your zone, you fired. It was easy. Yet there was swearing and screams of anger as something undead and rotting would pass out of the zone just before a toilet smashed right where it had been standing or the ground was skewered with twenty arrows instead of the shambling dead.

Juan activated the traps on Nerit's command. The fire jet traps, the quick drying cement traps, the stake traps. He listened and obeyed. He never saw the shuffling family of four complete with a toddler get stuck in the quick drying cement and flail about uselessly until the snipers shot off their heads. He didn't see the former nurse with both arms missing ignite into a torch as a gas jet went off. Nor the zombified firemen get skewered on the stake traps. But he would hear "Good job" from Nerit and smile with satisfaction.

Katie worked with feverish intensity loading up her crossbow, then waiting for something to move into her zone. Every time the shambling dead went down under the hail of her arrows, she would grin fiercely and reload. More than once she felt Jenni's presence nearby and it pushed her to keep going even when the heat and the smell seemed overwhelming.

"This is for Ken, fuckers," Lenore said further down the wall as her crossbow split zombies apart pouring their putrid innards onto the ground. She would pump her fist in the air then reload to do it all over again.

Jason helped man the slingshot. The teenagers launched Molotov cocktails with startling accuracy at the undead. They all wore t-shirts with the words "For Roger" written on them with a sharpie pen. Jason's read on the back: "For my Mom."

Rune ran across rooftops to gun down anything trying to come up the side streets. Most of the traps had already gone off with zombies dangling from the razor wire. He took out anything that stirred down the side streets. Most of the first zombies were still trailing off into the distance in two long columns.

Linda and Bette reloaded their catapult countless times. The discarded junk of the old world flew out over the battlefield, picking up force as it fell to earth and landing amongst the dead with brutal devastation. They would high five whenever they got a particularly gruesome death. Their favorite was a zombie priest who lost his head to a flying toaster oven.

Calhoun, followed by his pack of dogs, ran along the wall activating the traps closest to the fort. If the zombies began to congregate in one area, he would trip a variety of swinging arms made of old telephone lines and lawnmower blades. The big swinging arms were his pride and joy. They'd swing through a group of zombies and obliterate anything they'd hit.

The helicopters, on standby, had one bad moment when confronted with a handful of terrified people demanding to be removed from the fort.

"And go where?" Greta asked calmly.

With no answer to her question, the people had slunk away.

Travis wielded one of the five bazookas the fort had. With Kevin's help, they loaded it up and sent zombies flying in pieces across the battlefield. Despite the tension in the air, they found themselves laughing more than once.

Katarina took out the living dead with terrible accuracy. Being a sniper meant she was a little more up close and personal with the undead as they went down. She could see their ravaged faces, their empty eyes, their mutilated forms before her bullet put them down. Every age, every walk of life, every race wandered into view and every single one was put to final rest. Having lived with fear so long, she was startled to feel peace instead. Instead of feeling rage against them, she felt sorry for them. Every bullet, she realized was a blessing to those creatures. A final exit from their hell.

Yolanda sat in the communication center and listened to teams reporting in and Nerit's voice steadily giving commands. Next to her sat her own pistol. If there was a breach in the wall, she would fight. And, of course, keep one bullet for herself.

In the opulent ballroom of the hotel, the elderly and children of the fort waited. Despite themselves, they had all watched from the windows as the dead had swarmed toward the fort. They had watched mesmerized as the dead had been met with fierce resistance. Now the battlefield was a ruin. Smoke filled the air. Fear and hope filled their hearts.

Katie was gagging on the putrid stench as she reloaded her crossbow. Nothing was moving in her zone anymore. Only a few of the twenty catapults along the wall were still firing, most of those on the east side.

"Is it done?" someone yelled from nearby.

"I don't have any in my zone," Lenore called out.

Katie lifted her walkie-talkie. "Hey, what is going on?"

From his point on the wall, Travis could see most of the west side of the battlefield. Only a few severely mutilated zombies were trying to pull themselves along the ground. Kevin craned his neck, trying to look past the smoke.

"This might be it," Travis said, his voice trembling. His body was shaking as the adrenaline rush left him.

"It might be," Kevin said in awe.

"Let's get the copter up," Travis said into his walkie-talkie. "Check on the status of the zombies."

Lenore glanced over at Bette and Linda as they struggled to get a few microwaves onto their catapult. "It might be done!"

"What?" Linda looked over the wall at the decimated battlefield.

"Babe, nothing is shambling down there," Bette said in awe.

"Muthafuckin' zombies are dead," Lenore said with satisfaction.

"There might be more," Linda said pragmatically. "We can't get our hopes up yet."

A lone helicopter lifted up over the hotel and swung out over the hills.

Katie sat down in the chair next to her massive crossbow, her arms wrapped around her stomach. She tried not to breath too deeply through the kerchief over her mouth. The smell was unbearable, but the view was amazing. The enormous horde of the dead was not in view. Of course, maybe a second wave was on its way.

Nerit surveyed the map of the battlefield as she waited for the word. Eric stood near her, his face covered in a silk handkerchief. His hands were bloody from loading the catapult near her position. Stacey was sitting on the wall, wiping her face with her shirt. They were sweaty, dirty, and afraid to hope for the best.

"Think they're scared off? Think we did it?" Eric asked.

An eerie silence filled the morning. The sound of the catapults, explosions, and other weaponry had faded away. There was only a dull hum that Nerit realized was the moans of the dead in the distance.

"Possibly," she answered, but slowly smiled. Her map spoke of victory. But if there was another wave coming...

There was a burst of static over the walkie-talkie.

"That's it," Greta's voice cackled through the static. "Holy God in Heaven, that's it. We got two columns heading to the east and west and the ones that hit us straight on....boys and girls..what you see in front of you is it!"

Travis heard the news and snatched up his walkie-talkie. "Yolanda, make an announcement!"

"I'll try, but I'm crying!" she hollered back at him through walkie-talkie.

Within seconds, Yolanda's voice boomed through the fort speakers, announcing victory.

"Holy shit," Bette whispered, then was wrapped up in Linda's arms and they both began to scream with joy.

Rune sat on the wall, dangling his feet over the edge. Looking down past his knees, he saw a cluster of body parts. "Well, it was a good day to die, but oh well," he said and lit up a cigarette. Then he grinned as he realized his bike stood unscathed. "Well, hot damn," he said.

Katarina stood up slowly and began to cry.

Lenore sat back in the chair next to her crossbow and sighed softly. Nodding to herself, she pulled out a soda and popped the top. "Damn zombies shouldn't have touched my best friend," she muttered. Toasting the massacred zombies, she said, "For Felix and Ken. Rest in peace, my brothers."

Katie ran up to Travis and launched herself into his arms. He grabbed her tightly as they both laughed with delight and he swung her around. Juan joined them, tears streaming down his face, and they drew him into their embrace. Juan kissed both of them, whooping with joy. Nerit tackled all of them, laughing with joy. They wrapped her up in their enormous hug as Kevin joined in. Laughing and kissing each other, they were all crying and talking at the same time.

Jack pushed his way into the middle of them, barking with excitement and Jason wormed his way under his Dad's arm. Katie kissed the teenager's cheek and made him blush as Juan ruffled the boy's hair lovingly.

"We did it!" Travis shouted it to the heavens and the helicopter circling over head.

"I knew we would," Nerit said with a big grin. "I knew it!"

"It was almost too easy," Kevin exclaimed.

"You call that easy?" Nerit smacked Kevin's arm.

"Planning man! We planned it out and we did it!" Juan whooped. "We were a little late on the 'organize before they rise' part of the Zombie Survival Guide, but we were ready when they fucking got here."

"Thanks to Jason here," Katie said, squeezing the boy tighter.

Katarina dove into the middle of them. Nerit caught her up in a tight hug and Kevin high-fived her. "Bill would have loved this!" She burst into tears again, but she was smiling.

Others began to join them and hugs were tight and happy. They looked over the battlefield at the destroyed bodies of the dead and slowly it dawned on them that they had not lost one person in the battle. More tears came as relief set in.

Travis hooked his arm around Katie's shoulder and kissed her firmly just as Eric and Stacey showed up. Lenore and Rune came to join them and everyone started hugging and kissing each other again.

"We did it," Nerit said over the din of voices. "Look out there. Look at it. We all did this. We survived. And this is life. Our life. The fort stood."

Slowly, they fell into silence as the enormity of it all gripped the defenders of the small town. Gathered in groups all over the fort, they stared through windows, or from the rooftops, or from the wall itself, and they saw the dead littered across the ground. Since the first day of the rising, they had never had such a sweet victory.

"What a mess," Katie finally said. But in her heart, she knew that every second of every day from the first day had been worth it to feel this moment of victory. Jenni had been right. It had been worth it. She snuggled into Travis' side more firmly and smiled as Juan kissed her cheek. Wrapping her arms around Jason, she felt secure in the family she and Jenni had created. Jack yawned at her feet and looked up at her with his "I want a cookie" look.

"Yep, that is one helluva mess," Juan agreed. "Loca would be proud."

Calhoun suddenly shoved his way past them, his entourage of mutts following him. He looked one way, then the other surveying the carnage.

"We did it, Calhoun," Travis said proudly.

"We did a damn good job. The clones are not much more than chopped liver now," Nerit said to the old guy.

Calhoun nodded solemnly, turning to look at them. "I ain't cleaning it up," he said firmly then strode away, his satellite dish hat wobbling on his head with his dogs trailing behind.

The laughter that erupted was glorious and heartfelt. People started crying all over again. Katie was laughing so hard her sides hurt. Below them, the big bulldozers were coming out to clear the area and eliminate any of the zombies that might be immobilized, but still a threat. The fire traps went off again, refreshing the fire line to chase away any stragglers.

Travis, Juan, Eric and Kevin were all talking so fast and over each other, joyful expressions on their faces, that Katie barely understood what they were saying. The first tremor rippling over her stomach shocked her then she felt a warm gush of water flowing down her legs.

"Oh, God," she exclaimed. She looked up at Travis with a startled expression on her face. "My water just broke!"

Then a whole new kind of chaos broke out as everyone tried to help her back to the hotel.

Below the walls, the bulldozers crushed the zombie bodies into mulch and swept away the debris of the battle. Snipers took out a few remaining zombies staggering along the side streets. In the distance, the zombie hordes began to vanish from view.

The war was over.

2. The New Beginning

Katie stared down at the little face tucked into the pink blanket and felt as though she would never stop smiling. It was a mushed up, funny little face, but she could see shades of Travis in the shape of her daughter's nose and eyebrows coupled with her own mouth and eyes. The tiny little feet that had pushed against her bladder at the worst times were now kicking slightly under the blanket. The tiny little hands that had made funny little bumps under her skin now clutched her fingers. Tears slipped down her nose and turned the pink blanket rose in tiny spots.

Beside her, Travis was in silent awe. He kept touching their little girl, then Katie. His kisses adorned his wife's check and neck. He was overwhelmed and so was she.

The word from the outside world was that the zombie hordes were miles away now. The cleanup crews were continuing to clear out any last vestiges of the undead from the outer walls. They had won and the fort was secure. It was a wonderful world to bring their daughter into.

"I see you so clearly in her face," Travis murmured in Katie's ear.

"I see you," Katie softly whispered back.

Her husband kissed her neck again. "I love you so much."

Katie giggled. "Good, because you're a Daddy now and I'm not diaper changing alone!"

"I know! It's amazing. We're parents!" He reached over her to touch the tiny little pink fist again. "What are we naming her, Mommy?"

Katie returned her gaze to her daughter. She was beaming with happiness despite her exhaustion. "Bryce Jennily Kiel-Buchanan."

"Bruce, Jenni, and Lydia. It's perfect." Travis bent over and kissed the baby. "You're the first, Bryce. The first baby of our little fort. And soon you'll have other children joining you. You're gonna be the first generation of our new world."

Katie looked up at Travis curiously. "Other children?"

"Stacey told Eric right after they dragged you in here that she's next. She's about three months along."

Katie grinned as she burst into tears again. "We did something amazing today, didn't we?"

Travis nodded as he nuzzled her cheek. "Yes, we did."

Together, they gazed down at their newborn daughter in awe. Bryce's tiny little mouth yawned as she dozed off.

"It's a new world," Katie said softly.

Travis laid a soft, but passionate kiss on his wife's lips, then answered, "Yes, it is. A new beautiful world."

Author's Note

If you have jumped to the end of the book to see how it ends, I suggest you stop reading now. I realize many fans of this series are anxious to know who lives, who dies, and if there is a happily ever after, but you really shouldn't spoil yourself.

Trust me.

The journey you have been on with these characters has been long. To skip around to find out their fate is not really fair to them or to you. So flip to the front of the book and start reading this last leg of the journey that started with those tiny little fingers under the door...

...so now that leaves those of you who have read the book or just decided to be spoiled despite my warning. That's okay. I know it can be hard not to flip to the back of the book when things are getting rough for our beloved characters.

By now, you know that the death toll in this novel is high. Of course, I can never beat the first novel where I killed the world off except for a few survivors. And, honestly, if I kept to zombie tradition, no one would be standing at the end of this novel. But, you see, I think the doomsayers have it wrong.

The A"s The World Dies Zombie Trilogy" was inspired not only by the heroics of 9-11, but of other disasters as well. The media and writers love to concentrate on the terrors and evils of natural and man-made disasters. I am always fascinated by the heroics and selflessness of many people in times of crisis. Watching just every day folks scrambling to save complete strangers without much thought to their own safety is inspiring. I've sat mesmerized in front of the TV watching brave people try to dig through rubble, mud, and debris to save others, or dive into the ocean to save someone who has been attacked by a shark, or scramble to get supplies to desperate survivors they don't even know.

It is popular to buy into the concept that if our world went to hell, people would be reduced to barbarians. I think an element of the survivors would be just that, but I also believe that a greater number would work hard to rebuild our communities.

Together we stand or alone we die.

Looking over the long history of humankind, we have not always been the noblest of God's creations, but we have managed to rise above our faults to build nations, vast cities, communities, and families. Every day we live our lives within the confines of the rules we have created for ourselves and expect others to do the same thing. We aren't perfect, but we're doing a much better job than we give ourselves credit.

The "As The World Dies Trilogy" is the tale of a human settlement carving out a new life in the midst of a hostile environment. It is a story humanity has repeated over and over again throughout history. And like history, "As The World Dies" is a story about people.

If you have read this last tale or skipped around to check out the fates of your favorite characters, you now know that major characters die in this book. In fact, one of the two leads dies saving the lives of those she loves. This was not easy to write, I can assure you, but I knew it was her fate from the moment I wrote about those tiny fingers pressed under the door. But that is the reality of being a pioneer in a hostile country. Death and life always dance together and I could not deny that reality.

When this series began, I stated that originally I believed I was writing a short story. That idea lasted for less than three hours. In a very short time, I knew how this story ended and the major plot points along the way. I always knew who would live and who would die except for one death that was a real shocker. The journey from the tiny fingers under the door to the newborn fingers gripping Katie's fingers was long and sometimes overwhelming. It feels solid to have the series end with the beginning of Katie's family after starting with the death of Jenni's family.

But is this the end for the fort on the hill?

I am planning a short story volume that will highlight some of the supporting cast in the series. It will be released in 2010. And I will never rule out diving back into deadlands to see how Bryce, Jason and Juan's children are shaping their new world as they grow older.

Writing this last volume in the trilogy has not always been easy, but it tells the story I wanted to tell. It is the tale of two women who find a rare and powerful friendship at the end of the world and help rebuild a new one through love and sacrifice.

It's been one hellvua ride with Jenni and Katie. I hope you enjoyed it as much as I did.

Eternally,
Rhiannon

About the Author

Rhiannon Frater works and lives in Austin, Texas. She became an Independent Author at the urging of her husband.

She loves reading, movies, gaming, and hanging out with friends and family when she's not tapping away at her computer on her latest story. She also loves hearing from her fans and tries to respond to everyone who emails her.

To contact the author directly, email her at:
gothgoddessrhia@gmail.com.

For more information on her upcoming novels and other news, check out her blog at
www.rhiannonfrater.blogspot.com

Zombies, Vampires, and Texans! Oh, my!
The Novels of Rhiannon Frater

As The World Dies: The First Days

Two very different women flee into the Texas Hill Country on the first day of the zombie rising. Together they struggle to rescue loved ones, find other survivors, and avoid the hungry undead.

As The World Dies: Fighting to Survive

Katie and Jenni have found new lives with the survivors of their makeshift safe haven, but danger still lurks. Internal conflicts worsen among the survivors, as the fort is threatened not only by the zombie hordes, but marauding bandits.

Pretty When She Dies
A Vampire Novel

In East Texas, a young woman awakens buried under the forest floor. After struggling out of her grave, she not only faces her terrible new existence but her sadistic creator, The Summoner. Abandoning her old life, she travels across Texas hoping to find answers to her new nature and find a way to defeat the most powerful Necromancer of all time.